PRAISE FOR THE
SECRET HISTORIES NOVELS

Property of a Lady Faire

"Tons of plot, nonstop semicomic action, and further revelations about the entire Drood brood and their mysterious mission—what's not to enjoy?" —*Kirkus Reviews*

"It's inventive, it's lively, and it's not meant to probe the meanings of Life. There's lots of frantic action and mindless violence, which is one of the reasons this series is so popular. Simon R. Green also pens the Nightside series and the Ghost Finders books and I always enjoy reading his work. His writing is like taking a whirl on a Snap-the-Whip ride in an amusement park with a sound track of comedy albums . . . and it works."
—Kings River Life Magazine

"Green's worldwide legions of fans are sure to enjoy this newest entry into the Histories, as it represents all that readers have come to desire in an Eddie Drood and Molly Metcalf story: action, romance, intrigue, surprises around every corner, and an impossible threat defeated by heroism." —SFRevu

"Jumping from battle to battle, the action never stops in this eighth series entry that attempts to cross James Bond–style secret agent hijinks with urban fantasy. Fun, escapist fare."
—*Library Journal*

"Green's imagination seems boundless, and this eighth installment of his snarky, dark paranormal-noir Eddie Drood series is only further proof of that. Green also manages to weave genuinely moving moments and deeply poignant relationships into the colorful and irresistibly humorous scenes, creating a story that is superbly well balanced and instantly engaging."
—*Romantic Times*

"If you enjoy humorous action-adventure stories with a paranormal flair, you really should pick up the Secret Histories series. . . . *Property of a Lady Faire* is lighthearted adventure full of a great balance of humor and action."
—That's What I'm Talking About

continued . . .

Casino Infernale

"An eerie and imaginative new adventure. Green blends Love-craftian mystery with the world-building power of H. G. Wells, adding his own flair to create a quick-witted, fast-paced story . . . a cracking-good, emotional read."   —*RT Book Reviews*

"If you've ever read anything by Simon R. Green, you probably know exactly how things will go. It's going to be loud, messy, funny, weird, without restraint or decorum, and a whole lot of fun. Because Green writes with a freewheeling passion that's hard to deny. He always delivers a solid story with heaping doses of extreme creativity, ultraviolence, and keen Moments of Cool. Whether he's writing science fiction, space opera, epic fantasy, urban fantasy, or even horror, he barrels down the track at full speed, and God help anyone who gets in his way. Logic and decorum give way, and there's no such thing as 'too much'. . . . I love these books."   —Tor.com

Live and Let Drood

"A terrific, adventurous blend of genres, delivering high-octane heroism on a road lined with razor blades. . . . Fans of Green's genre-bending tales of high adventure will love this latest installment of his Secret Histories series. . . . Eddie Drood and his world are a smorgasbord for fans of urban fantasy and espionage thrillers alike. Highly recommended."   —SFRevu

For Heaven's Eyes Only

"Green continues to deliver enjoyable, fast-paced, and fun entertainment. This one is not to be missed."   —SFRevu

"Clever world building, madcap characters, cheeky one-liners, and a James Bond feel make this series stand out, and a surprise ending will have readers eagerly anticipating the next Eddie Drood adventure."   —*Publishers Weekly*

From Hell with Love

"Heroes and villains strut their stuff across a worldwide stage, and the end result is something so entertaining, it's almost a guilty pleasure. The cliff-hanger pretty much guarantees readers will be back for the next in the series, but I'd come back anyway just to see what the heck happens next."   —SFRevu

"*From Hell with Love* is both an intelligently written novel that advances the story of the characters while telling a ripping good yarn."   —The Green Man Review

The Spy Who Haunted Me

"As usual, the narrative moves at a fast clip and the sarcasm flows freely. Another action-packed melding of spy story and fantasy, featuring suave sleuthing, magical powers, and a generous dash of dry wit." —*Kirkus Reviews*

"Eddie gets to the bottom of things with style and a particularly cynical sense of humor. Scrics spinner Green's Drood books are fun, funny, and action-packed, and Eddie is one of his most entertaining creations." —*Booklist*

"No one delivers a story quite like [Green].... I thoroughly enjoyed *The Spy Who Haunted Me*, and I'll cheerfully recommend it to anyone who wants some wide-screen, no-holds-barred, big ideas and snappy execution thereof urban fantasy adventure." —The Green Man Review

Daemons Are Forever

"Green loves the wide-screen splash of cinematic battles against zombie hordes, and genuine traces of tragedy and nobility underlie the nonstop punning banter and pop-culture references, lending surprising nuance to this merry metaphysical romp." —*Publishers Weekly*

"A rapid-fire paranormal suspense ... a surprisingly moving tale of self-sacrifice and hope in the midst of chaos and loss. This excellent follow-up to *The Man with the Golden Torc* will have readers applauding the reluctant hero and anxiously awaiting his further adventures." —Monsters and Critics

The Man with the Golden Torc

"Packed with enough humor, action, and plot twists to satisfy fans who prefer their adventure shaken, not stirred.... Readers who recognize the pun on Ian Fleming's James Bond title will find the secret agent in question has more up his sleeve than a fancy car and some high-tech gadgets." —*Publishers Weekly*

"Take some James Bond, and throw in some of Green's own Nightside, and mix liberally with the epic over-the-top action of his Deathstalker novels, and you're somewhere in the right neighborhood for describing *The Man with the Golden Torc*. It has everything one comes to expect from Green's work: distinctive characters, stylized ultraviolence, more mad ideas per page than most writers get in a lifetime, and a wild roller-coaster plot that doesn't let up." —The Green Man Review

Property of a Lady Faire

A Secret Histories Novel

Simon R. Green

A ROC BOOK

ROC
Published by the Penguin Group
Penguin Group (USA) LLC, 375 Hudson Street,
New York, New York 10014

USA | Canada | UK | Ireland | Australia | New Zealand | India | South Africa | China
penguin.com
A Penguin Random House Company

Published by Roc, an imprint of New American Library, a division of Penguin
Group (USA) LLC. Previously published in a Roc hardcover edition.

First Roc Mass Market Printing, June 2015

ISBN 978-0-451-41432-8

Printed in the United States of America
10 9 8 7 6 5 4 3 2 1

CHAPTER ONE

Who Wants to Know?

I was just breaking out of a Top Security section of the Vatican, after an entirely successful burglary, when a voice spoke my name. I had been padding very quietly down a corridor that wasn't on any plan, in a building that didn't officially exist, and the last thing I expected was to hear my name spoken aloud by a voice I was almost sure I recognised. I stopped and looked quickly about me. I was half-way down a long, unlit hallway, heavy with shadows, with not a light on anywhere in the dozen or so adjoining offices. I was completely alone.

I knew that, because I'd gone to great pains and trouble to make sure of it. Because if the Vatican Security Forces ever found a Drood field agent operating anywhere inside the bounds of the holy city, they would quite definitely never forgive me. The Church might have made occasional use of the Droods down the centuries but has never trusted my family an inch. And I think it is only fair to say, vice versa.

The corridor was so dark I could only just make out its far end, but I was positive there wasn't another soul anywhere near me. The deep shadows lay undisturbed, and it was so quiet all I could hear was my own slow, controlled breathing. And then the Merlin Glass shot up out of my pocket to hang on the air right in front of my face. I didn't quite jump out of my skin, and I didn't actually make the strangulated scream I very much wanted to, but I did regard the hand mirror hovering before me with more than usual interest. Because if your very secret mission has just been utterly compromised and is now lying tits up in the gutter, you might as well enjoy it.

The sorcerer Merlin Satanspawn—and yes, I do mean the one you're thinking of—had made a present of the Glass to my family some fifteen hundred years ago. We're still trying to decide whether that was a kindly act or not. Ever since the Merlin Glass fell into my hands, not that long ago, it has proved itself to be highly useful, intensely irritating, and constantly surprising. Not least because I can never lay my hand on the operating manual when I need it.

The Glass looks like a perfectly ordinary hand mirror, with a chased silver handle and back. It can show me views of anywhere on Earth, and grow into a dimensional Doorway big enough to take me there. I'd grown used to that. But I wasn't at all used to seeing my reflection vanish from the mirror and be replaced by the shifty features of the notorious Harry Fabulous.

I grabbed the mirror by its handle and pulled it close to my face. A pale yellow light was spilling out of the Glass from wherever Harry was, and I didn't want it to attract unnecessary attention. I was almost out of this very secret part of the Vatican, but *almost* isn't *is*. Burglars should not hang around at the scenes of their crimes, not if they want to grow up to be very old burglars—particularly if the local security forces are authorised to use extreme and distressing levels of violence. But Harry Fabulous had got my attention. No one had ever used the mysterious Merlin Glass as a mobile phone before. I hadn't even known that was possible.

I tried the door handle on the nearest office, and it turned easily in my grasp. I pushed the door open and slipped silently into the darkened room, pulling the door almost but not completely shut after me. Just in case I needed to make a sudden and hurried exit. The pale yellow light from the hand mirror showed me the rough outlines of furniture and filing cabinets, and not much else. I looked into the Merlin Glass and gave Harry Fabulous my best intimidating glare.

"This had better be important, Harry," I said quietly. "I am rather busy just at the moment. How did you get this number, anyway?"

"Trust me; this is really very important, Eddie," said Harry, smiling nervously. "And I mean seriously important, with a heaping side order of urgent. As to how I was able to tap into the Merlin Glass, you really don't want to know. It would only keep you up nights."

There was no point in pressing Harry. If he wasn't prepared to give up his source, it was only because he was more scared of whomever he was working for than he was of me. Mind you, Harry Fabulous was scared of a great many people and things, usually with good reason. Harry is a creature of the shadows, or at least those very grey areas where Law and Morality and Good Sense are only passing things. Harry is a master of the illegal deal, the crafty con, and the kind of borderline business agreement you just know you'll end up regretting later. Harry Fabulous is your go-to guy for all the things you're not supposed to want, all the things that are supposed to be impossible to get. Whether it's a drug or a dream, a girl or a grimoire, a memory from yesterday or a promise of tomorrow, Harry has sources. He can get you anything, for the right price.

He's not much to look at, but then his kind never is. In his business, it's never a good idea to stand out from the crowd. A shabby man in shabby clothes, with a hard-worn face and unreadable eyes, Harry always said he could run a game on God, and be well out of town before the penny dropped. But then something went horribly wrong for Harry Fabulous, in a secret back room in one of those very private Members Only clubs well off the main drag in the Nightside . . . And now Harry leads a desperate life of penance and atonement, to make up for . . . whatever it was he did. Doing good deeds, for the good of his soul. Before it's too late. He hustles around, happy to be helpful to all the right people, mediating between people and groups who couldn't otherwise talk to one another.

Harry Fabulous wouldn't normally say boo to a Drood, so for him to contact me at all was . . . interesting.

"What do you want, Harry?" I said. "And can't it wait till I've broken out of the Vatican?"

"Not really, no," said Harry. "I have a client in desperate need of your help. As in right now!"

"Keep your voice down!" I said, glancing quickly out through the crack at the door. The corridor still looked empty, but I wasn't as convinced of that as I had been. I couldn't shake off the feeling that something was creeping up on me. And not in a good way.

"What are you doing in the Vatican, Eddie?" said Harry.

"I could tell you," I said, "but then I'd have to exorcise you."

"Come on, Eddie, you know me," said Harry. "I am the soul of discretion. Mostly."

"I do know you, Harry Fabulous," I said, "and I would not trust you as far as I could throw a wet camel."

"Lot of people say that," Harry said sadly.

"Can we please get on with this? I am rather in the middle of something here . . ."

"Doing what?"

"Something I am entirely sure both my family and all the Powers That Be at the Vatican would not want you to know about."

"Fair enough," said Harry. "I currently represent the management of the Wulfshead Club. And no, I don't have a clue who they are, just like everyone else, so there's no point in asking me."

"Then how do you know it's really them?" I said craftily.

"They were very convincing," said Harry. "I still get the shakes when I think about it."

"All right," I said. "I'll come straight to the Wulfshead, as soon as I'm outside the Vatican buildings."

"No!" Harry said quickly. "You can't! The club's new privacy shields don't allow anyone to teleport in. Even the mighty Merlin Glass would bump its nose. I'll meet you in the alley outside the main London entrance. As soon as you can, Eddie. Please."

"Give me ten minutes," I said. "Unless I run into Security . . . then make it fifteen minutes."

Harry's face disappeared from the Merlin Glass, replaced by my own reflection. Even in the dim light of the empty office, I thought I looked tired and hard done by. As one of the most secret of the hidden world's secret agents, I go to a lot of trouble to appear ordinary and anonymous, but people like Harry Fabulous put years on me. I would have preferred for him to hang around just a little longer, to answer a few pointed questions about exactly why I was needed so urgently, but that was probably why he'd disappeared so quickly. I slipped the Merlin Glass back into my pocket and stood still for a moment, thinking.

I knew all about the Wulfshead Club. Everyone in my line of work does. A very private drinking establishment, for very private people. A covert bolt-hole, for those of us who operate in the hidden world. The Good, the Bad, and the In-between are always welcome, as long as they've got money to spend. More importantly, it's neutral ground for those of us who feel the need for somewhere safe and secure to let our hair down. Many of us who work in the supernatural Intelligence community tend to end up there. If only because we all need someone we can talk to, about the things we've seen and the things we've done, who won't judge us. The kinds of things only people like us ever get to know about.

The world doesn't need to know. It would only worry.

There are a great many secret entrances to the Wulfshead Club, in any number of cities, scattered around the world. Though getting in, or out, can be murder. The club's been around for as long as anyone can remember, in one form or another, but no one knows for sure who owns and runs it. Despite a clientele who make their business digging out answers, the Wulfshead's management remains determinedly anonymous. And they have never, ever, asked a member of my family for help before. I had to smile. This was just too good to turn down.

My head came up sharply as I heard soft running footsteps outside the office, approaching rapidly from the far end of the corridor. Not good. Not in any way good. I couldn't use the Merlin Glass to teleport out until I was completely outside the building and back in the official world.

I pulled the door open and slipped back out into the corridor, not making a sound. When you're a field agent for the Droods, moving unseen and unobserved comes as standard. I glared into the gloom at the far end of the corridor, back the way I'd come, and could just make out a number of dark, indistinct figures heading my way at more than human speed. Charging down the corridor, they shifted their shapes subtly as they moved. I couldn't hear any bells or sirens; the advancing shapes were doing nothing to raise the alarm. Presumably they intended to bring me down before anyone else found out I was ever there. I had to smile. Being chased by a small army of angry priests and warrior nuns was probably every good Catholic boy's worst nightmare. Good thing I was raised Church of England.

I ran down the corridor at full pelt, not even trying to be quiet or unobserved any more. My feet hammered on the floor, and my arms pumped at my sides as I made good speed, leaving my pursuers behind. I was still hoping to make my escape without having to fight my way out. I didn't want to make more of a fuss than was necessary. Scrapping with priests and nuns inside the Vatican, even the parts that don't officially exist, is never going to be profitable. And I really didn't want the Vatican Security Forces to even suspect they'd had a Drood in the house. Which was why I hadn't raised my incredible Drood armour. Just the presence of so much golden strange matter in the holy city would set off every alarm they had and bring everyone running at once.

I risked a glance back over my shoulder. My pursuers were catching up fast, moving so quietly now that their feet didn't even seem to be brushing the bare wooden floor. I could see robes and wimples, but no faces. Even as I looked, though, the dark shapes changed, flowing like water. Legs and arms lengthened, backs became hunched, and great black membranous wings stretched out, their tips brushing against the corridor walls, beating loudly on the still air. The whole atmosphere in the corridor changed, becoming horrid and oppressive. There was a sudden stench of blood and brimstone. It seemed the rumours were true, after all. The Vatican had contracted out for its most secret security forces, drawing on denizens from the Lower Reaches. The remote activating of the Merlin Glass must have alerted them to my presence.

I was in real trouble now.

I pounded down the corridor, forcing the last bit of speed out of my aching muscles. It had been a long night, and I'm not really built for running. I could hear my breathing coming fast and hard, and my heart was hammering in my chest. I finally reached the door at the far end, skidded to a halt, and rattled the handle. It was locked. Of course it was; it was that kind of night. I grabbed a handy piece of heavy marble statuary from its niche (almost certainly centuries old, and valuable beyond price) and used it to smash the lock. The statue came to pieces in my hand, but the door jumped open. I threw the pieces aside and charged through the opening. I didn't dare look back. I could hear the flapping of huge wings right behind me, like wet blankets on the air.

Outside, an old-fashioned black iron fire escape clung precariously to the ancient stone wall. I hurried up the steps, heading for the roof. Having to pass through the door one at a time should slow my pursuers down nicely, especially if they stopped to argue over who had precedence. I hauled myself up the shaking metal rungs, making a hell of a racket, grabbing at the railings with both hands to hurry myself along. I made it onto the slanting tile roof and then stopped to get my breath and my bearings.

I could hear heavy things hammering up the fire escape, their combined weight almost pulling the metal stairs away from the side of the building. I didn't look. I didn't want to see, didn't want to know. I could hear angry buzzing voices, only just trying to be human, saying bad things. I went to stand on the very edge of the roof, planting one foot on the iron guttering, and looked out over the view below.

It was a hell of a long drop down to the ground below. Hundreds of feet, at least. But I could see the whole of the holy city stretched out before me, the great white buildings glowing and gleaming in the fierce moonlight. You get to see some of the best views in the world in my job. Though mostly not for very long.

I took out the Merlin Glass, shook it till it was the size of a Door, and then gave it the correct Space Time coordinates and threw it off the edge of the roof. The Glass fell away into the moonlight, an open Door full of the bright lights of London. I took a deep breath and jumped off the roof after it.

I heard a roar of frustrated buzzing voices rush by behind me, but I didn't look back at the fire escape. Some things you just don't want to see. I went hurtling down, gathering speed all the time, the ground rushing up to greet me. Cool evening air battered at my face and tugged at my clothes. The fall would be more than enough to kill any ordinary man. Good thing I was a Drood. I subvocalised the activating Words, and the golden armour contained in the torc at my throat rushed out to cover me from head to toe in a moment.

I could hear flapping heavy wings behind me, as dark things launched themselves in pursuit, but I was concentrating on the open Door falling away before me. The added weight of my armour sent me hurtling down faster than ever, and it was the easiest thing in the world to catch up with the falling Merlin Glass and plunge right through it, without even brushing against the sides. The Door slammed shut the moment I was through, cutting off the last angry screams from my pursuers.

And I crashed back to earth in a dark and deserted back alley in London's old Soho. I hit the ground at appalling speed, but my armoured legs absorbed most of the impact. I stayed where I was for a moment, crouched on one knee in the crater I'd blasted out of the alley floor, getting my breathing back under control. It never ceases to amaze me, all the things I can do in my armour. I muttered the Words, and the golden strange matter flowed back into my torc. I straightened, adjusted my clothing, and grabbed the hand mirror–sized Merlin Glass out of mid-air, where it had been hovering above me. I slipped it carefully back into its hidden pocket, and only then looked around me.

After the bright moonlight of the Vatican, it felt something of a step down to be standing in the grimy amber light of a London street lamp, interrupted now and then by the flickering glare of malfunctioning neon signs. I was back in Soho, all right. For someone whose job description genuinely is globe-trotting secret agent, it's astonishing how often I end up hanging around in grimy back alleys in the seedier parts of civilisation.

The never-ending roar of London's traffic blasted by at the far end of the alleyway. All rushing shapes and blaring horns. The alley itself was dark and foul and smelled of appalling things. Quite definitely including fresh urine. Assorted garbage lay in scattered heaps, troubled only by rats with really strong stomachs. The stained brick walls were covered with the usual overlapping graffiti: *Dagon Has Risen! Cthulhu Has Bad Dreams.* And, more worryingly, *Eye Can See You.* And there, standing right at the end of the alley, sticking to the shadows because that was where he felt most at home: Harry Fabulous. He stepped forward, just a little, and nodded jerkily, doing his best to look like he was pleased to see me.

"Nice of you to drop in, Eddie. You Droods do love to make an entrance."

"Stick to what you're good at; that's what I always say. Why am I here, Harry?"

"Good of you to get here so quickly," he said, avoiding the question. "Here, let me show you into the Wulfshead."

He moved quickly over to the left-hand wall, being very careful where he put his feet, and muttered certain secret Words. A massive silver door appeared in the brick wall, as though the silver had shouldered the brickwork aside for being less important, or less real. The door was big enough to drive an elephant through, and it shone with its own dull light, painting the wall opposite with a shifting, uncertain glow. The solid silver door was deeply carved and etched with a great many threats and warnings, in angelic and demonic script. The Wulfshead Club doesn't discriminate. There was no bell, no knocker, not even a handle. It isn't meant to be easy to get in. Harry placed the palm of his left hand flat against the silver, and after a moment that stretched on just a bit longer than was comfortable, the door swung slowly back before him. He snatched his hand back and smiled weakly at me. There were beads of sweat on his face. I wasn't surprised. If your name isn't on the approved guest list, the door will bite your hand right off.

Bright, cheerful light spilled out through the door and into the alley. Harry hurried in, and I moved quickly to follow him. It only took me a moment to realise I wasn't in the Wulfshead. Instead, the door had let us into a small business office. All very basic—just a table and two chairs. No windows, no decorations; a door behind us and another door on the other side of the room. I had a very definite sense of being observed. I turned to look thoughtfully at Harry, and he backed quickly away, holding his hands out before him.

"It's all right, Eddie! Really! That far door leads into the club proper—I promise you!"

"What are we doing here, Harry?" I said, and he actually flinched away from something in my voice.

"This is one of the private offices used by the club's management. For when they . . . want to keep an eye on things. It's just somewhere private, where we can discuss the management's current . . . problem."

"And why are you speaking for them, Harry?"

"Because they're not stupid enough to reveal themselves to a Drood. And because I owe them," Harry said flatly. His words gave him a certain amount of courage, and he did his best to look at me defiantly. "They didn't want you in particular, and the Drood family in general, knowing who they are. You'd only take advantage ... And anyway, if you did know who they were, I'm pretty sure you wouldn't approve."

"Wouldn't surprise me," I said. "My family doesn't approve of most people. And nearly always with good reason. So why are the management asking for my help? What could be so bad?"

If anything, Harry seemed even more jumpy now. He looked quickly around him, at the bare walls and the closed doors, and edged a little closer.

"Are you sure you've finished your business with the Vatican, Eddie? No loose ends that might turn up to ... distract you?"

"It's all done," I said firmly. "And that is all I am going to say on the matter."

Harry Fabulous didn't need to know that I had broken into the Vatican not to steal something but to make them a present. I had taken in with me a single significant volume of forbidden lore, and deposited it in a certain place on a certain shelf, in the Vatican's Very Secret Library. This particular copy, an almost exact copy of the book already in place there, had been compiled by the Drood Librarian. Just a few small changes, overseen by the family. I replaced one with the other, and took the original out with me. Because there were certain things in the original that we didn't want the Church to know about. It would only have upset them and kept them up nights. Vatican Security might know someone had been poking around, but they wouldn't know who, or why.

Which added up to a completely successful mission in my book.

Harry still didn't look at all happy. "I just hope no one saw you arrive out of nowhere."

"Come on, Harry," I said. "That was old Soho. One of the few bits they haven't got around to gentrifying yet. You could set fire to a giant Wicker Man stuffed full of merchant bankers, and no one would give a damn. In fact, they'd probably applaud."

"I hate to put it this bluntly, but I'm going to because the management insisted," said Harry. "You can only enter the Wulfshead Club as Shaman Bond. The management can't allow Eddie Drood to set foot on the premises. Not after what happened the last time he was here. Apparently, it took ages to get all the bloodstains out."

"Understood," I said shortly.

The last time I'd had reason to come to the club as a Drood, it had been during the Great Satanic Conspiracy. I'd forced my way in, in my armour, because I didn't want Shaman Bond associated with what I was about to do. What I had to do. I needed answers to some questions, very urgently, and I didn't have the time to be patient or reasonable. So I just beat them out of the man. And a few good people who got in the way. I looked thoughtfully at Harry.

"How long has the club's management known that Shaman Bond is a cover identity for Eddie Drood?"

"I find it best not to ask them questions," said Harry. "Are you sure you don't know who they are?"

"I'm sure my family could find out," I said. "If we ever really wanted to know. But they're not important enough. For now."

Harry sighed, and sat down on one of the chairs. He

looked tired. I pulled up the other chair, sat down facing him, and then looked at him expectantly.

"There's trouble at the Wulfshead Club," said Harry. "We need you—that is, we need Shaman Bond—to ask questions quietly and discreetly, among the club's clientele. Because secrets are leaking out of the club. Things said in confidence here have started turning up in the outside world. Which is supposed to be impossible. The club management guarantee that whatever happens in the Wulfshead stays in the Wulfshead. You can say anything, do anything, and no one will ever know. That's why people like you and I come here. But now, secrets are getting out, and often appearing where they can do the most damage to everyone involved."

"How long has this been going on?" I said. I was honestly shocked. Wulfshead security was supposed to be second to none.

"Almost three weeks now," said Harry. "The management thought they could handle it themselves at first. But it seems they can't. So they found me, to find you. They want you to discover exactly how the club's privacy is being compromised, and why, and who's behind it. And then they want you to put a stop to it."

"But why me, of all people?" I said, honestly curious. "I mean, given the mess I made the last time I was here?"

"That was a Drood," said Harry. "You expect things like that from Droods. The management wants Shaman Bond. Because he is a regular here, and knows everyone. And everyone knows him."

I frowned. "They think this is an inside job?"

"Has to be," said Harry. "Someone here is telling tales out of school. We need you to find out who."

"What do I get out of it?"

"I have been instructed to tell you," Harry said carefully, "whatever you want. The club's management agree to owe you a favour. You personally, that is; not your family. There are limits. It will be a personal favour to you, that you can call in at any time."

"Sounds good to me," I said cheerfully. "But you do realise I won't be able to keep this from my family?"

"Understood," said Harry. "The management merely asks that you be . . . discreet in how much you tell them."

"Understood," I said. A thought occurred to me. "If the club's management is so concerned about what's going on, why haven't they called in their own security big guns? The Roaring Boys?"

Harry winced. "Because you don't use a nuke to crack a walnut. The Roaring Boys . . . do tend to favour a scorched-earth policy. You can do this, Eddie. People will talk to Shaman Bond, where they wouldn't talk to anyone else. Because they think he's one of them."

He got up abruptly, strode over to the opposite door, and pulled it open. Savagely bright lights and disturbingly loud music blasted in from the club beyond. I rose unhurriedly and strolled to the door. Wild drinks and wilder music, just like always. I stepped through the door into the club, then stopped and looked back as I realised Harry Fabulous had stayed in the office.

"You not joining me, Harry?"

"Best not," he said. "I don't need the temptation. Can't afford to risk it these days."

"What did you do, Harry?" I said.

He smiled briefly. "Let's just say I met someone who was better at the art of the big con than I was."

He shut the door firmly in my face, and I moved on, into the Wulfshead Club.

*   *   *

The joint was jumping—loud and colourful and packed with all the usual unusual suspects. People coming and going, along with a few individuals who weren't in any way people, talking in small groups or muttering in corners or crowding together at the long bar. Winding down after a long day, or night; or gathering the courage of their convictions before they went out to do appalling things in the world. Some were plotting cons, or jobs, or glorious insurrection; others were just letting their hair down in convivial company. Lots of loud, blaring music. Apparently tonight was Let's Celebrate Sixties Film Music Night. I recognised the theme from the original version of *The Italian Job*: "We Are the Self-Preservation Society." A lot of people were singing along.

I strolled easily through the packed crowd, smiling and nodding, and being smiled at and nodded to. Shaman Bond has a carefully cultivated reputation for being part of the Scene: a well-known face, always around, always just turning up . . . always on the lookout for a little profitable trouble to get into. No one was surprised to see Shaman Bond at the Wulfshead, because no one was ever surprised to see him anywhere. I clapped my hand on a few shoulders, kissed a few cheeks, and kept moving.

Everywhere I looked, people were drinking and dancing and making deals. Laughing and shouting in the hot, sweaty atmosphere, the bright lights shining in their eyes and in their minds. Bright primary colours blasted down from above, constantly changing, while the walls were covered with giant flat plasma screens showing ever-changing views from secret locations around the world. Many of which didn't officially exist. Scenes from underground bunkers and secret laboratories, the hidden lairs of the

Good, the Bad, and the Uncanny. And even interesting peeks into the bedrooms of the rich and famous. (Along with other, less salubrious locations.) Lots and lots of well-known faces, doing all sorts of things that would do their public image no good at all.

I couldn't help wondering whether someone whose secret life had been spied on, and perhaps revealed, might not have decided on some appropriate revenge.

I headed for the long high-tech bar at the far end of the club, a nightmare Art Deco structure of gleaming steel and glass, with computer-assisted access to more kinds of booze than most people even know exist. You want a Wolfsbane cocktail, with a silver parasol in it? Or perhaps angel's tears, with a depleted uranium swizzle stick? Or perhaps you desire a deep purple liqueur distilled from a kind of moss found only on Mars? Then it's no wonder you've come to the Wulfshead Club.

It is said by many and believed by even more that the club management keep their bar stock securely locked away in a pocket dimension only tangentially connected to the bar. Because the bar staff are afraid of it.

I eased my way through the crowd, being pleasant and friendly to all the right people, because it's never wise to start a fight you can't be sure of winning. I caught the nearest barman's eye and ordered my usual bottle of Beck's. It arrived almost immediately, ice cold, with little drops of water beading on the glass. I nodded familiarly to the barman. His face was familiar, but it was hard to tell whether we'd ever actually met before—on account of there being a dozen or so barmen moving up and down the long bar, all of them with exactly the same face. Because they were clones. It's a lot easier to be sure of the honesty of your staff if you grow them all in vats.

I put my back against the bar and looked around me. Just Shaman Bond, chilling out, soaking up the atmosphere. Fitting in, letting myself become part of the crowd and part of the scene, so people would just accept my presence. So I could take advantage of them. I felt a little alone, even in the midst of so many, being there without my partner and my love, the wild witch Molly Metcalf. But I couldn't call her to come and join me, because it was widely known, in places like this, that Molly Metcalf was currently stepping out with a Drood.

I couldn't ask her to help out on the Vatican job either. Because while I could get in without being noticed, Molly's presence would have set off even more security alarms than my Drood armour. Molly had done many impressive and destructive things in her time, to the detriment of organised religions. And as a result, they all really disapproved of her. That's what you get for boasting you've been to Heaven and Hell and everywhere in between.

I studied the crowd carefully, taking my time. You can find all sorts at the Wulfshead—if they don't find you first. I made no move to approach anyone specific, or join in any conversation. Not yet. I just kept my ears and eyes open: seeing who was in tonight, and who they were with; who wasn't there but perhaps should have been; and who was getting involved with things and people they would quite definitely come to regret in the morning. Love and lust, or things very like them, hung heavily on the hot and sweaty air. Temptation comes as standard at the Wulfshead. No wonder Harry Fabulous was hiding. I tilted my head surreptitiously this way and that, listening in on the latest gossip. Who was out, who was having who, who'd died, and who was responsible.

There was a lot of talk about what was going on with the Shadow Banks, just recently. Those secret underground financial institutions that funded a lot of the bigger supernatural crimes, and criminals, on the quiet. Something significant had happened, after the last Casino Infernale in France, because the Shadow Banks had stopped loaning money. To anyone. Which was . . . unheard of. A lot of people in the Wulfshead were very unhappy about this. Can't do the crimes if you don't have the funding. Everyone knew that. There was a lot of talk, but no one knew anything for certain.

I could have told them. How I broke the bank at Casino Infernale . . . But I didn't. Because that was down to Eddie Drood. And still the conversations rose and fell . . .

Have you heard about the Great Game this year? They say it's going to be bigger than ever . . . I hear the man in Cell 13 is finally getting out . . . I heard the Lady Faire has just sent out invitations to attend her annual Ball, for all past and present friends and lovers. Is she handling everything herself? I wouldn't be at all surprised . . . I hear it's all kicking off in the Nightside, with the return of the Celestial Children . . . I hear, I hear . . .

Everyone had heard all kinds of things, but that didn't necessarily make any of them true. There was a lot of gossip about what the Droods were up to—nearly all of it wrong, but worrying. Which was as it should be.

There were certainly a hell of a lot of people in tonight. Packed together so tight you could hardly breathe. Some I knew, some I didn't. Monkton Farley, the famous consulting detective, was propping up the bar not far from me. Tall and whipcord lean, with a hard-boned face and flashing eyes, dressed very smartly, as always, with a vulgarly large diamond tiepin and immaculate white spats. Holding forth, very much as usual, to a small crowd of his wide-eyed and devoted fans, all of them hanging on his every word as he related his latest triumph. There's no denying he's a really good detective, with a razor-sharp mind; but there's also no denying he's an arrogant, stuck-up little tit. A hard man to dislike—but worth the effort.

Not too far away, ostentatiously ignoring Monkton Farley, was Ellen de Gustibus. She eats monsters. A pleasant enough sort, but it's still hard to look at her without feeling a certain chill. She really does eat monsters. Some agents of the Good are scarier than others. A tall, statuesque blonde in a rose-red basque and fishnet stockings, Ellen also favoured a bulky black leather jacket and stiletto heels so high they could be used in close combat, and often had been. She wore a hell of a lot of makeup, under spiky blonde hair, and was always smiling and laughing. And nearly always ready to buy the next round. Her crowd of wide-eyed admirers was even bigger than Farley's, and her stories were a lot more fun.

No one ever bothers Ellen de Gustibus. If anyone even tries, she just takes out a toothpick and rolls it round her mouth in a meaningful sort of way. Apparently, she'd just got back from cleaning out a nest of vampires in Budapest.

"How did you find them, Ellen?" asked a fan adoringly.

"Tasty," said Ellen.

Also present, unfortunately for all, was the Painted Ghoul. The clown at midnight himself, dressed in a bloodstained clown's costume composed of deliberately clashing colours. The Painted Ghoul's face was daubed with distressing patterns, and when he smiled his big red smile, you could see he'd filed his teeth into sharp points. His over-bright eyes were full of a malevolent glee. There's nothing funny about a clown with an erection.

I turned my back on him to look elsewhere, because he just lives for the attention, and nodded to Waterloo Lillian, a tall showgirl in a spangly outfit, with ostrich feathers in her piled-up hair and a bravely prominent Adam's apple.

"Have you heard anything about the Indigo Spirit?" I said, deliberately keeping it vague.

"Oh, him," said Lillian, sipping delicately from his champagne glass with an extended little finger. "He doesn't come around here anymore. Not since he got his head handed to him by a Drood a while back. I hear he does his drinking in the Nightside now. Because he knows he can't trust anyone here."

I felt bad about that, but I couldn't say anything. I hadn't meant to hurt him so badly. He just . . . got in the way.

"How about Charlatan Joe?" I asked, as casually as I could.

Waterloo Lillian sniffed loudly, the tall ostrich feathers shivering as he shook his head dismissively.

"The club management banned him permanently, for being dumb enough to bring the wrath of the Droods down on us in the first place. I mean, yes, this is supposed to be a sanctuary for one and all, but there are limits. And it's not like anyone misses Charlatan Joe, after all."

I moved away. I wasn't prepared to feel any more guilty. I'd done my penance.

Also present at the Wulfshead that night was Jumping Jack Flashman. Wearing a mind-blowingly colourful three-piece suit so bright and distinctive that blind people would have winced at it, complete with a black carnation in his buttonhole. He was looking even more smug than usual—which could only mean he'd just pulled off a really big score. Everyone knew he was a thief and a burglar, but we all felt safe when he was around. Partly because he was smart enough not to shit where he lived, but mostly because he stole only from the Very Rich and Prosperous. And no one who drinks in the Wulfshead makes enough money to qualify as one of Jumping Jack's targets. Tall and gangling, and handsome enough in a weak sort of way, Jumping Jack had fey blue eyes, dark stringy hair, and a drooping porn star's moustache.

He bellied up to the bar, grandly offering to buy drinks for one and all, and loudly announced he'd already set up his next challenge. A victim who would make everyone sit up and take notice. We all just laughed and nodded, because that was what he always said. No one doubted he could bring it off, though. No one did the short-range teleport burglary better than Jumping Jack Flashman.

I looked around, carefully, but no one seemed to be paying undue attention. Even though you would have thought that was just the kind of secret information the people spying on the club would want to know.

I moved unhurriedly on through the crowd, working the room with easy grace, chatting amiably with one and all, and just sort of casually bringing up the subject of secrets going missing. It seemed like everyone had heard something, though rarely the same something, but no one knew anything for sure. They weren't even particularly on their guard, or watching what they were saying. This was the Wulfshead, after all. They still felt safe here, because they always had been.

Monkton Farley bristled at the very thought, but he

made a point of dismissing his faithful devotees so we could discuss the matter privately.

"The whole point of drinking in an establishment like this," he said, "is that you can feel free to speak openly. Share a confidence, in the certainty that it will remain an understanding between the persons concerned. If that is no longer true, I may have to take my custom elsewhere."

"And we should miss you so, Monkton," said Ellen de Gustibus, easing in beside us and considering us solemnly over a very large drink. "But what secrets might you have, Monkton, that you're so concerned about? You're always saying your life is an open book."

"My professional life remains transparent to all," said Farley with quiet dignity. "But damn it all, a chap's private life should remain just that. The whole point of secrets is that they should stay secret."

"Two may keep a secret, if one of them is dead," Ellen said wisely.

The Painted Ghoul sniggered loudly as he forced his way into our group.

"I have no secrets, because I wear my heart on my sleeve. Look! There it is!"

We all looked, despite ourselves, and sure enough there was a human heart stitched to his billowing silk sleeve. It was still beating, slowly. The Painted Ghoul took a firm grip and wrenched the heart away. We all winced just a bit, as we heard the stitches tear. The Painted Ghoul offered the heart to each of us in turn, but we all declined. Even Ellen. Perhaps she was full, after Budapest. The clown shrugged and bit deeply into the heart. Blood dripped thickly from his chin, as he chewed happily.

He didn't care; but he loved it that we did.

"Your loss," he said indistinctly.

"I wouldn't touch anything you'd touched, clown," said Ellen. "I have scruples."

"Really?" leered the Painted Ghoul.

"Yes," said Ellen. "Bags full of them."

The clown actually stopped chewing for a moment.

"I think it's the Droods," Monkton Farley said abruptly. "They're the ones behind all this."

"Why?" I said.

"Because it always is the Droods!" Farley answered.

"Well, yes," said Ellen. "Very nearly always. But I don't think they'd go to all the trouble of listening in on our secrets just to give them away for free. The Droods use the secrets they acquire for leverage. Or blackmail. Or store them away for some future time, when they might come in handy."

"Nothing sells for a better price than a secret," said the Painted Ghoul.

"You should know," said Farley.

"You wound me, sir!" said the clown, throwing what was left of the heart to the floor and wiping his bloody fingers on the front of his outfit. "I tell everyone everything, just to see the look on their faces."

"Whoever it is that's listening in," said Ellen, "they're becoming a real nuisance. I come here to relax, far away from a judgemental world. Can't you figure out what's going on here, Monkton? Please? Pretty please?"

She actually went so far as to flutter her eyelashes at him. Monkton Farley smiled, despite himself. He never could resist a pretty face.

"I am a detective, and the current situation does ... intrigue me. I know for a fact that the Wulfshead Security people have turned the whole bar inside out, and failed to discover even a hint of a scientific or supernatural eavesdropping device. There's nothing here that isn't supposed to be here. Which suggests to me that this has to be some kind of inside job. And whoever is behind all this ... would have to be pretty damned powerful in their own right, not to be scared of what the Wulfshead management might do, if they ever find out."

We all looked at each other. We were all thinking of the Roaring Boys, but none of us wanted to say their name out loud, in case that was enough to make them appear. The last time the club management unleashed them, after that unfortunate business at last year's New Year's Eve celebrations, the police were fishing bodies and bits of bodies out of the Thames for more than three weeks. And the media never said a word. Funny, that ...

"Who do you think it is, Shaman?" said Ellen. "You've usually got your ear closer to the ground than anyone else."

"Yes," I said, "but I've been away. It does seem to me, though, that we're all missing the obvious question. Who profits? Who stands to make the most, out of all our secrets being made public? Or ... if they're not doing it for the money, what are they getting out of it? I mean, just setting up an operation like this can't have been cheap ..."

"Good point, Shaman," said Farley, frowning heavily. "If it's not about the money, it must be about the secrets themselves. Who wants to know?"

Jumping Jack Flashman just happened to be passing by at that moment, heading to the bar for a refill. He smiled charmingly on us all.

"Don't look at me; I only steal proper valuables. Secrets and information are just too hard to sell. You need brokers, and middlemen, and binding agreements ... I prefer to keep things simple. Nobody really cares if you just steal their valuables. Everybody's insured these days."

I went with him to the bar and ordered myself another bottle of Beck's. Talking is thirsty work. The barman who served me might have been the same one as before, or he might not. It didn't matter; they all had the same colourless professional personality. Though this particular clone must not have known me as well as some of the others, because he tried to interest me in some of the evening's special offers.

"Could I interest you in our special Dirty Pink Champagne, sir? Tinted, or perhaps more properly tainted, with a delicate diffusion of demon's blood? Atlantean ale? Lemurian lager? Ponce de Leon Sparkling Water, takes years off you. Or there's our new Cannibal Cognac—comes complete with a human finger at the bottom of every bottle. For when eating the worm just isn't enough . . ."

I looked at the bartender, and he decided he was urgently needed somewhere else. I put my back to the bar again, and looked up and down the length of the club. The place was packed, everybody talking at the tops of their voices, and men and women and certain others were huddling together in corners, doing things that would have been illegal if only the Government had known about them. That said, everyone was playing nice, because the club had raised its security levels. There were golem bouncers at every exit, standing unnaturally still in their oversized formal tuxedos. Their eyes burned fiercely, the yellow flames jumping slightly with every movement in the air. The golems were on guard, and they missed nothing.

And then I heard Ellen de Gustibus say, "Hey! Where did the Painted Ghoul go? He was standing right beside me just a moment ago!"

We all looked around quickly, but there was no sign of the clown at midnight anywhere. Which was ... more than odd. He wasn't the sort to just leave without making a big production out of it and upsetting as many people as possible ... And given the sheer press of the crowd, there was no way he could have gone far in just a few moments. Even as I looked around, there were more raised voices up and down the length of the club as people suddenly noticed that people they'd been talking to only a moment before just weren't there any longer. More and more names were shouted of people who'd disappeared. The music shut down abruptly as someone behind the bar realised something was seriously wrong. Panicking voices rose up throughout the club, demanding to know what the hell was going on.

It was only then that I realised how much the crowd had thinned out in the last few moments. The club was nowhere near as packed as it had been. Other people had already realised that, and were making a mad dash for the exits. Only to find that the doors wouldn't open. And I was pretty sure that wasn't down to the club management. We were being held where we were, like rats in a trap. People surged desperately this way and that, looking around for an enemy—or just someone handy to strike out at.

People at the sealed doors were yelling at the golems, demanding that they do something, but the tall, hulking figures didn't speak or move. Their grey stone faces remained utterly impassive, and the fire had gone out of their eyes, as though someone had turned them off. And the more I looked around, the more it seemed to me that there were even fewer people in the club than before. As though they were being taken when I wasn't looking. Just snatched away.

Suddenly the Wulfshead looked barely half full.

Men and women, friends and enemies, moved quickly to stand back to back so they could watch every direction at once and defend themselves against whatever was coming. Some threw accusations at one another, but most had already realised this had to be a threat from Outside. The shouting and screaming died quickly away, as people prepared to fight their corner. Weapons were appearing in everyone's hands. I turned and gestured urgently to the nearest barman.

"Why aren't the security measures kicking in?" I said loudly. "I thought they were supposed to defend us automatically, if the club ever came under attack from Outside?"

The barman looked back at me, confused. "I don't understand it! If there's a problem, any problem, the club should protect itself! If Security can't react, for fear of injuring the patrons, then all the doors should open automatically! And if that fails, then the Roaring Boys should appear, to sort things out. But nothing's activating! The computers back here are telling me they haven't been interfered with, or sabotaged, or even bypassed . . . They're just not activating. As though as far as they're concerned, nothing is wrong!"

I turned away from the barman as Monkton Farley grabbed me by the arm. His face was full of a sudden insight.

"Shaman! Have you noticed only people on the edges of the crowd have been disappearing! The people in the middle haven't been touched!"

"So whatever's grabbing people is only able to get at those people nearest the walls!" I said.

Farley fought his way into the crowd, yelling for everyone to stand together in the middle of the club and stay well away from the walls. Nobody argued. They were happy to go along with anything that might make them feel a little safer. They huddled together, back to back and shoulder to shoulder, glaring about them, defying any outsider to come too near. They all had some kind of weapon at the ready now. Everything from machine pistols to energy guns, enchanted knuckle-dusters to aboriginal pointing bones. We're an eclectic bunch at the Wulfshead.

There were even a few pieces of alien tech being brandished, dangerous enough to make me feel distinctly nervous. On the grounds that they looked powerful enough to destroy the whole club and everyone in it. I just hoped no one started shooting at shadows, because the moment one started, everyone else would be bound to join in.

I wanted very much to call on my armour so I could protect the crowd, as much as myself. But if I did that, everyone would know Shaman Bond was really a Drood. My cover identity would be lost forever. And I liked being Shaman Bond. I wasn't ready to give him up just yet. I put my right hand to my forehead, subvocalised the activating Words, and allowed just a trickle of strange matter to run down my neck from my torc, and then streak along my arm to my raised hand, until it could jump onto my face and form a pair of golden sunglasses. With so much going on around me, I was pretty sure no one would notice anything. And with the golden sunglasses in place, I could suddenly See the whole situation a great deal more clearly. I could See everything that was there, including the things I wasn't supposed to see.

The problem was the club's plasma screens. The huge screens covering the walls. Someone had tapped into them from Outside, and was watching everything that was going on inside the club from the other side of the screens. I could See them, dark figures sitting and listening on the far side of every screen—though they were almost certainly some distance away in reality.

This was how the secrets had been getting out. And no one had noticed because the screens were part of the club. Just taken for granted. They probably hadn't been physically altered, nothing to give away their new nature; they just had their signals piggybacked, so that the sound and vision went both ways.

I jumped up onto the bar and shouted at the crowd. Every eye and every weapon were immediately turned on me.

"It's the plasma screens!" I said. "Someone's made them two-way! Someone's looking in from Outside, so they can see and hear everything that happens here! And now they must be reaching through the screens to take people!"

I really shouldn't have been surprised when everyone present immediately opened fire on every plasma screen at once. I jumped down just in time and huddled up against the bar as all kinds of firepower were unleashed. The din was almost unbearable in the confined space. But when the shooting died raggedly away, and I looked up again, I saw that not a single screen had been so much as cracked. Whoever had tapped into them had clearly also reinforced them with all kinds of protections.

Everyone stood very still, looking around, and then a

whole bunch of dark hands burst out of every plasma screen at once, on the end of rapidly elongating dark, rubbery arms. The hands shot forward with incredible speed, grabbed the nearest people, and dragged them bodily towards the plasma screens, struggle as they might.

The dark hands clamped onto arms and shoulders with inhuman strength. Sometimes that was enough, if the victims had been caught off guard and off balance. The victims were dragged over to the screens, and then into and through them, all in a moment. If the victims fought back, then the hands would just hold them in place long enough for their arms to whip round and round them, wrapping them in dark, unrelenting coils. And then the arms would retract, dragging the still struggling victims through the plasma screens to whatever awaited them on the other side. People everywhere screamed and swore and fired their weapons wildly, and none of it did any good at all.

Of course, the kind of people you get at the Wulfshead Club often aren't the type to depend on weapons. Many were powerful enough or crafty enough to put up a fight on their own.

Monkton Farley ducked back and forth, hiding behind other people, using them as shields while he put his great mind to the problem of how to shut down the screens. He was already assembling an impressive bit of tech from various things he dug out of his pockets.

Ellen de Gustibus grabbed the nearest dark arm as it shot past her, held it firmly in place with both of her hands, and then took a large bite out of it. It bucked and jerked spasmodically as Ellen chewed her way through it. There wasn't any blood that I could see.

Waterloo Lillian stabbed an aboriginal bone at a dark hand as it went for him, and the hand just withered and fell apart. The attached arm disintegrated into dust. But even as Lillian whooped loudly in triumph, another dark arm looped itself quickly around him from behind. Half a dozen coils were enough to pin his arms to his sides, and then they squeezed hard, crushing all the breath out of him. The bone fell from Lillian's nerveless fingers, and his mascaraed eyes rolled up in his head. The arm dragged him off to the nearest screen.

Jumping Jack Flashman had already discovered he couldn't get out of the club. The main security shields were still in place. So he just went teleporting back and forth around the interior, appearing and disappearing before the hands or arms could get a grip on him. One dark arm did whip around him, but he was gone again before it could tighten. The next time he reappeared, though, a dark hand was waiting for him, hanging on the air. It formed itself into a fist and punched him hard in the side of the head the moment he appeared. The arm caught his unconscious body before it could hit the ground, looped around him, and hauled him away.

Whoever was in control on the other side of the plasma screens, it was clear they were no longer content just to take secrets. With their presence blown, they were taking the people who knew the secrets. And even with all this mayhem going on around me, I still couldn't help wondering . . . who could be brave enough, or stupid enough, or just plain desperate enough to make enemies of the club management? And all the friends and families and organisations attached to the people they'd taken? Even my family would hesitate to make so many significant dangerous enemies at once.

It wouldn't stop them, but they'd definitely think about it first.

A dark hand on the end of a rapidly lengthening arm came flying directly at me, only to slam to a halt at the very last moment. It hung quivering on the air, just a few inches short of my face, and then turned away, in search of another victim. I put a hand to my throat, where my torc was tingling wildly. The hand had detected the torc and turned away rather than antagonise the Droods. Which was . . . interesting. I looked quickly around, and then sent another trickle of golden strange matter down my arm, under my sleeve, to form an armoured glove over my right hand. I needed to do something before I was left standing alone in an empty club.

A dark hand flew past me. I grabbed it out of mid-air and crushed it with my golden glove. I felt bones crack and break in my grasp; and when I let the hand go, it whipped quickly back inside the nearest screen. Through my golden spectacles I watched it go, and saw vague figures moving agitatedly back and forth on the other side of the screen. One of them was clutching his hand to his chest, as though it was injured. And another figure . . . was quite definitely giving orders to the others. I punched the screen before me with my golden hand, and instead of cracking or breaking, the screen just let my armoured hand pass right through, into the place behind.

I concentrated hard, and my armour connected with the screen's operating systems, infiltrating their command structures. And then it seemed like the easiest thing in the world for me to reach all the way through the screen and grab the figure who'd been giving all the orders. I took a firm hold and hauled him back through the screen and into the Wulfshead Club. I threw him to the floor and stood over him . . . and was quietly astonished to discover that I knew him.

He just sprawled there, shaking and shuddering, not even trying to get up. He looked at me piteously, like a child expecting to be punished for something that really wasn't his fault. I made my golden sunglasses disappear so he could see my face clearly. I wanted him to be able to see just how angry I was.

It was Alan Diment, the current head of MI 13, the British Government's very own secret spy organisation, dedicated to protecting Queen and Country from unnatural threats. They weren't very big, or particularly well budgeted, but they tried hard. They handled all the day-to-day supernatural threats that my family, or the Department of Uncanny, were too busy to deal with. Normally they had enough sense not to mess with the Big Guys. And certainly not with established power bases like the Wulfshead Club. A lot of MI 13's higher-ups were supposed to be Members . . . Which was probably how they'd got access to the plasma screens in the first place.

Alan Diment was a middle-aged, grey little man, as quietly anonymous and nondescript as any professional secret agent should be. I knew him mainly as a courier, passed over for more important things for a whole bunch of good reasons. Diment was blonde and blue-eyed, in a minor aristocratic sort of way, the kind who got into Intelligence because that was what Daddy did. What his family had done, for generations. Only to discover that he wasn't any good at it.

The last time I encountered Alan Diment, very briefly, it was during the Great Satanic Conspiracy business. Which had turned out to be run by the previous head of MI 13, that treacherous little shit Philip MacAlpine. It also turned out that a lot of the higher echelons of MI 13 had been a part of the Conspiracy, and my family had to hunt them all down and kill them, root and branch. Because some things just can't be forgiven. Presumably Alan Diment had been one of the few older agents left untouched by the scandal. I had heard they'd put him in charge, but I'd never thought he'd be dumb enough to do something like this.

I grabbed him by the shirtfront, pulled him up off the floor, and slammed him back against the bar. I thrust my face right into his. He didn't even struggle, just looked back at me with his big, sad eyes. I showed him my golden fist, and his eyes widened even more as I made golden spikes rise out of the knuckles.

"You are in trouble, Alan," I said. "Real trouble. Tell me what you know. Tell me everything that's going on here. And this would not be a good time to grow a pair and fall back on your supposed authority."

"No one's dead! No one's hurt!" Diment said quickly. "This was just supposed to be an information-gathering operation! That is what spies do, after all, isn't it? Look, they made me be head of MI 13. I didn't want the job; I was looking forward to taking early retirement. But after that stupid Satanic Conspiracy thing wiped out all the top levels of the organisation, I was the only one left who knew how things worked. The only one with any real experience. I'd put the years in, so they gave me an office and a secretary and told me to get on with it. *Keep your head down,* they said, *and don't make any waves. Just hold the fort until we can find someone more suitable to do the job.*

"But . . . the Government had been through its own purge, because of the Conspiracy, and there were a lot of new faces around, settling into positions of power, desperate to make their mark. They were the ones who put the pressure on. They wanted to prove MI 13 was still fit for purpose. That it was still capable of bringing in the bacon ... I was told I had to do something, come up with some big new idea, to keep them from ... disposing of me.

"So I talked to a few old friends, chaps I went to school with, who were working for Black Heir. You know, the Government department tasked with clearing up the mess left behind after alien encounters ... Of course you know. These friends loaned me a few useful bits of alien tech, and I talked some of my people who were Members of the Wulfshead into quietly introducing that alien tech into the plasma screens. Wasn't difficult ... The club management may be absolute fiends when it comes to external security, but they never considered there might be a threat from inside their precious club.

"Anyway, I soon had some of my people sitting on the other side of the screens, keeping their eyes and ears open and writing down anything that seemed ... interesting. I sorted through it all and sent anything that seemed important Upstairs. And that should have been it. But then certain people in positions of power started deliberately releasing the secrets, to do damage to people they disapproved of. I think a lot of that was down to interdepartmental fighting ...

"They said they were very pleased with me! At first ... Enough to take the pressure off, for a while, but then they started getting greedy. They didn't just want the secrets, they wanted the people who knew the secrets. Because they weren't seen as people any more, just useful assets to be exploited. So the word came down, and it was more than my life was worth to say no. I was told to grab a few useful people from the Wulfshead tonight. They even gave me a shopping list. *Take a few,* they said,

not enough to draw anyone's attention. But no one expected you to be here. They took one look at you and
panicked. Said, 'Take everyone!' Make a clean sweep of
it, while we can. Before you figured out what was happening and shut it down. I told them it was a bad idea!
But they wouldn't listen . . ."

I turned Alan Diment around with my armoured
hand and showed him to the nearest plasma screen.

"You know who I am!" I said loudly. "Give back the
people you've taken, right now, and I'll give you back
your head of MI 13. With all his important parts still attached."

There wasn't even a pause. A voice from the other
side of the screen said, "Keep him."

Diment looked shocked, but not particularly surprised. I sighed inwardly and tried again.

"All right," I said. "You want to escalate? I can do
that. First, you've already seen that I can pass through
the screen. Don't make me come there in person and
show you just how much damage I can cause to things
and people when I'm in a mood. Second, do you really
want my family at your throats? Now, and forever?"

There was a long pause, and then all the dark hands
on their long black arms whipped back into the plasma
screens and were gone. The few people left in the club,
who'd managed to fight the hands off, raised their heads
and looked slowly about them. And then all the people
who'd been taken came flying back through the screens
into the club. They poured through in a rush, piling up on
the floor. Those still conscious cried out at the impact,
but didn't have enough strength left to make a fuss. No
one seemed badly injured; but a lot of them looked like
they'd been hit with some heavy-duty sedation. I glared

at the dark figures moving uneasily about on the other side of the screens.

"There had better not be anyone missing!" I said sternly. "Not even one. Or I will come and find you."

Four more bodies came flying through the screens. Interestingly, I didn't recognise any of them. But apparently someone thought they were important . . . I looked at Alan Diment.

"This was a really bad idea. Don't ever try it again. Not here, or anywhere else."

"I wouldn't," said Diment. "But someone else might."

I looked at him thoughtfully. "Who was it, exactly, who pressured you into doing this?"

"The current Government has an awful lot of new people in it," Diment said carefully. "Obsessed with secrets, and the power having those secrets would bring them . . ."

"Names," I said.

"Sorry," said Diment sadly. "You might kill me for not talking, but they definitely would, if I did."

I nodded, turned him around, and booted him back through the nearest plasma screen. It swallowed him up in a moment, and then every screen in the club went blank, shut down from the other side. I had no doubt that by the time the club's management had the screens up and running again, all ties to the other side would have been cut. Not a trace left behind, to point the finger at anyone.

People were getting to their feet now, and looking at each other and the blank plasma screens with equal confusion. Whatever they'd seen on the other side, and whatever had been done to them, they clearly didn't remember. I discreetly made my golden hand disappear, and then moved through the crowd, checking that everyone was all right. Ellen de Gustibus was leaning heavily on Monkton Farley, exhausted. He comforted her as best he could. He understood all there was to know about people, except how to be one. I gave him bonus marks for trying. Jumping Jack Flashman left through the nearest exit, the moment someone discovered they were working again. And the Painted Ghoul . . . just brushed himself down, briskly. As though this kind of thing happened to him all the time. And for all I knew, it did.

"Light my cigarette, lover," said Waterloo Lillian, and I did, though I had to hold his hand steady with my other hand while I did it.

"You all right?" I said.

"As close as I get," he said, smiling briefly. "Do you understand what just happened here?"

"Me?" I said. "No, I'm just passing through."

I spotted Harry Fabulous, slouching in the open doorway at the far end of the club, and excused myself. I wandered casually over, to have a quiet word. Harry half retreated into the shadows of the door, preferring not to be noticed or recognised by the clientele. He needn't have worried; everyone else was far too concerned with their own problems.

"I have been authorised to thank you," said Harry Fabulous. "The club's management are . . . reasonably happy with the way things have turned out. They wish me to assure you that they can take things from here. And do whatever may be necessary to ensure this never happens again."

"I'll still be having a word with my family," I said. "We'll sort out whoever it is in the current Government who's been getting ideas above their station. Can't have politicians messing around with things that really matter. One of us will have a quiet word with the Prime Minister. It's been a while since we made a PM cry, and wet himself." I gave Harry a firm look. "Remind your masters they owe me a favour. A big one."

"That was the agreement," Harry said steadily.

"So," I said, "can I take it I am no longer banned from the Wulfshead Club?"

"Shaman Bond never was," Harry said carefully. "But Eddie Drood still is. Because a lot of the clientele here would rise up and do their level best to strike him down, first time they saw him."

"I get that a lot," I said.

CHAPTER TWO

Where There's a Will, There's a Complication

Harry Fabulous made a point of escorting me to a particular back door, which he assured me would open directly onto the grounds of my family home, Drood Hall. I let him do it, because I was intrigued to see if the Wulfshead management really could bring that off. My family has always taken its personal security very seriously (especially after the Chinese Communists tried to nuke the Hall, back in the sixties) and I'd always been assured it was impossible for anyone to teleport directly onto Drood property. Just by offering to do it, the Wulfshead management were making a point. *See how powerful we are,* they were saying. *See what we can do, that no one else can.*

And sure enough, Harry opened an apparently unremarkable door at the very rear of the club, and bright sunlight spilled through the opening, pushing back the close, smoky air inside. I looked through the door, and there were the wide-open grounds leading up to Drood Hall. I looked the door over carefully, and then turned my gaze on Harry Fabulous, who did his best to bear up under it.

"I think my family will take this intrusion very seriously," I said. "This is simply not allowed, Harry. Tell the club management to rip this door out and destroy it."

Harry shrugged helplessly. "I'll tell them, Eddie, but they won't listen to me. You know that."

"They won't be listening to you, Harry. They'll be listening to me. I don't mind helping them out, in an emergency, but putting my family's security at risk is something else. You tell them either they shut this door permanently, or I will come back here with some of the more unpleasant members of my family, and we will shut down the Wulfshead Club, permanently. Suddenly and violently and with extreme prejudice."

"They didn't have to tell you about the door," Harry said carefully. "This isn't a threat; it's a peace offering. You should consider where they got the door from and who else might have one just like it. And no, I don't know, so there's absolutely no point in threatening me."

I considered the point, nodded, and stepped through the door. Immediately, I was back home, in the middle of the family grounds, brilliant green lawns stretching away in every direction, under a blazing blue sky. I heard the club door shut firmly behind me, and when I glanced back over my shoulder, it was gone. Not a trace left to show it had ever been there. Very well, Wulfshead management; message received and understood.

I strolled on through the grounds, taking my time, enjoying the scenery. Everywhere I looked, perfectly cut and professionally maintained lawns stretched away before me, big enough to land a whole fleet of planes on. Sprinklers filled the air with a moist haze, and stepping through them allowed me to enjoy a cool and refreshing moment in the blazing summer heat. The old hedge maze was still there, its spiky green walls towering over me as I passed. Of course, the old monster it had been constructed to imprison was long gone now, safely dumped and abandoned in another dimension. But I was sure we could find something equally bad and dangerous that deserved trapping inside the maze. Though I didn't think I'd raise the idea with my family. Given our track record, they'd probably try to throw me in.

A little further on, I paused to enjoy the massive flower gardens, laid out in intricate shapes and mosaics and boasting more than a few multicoloured blooms not at all native to this world, or even this reality. Some of them still moved to follow an entirely different sun than ours. A wide circle of red, white, and blue roses had been planted to resemble a great eye that winked slowly at me as I passed. I didn't wink back. It's best not to encourage them.

A whole crowd of peacocks paraded proudly by, filling the air with their loud, discordant cries. All part of our early-warning system. High-tech and magical systems are all very well, but you can't beat a natural response. Machines and magics can be overcome, or even sabotaged, but the only way to shut the peacocks up would be to shoot them all in the head. And I think we'd notice that. The gryphons were out on patrol too, waddling importantly back and forth. They can see a short way into the future, which makes them ideal for spotting potential attacks and attackers, and being there waiting for the poor sods when they arrive. They're friendly enough creatures to the family, but they do like to track down dead things and then have a really good roll in them. Which is why they are never allowed inside the Hall. I waved at them, and kept moving.

I knew I was just putting off the moment when I would have to go inside, and make my report to the ruling Council. Not that I had anything to worry about; the mission had gone well, or at least well enough. But I just knew they'd find something to complain about. They always did. I hate debriefings. It's hard enough explaining why you did something, without having to explain why you didn't do something else that they thought you should have done.

And they always make such a fuss over my expenses.

Drood Hall rose up before me; huge and imposing, it dominated the grounds it was set in without even trying. My old family home. Very old. The centre structure was a great sprawling manor house, with ivy swarming all over the walls. It dated originally from Tudor times, and had been much added to down through the centuries. It still boasted the traditional black-and-white boarded frontage and heavy leaded-glass windows, all under a jutting gabled roof. Four great wings came later, massive and solid in the old Regency style, containing fifteen hundred rooms and a hell of a lot more Droods. We're a big family, and getting bigger. Soon enough we'll be packed to overflowing, and then it will be time to move on again. Floors and floors above me, the great roof rose and fell like a grey-tiled sea, complete with gargoyles, ornamental guttering, observatories and aeries, sprawling nests of antennae, and a series of landing pads for everything from autogyros to winged unicorns. Along with a hell of a lot of gun emplacements. I did mention that we take our security seriously, didn't I?

I always have mixed feelings every time I come back to stand before Drood Hall. The family made my life hell, all the time I was growing up, and I ran away to London to be a field agent first chance I got. But the Hall is still my home.

Suddenly Molly Metcalf, my love and my delight, was running towards me, emerging from a door in mid-air that hadn't been there just a moment before. Molly was allowed to open a door onto the Drood grounds from her personal forest, because she was my girlfriend and because there was absolutely no way of stopping her. The wild witch of the woods walked her own path, and woe betide anyone who got in her way. So the family made a special dispensation in her case, rather than have her do it anyway and just laugh in their faces when they got upset about it. I could see the massive ancient trees of her private forest through the door, stretching away forever—trees too big, too primal, to be part of today's world. Someday I was going to have to find out just where, or more likely when, her wood was situated.

Molly came running from the opening she'd made in the world, smiling broadly at me, arms stretched out wide. The door behind her disappeared as she sprinted across the lawns to greet me. Sweet, petite, and overwhelmingly feminine, Molly always reminded me of a delicate china doll with big bosoms. She had bobbed black hair, huge dark eyes, and a rosebud mouth red as sin itself. She was wearing a long, billowing dress of ruffled white silk, possibly chosen to lend a touch of colour to her pale skin. For someone who preferred to spend most of her time out of doors, Molly never took even a touch of tan.

My Molly, my love. There are an awful lot of strange and disturbing stories about the wild witch Molly Metcalf, and every single one of them is true. I know; I was there at the time, for most of them.

She crossed the open space between us at incredible speed, her bare feet barely disturbing the thick green grass, and then she slammed right into me, throwing her arms around me as she bowled me over and sent me flying backwards. I was braced for the impact, and it still knocked the breath out of me for a moment. Molly ended up lying on top of me, laughing breathlessly into my face as I lay flat on my back on the thick green grass. I held her in my arms, grinning back at her. I always enjoy having Molly lie on top of me; it's like her whole body from head to toe is saying, *Hello! I'm here!*

"All right," I said finally, "how did you know to find me here?"

She kissed me several times, and ran her fingers through my hair. "I always know where you are, sweetie. I keep track. How else can I look after you? How was the Vatican?"

I looked at her sternly. "That's family business. You weren't even supposed to know I was there."

"I refer you to my previous answer," said Molly, in her most sultry voice. "And you haven't answered my question. Any problems?"

"Nothing I couldn't handle," I said.

"Showoff . . ."

I kissed her, to shut her up, and then we both lay there together, on the grass, in each other's arms. She rested her head on my chest, riding my breathing.

"I haven't paid the Vatican a visit in years," she said finally. "It's well past time I dropped in again, just to annoy them."

"Please don't," I said. "I'm pretty sure they're still getting over the last time you were there. When you transformed all the statues of the Saints into female versions."

"I was making a point!" said Molly. "I changed them all back again, didn't I?"

"Yes," I said. "Eventually . . ."

Molly suddenly scowled at me, glaring right into my face from only a few inches away. "Why are we here, Eddie?"

"Why are any of us here?" I said, reasonably. "I can make a few informed guesses, if you like . . ."

She prodded me hard in the chest with one long, bony finger. "I mean, why are we here at Drood Hall when we should be smashing our way into the Department of Uncanny, roughing up the hired help and intimidating the security guards, before pinning the Regent of Shadows to his office wall and getting some answers out of him? Very definitely including why did he murder my parents?"

She didn't give me time to answer. Just got up off me, scrambled to her feet, and turned her back on me, glaring at Drood Hall with her arms tightly folded. I sighed, inwardly, and took my time getting to my feet. Giving myself time to work out exactly what I was going to say. It wasn't going to be easy, because there was no right thing to say, but it was important to me that we understood each other. I brushed crushed grass off my clothes, to let her know I was approaching, and then moved carefully in beside her. I had enough sense not to touch her.

"Visiting the Regent, my Grandfather, in search of answers . . . is next on my list of things to do," I said. "Right after I've talked to the Council."

"You had time to stop off for a drink at the Wulfs-head," said Molly, still not looking at me.

"That was business," I said. "And this spying on me is becoming less charming by the moment."

Molly turned her head to scowl at me, her dark eyes flashing dangerously. "You promised me that when we got back from France, we'd go straight to Uncanny and get some straight answers out of the Regent! I want to know who gave him the order to execute my mother and father! I want to know exactly who in your family was responsible!"

"And we will," I said. "I promised. But first, loath as I am to admit it, I do have duties and responsibilities to my family."

She looked away again. "That's always been your problem, Eddie. Always one more mission, one more thing that needs doing . . ."

"Molly . . ."

"Cut the cord, Eddie! Before I decide to do it for you, and in a way you won't like. What's holding you here?"

"Right now?" I said.

"You didn't have to come back here for a debriefing, and you know it!"

"You're right," I said. "I'm here because I was called back to attend the reading of my grandmother's will. The mission was just something to keep me busy till all the paperwork was in order."

Molly looked at me blankly. "But . . . Martha was killed ages ago! And they're only now getting around to the reading of the will? Why has it taken so long?"

"Things move slowly inside the family," I said. "Customs and protocols, and all that. And to be fair, we have all been very busy. Anyway, I have to be present for the reading, because apparently I'm mentioned in the will."

"Ooh!" said Molly, brightening immediately. "Any chance she's left you some money?"

"What do we need with money?" I said, suddenly suspicious. "Last time I looked, we had enough tucked away to last several lifetimes. Have you been shopping in the Nightside again?"

"Of course we don't need the money," said Molly, her voice maddeningly calm and reasonable. "It's the principle of the thing."

"No, it isn't," I said. "With you, it's never the principle of the thing. It's always all about the money!"

"So you do think she's left you something!"

"I don't know," I said. "The Armourer just said I was . . . mentioned in the will. And knowing Grandmother, almost certainly not in a good way."

Molly looked at me thoughtfully. "You know, most people have two sets of grandparents. I know the Regent, your grandfather Arthur, was Martha's first husband. Before she kicked him out of the family, and married Alistair . . . and that Emily was her daughter by that first marriage, who married your father, Charles . . . Or Diana and Patrick as they now like to be known . . . God, your family's complicated, Eddie. But where are your father's parents? What about his family?"

"Good question," I said. "I have no idea. The Droods never like to talk about outside relatives. Inside the Hall, it's only Droods who matter. Makes it easier to instill family loyalty and duty. I grew up thinking both my parents were dead, and my family never wanted to talk about either of them. When I finally got to meet my parents, there just wasn't time to stop and talk . . . And since they've gone missing again . . ."

"Complicated," said Molly. "Very complicated."

"It is something I think about," I said. "I like to believe that there's another family, out there in the world somewhere. People I could go to if I ever did turn my back on the Droods."

"Are you thinking of leaving, Eddie?" asked Molly, not quite as casually as I think she intended. "I mean, you know I'm all in favour of that, but working for the Department of Uncanny didn't really work out. Did it?"

"No," I said. "The Regent lied to me almost as much as the Droods did. But I would like to have the option to leave; if only I knew for sure there was somewhere else for me to go . . ."

Molly smiled at me brilliantly and slipped a companionable arm through mine, and I knew I was forgiven. For the moment.

"Come on," she said briskly. "Let's do this. Get it done, and over with, so we can concentrate on the things that really matter. I wonder how much your grandmother's left you . . ."

"I'm really not going to like it when next month's bills come in, am I?" I said.

"All I ever inherited from my family were two sisters who always irritated the crap out of me," said Molly.

"You never talk much about your family," I said.

"Bunch of deadbeats and hangers-on," she said. "I'd divorce the lot of them if I could just find a lawyer who wasn't afraid of them."

We strode briskly across the lawn, heading for Drood Hall. I could hear one of the underground robot gun emplacements, directly under our feet, stirring restlessly as we passed over it. I was safe enough, as a Drood, but the robot sensors didn't approve of Molly. The robot gun would probably have liked to come up out of the ground to take a good look at her, but it was just sentient enough to be very wary of her. Even the peacocks backed away, to give her plenty of room. Which made me think . . . and take a good look around. The huge grassy lawns stretched off into the distance, open and empty. Not a Drood to be seen anywhere—which was just a bit odd, on such a lovely summer's afternoon. Where was everyone? Which, of course, led me on to another thought.

"Molly," I said carefully, "where are your sisters right now?"

"No need to look over your shoulder, sweetie," said Molly, smiling. "I would warn you if there was any danger of them dropping in. If only so that you could keep up with me once I started running. No, the last I heard, Isabella had bullied her way onto an archaeological dig somewhere in darkest Peru, in search of the Great Demon Bear. And Louisa is currently scuba-diving among the sunken remains of the city of Lyonesse, somewhere off the Cornwall coast."

"At least she won't be bothering anyone there," I said.

Molly laughed briefly. "You've never been to Lyonesse, have you?"

And then we both looked up sharply as a flying saucer went tumbling through the sky overhead. Just a small one, not much bigger than a London bus, covered with all kinds of crackling lights. It shot this way and that, turned rapidly end over end, circled the Hall twice, and then dived down for a not particularly dangerous crash landing on one of the empty arrival pads on the Hall roof. Dazzling colours blew off in every direction, exploding in the sky like so many silent fireworks. Two teenage girls on winged unicorns quickly appeared on the scene, and hovered overhead while spraying the scene with anti-radiation foam, from long nozzles attached to sturdy packs on the unicorns' sides. Nobody emerged from the crashed flying saucer. Probably too embarrassed.

"A flying saucer?" said Molly. "Some of your lot, or just Visitors?"

"It's questions like that," I said, moving on, "that remind me why I prefer to stay away . . ."

The front door loomed up before us — the main entrance to Drood Hall, and everything it contained. I took a deep breath, and braced myself.

"Look," I said to Molly, "I have to go in and see my family. You don't. Are you sure you wouldn't rather go back and wait in your nice safe private forest, until all the shouting and bad temper has subsided?"

"Nonsense!" Molly said immediately. "Wouldn't miss it for the world. I promise I'll stand at the back, and be very quiet, and not attack anyone unless I feel I absolutely have to. Come on — a chance to watch your family lose their temper with each other, like the arrogant, entitled, elitist scum they are? I never miss a chance to feel superior . . . Besides, you really think I'd let you walk into the lions' den on your own? It's my job to watch your back, against friends and enemies and family." She squeezed my arm against her side possessively. "What do you think the previous Matriarch of all the Droods has left you in her will, Eddie?"

"Nothing I'd want, knowing her," I said.

"Maybe she's appointed you her official successor and made you head of the whole Drood family!"

"Only if she was really mad at me . . ."

I kicked the main door in, and Molly and I strode into Drood Hall like we were thinking of repossessing the place. I was immediately surprised to discover that there was no one there to meet us. Or to try to stop us from entering. It's usually one or the other. The Sarjeant-at-Arms was nearly always waiting, to say something sardonic and offensive, as though he felt it was his duty to make sure I knew I was not at all welcome. Like I needed him to tell me that. At the very least, the Sarjeant usually preferred to escort me through the Hall, to make sure I didn't go anywhere the family didn't want me going. It's not like he could actually stop me doing any damned thing I felt like, including stuffing some of the family silver in a big bag marked *Swag* and making off with it, but we both usually went along. For the good of the family.

But it's when there's no one around that I know for sure something's going on. Something I'm really not going to approve of.

First rule of an agent: Never let them see they've got you worried. I stuck my nose in the air and strode through the shadowy vestibule, and on into the main hallway, with Molly still hanging determinedly onto my arm. Light streamed in through dozens of long, narrow stained-glass windows, shimmering spotlights stabbing through the gloom, filling the long corridor with all the colours of the rainbow. Many of the stained-glass scenes depicted significant moments in my family's long history, all the heroes and legends of Drood times. The secret history of the world. After that, it was row upon row of paintings and portraits, showing off honoured family members. Most of them looking dour or constipated, with not a single smile to be seen among the lot of them. The fashions changed as the centuries passed, but they all did their best to look like secret masters of the world.

Eventually portraits gave way to photographs, as the

more modern generations appeared. And it was only when I got to the very end of the hallway that I spotted the small gap on one wall, where the photo of my parents used to be.

I remembered that photo. When I was a child growing up in Drood Hall, it was all I had to remember my father and mother by. The two of them together, not much older than I am now, smiling happily . . . And now the photo was gone, and they were gone, airbrushed out of Drood history.

I stood before the empty gap on the wall, staring at nothing, feeling like I'd just been punched in the heart. I had no other photo of my mother and my father. It had been allowed to hang there as long as the family thought they were honourably dead, lost in action in the field. But now we all knew they were alive, and working for the Department of Uncanny, the family had turned its back on them. Made them non-persons. Because no one is allowed to walk away from the family. After a while, Molly squeezed my arm reassuringly, and we walked on.

People started to appear, in the corridors and open spaces, as we made our way deeper into the Hall. Men and women hurried back and forth on family business, all of them far too busy to stop and chat. Some actually jumped skittishly when I looked at them. Some faces I recognised, and some I didn't. We're a big family. So big we have our own monthly in-Hall magazine, *Drood Times*. A big glossy thing, distributed only within the family. In fact, all copies are programmed to self-destruct if they're touched by anyone without Drood DNA. The magazine is full of family doings, always bright and cheerful, and packed with the latest gossip—and it depresses me beyond words. I don't tend to appear in it much, except as a Bad Example.

Of course I read it every month. Know thy enemy . . .

I smiled and nodded to one and all, and kept going. Some smiled and nodded back; some didn't. Molly doesn't really do the smiling and nodding thing, even under the best of circumstances. She just scowled around her, and the Droods who recognised her put on a really impressive burst of speed.

I kept a cautious eye on Molly, just in case she decided she'd been insulted, but she seemed far more interested in the many rare and expensive works of art that pop up everywhere in the Hall. Paintings and statues by world Masters, all of which have never seen the inside of a museum or gallery, and whose existence here explains certain gaps in the Masters' official output. Tribute, from a grateful world and its governments. Or placations, to please leave them alone. Depends on how you look at it. I didn't like the thoughtful way Molly was looking at some of the more easily moveable pieces, or the frankly larcenous look in her eye. So I hurried her along, just a little, in case her fingers started itching.

Finally, we came to the heart of Drood Hall, the great open chamber called the Sanctity. Off-limits to pretty much all the family, these days, except for the ruling Council. The Sanctity, where all the things that really matter are decided. Two large and muscular young Droods were standing guard in front of the closed double doors, and they both slammed to attention as Molly and I approached. They were trying hard to look brave and bold and officious, and not at all terribly worried. For all their size and bulk, they both looked like they really didn't want to be there. Doing what they were doing. Whatever that turned out to be. They stood their ground as Molly and I walked right up to them, determined to do their duty. They were Droods, after all.

"Edwin Drood, we recognise you!" the guard on the left said loudly. "We acknowledge your right to enter the Sanctity!"

"Well," I said, "that's nice. But then, I've always had that right. Really didn't need you to tell me that. Why are you guarding the Sanctity? Has someone tried to steal it?"

The guard swallowed hard, and pressed on with his carefully rehearsed speech, in an only slightly strangulated tone of voice.

"However, it is my duty to inform you, it has been decided by the Council that while you may enter for the reading of the Matriarch's will, Molly Metcalf may not. We have been given specific instructions that she is not to be allowed into the Sanctity."

"I hope there's a good reason for that," I said, in an only slightly dangerous tone of voice.

The guard looked like he wanted to whine piteously and wet himself, possibly simultaneously, but he pressed on. "It is a condition of the will that only those mentioned or directly affected by the terms of the will may be present during its reading. These are the words of the Council and nothing at all to do with me, so please don't let the witch turn me or my brother into something squishy."

I was getting ready to make a fuss, just on general principles, when Molly surprised me by nodding her head understandingly. She slipped her arm free of mine, stepped back, and smiled easily at me.

"It's all right, Eddie. I get it. Wills are always going to be private family things. You go on. Take your time. I'm sure I can find some trouble to get into."

I grinned back at her. "I'll listen for the bang."

Molly kissed me hard, just to scandalise the guards, and then swayed casually off down the corridor. Almost certainly with theft, abuse, and extensive property damage in mind. Serve my family right, for upsetting her. The guards seemed happy to see her go. So I gave them my best hard stare, and they immediately snapped to attention again, on either side of the doors. There was no real fun to be had in intimidating them; it was like bullying puppies. The double doors to the Sanctity swung slowly open on their own. I gave them a long, thoughtful look and walked in.

I entered the Sanctity with my head held high, and then relaxed despite myself as the warm rosy glow of the place fell on me like a benediction. The Sanctity isn't just the main meeting place of Drood pomp and power; it's also home to Ethel. Our strange visitor from another dimension, or reality. Or somewhere else. We don't know, and frankly, most of us are too scared to ask. She looks after us, supplies the strange matter of our armour, and baffles us all on a daily basis. She does seem to be genuinely fond of the family, but I can't shake the feeling that our other-dimensional patron really thinks she's raising Droods as pets.

The constant red glow is the only sure sign of her presence in this world, and all we've ever seen of her. Given that she claims to have downloaded herself into our material reality from a higher dimension, I suppose it's always possible that the red glow might be all there is of her. Certainly, just standing in the glow for any length of time makes you feel loved, cared for, and appreciated. Still doesn't do much to keep major arguments from breaking out during Council meetings, though. The Droods are just that kind of family.

Sitting around the single bare wooden table before me were the current members of the Drood ruling Council. My uncle Jack, the Armourer. William, the Librarian. The Serjeant-at-Arms. And, somewhat to my surprise, the landscape gardener, Capability Maggie. Who was hardly ever seen inside the Hall, because she much preferred to be outside, looking after the gardens and grounds. If anything, she looked even less happy to be there than I was.

They all looked at me in much the same way, as though I was late, untidy and unwelcome, and let in only on tolerance. I was used to that from my family.

"Eddie!" said a loud, happy, and entirely disembodied female voice. "Hello hello hello! Welcome back! How was the Vatican? Did you bring me back a present?"

"Hello, Ethel," I said, to the chamber at large. "Yes, the mission was successful, and no, I didn't bring anything back for you. I had to leave in something of a hurry, with hellhounds on my trail, and the Gift Shop was closed. Besides, they didn't have anything there you would have liked."

"You don't know that," Ethel said immediately. "They might have. You could have looked."

"You're very hard to buy for," I said. "What do you get for the other-dimensional entity who is everything?"

She giggled, which is an eerie thing in a disembodied voice.

I looked around the table, nodding briefly to each member of the Council in turn. I can be polite and civilised when I have to. The Armourer, my uncle Jack, was a tall man in late middle age, full of far too much nervous energy for his own good. Or, given his job, everyone else's. He was tapping the fingers of one hand on the table, and frowning hard as he concentrated on some new awful thing to throw at the family's enemies. Or someone he'd just seen on the television news who'd upset him. He wore a long lab coat that might have been white a long time before, but was now covered with chemical stains, acid burns, and what looked worryingly like teeth marks. Underneath the lab coat, the Armourer was wearing a grubby T-shirt bearing the legend *Yes I do hear voices, and they all know your name.* Two fluffy tufts of white hair peeked out above his ears—all that was left of a once impressive head of hair that had jumped ship many years earlier. He looked hard done by, but still hard enough to cope.

Back in his day, my uncle Jack had been one of the family's leading field agents, rushing around Cold War Europe stamping out super-science and supernatural bush-fires. He still looked like he could punch his weight, but years of working in the Armoury had bent him over in a permanent stoop. Either from constant hard work at the design table, or just from the strain of putting up with generations of genius lab assistants who were often as much a threat to each other as they were to the family's enemies. In my experience, they didn't seem to feel a day was complete if they hadn't shot, blown up, or mutated each other several times before lunch.

My uncle Jack had large engineer's hands and an enquiring mind without nearly enough limits. And he was quite possibly the only real ally I had in the family.

The Librarian, William, looked a lot more together than usual. He'd come a long way from the fragile, broken soul I'd rescued from an asylum for the more than usually criminally insane, where he'd been hiding out for so long he'd gone native. One of our enemies broke his mind quite thoroughly, and he was still putting himself back together. With a little help from his friends. His recent marriage to the telepath Ammonia Vom Acht had clearly done him a lot of good, though I understood this was still an ongoing process. He was sitting up straight, his eyes were focused, and he was paying attention to what was going on. All of which were quite definite improvements.

He wore a smart blue three-piece suit and fluffy white bunny slippers. He had a great mane of silver grey hair, and a face with rather more character than I was used to seeing. His pale eyes still had a tendency to drift off on some private matter of his own, as though he was thinking of something far more important. And for all I knew, he was.

An excellent Librarian, mind. He knew where every book in the huge family Library was, and what was in it. He just often had trouble remembering why he'd wanted the book in the first place. A kind soul, with far more problems than one man should have to cope with.

I moved forward and stood right in front of him, so I could be sure he knew I was there, and then I produced a small black leather-bound book and laid it on the table before him. There was a title on the cover, but I can't read Aramaic.

"There you go, William," I said. "Straight from the shelves of the deepest darkest part of the Vatican's Very Secret Library. They now have the duplicate copy you provided, not containing the bits we don't want them to know about."

William smiled happily, if just a bit vaguely. He patted the book fondly with one hand, like a wandering pet that had found its way home.

"Thank you, Eddie. How this little devil went missing from our Library and ended up so far away has yet to be determined, but it's good to have it back. The Vatican wouldn't have approved of what's in it, anyway; never have been famous for their sense of humour, the Vatican."

"See! See!" Ethel said loudly. "He got a present! Why don't I get a present? Why didn't you bring me back a book, Eddie?"

"What did you have in mind?" I said. "John the Baptist's *Desert Cookbook: A Hundred and One Things to Do with Locusts and Honey*?"

"Actually," said Ethel, "that does sound interesting . . ."

The Sarjeant-at-Arms stirred impatiently in his chair. He could be patient, when he had to, but essentially he was a man built for action. Not sitting around while other people whittered on about things that didn't matter. Big and brutal and permanently angry, the Sarjeant was in charge of family discipline, and he enjoyed every punishing moment of it. He was a thug and a bully, by choice, and always went out of his way to appear dangerous and threatening. Especially at Council meetings. As though he was only ever one moment away from a violent outburst. Or perhaps, just so he wouldn't be taken for granted.

He wore the stark black-and-white formal outfit of a Victorian butler, right down to the starched high collar, just like his predecessor, because that was the custom for the family Sarjeant-at-Arms. Even if no one still living remembered why. The Sarjeant liked the outfit. He thought it gave him presence and authority. Everyone else thought it made him look like a dick. He had a shaved head, brutal features, a cold gaze, and an unforgiving scowl. If he'd ever had a good side, he'd had it surgically removed ages ago. He didn't like me, or approve of me, but he put up with me because I could do things for the family that no one else could.

And because I killed his predecessor. Or at least, got him killed.

I smiled coldly at him, and he nodded coldly back.

"We need to talk," I said, to the table in general. "I just teleported directly onto the grounds through a door supplied by the Wulfshead Club management."

The Sarjeant immediately sat up straight in his chair. "That's not supposed to be possible! It's a blatant invasion of family security!"

"Exactly," I said. "The management did it to let us know it was possible. And, as they pointed out, if they have a door that can do that, where did they get it? And who else might have one? They didn't feel like volunteering the information, of course . . ."

"We improved the main shields after the Accelerated Men got in," said the Sarjeant, scowling thoughtfully. "The new ones were supposed to be one hundred per cent unbreakable . . ."

"Probably were, then," said the Armourer. "But the first rule of science and engineering is nothing lasts. There is a place in the Nightside where you can buy inter-dimensional Doors that will take you anywhere. Run by the Doormouse . . . fascinating little fellow. He knows Drood property is strictly off-limits . . . but I'd better put in a call."

"Anyone who comes here uninvited deserves every appalling thing that happens to them," said the Sarjeant. "I'll increase the security patrols."

"Kill them all," said the Librarian, just a bit unexpectedly.

"But who would dare?" said the Sarjeant. "And even, who's left? I thought we'd wiped out most of the Major Players in recent years . . ."

"That is a subject for another time," the Armourer said firmly. "We have to deal with the business at hand."

"Right!" said Capability Maggie. "Starting with, What the hell am I doing here?"

She glared at everyone impartially. As far as Capability Maggie was concerned, nothing we'd just discussed meant anything to her. And I was just someone else keeping her from her beloved gardens and grounds. A short, stocky blonde, Maggie wore her hair so close-cropped it was almost military, along with basic fatigues and heavy boots. I'd never known her to wear anything else. In fact, I'd never seen her inside the Hall before. I usually just glimpsed her in passing, off in the distance somewhere, doing something useful with compost. Up close, she had a sulky mouth, fierce grey eyes, and a general air of barely suppressed fury. She sat stiff-backed in her chair, arms folded defiantly, and looked very much as though she'd like to bite someone.

I pulled up the only empty chair, and sat down at the table. "All right, I'm here. Can we please get this over with, so I can get on with my life?"

"Damn right!" said Maggie.

"I want to know why my Ammonia can't attend the reading!" William said abruptly. "If I've got to leave the Library, I want her here with me. So I can be sure at least one person here is on my side. And to help me find my way back to the Library afterwards. Don't you all look at me like that. You know very well it moves around once you take your eye off it."

"Calm down, William," the Armourer said patiently.

"You know very well that only those directly concerned with the will can be present during the reading. I've explained it to you enough times . . ."

"Besides," said the Sarjeant-at-Arms, "she's not family. And, she's a telepath."

"She's my wife now!" snapped the Librarian, matching the Sarjeant glare for glare. "That means she's one of us now!"

"You know better than that," said the Sarjeant, not unkindly. "It takes more than just marriage to make someone a Drood. Especially when the newcomer has a mind powerful enough to smash through all our security screens. It's a good thing she doesn't live here full-time."

"She has to live most of her life in that remote cottage on the coast," said the Armourer. "It's the only way she can keep everyone else's thoughts outside her head."

"So she says," said the Sarjeant darkly.

"I always feel better when she's around," said William. "More focused . . . I trust her implicitly!"

"Yes," said the Sarjeant. "But you're still not the most stable member of the family, are you?"

William started to say something, and then stopped. "Actually . . . you have a point there, Cedric."

"But why do I have to be here?" demanded Maggie, very loudly. "None of this is anything to do with me! I do digging, and weeding, and general upkeep among flowery things, and I have never given a wet slap for anything the rest of the family does! Or its stupid secret world. So why have I been brought here, against my will, when there are so many more important things I should be doing? Flowers don't just grow themselves, you know!"

"I think you'll find they do," murmured the Librarian.

"We'll get to you in a moment, Maggie," said the Armourer, entirely unmoved by her raised voice at close quarters. He was used to dealing with excitable lab assistants, and they went armed. He looked around the table, at each of us in turn. "As Martha's only surviving child, I have been declared executor of her will, with authority over all matters arising."

"Why has it taken so long to get around to the reading?" I said, just a bit pointedly.

"The family's been a bit busy, of late," said the Sarjeant.

"Not that busy," I said.

"There are a great many traditional family protocols, for when a Matriarch dies," said the Armourer. "And even more, for when one is murdered. There were ... security aspects that had to be dealt with first. And even after that, there were certain conditions that had to be addressed, connected to the will. Mother always did believe in thinking ahead. I have already taken care of most of the relevant details, but there are a few clauses in the will so important that they require each of you to be present for the reading. So here we all are."

He produced a large parchment scroll, apparently from nowhere, and placed it carefully on the table before us. He unrolled the thick brown parchment slowly, and considered the contents thoughtfully. I could just make out Grandmother's distinctive spiky handwriting. The Armourer took a deep breath, and then plunged right in, beginning with Martha's statement of intent. All the usual stuff about being of sound body and mind (both of which I would have happily disputed, given the chance). And then he got down to the good stuff.

"It is my firm belief," said the Armourer, reading out Martha Drood's words in a calm, controlled voice, "that my position as Matriarch should be inherited by the next in line. Which, given that I have had the misfortune to out-live all the other candidates, falls on Margaret Drood, also known as Capability Maggie."

We all sat up straight at that, and looked at Maggie. She glared right back at us.

"I don't want it! Is that why I'm here? Really? I don't want to be the Matriarch, and have to run this batshit insane family! I am perfectly happy where I am, looking after the grounds. It's all I've ever wanted to do. Let someone else be Matriarch!"

"Told you," said William, to no one in particular.

I gave the Armourer a hard look. "I thought we'd all agreed that having a Matriarch in charge of this family is a really bad idea. Because the position is far too open to abuse of power. Martha being a really good example! My own grandmother tried to have me killed!"

"For the good of the family," said the Sarjeant-at-Arms.

I gave him a hard look, and he stirred uneasily in his chair, despite himself.

"Don't push your luck, Cedric," I said.

"I'm sorry, Eddie," said the Armourer. "But having a ruling Council in charge . . . just isn't working. You're not here often enough to see how badly it isn't working. We all have our own jobs to do, our own duties and respon-sibilities inside the family. You wouldn't believe how dif-ficult it is, just to get everyone together in the same place for a meeting. And it's even more difficult to get a deci-sion made. On anything! As a result, decisions tend to get made by whoever turns up. And then get changed, or overturned, by whoever turns up next! The family needs one person in charge, who can set general policy and give the job their full attention. The Council will still be there, to offer advice and keep an eye on things . . ."

"Oh, of course," I said. "Because that's always worked so well in the past."

The Armourer sighed loudly. "I know you believe in democracy within the family, Eddie. So do I. But you know as well as I do that if we did put this to the general vote, the family as a whole would just vote to appoint a new Matriarch. Because that's what they know, and that's what they feel safe with. You can't impose democracy; they have to want it. And most of them aren't ready yet. Real change . . . takes time."

Capability Maggie could see the way this was going, and wanted none of it.

"But why does it have to be me? I don't want to be the Matriarch! Keeping the Hall's grounds under control is a full-time job! A job no one else could do as well as me, and you know it. And I love doing it. It's all I ever wanted. Not least because it means I don't have to deal with people much. I've never been good with people. You know where you are with flowers . . . I'd make a lousy Matriarch!"

"Sounds perfect material, so far," said the Sarjeant. "Loud, aggressive, and not afraid to get her hands dirty."

Maggie rounded on me. "Why don't you take the job? You were in charge of the family for a while."

"Yes," I said, "I was. Long enough to discover I really wasn't up to the job, and that I never want to do it again. I make a good field agent, but a lousy leader. I cared far too much about what happened to people when I had to make hard decisions. I prefer to stand aside now, and act as the family's conscience. That's a full-time job in itself." I looked around the table. "But let us be very clear on this: if you put the wrong person in charge, and it all gets out of hand, again . . . I will come back and take over, like I did before. And those responsible for making me do that . . . will be made to suffer."

The Sarjeant sniffed loudly. "You talk big, boy, but you know you'd never do anything that might threaten the family."

"Don't put money on it, Cedric," I said. "I would disband and scatter this family to the four winds, rather than let them fall back into the madness of Zero Tolerance. The Droods are supposed to protect Humanity, not rule them. And besides, it's not like we're the only secret organisation guarding the world these days. There are hundreds of groups out there; you can't move for tripping over them. Everything from the London Knights to the Department of Uncanny. The world doesn't need us like it used to in the old days."

"You can't put any of them on the same level as us!" said the Sarjeant. "They're . . . amateurs! We're special. We're necessary. And we need . . . direction."

The Armourer looked thoughtfully at Maggie. "They do say . . . that the best person for a powerful position like this is often the one who doesn't want it."

"All right, then," Maggie said quickly. "I want it! I really want it! Oh, you have no idea how much I want it!"

"Good," said the Serjeant. "That's settled, then."

"What?" said Capability Maggie, really loudly.

I rose to my feet. "Congratulations on your new role, Maggie. Do your best, have a good time, try not to get too many people killed."

"Bastard," muttered Maggie.

I looked up and down the table. "You all wanted a Matriarch back in control, so be careful what you wish for, and all that. I'm out of here. You make whatever decisions you feel are necessary, to invest Maggie as the new Matriarch, and I'll go along. For the sake of a peaceful transition, I will stand well back ... and only intervene as and when I feel necessary."

"Typical," said the Sarjeant. "You want to have us dance to your tune, but you don't want the responsibilities."

"Exactly!" I said. "Glad to see we're finally on the same page, Sarjeant. Now if you'll all excuse me, I've got more important things to be getting on with."

"Stay where you are, Edwin!" said the Sarjeant, rising quickly to his feet. "You're not going anywhere!"

"You sure about that, Cedric?" I murmured. "You think you can stop me? Really would like to see you try ..."

"Sit down, both of you!" the Armourer said forcefully. "We're not finished with the reading of the will. That is why we're all here, remember?"

I sat down, and so did the Sarjeant. The Armourer doesn't raise his voice often, but when he does, everyone listens. He glared at the Sarjeant, and then at me, and shook his head slowly.

"I swear, you could both use a good slap round the head sometimes. You are here, Eddie, because Mother mentioned you specifically in her will."

"Oh, this can only end well," I said. "Ladies and gentlemen, hope has left the building. Running. With its arse on fire."

"If this is just about him, can I go now?" said Maggie. "I've got seedlings to set out. And a hell of a lot of instructions to pass on, if I'm going to have to give up my lovely gardens."

"No, you can't go," said the Armourer. "This concerns you too. Or at least, it might. Depending." He sat there for a long moment, looking at the parchment scroll. He didn't appear at all happy. "We don't need to go through all the clauses in the will; the new Matriarch and the Council can deal with those. But only after we've sorted this out. Eddie, your grandmother has left you a bequest."

"It's not good, is it?" I said. "I can tell just from looking at you that this is not in any way shape or form, good. Unless it's money. Is it money?"

"Not money, no," said the Armourer. "But she did leave you . . . something."

And he produced a small oblong black-lacquered box, about a foot long, and four inches by three, decorated with gold-leaf inlay and filigree. The Armourer placed the box carefully on the table before him, and we all leaned forward for a better look. I reached out and touched the box, very carefully, with one fingertip. Nothing happened, so I picked the box up and studied it closely. No lock, no hinges, no obvious way to open it at all. I shook the box, and it didn't rattle. Though I did notice the Armourer and the Sarjeant wince, just a little. I put the box down again.

"What is it, Uncle Jack? Did you make this for her?"

"No," said the Armourer. "Which rather begs the question, who did? None of us in the Council even knew the thing existed, until we found it with her will. And yes, my lab assistants and I have done our very best to open it. On the grounds of family security, of course. We failed. So we scanned the hell out of it, with every piece of equipment we have and a few I made specially. And all we were able to discover is the box is sealed on every level we can think of, and it has been designed so that only you, Eddie, and your specific DNA, can open it. We have no idea what that thing is, or what it's for. All the will has to say about the box is, *There is something inside that will make you Patriarch of the family, Eddie. Something that will place you in power, despite all obstacles, and ensure that no one in the family will be able to stand against you.*"

The Sarjeant looked at the box, and then at me, openly stunned. Clearly, the Armourer hadn't mentioned that to him before. William just looked interested. Maggie bounced up and down in her seat, going red in the face, openly outraged.

"Wait a minute! Wait a minute! First you force me to accept the position as Matriarch, and now this?"

"Thought you didn't want the job," I said.

"Well, yes, but . . ."

"Exactly," I said.

The Sarjeant glared at the little black box. "What the hell was the Matriarch thinking . . . It could be a weapon of some kind, I suppose. Or it could be information . . . very secret secrets, for control or blackmail . . ."

"Just like Martha," said the Librarian, just a bit unexpectedly. "Still trying to pull our strings, even from beyond the grave. If I were you, Eddie . . . I would take that box and throw it off the end of the world."

"Why would she give something like this to me, of all people?" I said, honestly mystified. "She made it very clear that she disapproved of everything I did and said and stood for, when I was in charge . . ."

"There's more," said the Armourer.

"Of course there is," I said. "Can everyone hear that sound? That is the sound of my heart, sinking."

"The clause in Martha's will that leaves you the box has a very definite condition attached," said the Armourer. His mouth pursed for a moment, in what looked very like a moue of distaste. "I am only authorised to give you this box, Eddie, on the condition that you agree to give up Molly Metcalf. And never see her again."

I looked at him and, give the man credit, whatever it was he was seeing in my face and in my eyes, his gaze didn't waver one bit.

"Okay," I said. "You must know that's never going to happen."

"Really?" said Maggie. "I mean, we are talking about undisputed control of the whole Drood family. Not that I want the job, of course."

"You must know you can't ever marry the witch," said the Sarjeant-at-Arms. And he surprised me there, by saying it in a fairly sympathetic tone. "There is no way Molly Metcalf can ever be a part of this family. Not after all the things she's done. You could marry her without the family's permission, of course, but then there would be no place for you here either."

"Really?" I said. "In this day and age?"

"Remember what happened to James?" the Armourer said steadily. "When he insisted on marrying, against Mother's wishes? To someone the family considered … unsuitable? James forced it through anyway, and in the end Mother went along, because he was the very best of our field agents, and because he always was her favourite … But they had to live outside the Hall. And after he lost her, and had to come back here because he had nowhere else to go … he was never the same, after that."

"Is the wild witch really more important to you than the family?" said the Sarjeant.

"Hell, yes," I said. "I can always trust Molly."

"Damn right!" said the Librarian firmly. "I would

have walked out in a moment, if anyone had tried to keep me from marrying my Ammonia."

We all managed a tactful silence, there.

"How typical of dear Grandma," I said finally. "Still trying to run my life, even after her death. Still convinced she knows what's best for me, and the family. Still trying to bribe or threaten me into doing what she wants ... Yes. That settles it."

I pushed the box away from me, back towards the Armourer. He looked at me steadily, kindly.

"Are you sure, Eddie?"

"I never wanted to be Patriarch again," I said. "And nothing that's happened here has changed my mind. I don't want to be in charge, and I don't care what's in the box."

"You're not even curious?" said Maggie.

"No," I said. "Could be a cat that's alive and dead at the same time, for all I care." I looked at the Armourer. "Is that all?"

"Yes," said the Armourer. "There are a great many other clauses, but none that concern you directly."

"Then there's no reason for me to hang around any longer, is there?" I said. "So, if you'll excuse me ... Molly is waiting."

I got up to leave, again. Everyone was staring at me, all of them shocked to some degree. Even the Librarian, in his own vague way. It was clear to me that none of them would have turned down the box if it had been offered to them, even if they would have used the power it gave them for quite different reasons. And equally clearly, they were all wondering why Martha hadn't offered it to them ...

"What should we do with the box?" said the Armourer.

"Disregarding all the obvious answers," I said, "do your best to destroy it, Uncle Jack. And if you can't, hide it away somewhere very secure, and never tell anyone what you did with it. Because no one in this family can be trusted with something that could give them undisputed control."

"How can you say that about the family?" said the Sarjeant.

"Experience," I said.

I nodded cheerfully to Maggie, but she just glared at me.

"By turning down that box, you've forced me to become Matriarch," she said. "I'll get you for this."

"Lots of people say that," I said.

I moved away from the table, and that was when the Sarjeant-at-Arms got up to face me. He moved carefully forward to block my way.

"Before you go, Edwin, there is one further matter."

"Oh yes, Cedric?" I said. "And what might that be?"

"You have something that belongs to the family," said the Sarjeant, calmly and coldly. "And we really can't allow you to leave the Hall while you still have it in your possession."

"Really not with you," I said. "What are we talking about, exactly?"

"The Merlin Glass," said the Armourer.

He met my gaze steadily when I looked back at him. William was off somewhere else again. Or perhaps pretending to be, so he wouldn't have to get involved. Maggie just looked confused.

"Ethel?" I said. "You've been very quiet through all this."

"None of my business," said the voice from the rosy red glow. "This is human stuff. I don't get involved."

I turned my attention back to the Sarjeant. "What brought this on, Cedric?"

"New Matriarch, new rules," he said. "Can't have something as powerful as the Merlin Glass out of our hands while a new Matriarch is finding her feet. When the Armourer first gave you the Glass, it was never intended you should keep it for your own exclusive use . . . The Glass was a gift from Merlin to the Droods, and it belongs with the family."

I looked at the Armourer again. "This wasn't your idea, was it, Uncle Jack?"

"This was a Council decision," the Armourer said carefully. "We all agreed. You can't keep the Glass, Eddie."

"Are you worried I might use it to bring down the Matriarch if I decide I disapprove?" I said.

"A wise man covers all the options," said the Sarjeant.

"So we decided to ask for the Glass back, while we're all together here," said the Armourer.

"Ask?" I said.

"We're being polite," said the Sarjeant-at-Arms. "For now."

"You're talking like you'll never get another chance," I said. "I will be back. We can discuss this then."

"We know where you're going," said the Sarjeant. "You're going to the Department of Uncanny to talk to the Regent of Shadows. To get answers out of him. We don't care about that. Skin him alive, for all I care. But you can't use one of the family's most powerful weapons for your own private war. Give it up, Edwin. That is a Council order."

"So much for being reasonable," I said. "I did try . . . Look, I need the Glass, for now. You can have it back when I'm finished with it. I think, after all I've done for this family, I'm entitled to a little latitude."

"That's not how it works, Eddie," said the Armourer. "You know that."

"Don't I just," I said.

"You can't be allowed to leave here with the Glass!" said the Sarjeant.

"Try to stop me, Cedric," I said, smiling slowly. And he flinched, just a little.

The Armourer was immediately up on his feet, glaring at me. "Are you seriously prepared to defy the family, Eddie?"

"Of course," I said. "It's what I do best."

Maggie was up on her feet too. "If I'm going to be Matriarch, I'm going to make decisions. They're right, Eddie. You have to give up the Merlin Glass."

"You don't even know what it is," I said.

"Doesn't matter. It's the principle of the thing!"

"Good for you!" I said. "That's the trick; sound decisive, even when you don't have a clue what you're talking about. You'll make a fine new Matriarch. Just not right now."

"No one member of the family can be considered more important, more powerful, than the Matriarch or her Council," said Maggie.

And suddenly she sounded less like a gardener and a lot more like someone in charge.

"Except," said the Librarian mildly, "Martha clearly thought Eddie was more important, or she wouldn't have left him the box. Would she? Hmmm?"

Everyone looked at William, but he had nothing more to say. Maggie glared at me, and I glared right back at her.

"Well done," I said. "Not even officially the Matriarch yet, and already you've learned the joys of abuse of power."

"Why should you have the Glass, and no one else?" she said.

"Because I've proved I can be trusted not to abuse it," I said. "I love my family. I really do. And everything it's supposed to stand for. But it's at times like this that I know for a fact . . . I wouldn't trust most of you further than I could throw a wet camel." I smiled widely at all of them. "Moments like this . . . are why I prefer to maintain a distance between me and Drood Hall. Good-bye."

I walked straight at the Sarjeant-at-Arms, and he stepped back and out of the way at the very last moment. I left the Sanctity, and didn't look back once.

The doors opened quietly before me, and closed firmly behind me. The two guards were still on duty. They stared straight ahead, refusing even to look at me. Which was probably just as well. I was in the mood to hit somebody, or something. I started down the corridor, and then stopped as I heard the double doors open behind me. I turned quickly and then relaxed, just a little, as the Armourer came hurrying out of the Sanctity. He waited for the doors to close, and then glowered at the two guards.

"Go for a walk."

"But we were told . . ."

"Go!"

They both left, at speed, neither of them looking back. The Armourer looked at me severely.

"Eddie, there's a limit to how many times you can walk out on the family and still hope to come back."

"I keep leaving, and I keep hoping the family will take

the hint," I said. "But somehow, they always find a reason to call me back."

"And if this is the last time?" said the Armourer.

"I'll send you a postcard from wherever I end up."

"What if you need something from us?"

"Then I think I've earned the right to just walk back in and ask for it," I said. "You know I'll never leave here for good, Uncle Jack. I can't. Because despite everything I still believe in what the Droods are supposed to be. Shamans, to the tribe. Shepherds, to Humanity. And I suppose . . . there are a few people here I would miss. Like you, Uncle Jack. But I have to go now. I have to go talk to my grandfather, at the Department of Uncanny."

The Armourer nodded slowly. "Of course you do. He killed Molly's parents. On the family's orders. He knows things . . . you need to know."

"How long have you known, Uncle Jack?"

"Always," he said. "But I couldn't tell you."

"So many things you kept from me," I said. "And you're still keeping secrets from me, after all this time."

"Because some secrets . . . just aren't mine to tell," he said.

"It's time for the truth to come out," I said. "All of it."

"It won't make you happy and it won't make you wise," the Armourer said gruffly. "You watch your back, boy. It's lonely out there in the cold."

He stepped forward and embraced me. I hugged him back, and then we let each other go. We've never been a touchy-feely family. The Armourer went back inside the Sanctity. And I stood there for a long moment, thinking.

I wasn't sure where to look for Molly. I listened carefully, but I couldn't hear any screams, or explosions. Which suggested she probably wasn't inside the Hall any longer. More likely she'd gone back out into the grounds; the one part of Drood Hall that reminded her of her beloved private forest. I looked at the black oblong box in my hand. I'd snatched it up off the table and concealed it about my person while we were all arguing, and no one had noticed. Sleight of hand is a very useful talent in a field agent.

I studied the box carefully, and it still refused to make any sense. Supposedly my DNA was enough to open it, but my touch wasn't doing anything. And I really hadn't felt like experimenting with the box while I was inside Drood Hall. I wouldn't put it past dear departed Grandmother to have concealed some kind of booby-trap inside. No, I needed somewhere safer . . . like Molly's forest. I grinned, despite myself. Whatever was inside the black box, I really didn't feel like leaving it in anyone else's hands. I wondered if anyone had noticed it had gone missing yet . . .

I took out the Merlin Glass, and told it to take me to Molly. Wherever she was.

CHAPTER THREE

After the Will, a Last Testament

The Merlin Glass dropped me off by the family's very own artificial lake, where I found Molly Metcalf keeping herself busy by tormenting the swans.

I took my time walking over to the edge of the lake. I didn't want to startle Molly, or the swans. The lawns stretched away in every direction, broad and gently undulating, like a dark green sea under a brilliant blue sky. The waters of the lake were deep and dark, with mad ripples spreading in every direction. The surface was disturbed by Molly running across it, waving her arms wildly at the retreating swans, and shouting obscenities after them.

I paused, to look down at the Merlin Glass in my hand. Such a small and innocent-looking thing, in its hand-mirror guise. I wasn't sure why I was so determined to hang on to it. The Glass was a useful enough item, but

I'd managed perfectly well without it for years. It had never even occurred to me that I wasn't going to give it back until the Sarjeant demanded that I hand it over. But now I couldn't shake the feeling that I was going to need it. And I also couldn't help feeling . . . that the Glass wanted to stay with me. Which was just a bit worrying. I put the hand mirror away in my pocket, and stood on the bank of the lake, looking out across the waters.

It's not an everyday sight, even in the weird and wondrous grounds of Drood Hall, to see a witch charging across the surface of a lake with her dress rucked up to her waist, in hot pursuit of a dozen panicked swans. Their great white bodies shot this way and that, wings flapping energetically, never able to build up enough speed to get into the air, because they kept having to change direction when Molly got too close. She went sprinting up and down the length of the lake, her toes digging just below the surface of the waters to give her more traction. I stayed where I was, if only to avoid the energetic splashing from all concerned. My armour has many fine and useful qualities, but walking on water isn't one of them.

"Molly?" I said, after a while. "Please stop doing that, and come over here and talk to me. I'm sure whatever the swans did, they're really very sorry now."

"Snotty, arrogant, entitled birdy things!" said Molly. Loudly. "They were looking down their noses at me!"

She stopped running, quite abruptly, and glared about her. The swans glided to a somewhat ruffled halt a safe distance away. Molly sniffed scornfully, and stomped across the water to join me. I reached down, and pulled her up onto the bank beside me. She was still scowling, which is never a good sign.

"Swans don't have noses," I said mildly.

"Well, whatever they have, they were looking down them at me! They don't like me. I could tell. Yes, I'm talking about you, you fluffy white bastards! You'd better stay at that end of the lake, or it's sandwich time for the lot of you!"

"You wouldn't like them, Molly," I said. "Swan meat is actually pretty bland and greasy. We have to supplement their feed with a special kind of corn just to make them palatable. Like the Royal swan-keepers do."

Molly looked at me. "Didn't I read somewhere that only the Royal family are allowed to eat swan?"

"We have a special dispensation," I said.

"The Queen told you that you could eat swan?"

"No, we told her that we could eat swan."

"I've had enough of this lake," said Molly. "And the swans. Let's go somewhere else, Eddie."

We strolled through the grounds together, heading for a pleasantly shady copse of elm trees. It all seemed very calm and peaceful, but long experience had taught me that you can't trust anything at Drood Hall to be what it appears to be.

"You should be more careful," I said. "Antagonising swans is never a good idea. Powerful creatures, you know. A swan can break your arm. If it's got a crowbar."

Molly laughed, despite herself. "I couldn't stay in the Hall," she said. "Far too dark and gloomy. And claustrophobic. And far too many people looking at me."

"Looking down their noses, perhaps?" I said. "Like the swans?"

"So," Molly said brightly, in her best *I am changing the subject now and you'd better go along* voice. "How was the family?"

"Much as usual," I said.

"Bad as that, eh?" said Molly.

"Yes," I said. "I'm pretty sure I've been banished again. Go, and never darken our doorstop—the whole bit."

"They should know by now," said Molly. "That never works. So, what did your grandmother leave you in her will? Was it money?"

"No," I said. "She just left me a keepsake. Something to remind me of the kind of person she was."

Molly waited until she was sure I had nothing more to say, and then she said, almost casually, "Have you finished your business here?"

"Yes," I said. "Nothing to hold me here now. It's time for us to go visit the Department of Uncanny, and have our long-delayed little chat with the Regent of Shadows. My grandfather, Arthur Drood."

"Good," said Molly. "I could use cheering up. I am just in the mood for some serious violence and extreme property damage."

"Never knew you when you weren't," I said.

"Flatterer," said Molly.

"We are going to try talking first," I said firmly. "If communications break down, then we move on to more distressing measures of persuasion."

"Wimp," said Molly.

"The Regent didn't just decide to kill your parents on his own," I said carefully. "Someone ordered him to do it. Some specific person, inside my family, condemned your parents to death, for reasons of their own."

"The Matriarch," said Molly.

"Not necessarily," I said. "There have always been advisers and Councils and powers behind the throne, in the Droods. Not to mention wheels within wheels, and departments that don't officially exist. In a family as big as mine there's room for pretty much everything. And the Droods have a long history of using outside agents to do the really dirty and deniable stuff."

Molly shot me a look. "So whoever made the decision, and gave the Regent his orders, might still be a person of importance in your family? And not necessarily one of the obvious ones?"

"Could be," I said.

"I will have my revenge on someone," said Molly.

"It could be any number of people!" I said. "That's the point! That's why we need to talk to the Regent, to get the full story. He was just the weapon; someone else pointed him at your parents."

"They're just as guilty," said Molly.

"I know," I said. "I'm just trying to say . . . it's complicated."

"You want it to be complicated, so I won't kill your grandfather," said Molly. "I'll listen, if he's ready to talk. I want to know everything. But what if he doesn't want to talk?"

"I won't let you kill him," I said carefully. "I can't let you do that. But I think we are quite definitely entitled to intimidate the hell out of him, should it prove necessary."

"You think it won't?" said Molly.

"He sent us to Trammell Island, expecting the truth to come out," I said. "He wanted us to know. He just couldn't bring himself to tell us in person. Now we know . . . I think he'll tell us the rest. I think he wants to."

"But if he doesn't?" insisted Molly.

"Look, we can't hurt him anyway!" I said. "He's got Kayleigh's Eye, remember? As long as he's wearing that amulet he's invulnerable to all forms of attack. And that very definitely includes your magic, and my armour."

Molly started to say something, and then stopped, and looked at me. "What, or who, is Kayleigh? Do you know?"

"Beats the hell out of me," I said. "I've heard of it, because . . . well, I've at least heard of most things. Comes with the job, and the territory. But I haven't a clue where the Eye comes from."

"God, demon, alien?" said Molly.

"Almost certainly in there somewhere," I said.

"I can always threaten to blow up the whole building," said Molly.

I looked at her. "For you, restraint is just something other people do, isn't it?"

She smiled at me dazzlingly. "I have always believed in extremes and excesses. Why settle for less?"

I took the Merlin Glass out again, and muttered the proper activating words to establish communication with the Department of Uncanny. Molly clapped a hand on my arm.

"Hold it! Are you really going to tell them we're coming? And throw away the whole element-of-surprise bit?"

"We need to be sure he's at home," I said. "I don't want to turn up there and find him gone. I don't think he'd make us chase him, but . . . I think his first reactions will tell us a lot about how this is going to go."

"Good point," said Molly. "Go on, then. Get on with it."

But when I looked into the hand mirror, no one was there. No reflection, no contact; the Glass was just full of an endless, buzzing static. Which was . . . unusual. I lowered the Glass, and looked at Molly.

"That's never happened before."

"Could they be blocking us?" said Molly. "If the Regent has decided he's not going to talk to us, and that as far as he's concerned we're now both persona non grata . . . the whole Department could be hiding behind heavy-duty security shields."

"The Regent wouldn't hide behind his own people," I said. "At the very least, he'd have left us a message. Some kind of explanation. No . . . Something's wrong at Uncanny. Get ready. We're going through."

I had the Merlin Glass lock onto the Department's coordinates, and it jumped out of my hand, growing rapidly in size to make a door big enough to walk through. I led the way, with Molly treading close on my heels, leaving Drood Hall and its grounds behind.

I expected to arrive in London, in the shadow of Big Ben, overlooking the Department of Uncanny's hidden entrance. Instead, Molly and I arrived inside the Department itself, in the waiting room, which shouldn't have been possible. Normally you have to pass through all kinds of shields and protections.

The smell hit me first. The unpleasant coppery smell of freshly spilled blood. The Merlin Glass shrank back down without having to be told, diving back into my pocket. I barely noticed. I couldn't believe what I was seeing.

The last time Molly and I had been here, the waiting room had been a cheerful, cosy place. Flowers in vases, pleasant paintings on brightly painted walls, even a deep shag pile carpet. But now, the whole place had been trashed. The flower vases had been smashed, the paintings ripped from the walls and reduced to shreds and tatters, and all the furniture torn to pieces. And there was blood everywhere, splashed across the walls and soaked into the carpet. No bodies, just blood. It looked like a bomb had gone off in an abattoir.

I armoured up, the golden strange matter flowing over me in a moment, encasing me from head to toe. Molly gestured sharply, and scintillating magics swirled around her, protecting her from all the dangers in the world. I studied the waiting room through my golden mask, using the expanded senses it provided, everything from infrared to ultraviolet. But whoever was responsible for all this madness didn't leave a single clue behind. Everything was still, and quiet. I looked at Molly, and she shook her head quickly.

"I'm not picking up a damned thing," she said. "No magical workings, no sorcerous radiations . . . Could it have been a bomb?"

"No chemical traces on the air," I said. "This looks more like . . . brute force. So much blood, but no bodies . . ."

"Someone got here before us," said Molly. "And it looks like they were even angrier than me. What do you think, Eddie?"

"We go on," I said. "Search the place, top to bottom. There may still be survivors who need our help."

"And if whoever did this is still here?"

"Then so much the worse for them," I said.

I led the way out of the blood-soaked waiting room. Molly came quickly forward to walk at my side. She didn't believe in being protected by other people. We moved cautiously through the silent corridors of Uncanny. The whole place had been smashed up, torn apart, in an almost inhuman display of sheer destruction. Almost immediately, we began to find bodies. Men and women lying twisted and

broken, alone and in piles. Some had weapons still in their
hands; none of them had died easily. They'd been butchered, slaughtered. Broken limbs and smashed-in heads.
Bent in two until their spines snapped. Guts torn out, and
thrown away. Violence and viciousness, almost for its own
sake.

Whoever did this had to have superhuman strength.

We moved on, stepping over and around the scattered
bodies, carefully checking every open doorway and corridor end, but there was never any sign of whoever was
responsible. Just more and more bodies. So many good
men and women left to lie where they fell, where they
died, often with hands outstretched for help that never
came. And blood, so much blood everywhere. The heavy
coppery stench was almost overwhelming, so thick on
the air I could taste it.

More and more of the dead were armed, for all the
good it had done them. They died defending their territory, and each other.

"Do you recognise anyone?" said Molly quietly.

"I don't think so," I said. "We met a whole bunch of
people, the last time we were here, but . . . I wasn't really
paying attention. I thought I had time . . . to get to know
everyone. I can't say anyone so far looks familiar. I don't
see my parents, or the Regent. Or his personal aide—you
remember, the Indian woman, Ankani."

"Maybe they got away," said Molly.

"I'd like to think so," I said. "But whoever did this was
very thorough."

"Look," said Molly, pointing at a huge, burly figure
that had been smashed half through a wall and left hanging out of it. "Is that . . . I think they called him the Phantom Berserker, didn't they?"

"It's what's left of him," I said.

I moved in, for a closer look. A massive Viking figure, complete with horned helmet and bear-skin cape, his whole body was broken and bloodied. He looked like he'd gone down fighting. There was blood dripping from his hands. But one side of his head had been completely caved in, and there was a great gaping wound in his chest where his heart used to be.

"I thought he was supposed to be dead," said Molly.

"He is now," I said, more harshly than I'd meant.

Molly stopped abruptly, and looked about her. "Shouldn't there be alarms going off?"

"Yes," I said. "There should. There should be all kinds of protections and defences in place, and my armour isn't picking up any of them. Which suggests . . . someone must have shut all the systems down, to allow this to happen. I'd put my money on an inside job. A traitor, inside the Department."

"I never wanted this," said Molly. "I was mad, I was angry, but I never wanted this . . ."

"Of course you didn't," I said.

We moved on, through a silent world of blood and bodies and senseless destruction. Doors had been smashed off their hinges, or hung lopsided from splintered frames. Every room and office we looked into had been thoroughly searched, and then trashed.

"Maybe they were angry from not finding what they were looking for," said Molly.

"Could be," I said. "A lot of the Department people were armed, but I'm not seeing any bullet holes, or scorch marks from energy weapons. As though the invaders just soaked up all the firepower and kept on coming . . ."

"I'm not picking up even the smallest traces of offensive magics," said Molly. "Everything we're seeing here is the result of brute force. As though a whole army went rampaging through the corridors, killing with their bare hands."

We moved on, very cautiously now. Looking and listening, and checking for booby-traps, or any other nasty surprise left behind by our unknown enemy. But there wasn't anything. As though the invaders didn't care what happened after they left. They were just here to do a job, and kill anyone who got in the way. Unless killing everybody *was* the job.

"They can't all have been killed, can they?" said Molly, as much to break the awful silence as anything. "Some might have got away . . ."

"It looks like they all stood their ground, defending their positions, and died doing it," I said. "Brave and honourable, to the last. My grandfather chose good people. But they had weapons! They must have taken down a hell of a lot of their attackers! So where are the enemy bodies?"

"Presumably the enemy picked up their dead and wounded and took them with them when they left," said Molly. "To make sure no one could identify who they were. But . . . who could be powerful enough to do something like this, Eddie? Who is there left that's got an army big enough to massacre everyone in Uncanny? I mean . . . we've wiped out most of the major bad guys, and their organisations, in the past few years. Who is there left, who could do this?"

"Good question," I said. "Makes me wonder . . . did we miss someone?"

I stopped, and looked at her seriously.

"You can never tell where an attack will come from . . .

I was at the Wulfshead Club earlier, remember? I'd been called in to help, because they were under attack from MI 13."

"What?" said Molly. "Those useless *X-Files* wannabes? I'm amazed they had the nerve. No, hold on, wait a minute . . . MI 13 couldn't have done this. They're an officially sanctioned Government organisation, just like the Department of Uncanny. Unless some kind of departmental civil war has broken out."

"No," I said. "That doesn't feel right. MI 13 lost most of its higher-ups, and its direction, during the Satanic Conspiracy. It's just a ghost of its former self. They were only spying on the Wulfshead Club to pick up gossip they could use as leverage, to get back in the game."

"All right," said Molly, "How about this? Maybe some part of your grandfather's murderous past finally came back to haunt him. Who knows how many other people he killed on your family's orders?"

I wanted to say *executed,* not murdered, but it wasn't the time.

We moved on, climbing over piled-up bodies, splashing through thick pools of blood. Most of it wasn't even tacky yet. Whatever had happened here, we hadn't missed it by much. I checked every room we passed, peering in through smashed-in doors. Computers had been ripped apart, safes torn right out of walls, their doors yanked clean off, and papers scattered everywhere. Someone had been looking for something . . . The entire Department of Uncanny had been systematically gutted. Everyone killed, everything destroyed, nothing spared. It was like walking through the ruins of a good man's dream.

It reminded me of how I'd felt when I walked through

the devastated ruins of the Other Hall, home to the other-dimensional Droods, slaughtered by some unknown enemy. I never did find out who. But this was different. I could do something about this.

"Where are we going?" Molly said abruptly. "I mean, are we heading anywhere in particular?"

"We're going to the Regent's office," I said.

"You think there's a chance he might still be alive?" Molly said carefully.

"There's always a chance," I said. "He could have barricaded himself in, and as long as he had Kayleigh's Eye . . . But no, I don't really expect to find him alive. Not when everyone else is dead. He wouldn't have run away, hidden away, and abandoned his people. Even though that would have been the sensible thing to do. He was the Regent of Shadows, and a legend in his own right. But he might have left us a message, something to tell us what the hell happened here."

Molly looked quickly around her. "Are you sure this is the right way? All these corridors look the same to me."

"I remember the way," I said. "Drood field agents are trained to remember things like that."

"Smugness is very unattractive in a man," said Molly.

We looked at each other, and tried to smile, but in this stinking abattoir it was hard to feel anything but horror and loss. The need to lash out at someone, anyone, was almost overpowering. I needed a name, an identity, for the bastards that had done this. So I could track them down and punish every damned one of them. And the bloodbath they had made here would be nothing compared to what I would do to them.

When I wore the golden armour, I felt stronger, faster, smarter. More alive . . . But it also meant my emotions were bigger, and ran deeper, for good and bad. Right then, I didn't care. I would do what I would do, and worry about the morality of it later.

"This wasn't an attack, or even an invasion," I said. "This was a massacre. These people weren't killed because they got in the way; their deaths were an end in themselves."

"How can you be sure of that?" said Molly.

"Because there aren't any wounded," I said. "Every single man and woman here was finished off before the killers moved on. And the sheer ferocity of the attack . . . No bullet holes, no explosions, no high tech or magics, not even any knife marks . . . This was all brute strength and savagery. I can't even tell whether this was an attack force or just one wildly powerful individual."

"Judging from the state of the bodies, I'd say animal," said Molly. "Or people acting like animals . . . Werewolf pack, perhaps?"

"The Department would have been prepared for something as obvious as that," I said. "They'd have had silver bullets, shaped curses . . . they could have fought off something that straight forward. No, this is different. This is something new."

Finally we came to the Regent's office. The door had been torn right out of its frame, and lay face down on the corridor floor. I made Molly stay back and wait while I checked out the surroundings through my mask. I couldn't See or hear anything. No booby-traps, no hidden devices . . . as though whoever had done this didn't care what happened afterwards, or who came looking. More fool them.

I stepped warily into the office, with Molly crowding

my back. It looked much as I remembered, more like a
retired gentleman's study than an office where important
decisions were made every day. A comfortable setting,
cosy and cheerful, with richly polished wood-panelled
walls. Bookshelves full of well-thumbed paperbacks,
rather than leather-clad first editions. But now . . . most
of the wood panels were cracked, or smashed in. Shelves
broken, books thrown everywhere. The tall grandfather
clock that had stood by the door had been overturned,
its clockwork guts spilled across the carpet. The single
virtual window had been smashed, and now showed
nothing at all. And all the drawers in the Regent's desk
had been pulled out, the contents scattered everywhere.

The Regent of Shadows was still sitting behind his
desk. My grandfather, Arthur Drood. Sitting upright,
with his head tilted back, staring up at the ceiling with
sightless eyes. And only a massive hole in his chest to
show where his heart should have been.

It wasn't just his heart they'd taken. I could still remember the Regent showing me the ancient amulet
known as Kayleigh's Eye, grafted onto his chest, apparently fused to the skin. The amulet had contained a huge
golden eye that seemed to stare at me knowingly. A very
potent device, from Somewhere Else, that should have
been able to defend the Regent from any attack. Except
it hadn't.

My grandfather looked . . . almost like himself. A man
of average height, a little on the skinny side, well-
preserved for a man of his age. Wearing a scruffy old
tweed suit with leather patches on the elbows. He had
iron grey hair, a military moustache, and pale blue eyes.
His face was slack, and empty, the whole front of his
clothes soaked in blood. His shirtfront had been ripped

open, to get at his chest, and the Eye. I moved slowly forward to stand over him, and then I armoured down. The stench of death and freshly spilled blood was almost overwhelming without the armour to shield me. But I needed to see this with my own eyes, not just as an armoured Drood. Molly looked quickly around her.

"Are you sure that's wise, Eddie? Really?"

"We're alone here," I said, not looking at her. "No one else left in the building."

Molly stood facing the Regent's body. It was hard to tell from her face what she was thinking. "How is this even possible?" she said finally. "No one could touch the Regent of Shadows while he had Kayleigh's Eye. I put a lot of thought into how I was going to get past the Eye's protection so I could get to him."

"The Eye isn't in the building any more," I said. "My armour would have picked up its emanations."

"Do you think *that* . . . is what they came here looking for?"

"No," I said. "They tore this place apart in their search, when everyone knew the Regent had the Eye. I think taking the amulet was just a bonus."

I stood looking at the dead man, not knowing what to do. I'd only just found my grandfather, after so many years of believing him dead, and now I'd lost him again. Someone had taken him away from me. Molly came over to stand beside me, trying to comfort me with her presence.

"This isn't the revenge I wanted," she said.

"I would never have let you hurt him," I said.

"I know. I just wanted answers, that's all. And now it looks like I'll never get them."

I dropped a hand on the Regent's shoulder, just to say

good-bye. And then I stepped quickly back, startled, as the corpse sat up straight and turned its head to look at me. The dead, staring eyes fixed on me, holding me in place.

"This is a last message for you, Eddie," said the corpse, in a soft, breathy voice. Little more than air disturbing dead vocal cords. Just a warning, left in a dead man's throat. "I know you and Molly have no reason to trust me after all I've kept from you, but I had no choice. I was trying to protect you. From the sins of the past, and the enemies of the future. You see, I didn't just kill for the Droods. I did other things for them too, trying to earn my way back into the family. Now it's too late for me to make a full explanation, or an atonement.

"My Department is under attack. Someone, or something, has got in. Which can only mean some traitor has betrayed us all. Shut down the security protections, and left us defenceless. There's a whole army inside this building. My people are doing what they can to hold them off, but they don't have enough weapons. Never thought they'd be needed, here. I wanted to go out and fight them, but Ankani locked me in. For my own protection, she said. I can hear my people screaming, hear them dying. I can hear the killers drawing nearer, heading my way.

"So, this is good-bye, Eddie. I wish I'd had more time, to get to know you better. Time to just . . . sit down together, and talk. But you always think there'll be more time, for things like that, until suddenly there isn't. I would have liked to tell you and Molly . . . everything. But a lot of it wasn't mine to tell."

The corpse turned its dead gaze away from me, and looked at the gap where the door had been.

"This isn't the end I saw for myself, but I can't say it comes as any surprise. Agents rarely die in their sleep. Be sure your sins will find you out . . . I hope they don't think I'm going to beg for my life. I will sit here, with my faithful old gun, and see how many of them I can take with me. Before they drag me down. I wonder if I'll know them, when they break down my door. Whether I'll recognise the face of my killer . . .

"I don't know where Charles and Emily are, Eddie. They're not here. They never made contact again, after they left Casino Infernale. Find them, Eddie. Find the traitor inside Uncanny. Find the people who did this. Avenge all these . . . good people."

And then the corpse gave up its ghost, and was still and silent again. The last words my grandfather would ever say to me had reached their end.

"He only spoke to you," said Molly.

"He knew I'd come," I said. "He knew I'd want to avenge him."

"Why should I help the man who murdered my parents?" said Molly.

"Because this isn't all about you," I said. "It's about my parents, and avenging all the people who died here. Men and women who just wanted to do good in the world. I can't do this without you, Molly."

She nodded, slowly. "Where do we start?"

"Damned if I know," I said.

And then we both stood very still, as the phone started ringing. The sudden sound was almost unbearably loud in the quiet. I checked the Regent's desk, but the phone wasn't there. In the end I had to get down on my hands and knees, and I found it on the floor. It had been smashed to pieces. The ringing wasn't coming from the phone. So I got up again and addressed the office at large.

"Hello? Eddie Drood speaking. Who is this?"

The ringing stopped, and a Voice spoke out of nowhere. Something in that Voice was enough to make both Molly and me wince. Like fingernails scraping down the blackboards of our souls.

"I destroyed the Department of Uncanny," said the Voice. "And everyone in it. Because they got in my way. They didn't have what I was looking for, so you're going to find it for me."

"And why would I do that?" I said.

"Because I have your parents," said the Voice. "Dear Charles and Emily. Your father and mother are in my keeping. Quite safe, for the moment, but I will kill them slowly and horribly if you don't do what I want you to do. I knew you'd come here, Eddie. Good little Drood that you are. And the wild witch herself, Molly Metcalf! I couldn't hope for better helpers."

"What do you want?" I said. "And who are you?"

"I want the Lazarus Stone," said the Voice. "You're going to find it for me, and bring it to me. Without alerting anyone else in the Drood family. If you talk to anyone, I'll know, and I'll kill Charles and Emily. I will know when you have the Stone, and then I'll contact you and tell you where and how to make the delivery. Let's hope you're as good as your reputations, Eddie Drood and Molly Metcalf."

The Voice fell silent. Molly and I looked at each other.

"What the hell is the Lazarus Stone?" I said. "I've never even heard of it, and I've at least heard of most things."

"Same here," said Molly. "Especially if they're valuable. But that name doesn't mean a thing to me."

"There's bound to be a reference to it somewhere in the Drood Library," I said. "But we can't talk to the Librarian . . . Can't talk to any of the family. I may be on the outs with them just now, but they'd still insist on getting involved. And I won't put my parents' lives at risk."

"Eddie," Molly said carefully, "they gambled away your soul at Casino Infernale!"

"I know!" I said. "But I can't let them down too."

I didn't look at the body of my grandfather. I didn't have to.

"All right," said Molly. "What are we going to do?"

"We're going back to Drood Hall," I said. "We're going to break in, without anyone knowing that we're there, and then we're going to talk to the one Drood that no one outside the family even knows exists. The Drood in Cell 13."

CHAPTER FOUR

The Drood in Cell 13

"All right," said Molly, in her *I am being very patient here but you'd better believe I am going to take a lot of convincing* voice, "how are we going to get back into Drood Hall without being noticed? How are we going to sneak into the best-protected and -defended location possibly in the entire world? I mean, yes, we did do it once, all those years ago, but we had all kinds of help then that we don't have now. And your family are bound to have filled in all those loopholes anyway."

"No problem," I said cheerfully, and perhaps a little more confidently than I actually felt. "After all the trouble we had breaking in last time, I decided to make life easier for myself in the future. So I could come and go as I pleased without having to bother anyone."

"And because you don't trust your family," said Molly.

"Exactly!" I said. "So I had the Merlin Glass set up an

emergency back door. A very subtle hidden entrance, built around the Glass itself, completely undetectable by any of the Hall's shields and protections. Just in case I ever felt the need to come visiting without an invitation. The Door doesn't exist until the Glass decides it does, and then we step through into any part of the Hall, without anyone knowing. Theoretically."

"What?" said Molly.

"Well," I said, "I've never actually needed to try it until now."

"I like it!" Molly said approvingly. "Very sneaky. And you never told me about this before because . . . ?"

"Because I never needed to try it before," I said.

"Also very sneaky," said Molly. "Well done. Hanging around with me has clearly widened your moral horizons. But . . . why do we have to go visit this person in Cell 13? Why can't we just drop straight into the Old Library? There's bound to be something in there about the Lazarus Stone."

"It's not that simple," I said. "Nothing happens in the Old Library that William doesn't know about. He's a lot sharper these days. The Voice said no help from my family. We have to assume that whoever's behind the Voice is still watching."

"But isn't the Drood in Cell 13 . . ."

"Technically, no. Because he isn't a member of the family any longer. The Voice shouldn't be able to observe us once we're safely inside the Hall's many shields and protections, but I don't feel like taking the chance. It's bad enough we're going to the Hall at all; I'm not prepared to put my parents' lives at risk by talking to anyone we don't have to."

"I could always ask my sisters for help," said Molly. "They're not Droods."

"You've got a point there," I said. "There are all kinds of really powerful people who you or I could go to for help. Why did the Voice specifically rule out just my family?"

"Because the Voice has a specific reason to be scared of Droods?" said Molly.

"Wouldn't surprise me," I said. "A lot of people have good reason to be scared of my family. Though that would seem to imply that . . . whoever the Voice is, he knows my family. And they know him. Interesting . . . Doesn't get us anywhere, but it is interesting . . ."

"I could have Isabella and Louisa here in minutes," said Molly.

"No," I said. "I think we need to do this ourselves. The more people we bring in, the more complicated the situation becomes. Who knows what other people might do, to get their hands on the Lazarus Stone? It must be pretty damned powerful, or valuable, if the Voice was prepared to wipe out the whole Department of Uncanny, just on the chance they might have it. No, we do this on our own, Molly. Because we know we can trust each other."

"All right, then," said Molly. "Let's get this show on the road. Where are we going, exactly?"

"To the one part of Drood Hall where no one ever goes," I said. "If they've got any sense."

I took out the Merlin Glass, held the hand mirror close to my lips, and murmured the special set of spatial coordinates I'd programmed into it. Keeping my voice down, not because I didn't trust Molly but because I wasn't sure whether the Voice might still be listening.

The Merlin Glass jumped out of my hand and hung on the air before me. It spun round rapidly several times, and then grew quickly in size to form a Door. I couldn't keep from smiling. My uncle Jack isn't the only one who can do marvellous things with useful items. I may not be the engineering genius he is, but I have always paid careful attention when he speaks. Even if he doesn't always think so. Where the reflection in the Glass should have been, I could now see a dark and gloomy stone corridor. Molly squeezed in close beside me, and studied the opening dubiously.

"Is that it? I thought there'd be more . . . special effects, or something."

"It's a Door," I said. "And the essence here, as you have already pointed out, is sneakiness."

"But is that really it? The way to Cell 13?"

"I don't know," I said. "I've never been there before. Now follow me, stick close, and keep your voice down."

"Oh please," said Molly. "Like I've never burgled anywhere before."

I stopped to take one last look round the Regent's office, and at the Regent himself, still sitting in his chair, behind his desk.

"Good-bye, Grandfather," I said. "I wish I could have . . ." And then I stopped, because there were so many things I wished we could have. "If you're still listening, Voice," I said, "I will do whatever it takes to save my parents. And then I will hunt you down. Even if I have to go to the ends of the Earth and beyond."

I waited, but there was no response. So I just nodded to Molly, and we stepped through the Merlin Glass and into the depths of Drood Hall.

*   *   *

A long stone corridor fell away before us, just dull grey walls and a floor of bare flag-stones. Sparse illumination came from a line of naked light bulbs, hanging far apart so that there were long stretches of dark shadow between the pools of light. The air was cold, and still, and dusty. Not a place where people came unless they absolutely had to. Unless they were driven to it. The slightest sound seemed to echo on and on, hanging on the air. Drood Hall doesn't have dungeons; we have something worse.

I turned back to retrieve the Merlin Glass, but the Door hung back, avoiding my reaching hand. Instead it turned edge on in the narrow space, so that for a moment it seemed to disappear, and then it floated smoothly down the corridor ahead of us, like a guide or a guard in dangerous territory. It stopped when it realised I wasn't immediately following, and hovered on the air. There was a sense of impatience to it, as though it knew best what was needed here. I studied the Merlin Glass thoughtfully.

"It's never done this before, has it?" Molly said quietly. She was standing right beside me, her mouth brushing my ear.

"No," I said. "It hasn't. But that's the Merlin Glass for you, always full of surprises."

I did my best to keep my voice casual and unconcerned. This was the very worst moment the Glass could have chosen to develop a personality, and I didn't want Molly getting distracted from the business at hand.

"Is this why you didn't want to give the Glass back to your family?" said Molly. "So you could come and go from Drood Hall as you pleased?"

"No," I said, seizing gratefully on the change in subject. "That's not it. I don't actually know why I feel it's so important the Glass remains in my possession. I just have this feeling . . . that I'm going to need it."

Molly nodded. To a witch, premonitions are just warnings from the future, and always to be taken seriously. I didn't mention my inner conviction that the Glass wanted to stay with me. I didn't want to worry her. Molly looked up and down the long stone corridor. It stretched away into darkness in both directions, for as far as the eye could follow and then some. Molly didn't actually turn up her nose, but she looked like she wanted to.

"This is pretty basic, even for Drood Hall," she said. "I've never seen anything as . . . brutal as this, in the Hall before."

"Not many have," I said. "Most of my family prefer to believe that the Drood in Cell 13 doesn't exist. And for most of them, he doesn't. He's our equivalent of an urban legend, a cautionary tale. It's safer that way. You need special permission to approach him, along with very definite instructions on what you can and can't ask him. And that's for the visitor's protection. Just talking to the Drood in Cell 13 has been known to drive people crazy."

"Your family never ceases to intrigue and appal me," said Molly. "I thought my sisters were scary . . ."

"They are," I said.

Molly punched me in the arm.

"Ow," I said obligingly.

Molly looked dubiously down the corridor.

"Just how dangerous is this Drood in Cell 13?"

"You have no idea," I said. "He's not imprisoned here as a punishment, but because he's a danger to the whole family."

"So he is a prisoner?"

"Yes. But he asked to be locked away. He knew how dangerous he is."

"Is he crazy?"

"Hard to say . . ."

"What's his name?"

"Laurence Drood," I said. "Once the family Armourer. There was an accident, some two hundred years ago, or so. The details of the story are either lost, or blatantly contradictory. Either way, as a result of . . . whatever happened, Laurence now knows everything the family knows. Or has ever known. Including all the very secret things most of the family aren't even supposed to suspect. And unfortunately, it's a never-ending process. Every time the family learns something, Laurence knows."

"How is that even possible?" said Molly.

"We're the Droods," I said. "We all do ten impossible things before breakfast, just to get our hearts started. Don't hit me! Look, Molly . . . I don't think anyone in my family knows anything for sure where the Drood in Cell 13 is concerned, not after all this time. He knows, of course. But apparently he only tells people what he feels like telling. There are . . . stories, among the higher levels of the family. About people who managed to make their way down here, to ask the Drood in Cell 13 questions. About things they weren't supposed to know. It seems . . . he uses the things he tells to destroy people."

"Why would he do that?" said Molly.

"Because he can," I said. "Because he thinks it's funny . . . The point is, whatever information comes into Drood Hall, Laurence just soaks it up and stores it away in his amazing altered mind. It's impossible to hide anything from him. All of which makes him the perfect weapon to use against the Droods. That's why he asked to be locked away, from the world and the family, and that's why they went along. Put him down here, in the depths, out of sight and out of mind. It was either that or kill him, and who knows when he might prove useful? Or even necessary. It's always possible that some small piece of information, forgotten by everyone else, might prove essential to the safety and security of the family. Droods never throw away anything that might prove useful someday."

"Hang on," said Molly. "Laurence Drood is over two hundred years old?"

"Well over," I said. "And he's spent nearly all of it locked away, down here, in solitary confinement. So if he wasn't crazy when they locked him in . . ."

"Your family," said Molly, shaking her head.

"Trust me," I said. "I know."

I started forward, into the gloom of the long corridor, and the Merlin Glass retreated smoothly before me, hovering in mid-air. It wasn't just a Door any longer; its opening now showed me all the hidden secrets of the corridor ahead. What was really there. All the carefully concealed booby-traps and hidden protections. I wouldn't have seen any of them without using my armoured mask, and I didn't dare armour up down here. No wonder the Glass insisted on preceding me. But how did it know . . . ?

The Glass progressed down the corridor, quietly defusing booby-traps and shutting down protections. Molly leaned in close again.

"How is it doing that?"

"Beats the hell out of me," I said. "It's never done this before. I certainly never programmed it to do anything like this."

"Maybe the Armourer . . ."

"My uncle Jack would never make anything that might prove more powerful than the family's defences," I said.

"When we're finished with this," said Molly, "you need to let me take that thing apart. See what's going on in-side the Glass."

"Oh no you don't," I said, very firmly. "Merlin Satan-spawn made that Glass. You really think he didn't set some nasty surprises in place for anyone dumb enough to try to tamper with his work? You want to test your magics against possibly the greatest sorcerer of all time?"

"Well, if you're going to put it like that . . ."

"I am putting it like that."

Molly sniffed loudly. "Why isn't the Glass shutting ev-erything down, instead of just messing about, defusing and bypassing them one at a time?"

"Because," I said patiently, "shutting down all the pro-tections at once would set off all kinds of alarms. That's why I haven't armoured up. And why you mustn't use your magical shields. If my family even suspected some-one was trying to talk to the Drood in Cell 13, they'd start fumigating this corridor with flame-throwers and explosives, and then escalate."

"I could cope with that," said Molly. "I can take any-thing your family can come up with."

"Really?" I said. "Generations of Drood Armourers have put a lot of thought into keeping Laurence Drood safe, and isolated. Would you go up against my uncle Jack's ingenuity?"

"Well, if you're going to put it like that . . ."

The Merlin Glass stopped abruptly, so we did too. Through the opening I could see an overlay on reality, a clear vision on top of what I was supposed to see.

Trap-doors had been cunningly set among the floor's flag-stones, over terrifyingly long drops. Robot gun emplacements lay in wait behind apparently innocent stone walls. Shaped curses and floating hexes had been salted like mines the whole length of the corridor, floating unseen on the still air. And right ahead of us, two dimensional doors flickered in and out of reality, too quickly for the human mind to process. The Merlin Glass slowed the flickering right down, so I could see what lay behind the doors. I heard Molly gasp quietly beside me, and she clutched at my arm.

"Are those . . ."

"Yes," I said. "Drood scarecrows."

As one of my family's more infamous lines of defence, we keep scarecrows scattered across the grounds to deal with the more persistent and dangerous intruders. Savagely, and brutally. We make our scarecrows out of the dead bodies of our most hated enemies. Just because we can. I edged closer, to get a better look at them. Their faces were taut as parchment, with tufts of straw protruding from ears and mouths, but their eyes were still alive, and aware. Eternally suffering, endlessly hating, bound by unbreakable pacts to defend Drood Hall against all enemies. For as long as they lasted. If you listen in on the right supernatural frequencies, you can hear them screaming.

"Do you know them?" Molly said quietly. "Do you recognise either of them?"

"The clothes are unfamiliar," I said carefully. "I only know our most recent enemies, and there's no telling how long those two have been down here."

We both jumped despite ourselves, as the scarecrows stirred slowly, becoming aware that someone could see them. And then they fell still again, and the dimensional doors disappeared as the Merlin Glass put all the defences to sleep, one at a time. Until the corridor seen through the opening looked exactly like the one I could see with my own eyes.

"Did you know those . . . things were down here?" said Molly.

"No," I said. "I'm not sure anyone does, any more. Even the highest parts of my family prefer not to know what goes on down here."

"Is it safe for us to move on?"

"Only one way to find out . . ."

I moved slowly forward, Molly still clinging to my arm, and the Merlin Glass retreated steadily ahead of us. None of the booby-traps activated, and we walked right through the floating mines, unaffected. I was so tense from anticipation that all my muscles ached fiercely. The corridor stretched away ahead of us, as we moved from light into shadow and out again.

"Your family really doesn't want anyone talking to this guy," said Molly after a while. "Are there any human guards down here? Anywhere?"

"No," I said. "Never have been. Apparently just continued proximity to Laurence Drood can be enough to mess with people's minds."

Molly glared at me. "Liking this plan of yours less and less all the time, Eddie."

"We should be safe enough," I said, trying hard to sound calm and reassuring. "As long as we don't stick around too long."

"How long is too long?"

"Good question. How the hell should I know? I never thought I'd ever have to talk to the man."

"Isn't there anyone else we could talk to?" said Molly.

"I'm doing this for my parents," I said steadily. "Wouldn't you have done something like this for your parents?"

"My parents are dead," said Molly.

We walked on in silence, for a while, following the Merlin Glass. Either there weren't any more protections or hidden surprises left, or the Glass just wasn't bothering to show them any more.

"Eddie," said Molly, after a while, "if Laurence is the Drood in Cell 13, what about the other twelve cells? Are there other secret prisoners down here? Somewhere?"

"Not as far as I know," I said. "I think it's more like it took twelve attempts to produce a cell strong enough to hold Laurence Drood."

"I thought you said he asked to be locked away?"

"He's been down here a very long time," I said. "And as I understand it, he has been known to change his mind, on occasion."

"Terrific," said Molly. "What makes you think he's going to be in any mood to help us? Or even answer your questions?"

"Because there's one thing all the stories agree on," I said. "Laurence Drood just lives for the chance to tell people things that will seriously mess with their head."

"Terrific," said Molly. "You can do all the talking."

We came at last to what looked like a perfectly ordinary wooden door, set flush into a bare stone wall. A simple wooden slab, with no door handle, no bell or knocker, not even any obvious hinges. The Merlin Glass came to a sudden halt, on the far side of the door. Molly and I stood side by side and studied the wooden door carefully, from what we hoped was a safe distance.

"That's it?" said Molly. "This is the infamous Cell 13? Doesn't look very secure."

"Looks can be deceiving," I said. "In fact, that's probably my family's unofficial motto."

"You have an official motto?"

"Of course: *Don't fuck with the Droods*."

"I thought it was *Anything, for the family.*"

"Same thing. It's us versus the world, and the world had better beware."

"I can believe that." Molly scowled at the door. "How are we supposed to get in?"

"We can't," I said. "No one can. That's the point. No one gets in, no one gets out. Food and drink are teleported in. Uncle Jack told me how to gain access to the Drood in Cell 13, back when I was briefly running things around here. Just in case I needed to know something only Laurence Drood knows."

I armoured up my left hand, and then stopped and tensed, expecting all kinds of alarms to go crazy. But this close to Cell 13, different protocols took precedence. I placed my golden palm flat against the door, and said my name aloud. The wood of the door seemed to shudder under my touch, and then the whole door just faded away, replaced by a series of criss-crossing steel bars. Molly and I moved closer, together, to peer into the room beyond.

It seemed comfortable enough, for a cell in the depths of Drood Hall. Just a simple stone-walled room, with no window and only the most basic furniture. A man was lying on his back on the narrow single bed, wearing just a grubby white shirt and faded blue jeans. He ignored us, staring up at the ceiling. I said my name again, and he jumped up off the bed and stood quivering in the middle of the room. A small, slight man, who could have been any age at all, with a shock of white hair and wild, staring eyes. He looked at me, and then at Molly, his head cocked to one side like a bird.

And then he ran round and round the small room, his arms pumping at his sides, vaulting over the furniture and bouncing off the walls, building up speed. He went skittering up one of the walls like some terrible huge insect, dropped back down again, and ran round and round in tight circles, his arms flailing wildly. And then he launched himself at the steel-barred doorway, only stopping himself at the very last moment, to stare through the bars at Molly and me.

He wasn't even breathing hard.

His eyes were large and luminous, and didn't blink often enough. Up close, it was clear he was inhumanly thin, his shirt and jeans flapping loosely about him. The bones of his face pressed out against the taut skin. His smile was so wide it looked actually painful, revealing teeth like yellow-brown chisels. He all but vibrated with barely suppressed nervous energy. And above all, he had a strange, unnerving presence, as though there were more than one man standing before us.

When he finally spoke, the words seemed to just tumble all over each other in their eagerness to get out.

"Well well well, what have we here? Visitors! Oh yes ... Don't often get visitors, down here. Not allowed, oh no, very very rarely allowed. Because I upset people. Well! If they don't want to know the answers they shouldn't ask the questions. Should they? Don't bother answering, it's a rhetorical question. Still, I'm going to have to be on my very best behaviour with you two, aren't I? Hmmm? For Eddie Drood and Molly Metcalf? No nasty little head games, for the infamous wild witch and the most respected Drood of all. I shall tell you everything you want to know."

"Everything?" said Molly bluntly. "No lies, no evasions, no misleading half-truths?"

He grinned at her easily. "I do have a bit of a reputation, don't I? But you mustn't worry, you dear little thing you, you sisterly witch. I never lie. Not when a truth can do so much more damage."

"My Eddie needs your help," said Molly. "You mess with him, and I swear I will find a way to get to you."

"Nothing but the unvarnished and entirely unembellished truth for you!" said the Drood in Cell 13. "All for you! I love visitors . . . They always want to know things, but they're never happy when I tell them. I think it's because the world isn't what they think it is, and no one ever likes being told that."

He broke off, and fixed me with his burning gaze. "Do you know who and what I really am, Eddie Drood? The result of an accident, is that what they're still saying? Oh no no no . . . the real and secret truth, the sad sad reality is . . . that I did this to myself. I am the author of my own tragedy. The idea was for the family to have its own Living Library, just in case they lost the real thing. Like they did with the Old Library. I was family Armourer back then, all those years ago, and I worked with the Heart to find a way to download all the contents of the family Library into a single human mind. A living repository for all Drood knowledge. Except that the human mind was never meant to contain so much information . . .

"There were six volunteers, including me. I used to remember their names but now I choose not to . . . Anyway, the result of the experiment was three dead, two insane and later dead, and me. Poor poor Laurence . . . Of course,

I'm not the only one of my kind, these days. Once word got out that the idea was possible, was in fact doable, all kinds of other organisations had to try. With . . . differing results. You met one, Eddie! Remember the Karma Catechist? You bumped into him in Saint Baphomet's Hospital, in Harley Street! He knew all there was to know about magical systems, rituals, and forms of power. And much good it did him. He killed himself, you know."

"Yes, I know," I said. "I was there when he did it."

Molly looked at me sharply. "I didn't know that. You never told me about that."

"I'll tell you later," I said.

"But . . ."

"Hush," I said. "He's just trying to distract us, and turn us against each other."

Laurence laughed breathily. "Stick to what you're best at, that's what I always say."

"Do you really know everything?" I said.

"Well, not everything, no. I didn't know you were coming. I don't know why you're here, Eddie Drood and Molly Metcalf . . . and I don't know what you want with me. Go on. Surprise me, I dare you."

"What do you know about the Lazarus Stone?" I said.

Laurence stepped back from the bars, folded his arms tightly across his sunken chest, and looked at me curiously. "Well well well . . . It's been ever such a long time since anyone mentioned that name to me. The Lazarus Stone . . . possibly the single most dangerous individual item in the whole damned world. Yes . . . It's usually thought to be a small piece of the great stone that was rolled away from Lazarus' tomb, so Jesus could raise him from the dead. People think the Lazarus Stone can bring loved ones back from the dead, and make them live again. Because people are stupid. All nonsense, of course. Just romantic religious bullshit. A fake exotic history, to conceal the Stone's far more dangerous nature.

"The Lazarus Stone isn't actually a stone, and it doesn't really bring the dead back to life . . . As such. No no no . . . It's some kind of mechanism, almost certainly alien in origin, and it's all to do with Time Travel. Supposedly, and I say this because I don't know anyone who's actually used the thing successfully . . . Supposedly the Lazarus Stone can reach back through Time, and pluck any person from the Past, just before History says they died. Then bring them forward into the Present Day. So that someone who was dead can live again. This of course rewrites History. Often in unexpected and highly disturbing ways. So it is possible that the Lazarus Stone has been used and I just didn't notice. No one would, except for the people involved. I wonder if they thought it was worth it, in the end . . . I loathe Time Travel. You put butter in a pocket watch and it's bound to mess up the works even if it is the very best butter. Our family did possess the Stone briefly, but the Regent of Shadows took it with him when he left."

"What?" I said. "Why?"

Laurence leaned in close to the bars, and slipped me a sly wink. "Ask your uncle Jack! And do it quickly, oh yes; accessing me sets off all kinds of silent alarms, up above. And you can be sure they'll all come running to shut me up before I say something they think I shouldn't. Before I can say things about the family that the family doesn't want anyone to know."

He shoved his face right up against the bars, glaring at me. "Too late! Too late!"

I took a step back, reached out and took hold of the

Merlin Glass, and shook it down to hand-mirror size. I showed it to Laurence.

"Do you know what this is?"

"Of course I know!" said Laurence, pouting just a bit. He thrust a hand through the bars and tried to snatch the mirror from me, but I was careful to stay just out of reach. Laurence sneered at me, and stepped back. He pulled a white hair from his head, studied it intently, and then threw it away. He waved at the hand mirror, as though he could see someone in the reflection as well as himself, and then smiled at me guilelessly.

"That is the Merlin Glass, and you only think you know what it is and what it's for. It's not a toy. Or even a useful device. That . . . is Merlin Satanspawn's last revenge upon our family."

"What do you mean?" I said.

He shook his head several times, and then smiled craftily at me. "Let me out of here and I'll tell you. No? You're smarter than you look, Eddie Drood. Are you sure? I could tell you so many things."

"I thought you wanted to be locked up down here," said Molly.

"That was then," said Laurence. "This is now. They're different. The family will never let me out. I know that. When I let them imprison me, I never thought I'd live this long . . . But then, who knows how long a Living Library will last? Information is immortal, and Truth wants to be free! I am the family's memory, and as long as the family goes on, so must I . . . After I've spent all these years soaking up Drood information and Drood secrets, they can't ever allow me to fall into someone else's hands. Far too dangerous . . . But one day I will know all there is to know, including all the things they've managed to keep from me, and then . . . I'll just walk right out of here and there will be nothing they can do to stop me! And oh, the fun I'll have, walking up and down in the world, and playing with it . . ."

He laughed softly, a cold, horrible, and barely human sound. He broke off abruptly and looked at Molly.

"There's something you want to ask me, little witch. About the Regent of Shadows, and just how dark the shadows get."

"Yes," said Molly. "Do you know who gave him his orders after he left the family?"

"Of course!" said Laurence. "I know everything! That's the point. Arthur Drood, Grandfather to Eddie, late husband of the late Matriarch Martha. The Drood with a conscience, they used to call him . . . though that didn't last long once he was out alone in the cold cold world. The Droods used him to do their dirty work. All the secret executions and deniable operations thought to be too much even for Droods. They held the possibility of being allowed to return over him, of being welcomed back into the bosom of the family . . . and he did want that so very badly."

"Who was it?" Molly said harshly. "Who, specifically, gave him his orders? Who told him to kill my parents? Was it the Matriarch?"

"Oh, she was just one of many," Laurence said offhandedly. "A lot of people in the upper registers of the family used the Regent, for their own reasons, to do the things they weren't supposed to do. He did so many bad things, and so many good . . . before he finally wised up. And realised the family never had any intention of taking him back. He told them all to go to Hell and walked away, and set up his own organisation. The Regent of

Shadows, doing good, doing penance, for the atonement of sins."

Laurence abruptly turned his back on us, went back to his bed, and lay down again, staring up at the ceiling. As though all the energy had suddenly gone out of him. When he spoke again his voice was flat, almost uninterested.

"The Regent killed an awful lot of people who needed killing. And I'm afraid that includes your mother and father, Molly Metcalf. They did do so many awful things as part of the White Horse Faction, that you never knew about. Because they never wanted you to know what kind of people they really were."

"Shut up!" said Molly. "Shut up!"

She turned away from the bars, hugging herself tightly, as though to hold herself together. Laurence's soft laughter drifted out of the cell.

"You see, Eddie? People come to me and they say they want the truth, but they don't. Not really. You'd better go now. People are coming. And they really won't be happy to see you here."

"Will you tell them I was here?" I said.

"Only if they ask." He laughed happily. "I know everything there is to know, but you need to know the right questions to ask. And you didn't ask the right questions, Eddie Drood and Molly Metcalf."

CHAPTER FIVE

A Short History of the Lazarus Stone

Molly looked at me. "I don't hear anyone coming. Do you hear anyone coming?"

"No," I said. "But given this is a man who is supposed to know everything about my family, I am completely prepared to take his word for it. And if there really are Drood security forces on their way here, I don't think we should be here when they turn up. They are not going to be in a good mood, or even a little bit understanding about this."

"Let them come," said Molly. "I can take them."

I had to smile. "That's why we're leaving. Because I don't want to have to watch members of my family being seriously damaged. I might want to come back here, someday."

"Don't see why," said Molly. "You know this place is bad for you."

In Cell 13, Laurence Drood was quietly singing, "We'll meet again, don't know where, don't know when . . ."

I shook the Merlin Glass out to door size, subvocalised a new set of coordinates, and then pushed Molly through the moment the Door opened. I rushed through after her, not giving her time to argue, and immediately closed the Door down again. I tucked the hand mirror away in my pocket, and looked quickly about me. We'd arrived in a dark, shadowy corner, surrounded on all sides by high banks of machinery. There was enough dust around to suggest that this particular location was as overlooked now as it had been when I was a lot younger. Molly glared at me, but had enough sense to keep her voice down even as she yelled at me.

"Don't ever push! I hate being hurried! Where the hell are we now?"

"In the Armoury," I said, just as quietly. "Tucked away in an area that isn't much used. I used to hide here all the time when I was just a kid, avoiding lessons so I could watch my uncle Jack at work. Because whatever he was up to was always going to be more interesting than whatever school was trying to cram down my throat that day. I'm pretty sure Uncle Jack knew I was here all along, but he never said a word."

"What are we doing in the Armoury?" said Molly, just a bit dangerously.

"You heard the Living Loony," I said. "*Ask your Uncle Jack*, he said, which means he knows Uncle Jack knows something about the Lazarus Stone. Of course he would— if it's a weapon, the Armourer always knows about it. So I need to talk to him, quietly and very privately."

"The Voice said you weren't to talk to your family," Molly said carefully.

"I know," I said. "I'm banking on the fact that the Armoury's shields and protections are the most powerful in the Hall. Just to make sure that whatever happens in the Armoury stays in the Armoury. No matter how appalling, destructive, or violently explosive it might be. I really can't see how the Voice could eavesdrop on us here. Even God probably has to concentrate to listen in . . . Anyway, I need to talk to Uncle Jack."

"Hold it," said Molly. "If the Armoury's protections are that good . . . How did we get in? How could the Merlin Glass . . . Oh, wait a minute. Is this another of your secret back doors?"

"No," I said. "One of the Armourer's. He's never trusted the Merlin Glass. Especially since it merged with its duplicate from the Other Hall. So he took measures, to ensure I could always bring the Glass straight to him if it started misbehaving."

"Your family is seriously paranoid," said Molly.

"With good reason," I said. "Most of the universe really is out to get us."

"True."

I peered cautiously round the corner of the nearest machine, and looked out across the Drood family Armoury. As always, it was a busy place, with dozens of experiments going on simultaneously, a whole bunch of complicated machines doing inscrutable things, and lab assistants running wild everywhere. Rows upon rows of work-benches, design tables, and assembly points, and all kinds of weapons being tried out for the very first time, nearly always without any reasonable safety precautions. Uncle Jack's assistants were always so eager for a chance to prove how clever they were, it often seemed genius had taken up a lot of the space in their brains that was normally reserved for self-preservation instincts.

One assistant with two heads was arguing coldly with himself as to whose fault that was. Something large and wolfish in the ragged remains of a lab coat ran happily back and forth on all fours, pursued by several other assistants with nets and Tasers. And a young lady with far too much frizzy red hair walked calmly across the stone ceiling, upside down and apparently entirely unconcerned, as she pursued a giant eyeball equipped with its own flapping batwings. And all she had was a really big butterfly net.

Just another day in the Armoury.

There were loud bangs, even louder shrieks and curses, and several slowly dispersing clouds of smoke. Off in the distance I could just make out the Armourer himself, watching approvingly while some of the younger lab assistants blew the hell out of what was left of the firing range, with really big guns.

I pulled my head back in, and gave Molly my best serious look. "I need you to set up a distraction. Something that will grab everyone's attention, and pull all the lab assistants away from Uncle Jack so I can get him to myself. Something loud and scary and dangerous, but preferably also something that isn't actually going to damage anyone."

Molly snorted loudly. "Come on, Eddie, these are your uncle Jack's assistants we're talking about. You couldn't upset them with any less than a nuclear grenade. You can't damage them! They're like cockroaches. They always bounce back."

"This would be a really bad time to prove otherwise," I said. "I need the Armourer's help, and willing cooperation."

"Oh, all right. Something highly scary and threatening but not actually deadly coming straight up, just for you."

Molly reached down and plucked a single silver shape from the delicate charm bracelet around her left ankle. She stood up, peered around the corner of the machinery, and threw the charm the whole length of the lab. A dragon suddenly appeared inside the Armoury. A massive creature, with a huge golden-scaled body and vast flapping membranous wings. It shrieked harshly, and lowered a horrid horned head on the end of a long snakelike neck. Its clawed feet dug deep furrows in the concrete floor, and a barbed tail lashed back and forth behind it, throwing heavy equipment this way and that. Its eyes glowed blood-red, and its gaping mouth was packed full of large serrated teeth. It was actually very impressive, given that it wasn't real. As such.

The dragon filled all the available space at the far end of the Armoury, its curved back slamming up against the stone ceiling, while its great head swept this way and that to menace everyone in reach. The wings flailed wildly, creating heavy gusting winds to blow away everything that wasn't actually nailed down. But the lab assistants didn't stop to gape at the dragon, even for a moment. They took one look at the thing and immediately grabbed the nearest weapon and opened fire. They blasted away at the dragon with guns, energy weapons, magical artefacts and a whole bunch of strange things I didn't even recognise. The dragon soaked it all up, without taking any damage.

Uncle Jack was right on the ball, of course. He rummaged around in his desk drawer and came up with a bulky high-tech thing that looked like it had been cobbled together from half a dozen other items just that morning. And for all I knew, it had. Uncle Jack does love to tinker. He slapped the piece of tech a few times, till it was ready to do what he wanted, and then a dimensional gateway appeared, directly behind the dragon. A great circle cut out of Space, with rogue energies sparking and spitting all around the circumference, and beyond it, a view of Somewhere Else.

Molly muttered a few Words, and the dragon seemed to back away from all the armed figures, retreating through the dimensional gateway and out of the Armoury. The lab assistants pressed forward after it, caught up in the moment, still firing everything they had. They all passed through the gateway, except for the Armourer, who stood his ground. He looked more resigned than upset, as though a suddenly appearing dragon was just another annoyance to interrupt his day.

The massive creature reared up on the other side of the gateway, holding the attention of the lab assistants, so they wouldn't realise they weren't inside the Armoury any longer. And also so they wouldn't realise their weapons weren't having any effect. Molly shot me a quick grin.

"I'll have to go join the dragon, or it'll disappear the moment the gateway closes. I'll keep the lab assistants occupied for as long as I can, so you can talk with your uncle. But keep it short, Eddie. It only takes one smarter than average lab rat to shout *Illusion!* and the game's over."

She snapped her fingers and teleported away, air rushing in to fill the gap she'd left. I glimpsed her briefly on the other side of the gateway, half hidden behind one of the dragon's legs. And then the circle snapped shut, and they were all gone. The dragon, the assistants, and Molly. It was suddenly very quiet and peaceful in the Armoury.

I moved out from behind the machine stacks, and headed for the Armourer. He dropped the piece of improvised tech on his desk, and scratched at his bald head thoughtfully. Anyone else would have handled such a powerful piece of equipment more carefully, not to mention respectfully, but the Armourer built his toys to take punishment. He knew they had to work out in the field, often under harsh conditions. He sat down at his workstation and drummed the fingers of one hand on the desktop. I hadn't got within ten feet of him when his head come up.

"Hello, Eddie. I knew you wouldn't be able to stay away for long."

"You knew I was here," I said.

"Of course!" he growled. "I always know . . . Nothing happens in my Armoury that I don't know about. It's a necessary survival skill. Even if I am getting old, and tired. I've spent too many years buried away down here, Eddie. Time . . . for a change, I think. Time for a younger Drood to come in and take over. Someone who's got the energy to keep up with all the madness the current crop of lab assistants specialise in. Some days . . . I feel that when I wake up in the morning I should give myself a round of applause just for making it through the night."

"Don't talk like that, Uncle Jack," I said. "You'll outlive us all."

"Well," said the Armourer, "I am working on something . . ."

He suddenly spun round on his swivel chair, so he could smile at me. I smiled back, pulled up a chair, and sat down opposite him.

"Now," said the Armourer, "nice to see you again, Eddie. Where's Molly?"

"Off with the dragon," I said. "She has to be close, to keep the illusion going. You did know it was . . . Of course you did."

"How about a nice cup of tea?" said the Armourer. "Maybe a few Jaffa Cakes? No? Then perhaps you'd like to tell me why you've turned up here again, so soon after stomping out on the family? And please tell me you have Mother's little black box. Everyone else was going crazy looking for it, when they weren't accusing each other of taking it."

"I've put it somewhere safe," I said. "But that's not why I'm here."

I felt the need to choose my words carefully, so I sat back in my chair and looked around. The Armourer's desk was covered with assorted scraps of unnatural technology, where he was working on a dozen different things at once, as usual. His computer was wrapped in mistletoe and long strings of garlic; I've never liked to ask why. And there were papers all over the place, designs and lists and results, all covered with the Armourer's usual unreadable scrawl. I looked back at my uncle Jack. He was still sitting patiently, but I wasn't ready, so I looked round at the Armoury.

It hadn't changed much, but then, it never did. For all the destructive and appallingly dangerous things that happened all over the place on a regular basis, the Armoury itself was extremely resilient. A massive stone cavern, it was set deep in the bedrock under the West Wing. Originally the family's wine cellars, it was all bare plaster walls now, decorated with multicoloured spaghetti of electrical wiring, tacked up all over the place. Some of it hung down from the high stone ceiling, in tangled masses that no one had dared tackle in years. The fluorescent lighting was almost brutally bright, so anything that escaped would have a hard time finding a shadow to hide in, and the air-conditioning grumbled to itself and worked when it felt like it.

Harsh chemical stinks fought it out with the cloying aromas of freshly pressed herbs, along with the lingering smell of cordite that always hung around the firing range. Everywhere you looked, there was always bound to be something interesting and unusual and deeply worrying.

I couldn't put it off any longer, so I looked back at the Armourer.

"I need your help, Uncle Jack," I said steadily. "I can't tell you why, and you can't tell anyone I was here, or what we talked about. I can only talk to you now because I'm putting all my faith in the Armoury's shields, to keep out unfriendly eyes and ears."

"Business as usual," said the Armourer. "You only ever come to see your old uncle when you want something. What is it this time, Eddie?"

"I need you to tell me all you know about the Regent of Shadows and the Lazarus Stone."

"Oh bloody hell!" said the Armourer, quite loudly. He glared at me, his mouth a flat, angry line, but I could tell he wasn't mad at me. He breathed deeply a few times, and thrust his hands deep into his coat pockets. "I always knew that bloody thing would come back to bite us all on the arse, some day. What do you want with that, Eddie? I mean, bringing back people who are supposed to be safely dead and gone . . . as if we didn't have enough problems already."

"Isn't there anyone you'd bring back, if you could?" I said.

He met my gaze coldly. "No. You should know better

than to ask that, Eddie. There's a reason why we don't allow ghosts to hang around Drood Hall. A reason why we respect our fallen dead, but we don't listen to them. You can't look back if you want to keep moving on. We've known that in the family for generations. You have to let people go. No matter how much you might miss them."

"Is that why you told me my parents were dead, for all those years, when you knew they weren't?" I said.

"That was different," said the Armourer. "I had to protect you, and them."

"I know," I said.

"So many burdens," said the Armourer. "No wonder I feel tired all the time. But *Anything, for the family.*"

He looked at me, as though waiting for me to repeat the family creed, and when I didn't he moved on.

"Now, where was I . . . Oh yes! Yes . . . The Lazarus Stone." His mouth compressed again, as though nursing a bitter taste. "Certain elements within this family acquired the Stone years ago, almost certainly from some highly disreputable source in the Nightside. And yes, Eddie, I know Droods are banned from that awful place by ancient pacts and agreements. If these members of our family had been found out, there would have been all kinds of repercussions. And there's no telling where the fallout might have ended. There's never been any shortage of people in this family who would welcome a chance to go to war against the Nightside. Wipe it out completely, once and for all."

"Why haven't we?" I said. "I visited the place once, and I loathed everything about it."

"The Nightside is allowed to maintain its unsavoury existence because it is necessary," the Armourer said firmly. "It serves a purpose."

I waited for a while, but he had nothing else to say.

"That's it?" I said.

"That's enough," said the Armourer. "Now, moving on . . . These people, inside the family, went on to form the Zero Tolerance faction, and Manifest Destiny. And I don't need to remind you how close they came to subverting and taking over the whole damned family. They weren't above breaking mere rules in the name of a greater cause. They wanted to use the Lazarus Stone to bring back some of our greatest and most successful Droods, from out of the Past. Create an army of heroes and warriors and assassins, to tip the balance in the ongoing war between the Droods and all our many enemies.

"They wanted to win the war forever. No more compromise, no more agreements; they were going to put an end to the war by killing everyone on the other side. And anyone who sided with them. And anyone who just got in the way. The Droods would rule, and to hell with the collateral damage . . ." The Armourer laughed harshly. "Like that was a new idea. If it had really been that simple, the family would have done it long ago. And these people didn't care about all the changes such disturbances in Time would make to History, because they didn't like where History had brought them anyway. I have to say, Eddie, I'm not actually convinced any of this is actually possible . . ."

"It could be," I said. "I have seen History rewritten . . ."

I remembered the Red King, and the Sceneshifters. I was the only person still living who could, because I was there when the severed head of the Red King, preserved and controlled against his wishes, finally woke from his dreaming. The Sceneshifters had been this really secret group who moved things around in the background when people weren't looking. Rewriting History in small telling ways, to achieve their own ends. But small changes accumulate, and the Sceneshifters weren't always in control of what happened. Apparently, there used to be pyramids in Scotland. A major tourist attraction. But no one remembers them any more.

The Droods knew about the Sceneshifters, but didn't believe they were important enough or powerful enough to worry about. I met the Sceneshifters when I was on the run from my family, and I was so appalled at what they were up to that I put a bullet through the Red King's severed head. He woke up from his long dreaming and he woke up mad, and made the Sceneshifters never happened. I was lucky to get out of there alive. And still real. A cautionary tale . . .

The Armourer waited until he realised I had nothing more to say on the subject, and then he continued with his story.

"You youngsters, you think you invented secrets. Now, this all goes back to when your grandfather Arthur, the Regent, was doing dirty work for the family. They used my father cruelly, and there was nothing I could do . . ."

I leaned forward. I couldn't help myself. "Do you know who in the family gave the Regent his orders, and chose his targets for him?"

"Are you asking this for yourself?" said the Armourer. "Or for Molly?"

"Does it matter?" I said.

"I suppose not . . . It was mostly the people who went on to create Zero Tolerance. And Mother, of course, as Matriarch, because my father never could say no to her. And make it stick. But as to who ordered the Regent to kill Molly's parents . . . I couldn't tell you. I was out of the loop in those days, mostly by my own choice. I could see which way the wind was blowing, and I didn't want any part in it. I just kept myself busy in the Armoury and kept my head down. Eddie . . . it could have been any of a dozen people, most of whom are dead now anyway. Does it really matter? The family gave the order, so the family must take responsibility."

The Armourer paused, and looked at me thoughtfully. "And Molly's parents did have it coming, Eddie. Your Molly made quite a name for herself, back in the day, as a supernatural terrorist . . . But all of that was nothing compared to some of the things her parents did, in the name of the White Horse Faction. They put the terror in terrorism . . . They had to be stopped."

"Are you going to tell Molly that, or should I?" I said.

"Probably best if nobody does," said the Armourer. "Better for all concerned . . . Anyway, when your grand-father finally realised he was just being used, and walked away from his family for the second time, he took a num-ber of useful things with him. Partly to punish the family, partly to help fund his new organisation. And one of the things he took . . . was the Lazarus Stone. Because he didn't trust what the Zero Tolerance people might do with it.

"There was a hell of a row in the family, afterwards, when they discovered the Stone was gone. But by the time they'd worked out who'd taken it, your grandfather had already made himself into the Regent of Shadows, a man of influence and power in his own right. And the Matriarch wasn't ready to go to war with him over a few missing items. The Zero Tolerance people couldn't ex-plain how important the Stone was without revealing their own intentions . . . And then, of course, a lot of things happened, which you know very well because you were there for most of them, and the Lazarus Stone ... was forgotten. I knew Father had it, because I helped him steal it. You must understand, Eddie—the Regent didn't take the Stone because he wanted to use it; he just didn't want anyone else to use it."

I looked at him steadily. We'd finally got to the point I'd been dreading.

"You do know what's happened, Uncle Jack ... at the Department of Uncanny?"

"Of course I know," he said. "All hell's breaking loose up in the War Room, though no one's decided what to do yet. Yes, Eddie, I know. They told me as soon as the news came in. My father is dead. Finally dead for real, lost to us all. It's been a hard few years for me, Eddie. First I lost my brother James, and then my mother, the Matriarch, and now my father. And my son, Timothy, of course, but then ... he was lost to me years ago. Still, the family endures. The family goes on. That's what they teach us, and it is a comfort, I suppose." He looked at me sharply. "You were there, Eddie. How were they able to kill the Regent? He had Kayleigh's Eye! I gave it to him before he left, to keep him safe!"

"Somebody took it from him," I said. "Ripped it right out of his chest. How is that even possible, Uncle Jack?"

"I don't know," said the Armourer. "Nothing magical or high tech could even touch it ... Brute force, maybe. Do you know who, or what, was able to destroy the whole Department of Uncanny?"

"No," I said. "It was all over by the time Molly and I got there. No evidence left anywhere, to point a finger."

"The family thinks you did it."

"What?"

I started to get up, but the Armourer gestured sharply for me to sit down again.

"I don't believe a word of it," he said. "And neither will they, once they've calmed down a bit. But apparently you and Molly were seen fleeing the scene after the massacre. And it's not just the family. The word is out everywhere that you're responsible. That Molly took her revenge on the Regent for the killing of her parents, and the two of you wiped out everyone else when they tried to stop you."

"That's not what happened!" I said.

"I know," said the Armourer. "I wasn't born yesterday! But mostly, everyone else wants your blood for this. Pretty much every organisation in our line of work is on the lookout for you two." The Armourer scowled briefly. "This is all so well organised, you'd think someone arranged it . . . I can turn the family around, but it's going to take time. Are you sure you wouldn't rather drop this mission of yours, just for now, so you can beg the family's forgiveness and accept their protection? For Molly's sake, as well as yours?"

"I can't," I said. "And if you knew why, you wouldn't want me to."

"Oh," said the Armourer, nodding wisely. "One of those cases, eh? But, Eddie, how were they able to get to the Regent? Do you know?"

"Grandfather left me a final message," I said. "It seems there was a traitor inside the Department, who lowered all the shields and let the enemy in. He didn't know who. They were there for the Lazarus Stone. But I have reason to believe the Regent didn't have it."

"Of course not," said the Armourer. "He gave it to James, long ago."

"What?" I said.

The Armourer winced. "Please stop doing that, Eddie. It goes right through me. Now, where was I . . . Oh yes. You have to remember, Eddie, that while I was in touch with your grandfather on and off through the years, it all had to be very much under the radar. The family couldn't know. For my safety, and yours, and your parents'. So a lot happened that I only heard about later, after the fact. The Regent gave the Lazarus Stone to your uncle James, because James asked him for it. And James . . . gave the Stone to the Lady Faire."

"What?"

"Eddie, either you keep the volume down or I will plunge you into a bath of industrial-strength tranquiliser! We don't want the rest of the family coming down here to see what's going on. Do we?"

"But he gave it away? To the Lady Faire? Why would he do that?"

"Because there's no fool like an old fool," said the Armourer. "James had an affair with the Lady, perhaps because he was getting on and needed one more chance to play his legend. To be the illustrious Grey Fox . . . To prove to himself that he wasn't getting *old*. Other people buy a Porsche . . . You do know who and what the Lady Faire is, Eddie?"

"Not really," I admitted. "Just rumours. You do hear things, out in the field, whether you want to or not. Isn't she supposed to be . . . well, the ultimate courtesan?"

"The Lady Faire is much more than that," the Armourer said sternly. "The Lady Faire is a ladything. You know, like a ladyboy, only even more so. Oh, do try to keep up, Eddie—we're both a bit old for me to be explaining the birds and bees to you. The Lady Faire is an omnisexual, the ultimate sexual object. All things to all people, and indeed, all people to all things ..."

"I have no idea what that means," I said.

"You've led a sheltered life, haven't you, boy?" said the Armourer. "We used to get out a lot more, when I was a field agent. It was expected of us. You could learn a hell of a lot more through pillow talk than through burgling an office ... Look, the Lady Faire is ... Oh well, we might as well use the term ... *She*'s not male or female, but a combination of both. A whole that is supposed to be far greater than the sum of its parts. If you'll pardon the expression. She's beautiful, bewitching, irresistible—the ultimate honey trap. You know, seduce them, wring all their secrets out of them, and then throw them to the wolves. The Lady Faire is every love and lover you ever dreamed of, especially the ones where you wake up screaming, in a cold sweat. One of the Baron Frankenstein's more inventive creations, when he was getting old, and a bit kinky."

"Did you ever meet her?" I said, fascinated despite myself.

"Just the once. Years ago, when I was working a case in Los Angeles with your uncle James. He introduced me to the Lady Faire at a Hollywood party. Every star and diva you can think of was there, but no one had eyes for anyone but the Lady Faire. I have to say, I was a bit creeped out by her, myself. Her magic doesn't work on everyone, you know. There is such a thing as too sweet ... But it was obvious to me even then that James was smitten with her. So, years later, he decides he's in love with her, and gives her the Lazarus Stone. Because she said she needed it to get her out of a bind. Don't ask me what that was all about. James never told me. I'm not even sure he got all the details from the Lady Faire ...

"Of course, the family never knew anything of this. They would not have approved. They've made a hell of a lot of allowances for James, down the years, because he was the Grey Fox, the greatest field agent we ever had. But an affair with the Lady Faire? That would definitely have been a step too far. Anyway, according to what James finally told me, the Stone was only supposed to be on loan. A temporary gift. But, love is blind . . . James never saw the Lazarus Stone again.

"And then he died . . . After that, I had too many other things to worry about, and I just forgot about the Stone. Until you reminded me. To the best of my knowledge the Lady Faire still has it. Far as I know, she's never used it. Though, of course, how could I be sure? How could anyone?"

"Does anyone else know she has the Stone?"

"I don't see how. But information has a way of getting out."

"I have to get hold of the Lazarus Stone," I said. "And no, I can't tell you why. Are you positive the Lady still has it?"

"Oh yes," said the Armourer. "I'd definitely have heard if it had turned up with someone else. The family does like to keep a close eye on all the Major Players. Though it has to be said, the Lady Faire is semi-retired these days. Keeps people off her back by threatening to publish her memoirs. In fact . . . she's just sent out the invitations to her annual Ball, a get-together for all her lovers and friends. Past, present, and future. No address given, no date or time; you either know where and how to find her, or you don't deserve to get in. And at the moment the family doesn't know."

"How can we not know?" I said. "Given that we keep such a close eye on all the Major Players?"

"I think the family prefers to keep its distance," said the Armourer. "As long as she stays semi-retired, we don't care where she is. And she never was as important, or significant, as her legend liked to make out. But it does mean you'll have to locate the venue for the Ball yourself, Eddie. And you can't go after her as a Drood. We can't be seen to be openly connected with her."

"Even though I'm currently a rogue and a mass murderer?"

"Perhaps especially because of that."

"All right," I said. "I can't involve the Droods in what I'm doing anyway. I'll just have to do this as Shaman Bond."

I stopped, and looked at him thoughtfully.

"While I'm here . . . I need to talk to you about the Merlin Glass. It's started . . . doing things. Acting independently . . ."

"Ah," said the Armourer, "I was afraid of that."

"You were? Then why didn't you warn me!"

"I did," said the Armourer. "Never trust a gift from Merlin Satanspawn. The clue is in the name, after all . . . I believe there is some kind of living thing, trapped or perhaps lurking, inside the Glass. Sometimes you can just catch a glimpse of it moving, somewhere in the background of your reflection. I wonder whether it might be some last trace of Merlin himself, trying for a comeback . . .

"And of course, what you have now is a combination of the original broken Glass and the duplicate Glass you found in the Other Hall. Merged together in a way I fully admit I don't understand at all. God alone knows what the Other Merlin might have hidden in his Glass."

He sighed heavily, seeming suddenly that much older, and tireder.

"This is why I wanted you to give the Merlin Glass back. So I could run some exhaustive tests on it. I don't think it's safe to handle any more. If it ever was."

"You can have it back," I said. "After I've finished this mission."

And then we both looked round sharply. A lot of people outside the Armoury were heading our way.

"Your assistants must have figured out the dragon was just an illusion," I said. "I was hoping we'd have more time . . . I'd better get out of here."

"I can't help you, Eddie," said the Armourer, as we both rose to our feet. "Can't even give you any new toys for your mission."

"Where did you send the dragon?" I said. "Molly went to join it."

"Just out into the grounds," said the Armourer. "Give my best to the Lady Faire when you find her. See if she remembers me. Or James."

I opened up the Merlin Glass, and was gone.

CHAPTER SIX

False Knight on the Road

'd told the Merlin Glass to take me straight to Molly, and I can't say I was completely surprised when I stepped through the Glass into an area of almost entirely devastated Drood grounds. A great circle of scorched and blackened grass stood before a copse of trees, all of which were on fire. The heat from the flames was enough to stop me in my tracks, while a thick cloud of black smoke boiled up into the sky from what had been a favoured picnicking spot for young Droods. All around the scorched grass, the wide-open lawn was pockmarked with impact craters, heavy-duty bullet holes, and signs of extensive use of high explosives. All the usual local wildlife was conspicuous by its absence. Except for the wild witch herself, Molly Metcalf, standing quietly and demurely to one side. She smiled innocently at me.

"Can't take you anywhere," I growled.

"Wasn't my fault!" she said immediately. "This was all done by the lab assistants doing their level best to take out a dragon that wasn't really there, with enough fire-power to win a war. They can be very enthusiastic, those lab assistants. Especially when they've got all kinds of guns and a really big target."

"Why didn't you just drop the illusion, once you were safely out of the Armoury?" I said.

She shrugged. "I wanted to buy you some time. And the lab assistants were having so much fun . . ."

I shook my head slowly. "Capability Maggie is not going to be pleased."

"You made that name up!" said Molly.

"I wish," I said. "She's in charge of looking after the Drood grounds. Or at least she was; she's just been made the new Matriarch of all the Droods."

"All right," said Molly. "Now your family has another Matriarch I'm not going to listen to."

"Could you at least put out the trees?" I said. "As a sign of goodwill, and a personal favour to me?"

"Oh well," said Molly. "If you're asking nicely . . ."

She glared at the burning copse, and all the flames snapped off in a moment, revealing the dead, spiky remains of half-consumed trees. The copse now looked, if anything, rather worse. Molly saw the look on my face, and heaved her best martyred sigh. She gestured broadly with one hand, and all the charred bark jumped off the trees, falling to the ground like so much soot, revealing fresh new growth underneath. The elm trees jerked and swayed in an unfelt breeze, twisting and stretching themselves back to full size again. New leaves flourished everywhere.

The huge circle of scorched grass jumped into the air, and by the time it had reseated itself in the earth, everything was a vibrant shade of green again. The blast holes and exploded craters healed in a moment, with nothing left to show they had ever been there. And a whole bunch of new flowers burst up out of the earth, like so many Technicolor exclamation points.

The last few vestiges of black smoke drifted away on the breeze. Birds started singing again.

"You see?" said Molly. "I'm not just here for the bad things in life."

"Thank you," I said. "I'm sure that will go a long way towards helping with your current status in my family."

She looked at me. "My current status? I thought this was all about you?"

"Unfortunately, as it turns out, not," I said. "They've put you back on the supernatural terrorist list."

Molly smirked, actually flattered. "Been a long time since I thought of myself as that. Happy days . . . All right, what am I supposed to have done now? And it had better be something particularly stylish and impressive, or I'll walk right back in there and demand to know why they thought it was me. I mean, I have my standards."

"We're supposed to have murdered everyone at the Department of Uncanny," I said. "Including my grandfather, the Regent of Shadows."

Molly stared at me for a long moment. "Who the hell thinks *that*? I have only ever killed people who needed killing! Everyone knows that."

"Pretty much everyone in our line of work believes we're guilty," I said. "Very definitely including my family. So I think we should get the hell out of Dodge. Right now."

"Fine by me," Molly said immediately. "You should never come home, Eddie. This place has always been bad for you. Let's go back to my forest. No one can track us there, and we can talk freely without fear of anyone listening in."

I looked back at the Merlin Glass, still floating on the air in full Door mode. The opening was full of quietly buzzing static, as it waited for new instructions. I looked at it for a long moment, before subvocalising the coordinates for Molly's wild woods. I wasn't entirely confident about trusting Molly to the Glass, after everything the Armourer had said, but it didn't seem I had much of a choice. The Glass was the only real option I had for staying ahead of my enemies. My many enemies. I could have asked Molly to teleport us, but I didn't like to. That kind of spell was a major drain on her magical reserves, and I was pretty sure we were going to need those in the not-too-distant future. So I waited for the woods to appear on the other side of the Glass, and then strode quickly through, with Molly right behind me.

It was good to be back in the wild woods again. The moment I stood among the huge and ancient trees, I felt half my cares just slip away, like a weight I no longer needed to carry. I stood a little taller, and breathed more easily. Tall and vast and heavy with foliage, the great trees spread away in all directions, as far as the eye could see ... and farther. The primordial forest, of Olde Englande. From when life was new and free, and we all lived in the woods because there was nowhere else.

The air was heavy with rich and pungent scents, of earth and grass, leaves and flowers and other living things. A low wind gusted through the trees, carrying the songs of all sorts of birds, only some of which I recognised. Creatures large and small moved in the shadows among the trees, going about their business, entirely unconcerned with human visitors but preferring to keep their distance nonetheless. Just as well. They usually made rude remarks when they saw it was me. The forest wildlife was very protective when it came to Molly.

The Merlin Glass quickly shrank back down to hand-mirror size the moment Molly and I had passed through. As though it was limited by the old magics working in the wild woods. Or perhaps it just wanted to be put away and not thought about for a while. Until it was needed again. Looking back, it surprised me how quickly I'd become . . . not dependent upon the Glass, but certainly used to it. I don't normally like relying on devices, even the Armourer's ingenious little toys. Better to depend on your wits in the field; they're less likely to let you down at a critical juncture. But the Glass was just so useful . . . I should have distrusted it long before this. Unless it was somehow influencing me. I tucked the hand mirror away in my pocket. It felt like storing a live grenade . . . that was just waiting for the right moment to go off.

Molly slipped her arm through mine and we strolled along together, through the tall trees. There were no open paths, as such, but Molly always knew which way to go, and the heavy vegetation seemed to just lean back out of the way, to let her pass. The trees' branches bent ponderously together overhead, forming a thick, dark canopy, through which golden shafts of sunlight dropped down like shimmering spotlights. Birdsong rose up on either side of us, close and sweet and tuneful. A breeze caressed my face, filling my head with restful scents and a pleasant sense of languor. I could feel the day-long tension seeping slowly out of my muscles. It occurred to me then that it was always summer here in the wild woods, no matter what time or season it might be anywhere else in the world. Whenever Molly brought me here, it was always summer.

"One of these days," I said, as casually as I could, "you're going to have to trust me enough to tell me exactly where your private forest really is. Or perhaps the more proper question would be *when* it really is."

"One of these days," said Molly just as casually, looking straight ahead. "It isn't that I don't trust you, sweetie. It's just that some secrets aren't mine to share. I don't own this place; I just get to visit. I'm a guest here, just like you."

"Then who does own the wild woods?" I said. "Who do you need to ask, for permission to come here?"

"You see?" said Molly, squeezing my arm against her side companionably. "Questions just lead to more questions, with no guarantee of an answer. Or at least, an answer you could live with."

"We lead such complicated lives," I said, after a moment.

"You need to tell me what's been happening," Molly said sternly. "What did you talk to your uncle Jack about? And how did we end up as fall guys for the Uncanny massacre?"

I brought her up to date, and not surprisingly she jumped on the one thing that really mattered to her.

"So, no one in all your family knows, any more, who gave the Regent his orders to kill my parents? Or even why?"

"Uncle Jack doesn't believe so," I said carefully. "I suppose it's always possible there could be a record somewhere, tucked away in some vault in the family archives, and I promise we will look later, when this current mess is finally over, but I wouldn't put any money on it. This is all deniable operations stuff, and the people involved would have been bound to cover their tracks. Destroy all the paper trails, and there's no incriminating evidence . . ."

"I need to know," said Molly.

"I know," I said.

I hadn't told her about the Merlin Glass. Partly because I didn't want her distracted from our current mission until my parents were safe again. And partly because I was worried that the Glass might be listening. I didn't want to put Molly in danger from the Glass. Or from whatever might be lurking inside it.

"I have heard of the Lady Faire," said Molly. "As a name, and a legend. One of those renowned personages always popping up on the edges of things. Up in Really High Society, where the air isn't just rarefied, it's designer, and only the very best and the very worst kind of people get to mingle. I haven't a clue where she is right now. I've never mixed in those kinds of circles, even before I met you and got civilised. It's not like she and I had anything in common, after all. The Lady Faire used seduction and fascination to destroy her enemies and achieve her ends, whereas I always favoured . . ."

"Destruction?" I said.

"You say the nicest things, sweetie. I never met the Lady Faire because I never got invited to those sorts of parties. I'm a simple girl at heart. I couldn't even tell you what she looks like . . ."

"I should have asked the Armourer for a photo, before I left," I said. "I don't know much more than the legend, myself."

"There might not be any photos," said Molly. "If she's as secretive as everyone says."

"Oh, there's bound to be one somewhere," I said. "My family has files on everyone who is anyone."

"And yet they're saying they don't know where she is right now?"

"I think it's more . . . they don't want to know."

"Ah," Molly said wisely. "There's a story there. I can smell it."

"Wouldn't surprise me," I said.

I had told her about Uncle James, but neither of us mentioned him. Of such small concessions and agreements are relationships made.

"The Lady Faire does get around," said Molly. "According to the stories, barroom gossip, and general character assassination I've heard . . . she's set up shop in every major city on the planet at one time or another. Chasing the Intelligence community from one hotspot to another, like the glamorous little parasite she is. And even to a few dark and disturbing neighbourhoods that aren't on any official map. The Lady Faire goes where the action is. She was the toast of San Francisco society through most of the Seventies, and Queen of the Night in Bangkok in the Nineties. And you don't even want to know what she got up to in the Nightside, for almost two years."

"I know what she got up to in Soho, in the Sixties," I said. "I was the Drood field agent in London for several years, remember. And they were still telling stories about her conquests and exploits, some fifty years after she left. Most of which I prefer not to believe, for my own peace of mind."

"Believe them all," said Molly. "Especially the really bad ones. Because they're the ones she's most proud of. I used to be a real party animal, back in the day . . . But the word was and is that no one can party like the Lady Faire."

I frowned. "She'd been around for quite a while, even

before Soho in the Sixties . . . So how old do you suppose she is?"

"She's one of the Baron Frankenstein's creations," said Molly, shrugging. "She could be alive, or dead, or any number of states in between."

"Fair enough," I said. "But where do we look for her now? Where can we go where they'd know?"

"The Wulfshead," said Molly. "They always know the very best gossip. And I could use a drink."

"Never knew you when you couldn't," I said. "But I was just there, remember? They've got their own problems, cleaning up after the MI 13 intrusion. I doubt there'll be many patrons around for a while."

"Strangefellows!" said Molly, clapping her hands together delightedly. "Everyone goes to Strangefellows!"

"Only because no one else will have them," I said. "I keep telling you: Droods can't go into the Nightside. And I'm not letting you go in there alone."

"Why not?" said Molly, immediately bristling. "I can look after myself!"

"Wouldn't doubt it for a moment," I said. "But you are just a little bit too prone to temptation and getting distracted, in the Nightside."

"Well, yes," said Molly. "That's what it's for . . . But there are a great many powerful and determined people and organisations looking for us right this minute. And the Nightside is the one sanctuary and neutral ground that everybody recognises."

"I can't go in as a Drood," I said. "People would notice. And the whole point of our current situation is that we don't want to be noticed. By anyone. Not until we've got our hands on the Lazarus Stone, and got my parents back safely."

Molly pouted sulkily. "You could always go in as Shaman Bond."

"No, I couldn't," I said. "They'd know."

"You're right," said Molly. "They would. It's the Nightside."

"Wherever we go, someone is bound to recognise one or both of us," I said. "Shaman Bond's reputation might be smaller than yours, but it's just as widespread. And no matter how fast an in and out we make it, word will get back to my family, and they'll come after us. Along with all the other organisations in our line of work, everyone from the London Knights to the Soulhunters. I'm not sure it's safe for us to show our faces anywhere."

Molly smiled, and rested her head against my shoulder. "Takes you back, doesn't it? To when you and I first got together? On the run from everyone, with the whole world at our backs and at our throats?"

"Only you could get nostalgic about that part of our lives," I said. "I really hoped we'd put that behind us. I'm not built for running. No, we need a plan. And for that, we need information. And for that we need . . . the OverNet."

"Oh bloody hell," said Molly, stepping away from me and looking down her nose in disgust. "Really?"

The OverNet is the dark, shadowy side of the Internet, a secret overlay unsuspected by even the fiercest hackers, dealing exclusively with supernatural and super-science matters. The kind of sites even the most feral conspiracy nuts have never dreamed actually existed. All the information on the hidden world is there, somewhere, on the OverNet. If you can find it, if you can find your way in, and if you can get back out again with your mind and your soul still attached. An endless repository of strange facts, unnatural gossip, and really secret shit, everything you ever wanted to know that most people have enough sense to leave strictly alone.

"The OverNet can be very useful," Molly said carefully, in her best tactful tone, "but it's not exactly *reliable*, now is it? I mean, a lot of it is just nasty people, and other things, dishing the dirt on one another."

"I know," I said, "But it is a very good place to ask questions. Someone will know something about the Lady Faire, or point us in the direction of someone who does. It's the best place to start. Now, I can't log on through any of my usual Drood connections, and even the most secure underground cybercafés won't be safe for us, under current conditions. I can't even use the computer in my London flat; the family will be looking up all my known addresses and setting people to watch for us. The Voice said no talking to my family. I think I've already pushed that as far as I dare."

"We could always go back to my old place in Ladbrook Grove," said Molly. "I sublet it to myself, under an assumed identity, just in case I ever needed to go back. Or one of my sisters needed somewhere to crash in a hurry. Because I didn't want them staying with us. There's a Door here in the wild woods that will take us right there."

"No," I said. "We can't do that. My family has that address on file; it's how I found you in the first place. They're bound to have the place staked out by now."

"Hold everything, hit the brake, go previous," said Molly, just a bit dangerously. "Your family has a file on me?"

"Of course," I said. "We keep files on everyone who is anyone."

"But I'm almost a part of your family now! I'm with you!"

"We keep files on everyone. Especially members of the family."

"Droods are weird," said Molly.

"Why do you think I left, first chance I got?"

"All right, where do you think we should go?"

"I think we need to go to one of my underground safe houses," I said. "One of my off-the-map and under-the-radar addresses that aren't in any file. Very secure bolt-holes that I maintain just for occasions like this. When I don't want anyone to know where I am, very definitely including my family."

"Are we talking deniable operations again?" said Molly.

"Yes," I said. "Because the world's like that sometimes. Especially the world of the secret agent. When the left hand mustn't know who the right hand's killing."

"Like my parents?" said Molly.

I just looked at her. I had nothing to say. There was nothing I could say. In the end, Molly looked away.

"Am I to understand that you still have several of these . . . safe houses?"

"Yes," I said. "Scattered here and there and all over the place. Because you never know when you can't go home again. Like right now."

And then I stopped, and looked thoughtfully at Molly. She looked right back at me.

"What?" she said suspiciously. "You've got that *I'm only doing this for your own good* look on your face. You should know by now it's not going to get you anywhere."

"This mission is all about getting my parents back," I said steadily. "And the only way to do that is by stealing a major Object of Power from a living legend. Even if we do bring it off, the odds are we'll end up paying for that crime for the rest of our lives, one way or another. You don't have to be involved in this, Molly. I'd understand, I really would. You could sit this one out, safe here in your forest, till it was all over. I can take the blame, for the death of my grandfather and of everyone else who died at the Department of Uncanny. For once it really is all about me, and my parents. You don't have to take the fall with me."

Molly sighed heavily, and stepped forward to stand right in front of me. And then she slapped my face, hard.

"I go where you go," she said fiercely. "Now and forever. You should know that."

My face stung, and my ears were ringing, but I still couldn't help smiling. "I do know that," I said. "I just need to be reminded now and again."

"Kiss it better!" Molly said brightly, and kissed me happily on the mouth. "So!" she said, bouncing eagerly up and down on her toes. "Where are we going?"

"You won't like it," I said.

I took the Merlin Glass out again, doing my best to treat it perfectly normally. I gave it the coordinates for a particular safe house I hadn't used in years, and the Glass immediately jumped out of my hand and swelled up to Door size, hanging on the air before me. A grim grey street scene showed on the far side of the Glass, and Molly and I stepped through the Door and into the city of Newcastle upon Tyne, in the far North of England.

The first change I noticed was the light. The golden summer of the wild woods was cut off abruptly, replaced by the dour, overcast, and somehow grimy light of a city street on a dark and gloomy autumn afternoon. A cold wind went scudding down the street, blowing leaves and other small things along the pavements. Two long terraces of mostly anonymous housing swept up and down the street.

Molly and I were standing in the middle of Bayswater Road. Rumbling sounds of distant traffic replaced the wild birdsong. The only bird noises you were likely to hear in this neighbourhood were the pigeons, coughing consumptively. Molly shuddered suddenly. I understood. It wasn't the grey light or the cold wind; it was how dark and oppressive and claustrophobic the city felt, after the wild, open freedom of the forest.

"Everything's so grey," said Molly. "Even the air. We're up North, aren't we?"

"Newcastle," I said cheerfully. "A big bustling modern city, with impressive nightlife and a thriving cultural scene." I looked around. "Not here, particularly, which is part of what makes it such a perfect place to hide."

I looked carefully up and down the street. Everything seemed calm and normal enough. No traffic, and just a few nondescript individuals trudging along the pavements, intent on their own business and paying no attention at all to their surroundings. Not even a twitch of a curtain at any of the windows, from someone looking out.

"This is an area mostly occupied by students," I said to Molly. "So people here are used to seeing new faces all the time. Just another reason why I chose this place. This way."

I led Molly down the street, counting off the terraced houses in my head, until I came to a door that looked familiar. It also looked cheap and shabby and uncared for, which was sort of the point. I didn't want anything that would stand out or attract attention. Best of all, who would look for a Drood in a setting like this? I produced a key ring I didn't use every day, and searched through the assorted keys until I found the one that unlocked the waiting front door. The lock turned easily enough, but the door had settled into its frame and didn't want to budge. Molly looked on, smirking, as I had to put my shoulder to it. The door finally stopped resisting, and let us in. I hit the switch just inside, and was quietly relieved when the light came on. I had set up direct debits for everything through a shell company, but you never know.

The long, narrow entrance hall was gloomy, quiet, and dusty. It clearly hadn't been used for quite a while. Which was as it should be. The air was still and dry. I looked carefully at the bare wooden floorboards and saw that the thick layer of dust was entirely undisturbed, apart from some rat scratchings and what looked like recent droppings. No one had been here.

I moved quickly from room to room, slamming open the doors and checking out the rooms. My footsteps sounded loud and carrying on the quiet, as though the house resented its long peace being disturbed. I came back out into the hall, and Molly was standing exactly where I'd left her, looking around in a way that made it very clear she had no wish to go anywhere else until somebody did some serious cleaning. I didn't blame her. There was no carpeting on any of the floors, no prints or posters or decorations on any of the bare plaster walls, and the secondhand furniture had been chosen for its cheapness and utility.

"Yes, it's a dump!" I said cheerfully. "You'd probably have to spend serious money on an upgrade before it was good enough to be condemned. That's the point."

"How can you stand to live in a place like this?" said Molly.

"I don't," I said. "This isn't a home, it's a bolt-hole. A

place to hide out that no one would want to look inside. It has four walls and a roof, and a door I can barricade. That's all you need in a bolt-hole."

"I don't like to think of you living in places like this," said Molly. "The cold and seedy side of the secret agent life."

"For years, places like this were all I knew," I said. "Hiding in unlit rooms, watching unobserved, checking out secrets or people, until it was safe to move on. Not a lot of glamour in the life of a Drood field agent. Until I met you."

She smiled briefly, and then wrinkled her nose. "What is that *smell*?"

"Any number of really unpleasant answers cross my mind," I said. "I find it best not to inquire. Don't get comfortable. We're not staying here long."

"Best news I've had so far," said Molly.

I armoured up and looked around through my golden mask, checking the house's security settings. None of the booby-traps had been tripped, and none of the shields and protections had been forced. Everything seemed to be just as I'd left it. I had to stop and think for a moment to work out that it had been eight years since I was last here, body-guarding an art historian who'd found something nasty living in an old painting. Eight years . . . probably not a good idea to look inside the fridge. I armoured down again.

Molly made her way steadily down the hall, peering through the open doorways and quietly expressing extreme disgust for everything she saw. I didn't blame her. It was all cheap and cheerful, where it wasn't damp and dusty. There were cobwebs in the corners, and the sound of small scuttling things.

"It is a bit of a mess, I agree," I said. "Just a little more than I was expecting . . . I used to have this cheerful little Pixie who kept the place spic and span, but as I haven't paid her in years . . . Look, we won't be here long. I just need to access the computer, and then we'll be on our way. Hold your nose if you think that will help. Or your breath. I can't open a window; that would tell the whole world someone was here."

Molly stood in the middle of the hallway, her arms folded tightly across her chest. Never a good sign.

"I am not sitting down anywhere," she said. "The whole place looks unhealthy. I might catch something."

"Come into the study, Molly," I said encouragingly. "You'll like the study."

I led her to the end of the hall, and sent a tendril of golden strange matter down my arm from my torc to form a golden glove over my right hand. And then I carefully extruded a key from one finger and unlocked the study door. I waited a moment, just to be sure the key had shut down all the various nasty deathtraps protecting the room, and then pushed the door open. The study seemed calm and quiet, so I led Molly inside. She looked around and sniffed loudly, but I could tell she was impressed, really.

The walls were all spotless white tiles, with not a speck of dust or dirt anywhere. The floor was so clean you could have performed major surgery on it. The computer system set up on the only table looked just as it had the day I'd left it. I pulled out the only chair and sat down at the keyboard. Molly moved in close behind me, so she could peer over my shoulder.

"I programmed this room to look after itself," I said. "And protect and defend the computer, of course. If the wrong key tried the door's lock, the room would have blown up the whole building. Drood tech must never be allowed to fall into enemy hands. Aren't you glad I told you that after I tried the key? Thought so."

"Blow up the house and to hell with the neighbours," said Molly. "That's the Drood way, all right."

I fired up the computer and logged in, using one of my old Shaman Bond online identities. Just in case someone tried chasing the connection. The monitor screen showed me a screensaver of a Soho street at midnight, with something odd lurking in the background.

"We're going to have to be quick," I said, tapping away at the keyboard with my usual two fingers. "Just my being online will attract the attention of my family. And then they'll wonder what Shaman Bond is doing in New-castle, and someone will come running to find out. And this will be another of my secret bolt-holes I can't come back to. I really must find the time to set up some new ones. You can never have enough hiding places. Okay, let's do this. Get the info and get out."

"Fine by me," said Molly, her chin on my shoulder and the side of her face pressed against mine as she studied the monitor screen. I found her presence comforting. I slipped easily into the OverNet and moved rapidly from one site to another, following one promising link to the next. Images came and went quickly on the screen, as I went looking for the Lady Faire.

"You know," said Molly, "you don't need all these safe houses and bolt-holes any more, Eddie. You can always stay in my forest. No one can get to you there. You'd be safe with me. Not even Droods can enter my wild woods without my permission."

"That's very kind of you," I said, keeping my gaze

fixed on the screen. "But I've never liked to be dependent on the kindness of others. Besides, your forest doesn't have computers."

"Lot you know," Molly said easily. "You'd be amazed at what I've got there, tucked away. The wild woods are a lot bigger than you think."

"How on earth can you have computers in the woods? Where's your power supply, and your connections? How could . . . No. No, I'm not going to be distracted. You can tell me all about it later, and I'll disbelieve you then."

"Suit yourself," said Molly.

I went rummaging roughly through the OverNet, searching for information on the Lady Faire. I did get distracted by a few things along the way, because you can't help it. Even Drood tech can't protect you from all the unwanted pop-ups and unnatural ads that infest the OverNet. *Would you like to meet other pagans in your area?* said one insistent message. I had to wonder, what did they mean, *other*? What sort of list was Shaman Bond on? Another ad wanted me to *Join the Satanic Swingers Club! You'll have a Hell of a good time!* There were photos attached, but I didn't have the time. And then there was *Hello, I am an Elven Prince with a large fortune in fairie gold that I need to transfer into your reality. If you will just give me all your bank details . . .* I'm amazed anyone still falls for that one.

I finally left the distractions behind and moved on, in hot pursuit of the Lady Faire. There was no shortage of stories about her past exploits, most of them wildly contradictory in the details. That's legends for you. The Lady who's been everywhere and had everyone . . . A lot of the accounts tended to quickly degenerate into *He said, She said, They said . . .* And there was no shortage of fan sites for the Lady Faire, all unofficial. Some were even set up to worship her, quite literally, as a living goddess. These people were praying to her, even sending her gifts and supplications, pleading for intervention in their personal lives and solutions to their problems.

It didn't look like the Lady Faire ever responded to their entreaties, or talked directly to any of them. In fact, I couldn't find a single instance of her communicating with anyone. There were just as many sites condemning her as everything from a Bad Example to a female Antichrist. Angry accusations, death threats, calls for jihad . . . It did seem that some sites were actually at war with one another, with mounting real-life casualties. These people took the Lady Faire very seriously. And yet, strangely, there wasn't a single photo of her to be found anywhere. Not even on the most rabid and obsessive fan sites. Instead, there were any number of artist's impressions, everything from court sketches to fully painted portraits.

And every single one of them different.

I finally ended up on the message boards. As Shaman Bond, naturally. Because the whole point of my cover identity was that Shaman could turn up anywhere and no one was ever surprised. I chatted with a lot of people who claimed to know the Lady Faire, or more usually knew people who knew her, but while everyone had heard about her annual Ball, none of them had any idea where it was being held. Until finally I made contact with Dead Boy.

Dead Boy came to the Nightside as a teenager and was immediately mugged and murdered. He made a deal he still won't talk about, to come back from the dead and avenge his murder. But he should have read the small print. He's stuck in his risen corpse, unable to leave, possessing his own dead body. At least until his body wears out. He's something of a party animal, and he does get around.

I know where the Lady Faire's Ball is being held, he said. *I just got my invitation.*

"Okay," said Molly, her chin still resting comfortably on my shoulder. "The Lady Faire only gives out invitations to her lovers. Which means she, he, or it has had sex with Dead Boy. Who is, after all, dead. Now that's just creepy. I mean, I like to think I'm open-minded about most things, especially if I haven't got around to trying them yet, but even I draw the line at sleeping with someone who smells strongly of formaldehyde. Even if they are still moving around."

"I am very pleased to hear that," I said.

Get you to the Winter Palace, said Dead Boy. *And beware the Ice Queen.*

He withdrew completely from the OverNet before I could ask any questions.

I sat back in my chair, and Molly put her arms around me. I was thinking hard. The monitor hummed impatiently before me.

"Okay," said Molly. "The Winter Palace . . . That name definitely rings a bell, but I can't place it."

"The Winter Palace is very exclusive," I said. "Very elite. In fact, I think you have to own or run a small country just to get past the doorman. Never been there myself, but I have heard stories about it. From my uncle James."

"He's been there?"

"The Grey Fox has been everywhere."

"Well, where is the Winter Palace?"

"Ultima Thule," I said. "The last really cool place in the world. I hope you packed your thermal underwear."

And then I broke off, as the monitor screen suddenly went blank. My first thought was some Trojan must have got past my filters, but then a gleaming golden Drood mask appeared on my screen, featureless and implacable, seeming to stare right out at me, as though it could see everything.

"What is that?" said Molly. "Eddie, what is that thing?"

"My family have found us," I said numbly. "They've hacked into the OverNet connection. I didn't think they could do that."

"Then do something!" said Molly. "Shut down the computer!"

"I can't!" I said. "It should have shut itself down the moment it realised something was wrong. My family have overridden the security protocols from their end."

I hammered away at the keyboard, trying to call up something that would protect me, and as I did, the golden face started to talk to me.

"Where are you, Eddie? The family needs you to come home. You need to come home. Now. Eddie needs to come home now."

I hunched my shoulders against the hypnotic words. "No, he bloody doesn't," I said.

"What is that awful voice?" said Molly. "It doesn't even sound human . . ."

"Psychological warfare," I said. "Don't listen to it."

I gave up trying to shut down the computer, and pulled the plug. Everything went dead, but the golden face was still on the screen, still talking. So I armoured up my fist and smashed the computer with one vicious blow. Sparks flew, and black smoke curled out of the collapsed sides of the machine. The golden face disappeared from the monitor screen, its voice cut off in mid-sentence.

I hit the computer again, just to be sure. Broken pieces scattered across the desk.

I retrieved the glove to my torc, pushed back my chair, and got to my feet. Molly stayed with me, her hands on my shoulders, talking calmly but urgently, but I wasn't listening. My family had found me. They'd be here soon to take me home. By force, if necessary. And this time I would never get away. Never be free again. They'd see to that. Even if it meant I ended up as the Drood in Cell 14.

All the house's security alarms went off at once. Bells and sirens and flashing lights, in every room throughout the house. I hadn't realised I'd installed so many. I shouted the various suppressing words, and one by one the alarms shut down. I turned to Molly.

"My family can't be here already," I said. "They just can't."

"Are you sure they didn't know about this place?" said Molly.

"No one knew!" I said. "That's the whole point of an underground bolt-hole! I only ever brought one other person here. And she wouldn't have said anything."

"Why not?"

"Because she's dead."

"What happened to her?"

"A painting ate her."

I hurried over to the study's only window and looked down into the street. Molly crowded in beside me. Dozens of soldiers in dark uniforms were moving quickly from house to house, calling out the occupants and then hurrying them away. Soldiers with body armour and automatic weapons, being very professional, and not taking no for an answer from anybody. There had to be at least a hundred of them, a very efficient small army, anonymous behind black-visored helmets. Some of the people didn't want to be evacuated from their homes, but when faced with even the slightest opposition or resistance, the soldiers went straight to brute force. Some of the students started shouting about their rights, and I winced as I saw rifle butts connecting with heads and ribs, and limp bodies being dragged away. Most people went quietly. Having an automatic weapon shoved right in their face does tend to take the fight out of most people.

Someone wanted the street emptied. Someone didn't want any witnesses for what was going to happen next.

As fast as people spilled out of their houses, soldiers led or dragged them away to the far ends of the street, where more soldiers were waiting to move them on to a secure area. It was all very well organised. The whole terrified populace was emptied out in minutes, with no one left behind. Except Molly and me. My safe house was being conspicuously avoided by the soldiers. Left until last. But eventually the dark-uniformed soldiers came, and formed a crowd bristling with weapons before my door. Someone leaned heavily on the doorbell, and followed it up almost immediately with a loud, hammering fist.

"Who are these people?" said Molly. "SAS?"

"No," I said. "Come on, Molly, we've seen these uniforms and tactics before. These are MI 13 shock troops. Remember when they attacked us outside my old flat in Knightsbridge?"

"Of course," said Molly. "Silly buggers. They came in mob-handed, complete with helicopter gunships and armoured vehicles. Didn't do them a whole lot of good against us."

"We kicked their arses," I said. "You'd think they'd

know better than to annoy us again . . . Will you listen to the noise they're making at my front door? Idiots. With the shields I put in place, they couldn't break that door down with a depleted-uranium battering ram. But I suppose we'd better go down and talk to the uniformed thugs, if only to find out what they want. And how they knew we were here. I also wish to make a very strong complaint about how they've been treating the innocent people of this street. First rule of fights in the hidden world: it's not supposed to spill over into the real world, and affect innocent bystanders. I will not have civilians hurt because of me."

"You tell them, Eddie," said Molly. "Be firm." And then she kissed me hard.

"What was that for?" I said.

"Because you immediately assumed that this was all your fault. It isn't. Everything bad that's happening here is down to the uniformed thugs. So let's go kick their nasty arses. I'm just in the mood to punch people in the face, knock them down, and stamp on their throats."

"Never knew you when you weren't," I said generously.

We sauntered down the hall to the front door, and I yanked it suddenly open, surprising a large burly type in mid-knock. I thrust my face right into his visored helmet and gave him my best *You're in trouble, pal* glare. There were several black-uniformed soldiers at my door, and they all backed quickly away, covering Molly and me with their automatic weapons. I stepped outside, with Molly right beside me, and the door quietly shut itself. Which meant all the house's shields were now back in place and fully armed. If anyone did try to break in, the whole place would go *Boom!* in a loud and thorough manner. I smiled easily at the soldiers crowded together before me.

"Yes?" I said loudly. "Can I help you? You're not the armed wing of the Jehovah's Witnesses, are you?"

"Oh shit," said the first solider. "It *is* them!"

"It's them!" said a second solider.

"I said that!" said the first.

"But it really is *them*!" said the second. "It's Eddie Drood and Molly Metcalf!"

"They are why we're here," said the first.

"Well, yes," said the second. "But I really was sort of hoping someone else would find them."

"This is the correct address," said the first. "Where the boss said they'd be."

"I was really hoping they wouldn't be home," said a gloomy third voice. "She turns people into things."

"You are all seriously letting the side down!" said the first. "Pull yourselves together! We have our guns, and we have the drop on them!"

"It won't help," said the second.

I looked at Molly. "No one does a decent threat any more. I can remember when armoured thugs had style."

"You just can't get the help, these days," said Molly. "I blame bad toilet training."

"Hands up!" said the first soldier, jerking his gun at me, his voice probably a little higher-pitched than he intended. "Put your hands in the air, now! Then kneel down, and lie face down on the ground!"

"Yeah, right," said Molly. "Like that's going to happen."

"I really don't like the way you've been treating the people who live on this street," I said sternly. "There's no excuse for unnecessary brutality."

"We know who you are!" said the first soldier. "We

know what you are! Your armour doesn't scare us. We're prepared. We've all been issued specially prepared ammunition!"

"Heard that one before," I said.

I subvocalised my activating Words, and my golden armour exploded out of my torc and swept over me in a moment, enclosing me from head to toe. The soldiers cried out in shock as a gleaming gold statue appeared before them, the face a featureless golden mask. There's something about there not being any eyeholes that always puts the wind up people. I raised one golden fist, concentrated, and thick spikes rose from the knuckles. The soldiers fell back several steps despite themselves. And then Molly stepped forward, smiling sweetly, and wrapped herself in a shield of swirling magics, stray energies spitting and sparking on the air. The soldiers fell back even farther. They were right out in the middle of the street now, huddling together for comfort.

One of them panicked and opened fire, and suddenly all the soldiers were firing at once, blasting Molly and me with everything they had. The roar of so many automatic weapons all firing at once was deafening. Bullets slammed into my armour, raking me from head to foot, and I didn't flinch. I felt no impact, and the armour soaked up all the bullets. With my old armour, the bullets would have ricocheted, going everywhere. The new strange matter armour was more responsible, absorbing all the bullets as fast as they arrived. I wasn't entirely sure where my armour stored them, or what it did with the bullets afterwards. Did it perhaps crap them out the back later, when I wasn't looking? I wouldn't like to leave a trail ... The soldiers kept firing, and the bullets did me no harm at all; it was like firing into a bottomless golden pool.

Some of the soldiers targeted Molly, and found that even more upsetting. Their bullets turned into pretty butterflies in mid-air, which then flew away. And given the rate at which the automatic weapons were pumping out bullets, it wasn't long before the sky above us was full of clouds of brightly coloured butterflies, weaving pretty patterns in the air.

The soldiers kept on firing until they ran out of ammunition, and then they just sort of stood there, like they didn't know what to do. So I stepped forward and punched out the first solider, hitting him so hard in the face that his black visor split neatly in two. He fell backwards, hit the ground hard, and didn't move again. And while the others were looking at him, Molly stepped forward and kicked the second soldier so hard in the nuts it actually lifted him up into the air for a moment. He hit the ground hard, curled into a ball around his pain, and made high-pitched noises of distress. I was pretty sure he was wearing protective armour down there, because I heard it break. Molly looked at me.

"They have to learn respect."

"Oh, I'm sure they're both feeling very respectful," I said. I looked at the remaining soldiers. "I expect you'd like to surrender now, wouldn't you?"

And then Molly and I looked round, as more soldiers came running towards us from both ends of the street at once. Dozens of black uniforms, heavily armed and armoured, crashing down the street with grim determination. The soldiers who had been firing on us turned and ran to join the others. Or perhaps to hide behind them. I looked past the approaching soldiers. Both ends of Bayswater Road had been completely sealed off by parked military vehicles and barricades. But I couldn't see any helicopter gunships, or attack vehicles, of the kind MI 13 had used before. Just black-uniformed cannon fodder. What were they planning?

"Do they really think sealing off the street is going to stop us leaving?" said Molly.

"I think it's more to keep other people out than to keep us in," I said. "They don't want any witnesses for whatever it is they have planned."

"I don't like the feel of this," said Molly, looking back and forth uncertainly. "Something is heading our way, apart from these idiots. Something . . . bad. I can feel it, crawling on my skin. You know what, Eddie? This might be a good time to exercise the better part of valour and leg it through the Merlin Glass. Before the bad thing gets here."

"You want to leave?" I said. "And miss a good scrap? A chance to beat the stuffing out of a bunch of smug, obnoxious thugs? Are you sickening for something?"

"No," said Molly, with quiet dignity. "I am just pointing out that MI 13 is showing every indication of having planned all this very thoroughly. They've got something else up their sleeves, and I can't help feeling we would both be a lot better off if we weren't here when it arrived."

"Hell," I said, "it's come to something if you're being the voice of reason." I looked up and down the street. "I can't See anything unnatural. No sign of any high tech or magical energies. Come on, Molly, this is MI 13 we're talking about. They couldn't organise a hand job in a brothel. Their specially prepared ammunition didn't amount to much, did it?"

"Oh, go on then," said Molly. "Mindless violence and extreme behaviour it is. Twist my arm . . ."

The approaching soldiers slowed their pace as they drew near, spreading out to surround us. Molly and I moved unhurriedly to stand back to back. The soldiers formed quickly into ranks, covering us with their automatic weapons and barking orders at us from behind their anonymous black-visored helmets. I turned my golden mask back and forth, and soldiers flinched away from its eyeless gaze. It was one thing to hear all the stories about Drood armour, and quite another to have to face it in the real world. The soldiers in the front ranks tried to back away, but the ones behind were having none of that, and held them there. A few scuffles broke out, until their officers got them back under control.

And Molly and I hadn't even done anything yet. I just stood there, my spiked golden fists held out before me, while Molly's magics flickered dangerously around her, full of nasty possibilities. Finally, one of the officers came forward to face me. His uniform had no markings, but there was a silver badge on his helmet, just above the visor. He stopped a more than respectful distance away, his automatic weapon trained on my armoured face. For psychological value, no doubt. His back was stiff, his head held high, and when he finally spoke his voice was sharp and authoritative.

"Eddie Drood, surrender yourself and your woman, and give yourselves over to the authority of MI 13. Do it now, before things get ugly."

"You're already ugly," I said. "I've seen how your people handle innocent bystanders."

"And what's this *your woman* crap?" Molly said loudly from behind me. "I am Molly Metcalf, wild witch of the woods and a supernatural terrorist in my own right! And a serial transformer of piggy little men who annoy me into squelchy little snot things!"

"She really is," I said. "I'd back away now and ask for new orders from someone higher up the food chain, if I were in your shoes."

"I don't take orders from rogue agents and witches with delusions of grandeur," snapped the MI 13 officer.

"I do not have delusions!" said Molly very loudly.

"You've upset her now," I said to the officer. "I'd start running if I were you. Not that it'll do any good, of course . . ."

"We have orders to take both of you in, dead or alive," said the officer. "Guess which we'd prefer."

"Why can't people just be reasonable?" I said plaintively to Molly.

"No good asking me," said Molly. "I never did get the hang of reasonable."

I smiled, and shrugged at the officer. "Sorry, but you see how it is. Tell you what—why don't you and your uniformed bully boys just put down your weapons and surrender to Molly and me? And then we won't have to do terribly unpleasant things to all of you, that will make the survivors scream when they wake up at the hospital."

"Survivors," said Molly. "Always the optimist, Eddie."

The officer stepped back, and gestured sharply to a nearby soldier, who stepped smartly forward out of the ranks and aimed a rocket launcher directly at me. I started to say something, and he fired the thing at me, at point-blank range. The shell shot across the few yards separating us at incredible speed, the sound of its rocket blast almost overpowering. The sensors in my mask kicked in immediately, speeding up my sight and reflexes till the world and everything in it seemed to be moving in slow motion. I grabbed the shell out of mid-air and cradled it in my arms, hugging it to my chest. It exploded almost immediately, and my armour soaked up every bit of it. There wasn't even a shock wave to affect the soldiers around me. I'm considerate like that, sometimes. I'd crouched a little, to be sure of smothering the blast, and when I straightened up again, the soldiers made low, shocked sounds as they saw that my armour was entirely unmarked and unaffected.

The officer gestured quickly again, and another soldier came forward, this time armed with a flame-thrower. The fuel tank had all kinds of magical symbols scrawled across it, so I assumed the flames had been specially treated. Given the effect of the specially prepared ammunition earlier, I decided not to be impressed. So I just stood there, my arms casually folded, and let the soldier get on with it. He bathed my armour in a blast of roaring flames, sweeping the jet back and forth across me, and I didn't even feel warm.

Good to be a Drood.

The soldier gave up, turned the flame off, and stomped back into the ranks, where some of his friends patted him consolingly on the shoulder. There then followed something of a pause, as the officer quietly debated with his troops over what to do next. I don't think they'd expected there to be a *next*. There was even more discussion going on in the ranks at the back, most of it of a somewhat dispirited nature.

"You might have warned me about the flames," said Molly, behind me. "I mean, yes, I have been to Hell and back and there isn't a fire on this world that could actually get to me, but a warning would still have been the polite thing to do."

"Sorry," I said. "I was thinking . . . whoever sent these herberts out to annoy us must not have known much about Drood armour, or your magics. And given that this is MI 13, who have tangled with us before, to their cost . . . you'd expect them to know better."

I broke off, as Molly started chanting behind me. I could feel magical energies tingling on my armoured back. There then followed a series of explosions, and a whole bunch of screams, and then it all went quiet again. The soldiers in front of me looked past me and Molly, saw what she had just done, and appeared very upset. Several ripped off their helmets so they could be suddenly and violently sick.

"Well?" I said.

"Fine, thank you," Molly said cheerfully.

"You're being extreme again, aren't you?" I said.

"They started it," said Molly. "I believe in getting my overreaction in first."

"I have a strong feeling," I said thoughtfully, "that this—all of this—is just a distraction. Expendable foot soldiers, never expected to actually bring us in or take us down. They're just . . . something to keep us occupied until the really heavy shit turns up."

"Sounds like a plan to me," said Molly. "I wonder whose it is . . . Who's in charge of MI 13 these days?"

"Officially, Alan Diment," I said. "But he made it clear to me, back at the Wulfshead, that he's not much more than a figurehead. Being steered and pressured by people higher up."

"I think we should find those people and give them a good talking-to," said Molly.

"Sounds like a plan to me," I said. "Hello . . . something new is coming our way."

Molly came round to stand beside me as the ranks of soldiers parted to allow Alan Diment to approach us. He still looked like a minor civil servant, out for an afternoon walk and not at all happy about it. He kept his back straight and his head high, but he still gave the impression that he should be waving a large white flag. He passed through the soldiers, and stopped a very respectful distance away from me and Molly. He looked from me to Molly and back again, and when he finally spoke he sounded scared but determined.

"You know I didn't want any of this," he said. "None of it was my idea. I'd have known better."

"But you're here," I said. "Why is MI 13 so determined to take us down, dead or alive?"

"Because you destroyed our operation at the Wulfshead Club," said Diment. "And embarrassed my current lords and masters. You've made them lose face in the Intelligence community, and made them seem weak and useless to the Government that funds them. You must have known my masters would be just waiting for a chance to get back at you, and you gave them the perfect opportunity when you invaded the Department of Uncanny and slaughtered everyone there. What were you thinking? Did you really believe you could get away with that, just because of who you are? Every organisation in the hidden world is after you. Because if you'd turn on Uncanny, and your own grandfather . . . Well, nobody's safe. The word is, whoever takes you down gets a free pass from the Droods. And everyone wants that. Your family is really disappointed in you, Eddie. You let the side down by getting caught. Now the British Government wants you. And you too, Molly; don't feel left out. Both of you have been declared fair game. And MI 13 got here first."

"How?" I said. "How did you know we were here?" My voice cracked like a whip on the silence, but give Diment credit; he didn't flinch.

"Don't be silly, Eddie. I'm hardly going to tell you, am I? Might need to use that source again, someday."

"Molly and I didn't kill all those people at Uncanny," I said. "We've been set up."

"Well, yes, you would say that, wouldn't you?" said Diment. "The fact remains, you were seen leaving the scene of the crime."

"No, we bloody well weren't!" said Molly. "We teleported out!"

"So you were there," said Diment. "Thank you for confirming that. Makes this so much easier. I will say I was surprised to learn you were responsible for a mass murder, Eddie. You were always an agent first, and only ever a reluctant assassin. But you're a Drood, and she's the wild witch, so I suppose I shouldn't be surprised at all, really."

"Who saw us leaving the scene?" I said.

"Presumably someone trustworthy," said Diment. "Look, the Government has tasked MI 13 to bring you in, dead or alive. I would prefer alive, but if you insist on resisting . . ."

"Kill a Drood?" I said. "You're really ready to go to war with my family?"

"You're not listening, Eddie," Diment said patiently. "You have been officially disowned by your family. Declared rogue, and no longer protected. Surrender, Eddie. Do it now, while you're still in a position to strike some kind of deal."

"What kind of deal?" I said.

"Eddie?" said Molly, looking at me sharply.

"I'm just curious," I said.

"If you'll stand down and go willingly, you'll be allowed to hand over your armour on your own terms," Diment said carefully. "It is the armour my current lords and masters want, after all. Imagine what MI 13 could do with its own armoured agents."

"That is never going to happen," I said. "After what I saw at the Wulfshead today, it's clear your current lords and masters can't be trusted."

"That may or may not be the case," said Diment. "It doesn't make any difference. You don't have a choice, do you, Eddie?"

"I always have a choice," I said.

"Damn right," growled Molly. "And right now I am choosing to be completely unreasonable, and downright violent with it."

I smiled at her, behind my mask. "Exactly, Molly. Time to put these uniformed little snots in their place. But we need to do it fast and get the hell out before my family turns up to complicate things. Because you can bet one of our people inside MI 13 will have contacted them by now."

"You have people inside MI 13?" said Molly.

"We've got people inside every secret organisation," I said. "How else do you think we stay on top of everything?"

"That does explain a lot," said Diment.

"Are you still here, Alan?" I said pointedly.

"Your family wouldn't side with this bunch of creeps, would they?" said Molly. "I mean, they wouldn't allow you to be handed over to the Government. Would they?"

"Of course not," I said. "But they would let MI 13's troops wear us down, so they could move in afterwards once we were exhausted. And then . . . at the very least they'd demand to know what was really going on. And we can't tell them."

"Wait a minute, wait a minute," said Diment. "What do you mean, *what was really going on*? What am I missing?"

"Almost everything, Alan," I said. "Now hush—grown-ups talking."

"Oh . . . *shit*," said Molly.

I looked at her. "What?"

"Something's happening," said Molly. "And I really don't like the feel of it."

The black-uniformed soldiers all tilted their heads at the same time, receiving a new communication, and then they all turned and ran for the ends of the street as fast as they could move in their heavy body armour. Diment hurried after them, not even glancing back at Molly and me. Molly made as though to stop him, but I intervened. Diment was just a messenger boy. The soldiers hurried behind the road-blocks and then stood their ground, covering the street with their automatic weapons.

"They're waiting for something," said Molly.

"Seems likely," I said. "I wonder what . . . I mean, what could MI 13 have that they think could bring us down? That their own people are afraid of?"

"I love the way you keep asking me questions, like you think I've got any answers," said Molly. "I'm as much in the dark as you are!"

"Probably even more so," I said generously.

And then I broke off, and studied the street ahead of me carefully, through my mask. The natural energies of the world had just changed. Something was forming in the air. I could See strange lights, pulsing, and there was a growing sense of *presence* . . . of something from Outside forcing its way into our reality. Forcing the edges of the world apart, so it could shoulder its way through. Molly saw it too, and sucked in a sharp breath.

"Okay . . ." she said. "That doesn't look or feel like anything I'm familiar with . . . Feels nasty, though."

"This is high tech, not magic," I said. "Though admittedly, beyond a certain point it gets really hard to tell them apart. MI 13 is establishing some kind of Gateway, to let something through. And something pretty damned big too, given the size of the opening. Where the hell is MI 13 getting the kind of power they'd need, to open a Gateway this size? And what would they be bringing here, that they believe can take on a Drood in his armour?"

"Are you talking to somebody else?" said Molly. "Because I know for a fact I already told you I don't know anything!"

"Sorry," I said. "Just thinking out loud and trying not to panic . . . Given everything that you and I have already tackled, from Hungry Gods to a worldwide Satanic Conspiracy, what could MI 13 be bringing to the table on a Government department budget? Hold everything . . . Do you See those energies bleeding out from the edges of the Gateway?"

"Are you asking me, or is this just another . . . ?"

"Do you See them?"

"Yes! What are they?"

"Tachyons. Time particles . . . We're looking at a Time Gate! A transfer point, connecting one period in Time with another. Bringing something here, from the Past or the Future."

"Now that's just cheating," Molly said briskly. "And just a tiny bit alarming on any number of levels . . ."

"This kind of technology is way beyond anything MI 13 should have access to," I said, honestly shocked. "My family has always kept a very close eye on anyone messing around with Time. And there are Certain Others, who have been known to step in and make certain organisations and individuals never happened, just to put a stop to things like this."

"Could Black Heir be helping MI 13 out?" said Molly. "They're responsible for cleaning up all the weird tech left behind after alien incursions."

"Black Heir know better than to meddle with things beyond their remit," I said. "They survive by being useful, and not at all threatening. Oh, wait a minute . . . Yes! Got it! When MI 13 abducted those people from the Wulfshead Club earlier, one of them must have been an alien or a time traveller! There's always one or the other passing through. MI 13 must have confiscated their tech before throwing them back. The bloody fools . . . messing around with things they can't hope to understand or control, all in the name of ambition . . . This is what made Diment's bosses brave enough to take on a Drood. And the wild witch, yes. But what have they found, what are they summoning through that Gateway . . ."

"Brace yourself," said Molly. "The energies are changing. The Gateway's opening. Looks like the show's about to start."

"I wonder if they've got a T. rex," I said. "I've always wanted to have a go at a T. rex."

"You go right ahead," said Molly. "I'll stand way over there, and watch."

The Gateway hung on the air, halfway down the street, like a hole in reality itself. Strange lights flickered in and around it, while even stranger energies radiated away from the razor-sharp perimeter. Odd emanations pulsed and flared as the Gateway stabilised, enforcing and embedding itself in the world. Weird things began to happen in the street—other-dimensional fallout, warped probabilities. Half a dozen soldiers at the far end of the street turned suddenly inside out, flowering in bloody messes. Others melted, running away like candle wax. A few simply exploded. More disappeared, forced out of reality by the Gateway's overpowering presence.

Birds fell dead out of the sky, and it briefly rained blood.

Buildings on either side of the street began to slump, bulging out as though tugged forward by some strange new gravity. Windows exploded, under too much pressure. The ground shook and then cracked beneath our feet, and deep booming voices issued up from far below. The sky turned strange colours, and the air suddenly tasted sickly sweet. And then the Gateway firmed, a perfect circle, cut out of reality. Not as big as I'd feared—maybe thirty, forty feet in diameter... But just its presence here was seriously bad news. At least the world had stabilised around it now. Everything seemed back to normal, apart from the damage already caused. And of course the dead soldiers were still dead. I wondered if Diment's bosses thought their losses were worth it. Or if they even cared.

I tried to see what was going on beyond the Gateway, but that was too much, even for my mask. It was like looking at a different kind of Space, where the most basic rules were utterly different. Like one of those pictures that were all the rage a while back, where if you focused your eyes just right, you could see another image inside the picture. Three dimensions, hidden inside two. What was inside the Gateway was simply too complicated, or perhaps too real, for me to make sense of, even with my armour's help. Time has substance, but not any kind Humanity can comprehend. And then something stepped through the Gateway and into our world, and I stopped worrying about theoretical stuff.

I knew a real and present danger when I saw one.

"What the hell is that?" breathed Molly, pressing in close beside me.

"A blast from the past," I said. "From the Droods' past."

"I should have known," said Molly. "It's always about your family, isn't it?"

The new arrival was a man in full armour. Medieval plate armour, with strange curves and angles, gleaming bitter yellow like diseased candlelight. The figure was completely enclosed from head to toe, and carried a long sword on one hip and a battleaxe on the other. Its helm had a countenance as blank and featureless as mine. Nothing to give any indication of a human face behind it. The figure stood inhumanly still, but I had no doubt it was looking at me, and a terrible chill ran down my spine.

"I know what that is," I said. "I've never seen one personally, just pictures in a very old book, but . . ."

"It looks old," said Molly. "Or at least old-fashioned. Is it one of the London Knights?"

"No," I said. "Arthur would never have suffered a thing like that to sit at his round table. I never actually thought they were real, just a cautionary tale, to scare impressionable young Droods . . ."

"Eddie! What is that thing?"

"That is a False Knight," I said. "Magical armour—a living thing in its own right, permanently bound to its wearer. Metal forged from the pits of Hell, they say. Once put on, of your own free will, it can never be taken off. The wearer gives up being a man to become something more and less than a man. Made over, into a new and powerful thing. Unbeatable, untouchable. A False Knight.

"The armour feeds on blood and death and suffering. Everything it kills makes it stronger. It lives to kill, and kills to live. The False Knights were created centuries after Arthur's fall at Logres, intended as an answer to the Droods. There's a reason they call that period the Dark Ages. This was the last desperate gamble of the Order of Steel—bad guys, who believed Might Made Right and they were the mightiest of all. Only the Droods stood between them and a reign of blood and horror. To destroy the armoured Droods, the Order of Steel made a deal with the darkest force of the Dark Ages and gave themselves up, to be False Knights. A whole army of them.

"We destroyed them all, in one great battle. Over a thousand years ago, in Tintagel, in Cornwall."

Molly looked at me uncertainly. "You can take a False Knight, can't you?"

"One, probably," I said. "But there was more to the story . . ."

And that was when a great company of False Knights came striding through the Gateway, from out of the Past and one of my family's darkest legends. Row upon row and rank upon rank, filling the whole end of the street with their sickly gleaming armour. They marched in perfect lockstep, with inhuman timing and precision. The sound of their metal boots hammering down in unison filled the air, and echoed back from the surrounding buildings. Their arms swung heavily at their sides, their hands clenched into metal fists, and not one of them had a face on the front of his bitter yellow helmet. I'd never understood before just how disturbing that could be, even though I'd used the same trick myself, for so long. To look at something you know can see you, even though it doesn't have any eyes . . . The False Knights crashed to a halt as the last of them emerged from the Gateway. Standing so still, in their ranks, looking straight at me, and Molly.

The surviving MI 13 soldiers at that end of the street turned to run. One look at the False Knights was all it took to persuade them they wanted nothing more to do with any of this. Even their officers couldn't bully or threaten them into holding their ground. I couldn't see Diment anywhere, or his secret masters. No doubt they were watching, from somewhere they thought was safe. But nothing and no one was safe now, not with False Knights in the world.

"I was afraid of that," I said, as steadily as I could. My mouth was dry, my lips numb. I had to swallow hard a few times before I could continue. My skin was crawling under my armour, and I could feel my heart hammering painfully fast. "At the battle there was one company of False Knights who just vanished. My family never did find out what happened to them. Well, I guess we know now, don't we? Those damned fools running MI 13 opened up a Time Gate and brought them here. They have no idea what they've unleashed on this world . . ."

The Gateway disappeared behind the False Knights. Gone in a moment. Presumably whatever MI 13 had been using to generate the Gate had just run out of power.

"Damn," I said. "There goes one solution to the problem I was counting on . . ."

"Forcing them back through the Gateway and into the Past?" said Molly. "That was never going to work. You said yourself the company of False Knights vanished from the battle and your family never saw them again."

"I can't believe MI 13 thought they could control something like this!" I said.

"After what happened at the Wulfshead, and what they think happened at Uncanny, they probably panicked," said Molly. "They must have thought we'd be coming after them next. Eddie, we have been set up, big time. So what are we going to do? Get the hell out of here, and let your family deal with the False Knights when they turn up?"

"You'd do that?" I said.

"I know my limitations," said Molly. "And I am looking at a whole army of them right now."

"We can't leave," I said. "We can't let False Knights run loose in the world. We have to hold them here, keep them focused on us, keep any of them from escaping until my family gets here. If the Knights scatter, it could take the Droods generations to hunt them all down. And God knows how many people would die. The Knights need blood and death and suffering, to survive. And a company of False Knights could wipe out the entire population of this city in under an hour. I don't even want to think how powerful that much blood and slaughter would make them . . . They were created to be an answer to the Droods. A final answer. And even our own history books say they came pretty damned close."

"So!" Molly said brightly. "How did your family defeat a whole army of False Knights, back in the day?"

"The book didn't say."

"Terrific . . ."

"I've always supposed we used one of the Forbidden Weapons, from the Armageddon Codex," I said. "The kind we're only supposed to use when reality itself is under threat. They never get discussed in the history books, because we're not supposed to have them."

"And they're a very long way away," said Molly.

"And we couldn't use them anyway, without the supernatural fallout killing off most of the city," I said.

"Then think of something else!" said Molly. "Because I am getting seriously spooked just looking at those things! How are the two of us supposed to stop a whole army of Drood equivalents? I mean, I'm good, but I'm not that good. I'm not sure anyone is . . . Don't ever tell your family I said that."

"We can do this," I said. "We have to do this. We have to keep them occupied, keep them all here. Until someone arrives to save us."

"You really think we can take them?"

"You want the truth, or a comforting lie?"

"What do you think?"

"Yes, I think we can beat them," I said.

"Then so do I!" said Molly.

We nodded to each other, and then walked steadily down the street, side by side, to where the False Knights stood waiting, their faceless gaze still fixed on us. They probably hadn't thought the first thing they'd see in their new Time would be a Drood in his armour. Just as well; it was the only thing that would have held them here. The only thing in the world they had good reason to be afraid of. While the only thing I had on my side . . . was that they had experience of only the old Drood armour. They knew nothing of the strange matter armour Ethel had given my family. With its far greater properties.

MI 13 officers finally drove their remaining men out from behind the barricades and down the street to reinforce the False Knights. Or at least to observe what was happening. The moment they drew level, the False Knights turned on them and butchered them all. Swords and axes flared dully in the grey light, and blood splashed everywhere as severed limbs and heads flew through the air. The False Knights cut the soldiers down with ease, bitter yellow blades shearing clean through Kevlar armour without even slowing. The few rounds the soldiers got off ricocheted harmlessly from the Knights' armour. It was all over in a few moments, the False Knights moving inhumanly fast, with appalling grace and precision. Spurting blood splashed across the bitter yellow armour, which soaked it up immediately, leaving not a drop behind. Some of the Knights picked up pieces of dripping flesh and wiped their metal helms with it.

As though they were thirsty.

And just like that, it was over. Mutilated bodies, and pieces of bodies, were kicked carelessly to the sides of the road, and the False Knights resumed their ranks and looked at me and at Molly again. As though daring us to do something, anything, about the awful thing they'd just done.

"Why did they do that?" said Molly. "Why kill the soldiers when they were on the Knights' side?"

"No one is on the False Knights' side," I said. "That's the point."

The Knights held their gleaming swords and axes at the ready, and not one drop of blood fell from the heavy blades. The bitter yellow armour had soaked it all up. The Knights had had their first taste of their new world, and they liked it. I made myself move forward, and

Molly was immediately there beside me. That helped. I was facing one of my family's oldest and darkest nightmares, and I'm not sure I could have done it on my own.

One of the False Knights stepped forward out of the front rank. His metal boots slammed down hard as he came to meet me, and the ground cracked beneath his every step, as though he was too heavy, too real, for this world. He carried a long sword, with a hilt long enough for him to use both hands. I concentrated on my armour, and forced a change on it. Heavy collars rose up to protect my head and shoulders, while vicious spikes protruded from my elbows and knees. I even raised spikes on the knuckles of my golden gloves. The False Knight stopped and looked at me. He hadn't been expecting that. Droods hadn't been able to change their armour the last time he'd met them. For the first time he realised he wasn't facing the kind of Drood he knew. I grinned behind my featureless mask. They might be an army, and they might be clad in armour out of Hell itself. But they'd never met a Drood like me.

I gestured for Molly to hold her ground, and she stopped, reluctantly, glaring fiercely at the watching Knights. I grew a long golden sword out of my right glove. It shone with a bright, healthy light. I nodded to the False Knight, and he nodded to me, challenge given and accepted. And then we ran forward, charging straight at each other. We slammed together in the middle of the street, our swords rising and falling. And my strange matter sword sheared right through his bitter yellow blade. The end fell away, clattering on the ground, and as the False Knight hesitated, caught off guard, I brought my sword swinging round in a viciously fast arc . . . and cut off his head. The bitter yellow helm fell to the ground, and rolled away. The headless body fell stiffly backwards, like a felled tree. It clanged hollowly as it hit the ground, and not a drop of blood came out of it.

I turned to face the waiting ranks of False Knights, and laughed at them. The simple, unintimidated sound seemed to fill the empty street. Molly whooped loudly, and punched the air with her fist. And the whole army of False Knights came striding down the street, right at me, and Molly, to do together what one Knight had so signally failed to do. The ground shook and trembled under their weight, and the very air seemed to curdle around them, as though their presence alone was enough to poison the world.

Molly danced forward to face them, smiling unpleasantly. She raised both arms in the stance of summoning, and chanted a series of harsh ugly Words. A great raging wind blew up out of nowhere, and swept down the street to hit the Knights head-on. The wind overturned parked cars and sent them tumbling, and blew everything else around like leaves, but it didn't even slow the False Knights.

Molly cut off the wind the moment she realised it wasn't working. She summoned up fireballs and threw them at the Knights, fires hot enough to shimmer the air and melt everything in the mortal world ... but the flames just splashed harmlessly against the bitter yellow armour, and fell away, and the Knights kept on coming. Molly lifted her chin and squared her shoulders, and hit the first rank with her strongest transformation spell. The air between them crackled with violent magical energies, but nothing in the spell could touch the False Knights in their armour.

Molly scowled fiercely, concentrating on one Knight

right in front of her. She raised a hand, and then clenched it, hard. And the False Knight broke step, shuddering to a halt as his bitter yellow armour cracked and crinkled all around him. It scrunched up like tin foil, crushing the man within, collapsing in upon itself. The False Knight staggered, waved his arms wildly, and then fell to the ground as his armour closed in around him, crushing and compressing him, until there was just a crumpled ball of bitter yellow metal in the street.

Molly turned to look at me. Her face was drawn, and pale, and wet with sweat. She was shaking hard, only just able to keep her feet.

"Sorry, sweetie," she said, trying hard to smile. "That's it. That's all I've got. It took everything I had just to bring one of the bastards down."

"That's more than most could have managed," I said. "It's all right, Molly. You stand down, and let me go to work. I'll take it from here. But if it looks like I'm losing, get the hell out of here."

"I won't leave you, Eddie."

"You have to."

"You can't make me!"

"You don't understand, Molly! If they take you, they'll make you one of them! Wrap you up in their Hell armour, make you False too!"

"You go down, I go down with you," said Molly. "Fighting to my last breath. Because I wouldn't want to live without you anyway."

She couldn't see me smile behind my mask, so I nodded fondly to her.

"Together forever, my love," I said.

"Forever and a day," said Molly. "Now go kill those sons of bitches."

"Love to," I said.

I pulled the golden sword back inside my hand, strode over to the side of the street, and plucked the nearest street lamp out of the ground by its electrical roots. There was a shower of sparks as I hefted the long metal weight easily in my hands. And then I charged straight at the False Knights, using all the power of my armoured legs to close the gap between us in a few moments. I was in and among their front ranks before they even had time to react. Everyone always forgets that Drood armour is fast, as well as strong.

I swung the long steel lamp with all my strength, picking Knights up and throwing them this way and that. Their armour dented under the impact, but wouldn't crack or break. More pressed forward, but I kept the lamp post swinging, and they couldn't get past it. I slammed it into chests and heads, swept armoured legs out from under them, smashed them down, and swept them away. False Knights flew through the air, hit the ground, and rolled, then got up to come at me again. I couldn't hurt them. The bitter yellow armour protected them, just like mine protected me.

I threw the street lamp into the mass of them, and grew my golden sword again. I swung it with both hands, striking down on the bitter yellow armour with all my strength, and the strange matter blade cut deep. It sliced through their armour and out again, sheared clean through shoulders to cut off arms, and decapitated bitter yellow helms, but not one drop of blood flowed. And still the Knights pressed forward. I had to cut off their heads to stop them, one at a time, and as more and more of them crowded in around me, it got harder and harder to find the room to swing my sword.

They hit me again and again, with their swords and axes and huge brutal fists. Their blades couldn't penetrate my armour, but they were all so inhumanly strong that the sheer impact got through. Their attacks drove me this way and that, back and forth across the street, even as I fought them, and I cried out inside my mask as the blows hurt me, again and again. I hacked about me with my sword, doing what damage I could, overwhelmed by the crush of bodies.

I stabbed one False Knight right through his mask, my sword punching through his metal face and out the back of his helm, and even though the Knight fell, it didn't make a sound and there was no blood. I began to wonder if there was anyone, or anything, left alive inside the bitter yellow armour. I yanked the sword out, back-punching a Knight behind me with my spiked elbow, and kicked the legs out of another Knight in front of me. This opened up a little room, and I swung my sword in short, vicious arcs, going for their throats. A metal fist slammed into the side of my head with incredible force, and the pain was so bad it blinded me. My legs buckled, but I wouldn't let myself fall. I swung my sword relentlessly, panting harshly, until my vision cleared. My arms and back ached from the sheer effort of fighting, and for a moment all I could see were the faceless masks all around me, and the swords and axes rising and falling, trying to find a weak spot in my armour, or in me. As they beat me to death by inches.

I saw an opening, threw myself through it, and ran down the street, away from the overpowering numbers.

When I thought I'd opened up enough space, I lurched to a halt and turned to face them again. The False Knights were coming after me, taking their time. Savouring the moment. They knew I had nowhere to go. I glanced across at Molly. She hadn't moved from where I'd left her, leaning on a street lamp, holding herself up with the last of her strength. She looked almost as bad as I felt, but she smiled steadily back at me. Waiting to see what I would do next, because she had faith in me.

"Get ready to run," I said breathlessly. "I've got an idea, but if it doesn't pan out . . . I've got nothing else."

"Wait!" said Molly. "I've had an idea! What about the Merlin Glass?"

I looked at her stupidly, fighting to concentrate. My head ached like hell.

"What about the Glass?"

"Can't you use it, to send the False Knights away? Send them somewhere they couldn't survive?"

"That is a really good idea," I said. "Better than mine. I'll send the bastards to the Moon. One at a time, if I have to."

But when I passed my hand through my armoured side, the Merlin Glass wouldn't come out. The hand mirror jerked this way and that, avoiding my grasping fingers. As though . . . as though it was afraid of the False Knights. I swore briefly, and took my hand out.

"When this is over," I told it harshly, "we are going to have a serious discussion about which one of us is in charge here."

The False Knights were almost upon me. I put my hand back through my side, and drew my Colt Repeater from its hidden holster. The gun the Armourer gave me long ago. A very special gun, the Colt Repeater teleported ammo straight into the chambers so it could never run out, and I didn't even need to aim it exactly. The gun never missed. This was my original idea. My golden blade had pierced the False Knights' armour, so clearly strange matter trumped bitter yellow. If I surrounded every bullet I fired in golden armour, and punched a hole through their heads as I had with my sword . . . they should fall. I grinned coldly behind my mask, and aimed my Colt Repeater at the nearest Knight.

I shot it through its featureless face. The bitter yellow helm snapped back, and the False Knight crashed to the ground and didn't move again. The other Knights paused for a moment, as though they couldn't quite believe what had happened, and then they came on again. I shot them all down, one by one. Aiming and firing as quickly as I could, till my hand ached, picking off target after target. They didn't even try to defend themselves with different tactics, because they didn't understand what was happening. They couldn't understand what was killing them. They'd never seen a gun before. By the time they started to get the idea, I'd already thinned the ranks out so much it didn't matter. I shot them down without mercy or hesitation, because it was necessary. Not one of them got close to me. I backed away, step by step, still firing as the last of them tried to rush me, until the very last False Knight fell dead at my feet.

I laughed, shakily, at the piled-up bodies cluttering the street. "You really shouldn't have come here. Things have changed since your time. We're much better killers now."

They hadn't even tried to run. They knew they had nowhere to go. So they had just kept coming, kept trying to kill me. They were a lot like Droods, in their way.

I put the Colt Repeater away. My arm ached, and my hand shook as I held it out before me. The golden strange matter I'd used to coat my bullets ripped itself out of the fallen Knights, and shot back through the air into my waiting hand, melding back into the armour it had come from. I wasn't going to leave it lying around for MI 13 to pick up.

I armoured down, and almost collapsed without the armour to support me. I swayed on my feet and Molly was quickly there to hold me, and hold me up. I leaned heavily on her, and she made a soft angry sound as she saw how bad a beating I'd taken.

"I'm okay," I said, as much to myself as to Molly. "I just need to . . . get my breath."

"Let's get out of here," said Molly.

"I have to talk to Diment first."

"Him? Really?"

"Yes."

Molly looked around her. "How long before your family get here?"

"Not long. I can feel them, through my torc . . . So let's do this quickly."

I pulled myself away from Molly, and she watched me closely until she was sure I could stand unaided. I strode down the street, toward the barricade, keeping my back stiff and my head held high.

I caught Diment peeking round a corner of the barricade, and I gestured sharply for him to come out and talk to me. He didn't want to, but he did. He wasn't going to say no to me, after seeing what I'd done to the False Knights. He came forward and stood before me, doing his best not to look at all the armoured bodies.

"My family are on their way," I said. "You stay here and make a full report to them. You know, this could be a really good opportunity for you to drop your current lords and masters right in it. My family are going to be really angry at seeing False Knights here, and you can honestly say it wasn't your idea. You can point the finger at all those meddling little shits who've been messing you around. This could be your chance to actually run MI 13, with my family's support."

"Sounds like a plan," said Diment. "Where will you go now?"

"Away," I said. "Far away."

This time the Merlin Glass all but leaped into my hand, and Molly and I were gone in a moment.

CHAPTER SEVEN

Doors

Molly and I stepped through the Merlin Glass, and back into the computer room of my safe house, somewhat to Molly's surprise. I shut the Glass down quickly, to make sure Diment didn't get a glimpse of where we'd gone. Molly looked around her, as though to make sure she was where she thought she was, and then fixed me with a hard look.

"Explain."

"There's no way Diment will expect us to hang around," I said. "Which means he won't even think to check here. Last place he'd look."

"And you're sure about that?" said Molly.

"Reasonably sure," I said cheerfully. "Don't worry, the house's shields will hide and protect us."

"Even from your family, when they get here?"

"That's the idea," I said. "I want to see what happens

when they turn up and see the fallen False Knights. Because I need to be sure . . . that only MI 13 higher-ups were involved in bringing the Knights here."

Molly shook her head. "I'd say you were being paranoid, but I've met your family."

"You'll notice I'm still holding on to the Merlin Glass," I said. "Just in case we need to leave in a hurry."

Molly looked suspiciously at the hand mirror. "And not because you don't trust it?"

"Hush," I said. "It might be listening."

Molly started to say something, and then didn't. She suddenly looked very tired, and swayed on her feet. She'd exhausted herself, along with her magics. I was just as tired, bruised and battered from head to foot. So I took Molly in my arms and we held each other, and leaned on each other.

"How long can we stay here?" Molly murmured, her face pressed into my shoulder.

"Not long," I said. "But long enough to get our second wind."

She was so worn out that I was supporting her weight as well as my own, and I was so tired I could barely stand, but I did anyway. Because she needed me, and because I would rather die than let her down. After a while her legs straightened as she got some of her strength back, and she pushed me away. Molly has always believed in standing on her own two feet. I pulled the chair out from the desk and she sat down on it, just a bit heavily. I sat down carefully on the edge of the desk, not letting myself groan out loud. My muscles ached fiercely, but Molly didn't need to know just how badly the False Knights had hurt me.

"Why isn't your family already here?" she said crossly, not looking at me. "Just the arrival of something like the

False Knights in our world should have set off all kinds of alarms, back at the Hall."

"Undoubtedly," I said. "They're probably spitting blood and teeth in the War Room right now. But I rather suspect they've been busy, giving all their attention to tracking down those they believe responsible for the massacre at Uncanny."

"Your family can't really believe that was us! They must know better!"

"They know you know the Regent killed your parents, on Drood orders," I said carefully. "So it's not beyond the realm of possibility that things might have got . . . out of hand."

"Your family tried to kill me once before," said Molly. "When they thought I'd murdered the Matriarch. Damn near succeeded . . ."

"I will never allow that to happen again," I said. "I will stand between you and all harm."

"Even from your family?"

"Especially from my family."

We smiled at each other. It is good to say some things out loud, even when you both already know them. Molly looked at the computer on my desk, and then did a double take, sitting up straight in her chair.

"Hold everything! That computer is entirely intact and untouched! But I saw you smash it . . ."

"Drood tech," I said, just a bit smugly. "Built to last, look after itself, and put itself back together again after Drood temper tantrums. Uncle Jack does good work."

"Boys and their toys . . . ," said Molly.

"Agents and their equipment," I said severely.

And then I looked round sharply and moved over to the window to peer out into the street. Molly immediately levered herself out of her chair and hurried forward to stand beside me. Outside, Alan Diment was walking unhurriedly around the piled-up bodies and bits and pieces of the fallen False Knights, occasionally leaning over to peer at a decapitated head, or poke a body with the toe of his boot, just to be sure. He didn't look particularly upset, or disturbed. If anything, he looked . . . calm, even satisfied. Which wasn't what I would have expected from a mere functionary who'd just seen his operation go down in flames, and the people he was after disappear. Unless . . .

"I wonder," I said. "Did he know this would all go wrong, but did nothing and allowed it to happen? Just so it would discredit and bring down his loathed lords and masters?"

"He had the guts to take on the Wulfshead Club," said Molly.

"Crafty bugger," I said. "He's come a long way . . ."

"Our little boy is all grown up," said Molly.

A handful of black-uniformed MI 13 soldiers moved cautiously down the street, approaching slowly, with weapons at the ready. They looked like they'd crap themselves if a nearby dog farted. They passed the scattered remains of their fallen fellow soldiers, and shied away from the great pools of blood, giving the dead plenty of room. I looked for more soldiers to come and join them, but there weren't any more. Just these dozen or so men, with their dark visors pushed up, showing pale, shocked faces. They were professional types, and no doubt seasoned fighters, but they weren't used to meeting things so much worse than they were. I wondered where the rest of them were, and then realised this small number were all that had survived. The False Knights had slaughtered everyone else. I said as much to Molly, and she just shrugged.

"Do you care, Eddie? Really? Those uniformed scumbags would cheerfully have handed us over to . . . God knows who. To be locked up, or dissected, or just taken out back somewhere and executed."

"It's my job to protect people from things that aren't people any more," I said. "Even uniformed thugs and bully boys. It's a Drood's job to protect Humanity. No one ever said we had to like them. Or vice versa."

"The False Knights were . . . something of a surprise," said Molly, not looking at me. "You never mentioned them before. First the Drood in Cell 13, now the False Knights. Any more deep, dark secrets in your family's past?"

"More than you can possibly imagine," I said, trying to keep it light. "My family has secrets like a dog has fleas."

Molly turned abruptly away from the window and looked back at my computer. "Eddie, if that's your uncle Jack's work, how did it get here?"

"He gave it to me as a moving-in gift," I said. "The Armourer helped me set up all my safe houses, the approved ones and the underground ones. Who else do you think put in all the shields and defences? I'm a field agent, not an engineer. He's helped set up safe houses for all our agents. Admittedly I have more than most, because I have always had more reason than most to want to hide from my family . . . but Uncle Jack has always been very supportive."

"But that means this place isn't safe!" Molly said sharply. "He knows about it! He could lead your family straight here!" She stopped, and frowned. "Would he tell them?"

"Of course," I said. "He's fond of me, but this is family business. However, he would be the first to point out that while he knows all my safe houses, he has no way of knowing which one I'd go to first. And the family can't spare enough people to investigate all of them at once. They'll have to jump around the world, checking them one at a time. The odds are in our favour, Molly. We have time to get our breath back."

"But you want them to come here," Molly said slowly. "So you can . . . observe them. I'm not sure I'm following this, Eddie."

"Not sure I am myself," I said. "Far too many unanswered questions at the moment. When you're stuck in the middle of a mystery, information is ammunition. So, we wait." I forced out an easy smile for her. "And get our strength back, for major arse-kicking in the future."

She didn't look convinced. "Sometimes I think you trust your uncle Jack too much. Don't get me wrong—I like him. But he's old school Drood. And I've always known he has his own secrets, and his own agenda. I don't think he's always on your side."

"No one is," I said. "Except you, of course."

Molly smiled. "Nice catch."

"While we're waiting," I said. "We need to decide where we're going next."

"Ultima Thule," said Molly. "For the Lady Faire's annual Ball, at the Winter Palace."

"Well, yes," I said. "But we can't go there directly. Far too many shields in place. Ultima Thule is a world within a world, a private reality, with all the ways in and out carefully configured and heavily guarded."

"Too much even for the Merlin Glass?"

"The Winter Palace is supposed to be hard to get to,"

I said carefully. "That's why it's so popular as an exclusive retreat. For the kind of people who don't want to be interrupted in their very private pleasures. The Merlin Glass might be powerful enough to punch through all the shields and protections, but that would undoubtedly set off all kinds of alarms and bring the guards running. Or everyone might just pack up and leave, so they were all long gone when we got there. We can't risk that. So we need a sneaky way in. One that won't be noticed. We need a dimensional Door."

"You've been thinking about this," Molly said accusingly. "In fact, you are giving every indication of being downright devious and cunning. I approve."

"Good to know," I said. "One of the things I've been thinking about is that some unknown person has been providing unauthorised people with Doors that open onto Drood grounds. Which is not only never allowed, but is supposed to be impossible. Which means . . . whoever is providing these Doors must be a master at his work."

"Sounds like the Doormouse to me," Molly said immediately.

I looked sternly at her. "You just made that name up!"

"I did not! The Doormouse has been a fixture in the Nightside for ages, at his House of Doors. He's a master craftsman, making dimensional Doors to order."

"I know," I admitted. "I have heard of him. The Armourer's talked about him, on occasion. The Doormouse has been known to make Doors for the Droods, on occasion. Uncle Jack always says you can't beat a specialist. But why would someone with a good working relationship with my family, who knows what we do to people who annoy us, make Doors our enemies could use to breach our security? It doesn't make sense."

"I think we should go ask him," said Molly.

"Good idea," I said. "Maybe I can get some answers, and pressure or guilt the Doormouse into providing us with a sneaky back Door into Ultima Thule." I stopped, and looked at Molly. "Is he really a mouse?"

"Oh yes," said Molly, offhandedly. "Just not your ordinary everyday mouse."

"Sort of gathered that," I said. "You know the strangest people, Molly."

"I've met your family," said Molly.

And then we both looked out the window again, as we heard raised voices and new movement outside. Half a dozen Droods were marching down the street, heading for Alan Diment, their golden armour shining brightly, even under the grey northern skies. The uniformed soldiers scattered out of the Droods' way and stayed well back, keeping their automatic weapons pointed very carefully at the ground. They'd seen what one Drood in his armour could do, and they really didn't want to risk upsetting a whole bunch of them. The Droods didn't even glance in their direction.

"Don't worry," I murmured to Molly. "Even if the Armourer has told them about this address, they won't know we're here. They can't even see us looking out the window. The house shields will see to that."

"You'd better be right," said Molly, just as quietly. "Neither of us is in any condition to fight off six Droods in their armour. How did they get here? I didn't hear any transport, or sense any teleport energies."

"My family has many ways of getting around," I said. "But they're still here a lot faster than I expected. They must really want to find me and shut me down before anyone else does."

"The last time you were declared rogue," Molly said carefully, "your whole family was out to kill you."

"I think this time they want answers first," I said, trying hard to sound confident. "Of course we can't count on that. To the family, the only good rogue Drood is a dead rogue Drood."

The six armoured Droods gathered around the dead False Knights. I watched closely. They were all doing their best to appear calm and casual and in charge of the situation, but I could tell from their body language just how shocked and surprised they were. They hadn't expected anything like this. They clearly recognised the False Knights, just as I had, but I let out a breath I hadn't realised I was holding as it quickly became clear they didn't know how the False Knights got here. They didn't know about MI 13's Time Gate.

They all turned on Diment and took it in turns to growl questions at him. Give the man credit, he held up well in the face of open interrogation by six angry Droods. It helped that he obviously didn't know much, and what he did know pointed the blame very firmly somewhere else—at his current bosses. I wished I could hear what they were saying. Diment was doing a lot of nodding and compliant gesturing, and even more talking. One of the Droods suddenly armoured down, the better to glare at Diment, and I sucked in a sharp breath as I recognised the Sarjeant-at-Arms himself. Scowling and frustrated and very angry. He towered over Diment, barking questions at him, and Diment just kept smiling and talking, as persuasively as he knew how. Dropping his lords and masters right in it, with every word.

"Well, well," I said. "The Sarjeant-at-Arms, out in the field . . . He is taking this seriously. And, perhaps, personally."

Diment gestured at my safe house, having presumably got to my part in what happened, and the Droods all turned to look at my window. Molly and I both flinched back in spite of ourselves, but they only looked casually at the house for a moment, then turned back to Diment. The house's shields were still holding. The Sarjeant gestured for the other Droods to inspect the dead False Knights thoroughly, while he continued his interrogation of Diment. The Droods nodded quickly and moved away to form a circle round the bodies and bits of bodies. Some knelt down to study the bitter yellow armour close up, though they were all very careful not to touch anything.

"That was close," I said. "Too close for my liking. I think we should go visit the Doormouse. Right now. No, wait a minute . . . Am I right in thinking his House of Doors is situated in the Nightside?"

"Well, yes and no," said Molly.

"That is never a good start to any answer," I said. "Molly, I keep telling you, I can't enter the Nightside! Droods are banned, by long compact and agreement!"

"Even rogue Droods?"

"I think especially rogue Droods."

"Well, technically the House of Doors isn't necessarily actually inside the Nightside," said Molly. "You can access the Doormouse's establishment from the Nightside, but then, you can access it from a whole lot of places. The entrance may be in the Nightside, but the shop isn't. That's the whole point of Doors. They're short cuts, through Space. So the House of Doors is in the Nightside, but not of it. A bit."

"That is a technicality," I said. "But it's good enough for me. If the Merlin Glass is in a mood to cooperate . . ." I glared at the hand mirror, still firmly gripped in my hand. "You behave yourself, or I'll write dirty words on you with a bar of soap."

The Merlin Glass seemed to stare innocently back at me. I took another look out the window. The Sarjeant-at-Arms was looking straight at me from the middle of the road, standing very still. I stood just as still. Could he see me? His face was unreadable, his gaze steady. And then he turned away, and I started breathing again. If the Sarjeant had seen me, he'd chosen to let me go. Which wasn't like the Sarjeant-at-Arms. Unless he knew something I didn't. Which wouldn't surprise me in the least. Given my current situation, I was entirely ready to believe that everyone in the world knew more about what was really going on than I did.

So I needed to concentrate on what mattered: getting my hands on the Lazarus Stone, and rescuing my parents. I turned my back on the window and nodded abruptly to Molly. She provided the Merlin Glass with the spatial coordinates for the House of Doors, and the hand mirror jumped eagerly out of my hand, shaking itself out to Door size. A bright light shone through the Glass from the other side, and I stepped quickly through the Door, with Molly on my heels.

We arrived in a large and strikingly impressive reception area that was bigger than most shops. The Merlin Glass shut itself down immediately, shrank back to hand-mirror size, and all but forced itself into my grasp. I got the distinct impression it didn't like this new location. I put it away, and looked curiously about me.

"This is it!" Molly said proudly. "The House of Doors! For when you definitely, absolutely, have to be Somewhere Else in a hurry!"

"Where is this House of Doors, exactly, if it isn't in the Nightside?" I said.

"I don't think anybody knows, exactly," said Molly. "The Doormouse takes his privacy very seriously, and so would you if you were large and fluffy. You can only access his establishment through the Doors he makes. And yes, there is a hell of a lot of unseen security operating here, so let's try being polite first, okay?"

"Of course," I said. "First."

"Stand further away from me," said Molly.

The reception area was a large open space of quite staggering style and elegance. Thick white carpeting and walls so white they were positively luminous. Lots of large abstract paintings and intricate mosaics, heavy pieces of antique furnishings, and a number of low tables covered with strange things that might have been high tech, abstract sculpture, or just objets d'art. The track lighting was bright and cheerful, but I couldn't help noticing there wasn't any reception desk, or even a receptionist. At least there was no piped music, which argued for a certain level of civilised behaviour.

"Hey, Mouse!" yelled Molly. "Shop!"

I glared at her, and she smiled sweetly back. And just like that, there he was—the Doormouse, scurrying forward to meet us from the back of the reception area. A six-foot-tall, vaguely humanoid mouse, with dark chocolate-coloured fur, under a white lab coat that reminded me irresistibly of the Armourer. The Doormouse even had a neat little pocket protector in place, to back up his many colour-coded pens. He had a dark muzzle, laid-back ears, long twitching whiskers, and thoughtful, very human eyes. He looked cute, in an oversized and extremely disturbing and unnatural way. Mice just aren't supposed to be that big. I felt an overwhelming urge to put some traps down. The Doormouse hurried forward to join us, clapping his fuzzy paws together, and when he finally spoke, his voice was high-pitched, cheery, and not quite human.

"How did you get in here without an appointment?" he said loudly, bouncing up and down before us. "No one's supposed to be able to get in without—oh, it's you, Molly! I might have known. You never did have any respect for other people's privacy. Especially when there were valuables involved. Ah, well, at least it isn't your sisters. Don't tell them I said that. Hello, Molly! How are you, my dear?"

Molly started to say something, and then all the colour just drained out of her face, and she would have collapsed if I hadn't caught her in time. I made a loud, pained noise despite myself, as her weight almost dragged me down too. The damage I'd taken from the False Knights was catching up with me. The Doormouse leaned in close for a better look at Molly's pale face, and then he nodded quickly.

"It's dimensional shock! Seen it before, seen it before. Too many trips through too many Doors, with not enough time in between, crashes the nervous system. You'd better both come on through, into the Showroom. Yes, that's the ticket! Oh, my word, yes. Bring her through, Drood. Oh yes, I know who you are. I know a torc when I See one."

He led the way to the back of the reception area, chittering loudly to himself, scurrying along and then making himself wait until I caught up with him. It was all I could do to keep Molly staggering forward. Her eyes were half shut, and she was barely cooperating. I was worried. I hadn't seen her this exhausted in a long time.

She must have really drained her energies, fighting the False Knights. And I'd let her do it. I held her up, biting my lip against the fierce pains shooting through my abused body, and kept her moving.

And I still had the presence of mind to study the Doormouse unobtrusively. Very few people can See a Drood torc. That's rather the point.

The Doormouse led us through a very ordinary-looking door at the back, and on into his Showroom. Which turned out to be almost unbearably vast. One of the biggest enclosed spaces I've ever seen, and I've been around. I literally couldn't see the sides or the end of it. When I looked up, there wasn't a ceiling, just a layer of puffy white clouds. The Showroom was packed full of Doors, standing upright and unsupported, hovering a few inches above the colourless floor. They stood in long rows and ranks, stretching away into the far distance. They seemed to go on forever, Doors beyond counting, made from every kind of wood I could think of, in every shade and fashion. There were even some Doors made from metal and glass and crystal. Some burned and blazed with their own inner lights. And each and every Door had its own special handwritten card, describing its particular destination. I looked at a few of the closest as I held Molly up. The Doormouse had disappeared off somewhere.

Shadows Fall. Carcosa. Sinister Albion. Lud's Gate.

I was still getting my head around the sheer range in those destinations when the Doormouse came bustling back, carrying a tall glass of something hot and steaming in each furry paw. He thrust both glasses at me. I held Molly a little more securely, and she leaned her head on my shoulder and murmured something indistinct. I looked suspiciously at the proffered drinks.

"Oh, don't be so mistrustful, Eddie Drood!" said the Doormouse. "It's just a hot cordial, to restore your depleted energies. Perfectly safe, and very tasty. On the house!"

"Oh well," I said, "if it's on the house . . ."

Anywhen else, I would have held the Doormouse's nose and made him take a good drink of the stuff first, but Molly needed something to help her, and there was nothing else on offer. I accepted one glass, and took a careful sip. Because bad as Molly was, I wasn't about to give her anything I hadn't tried myself first. It tasted like mulled cider, and it went down smooth and easy. Almost before I knew what I was doing, I'd downed the lot. A small and very pleasant explosion went off in my stomach, and a delicious warmth rocketed through my body, wiping out all my pains. It felt like someone had just kicked me in the adrenal glands. I snapped wide awake in a moment, and grinned broadly at the Doormouse, who sighed heavily.

"You're supposed to sip it! Honestly, I go to all the trouble of brewing up something special, something you can savour, and you knock it back like it's a cheap muscatel."

"I like it!" I said happily. "What's it called?"

"Rocket fuel," growled the Doormouse. "Though that is of course metaphorical rather than descriptive. Go on, give Molly the other glass while it's still hot."

I handed him my empty glass and held the other to Molly's mouth. I eased a little of the steaming beverage past her slack lips, and she swallowed slowly, and then her eyes shot open. I tilted the glass so she could get a good mouthful, and she immediately stood up straight and grabbed the glass with both hands. She chugged it all down in several large gulps, and the Doormouse shook his head bitterly.

"I don't know why I bother . . . Next time I'll just give you a bottle of Snakebite each, and you can rough it out. I'm wasted on you, I really am."

Molly pushed herself away from me, tilted her glass all the way back to get at the last few drops, and then tossed the empty glass to the Doormouse. Her face was flushed with a healthy colour, and her eyes sparkled. She grinned at me, grabbed me and hugged me, and then pushed me away again so she could do her happy dance, right there on the spot. I couldn't help but laugh.

"Damn!" Molly said loudly, stretching so hard I could hear all her joints creaking at once. "That is the good stuff! I feel great! And I can feel my magics coming back!" She looked at me. "And you don't look like shit any more!"

I had to agree. All my bruises were gone, my muscles had stopped aching, and I felt like I could beat up a grizzly bear with both legs strapped behind my back. But since I have learned never to trust good luck or apparent miracles, I gave the Doormouse a hard look.

"Are we really back in top form, or do we just feel that way? Is this good feeling likely to wear off at some inopportune moment? Are there side effects we should be warned about in advance?"

"Typical Drood," said the Doormouse, entirely unmoved by my suspicions. "It's an old family remedy, nothing more." He put the two empty glasses down on a handy side table that I would have sworn wasn't there a moment before. He smiled benevolently on Molly and me. "It's all natural, and very good for you, and almost certainly won't cause any real damage on the genetic level. Though you might piss blue for a few hours."

"Will it put hair on my chest?" said Molly.

"Not like mine," said the Doormouse.

"Good to know," I said.

Molly laughed, threw her arms around the Door-mouse, and hugged him tightly. He suffered her to do that, his whiskers twitching occasionally, and then Molly stepped back and clapped him on the shoulder, hard enough to make him wince.

"Good to see you again, Mouse," she said. "It's been a while, hasn't it?"

"It has indeed," said the Doormouse. "And this is your young man, is it? Eddie Drood himself! Delighted to meet you, dear boy; please don't hug me. Any friend of Molly's . . . I won't ask what trouble you're both in, because it's none of my business and you probably wouldn't tell me anyway, but I'll do what I can to help. Please try not to break anything while you're here." He looked thoughtfully at Molly. "The last time I saw you we were in Strangefellows bar, and you'd just . . ."

"Not now," Molly said quickly. "Not in front of the Drood."

"Of course," said the Doormouse. He looked me over carefully. "Eddie Drood . . . I am of course honoured, and fascinated, to meet such a legendary figure at last, but I have to say I am just a little . . . concerned, to see you here. In my humble and *very fragile* establishment. Might I inquire why you've come to see me, Sir Drood? Have you, in fact, come to shut me down? I mean, this is about those Doors I made, isn't it? The Doors that open onto Drood property . . ."

"I would like to know what you thought you were doing, making such things," I said. "You must have known my family would not be at all pleased. They might nuke your establishment from orbit, just to be sure. No one overreacts like a Drood."

"I know!" said the Doormouse, wringing his paws together piteously.

"I think you'd better issue a recall," said Molly.

"I will certainly try," said the Doormouse. "Though I doubt anyone will listen. They are very popular. And no, I can't shut them down from here. Not once they've left the Storeroom."

"You don't install a hidden override, or back-door command?" I said.

The Doormouse looked honestly shocked. "If my customers even suspected such a thing, my sales would plummet! All my Doors are guaranteed to be self-repairing and self-perpetuating. A Door isn't just for convenience; it's forever! That's the point. That's what I sell—reliability."

"But why . . . ," I said.

"I was tricked!" the Doormouse said shrilly. "The original order came from inside Drood Hall. Apparently from the Matriarch Martha Drood herself. It had all the correct signatures and security code phrases attached . . . I did check! And it came through all the usual channels, with nothing out of the ordinary about it. Of course I thought it was a bit weird . . . but you don't challenge a Drood, after all. If this was what the Matriarch wanted, I had to assume there was a good reason."

"Martha Drood has been dead for some time," I said.

"I know that now! But I didn't know it then! I don't keep up with that sort of gossip. Don't read those magazines . . . I only found out the Nightside had a new set of Authorities when John Taylor popped in to tell me he was the new Walker. I think it's fair to say none of us saw that one coming . . . He's off on his honeymoon at the moment, so if you want to get away with anything here, now's probably a good time . . ."

"Didn't you wonder why my family would want people to have Doors that gave them access to the Drood grounds?" I insisted, refusing to be sidetracked.

"I didn't think it was any of my business," said the Doormouse, holding on to what was left of his dignity. "You Droods have always gone your own way, and your ways have always been a complete mystery to outsiders. If you want to bury a dragon's head in your backyard ... I just made the Doors and started shipping them out to the addresses provided. And sent my invoice in to the Hall, as usual. Which is, of course, when the sawdust hit the fan. I had to shut my phone off. I don't like being shouted at."

"How many of these Doors did you sell?" I said.

"Only forty-seven," the Doormouse said quickly. "I made a hundred, as requested, but not everyone has picked them up yet. Once it became clear these Doors weren't ... officially sanctioned, I locked them away. I can provide you with a list of everyone who's already received their Door ..."

"That's something," I said. "Don't give me the list; send it to the Hall, marked *Attention: Armourer*. And: *Really, really urgent*. He's almost certainly worked out a way to block the Doors by now, but it'll probably help him to know who might try to use them."

"The Armourer, of course!" said the Doormouse. "I know Jack Drood. He does good work. He often pops in here for a chat. Hell of a poker player too."

I gave him my very best hard look. "Uncle Jack visits the Nightside regularly, doesn't he? Even though he isn't supposed to."

The Doormouse shrugged, elaborately casually. "I couldn't possibly comment. I haven't heard anything at all about him being given special dispensation. I have nothing to say on the subject. On the grounds that Jack Drood can be a seriously scary individual when he chooses."

"What, that sweet old man?" said Molly.

"My uncle Jack was one of the family's top field agents, during the coldest part of the Cold War," I said. "A respected and feared troubleshooter in all the worst parts of the world, just like his brother, the Grey Fox."

"James Drood," said the Doormouse, nodding energetically. "I may or may not have met him, as well. Somewhere or other."

"Just how many members of my family come to the Nightside?" I said.

"I couldn't possibly comment," said the Doormouse. "On the grounds that I don't want to end up as a rug in Drood Hall."

"Look, this could be your chance to get back into the Droods' good books," said Molly. "We need a Door. A very special kind of Door."

"Oh well," said the Doormouse. "If it's for the Droods . . ."

I smiled. "Send them the invoice."

I looked around at the long rows of hovering Doors, heading off into the distance in every direction. It was like standing in a forest of very flat trees. And it had to be said: they weren't just Doors. I could feel their presence, like they were watching me. I turned back to the Doormouse with a certain sense of relief.

"How did you learn to make Doors?"

"I studied with old Carnacki, years and years ago," said the Doormouse. "When I was just a bright-eyed, bushy-tailed young hippy. When I was still human."

I started to say something, but the Doormouse had already turned away to address Molly.

"I had your sister Louisa in here, just the other day.

Or was it last year? Anyway, she wanted me to make her a very special kind of Door."

"Of course!" said Molly. "That's how she got to the Martian Tombs!"

"Please don't tell anyone!" said the Doormouse, glancing furtively around him. "Mars is supposed to be off-limits, especially the Tombs. I went there, once, just to test the Door, you understand. I couldn't get my fur to lie flat again for weeks afterwards."

"Do you know what's there?" I said. "Inside the Tombs?"

"No," said the Doormouse, very firmly. "And given all the connotations attached to the word *Tombs*, I don't want to. Ever. I didn't really want to make the Door, but your sister can be very persuasive, Molly. And very hard to say no to when she's got you by the throat."

"We need a Door to take us to Ultima Thule," I said loudly, to get us back on track again.

"Why on earth would you want to go there?" said the Doormouse. "Awful place! Cold enough to freeze the nuts off a squirrel . . ."

"It is necessary that Molly and I attend the Lady Faire's annual Ball, this year, at the Winter Palace," I said carefully. "And no, we don't have an invitation. We're going to crash. Which means we need to sneak in. Unnoticed."

"I'd say you weren't her type," said the Doormouse. "Except the whole point of the Lady Faire is that everyone and everything is. She's a ladything, you know! The only one of her kind, which is probably why she's so very . . . lonely. I did meet her once, in person. If that's the right term . . . At one of the late Immortal's parties, at Griffin Hall, here in the Nightside. Of course, that was before the Griffin and his wife and his Hall were all dragged down to Hell by the Devil himself . . . But then, that's the Nightside for you. Their cook used to make the most marvellous canapés. Stuffed baby Morlock."

"Stuffed with what?" said Molly, before I could stop her.

"Baby Eloi, probably," said the Doormouse. "An amazing creature, the Lady Faire, quite delightful. In her own singular way. Sweet and charming and most . . . overwhelming at close quarters. Like being hit over the head with the *Kama Sutra*. She was very kind to an old mouse . . ."

"You didn't!" said Molly.

"No, I didn't," said the Doormouse, drawing himself up to his full height so he could look down his muzzle at her. "I made an excuse, and ran. She isn't my type. Or, to put it another way, she scared the living crap out of me. Far too intense. But I do understand the attraction. She was made to turn people's heads. And I did used to be a person, long ago."

"I never knew you were human originally," said Molly. "You never said . . . Would you like me to turn you back?"

"No, I would not," said the Doormouse very firmly. "I am the way I am by choice. There were several of us, once. Very happy being hippies, in that long lost Summer of Love. But the world changed and moved on, and we didn't like the way it was going. So we made the decision to give up being human, and become something closer to how we actually saw ourselves. We are the Mice! Fear our playfulness! The others went off to form a commune in some small country town, but I was always much fonder of the bright lights. City mouse . . . I found a trade and a craft, working with Doors. Look at them! Aren't they marvellous?

"Every Door is a possibility, a chance to be Somewhere Else, to travel through all the places there are . . . all the worlds of if and maybe. A never-ending exploration into the works of God . . . No, my dear Molly, I am content as I am. Except for when Droods come into my life and mess it up, big time. You can't go directly to Ultima Thule, Eddie Drood! Even I couldn't make you a Door that would sneak you through that many layers of protection." He stopped abruptly, and thought about it. "Well, actually I could, but you'd probably have to blow up a sun to generate enough energy to power it. And you said you didn't want to be noticed."

"I thought you could make a Door to take anyone anywhere," Molly said innocently.

"I can!" the Doormouse said immediately, bristling. "I have made Doors to Heaven and Hell and Everywhere in Between! But there are always going to be . . . problems. Side effects. Look, you'd better come with me."

And he scurried off into the long ranks, darting in and out of the hanging Doors. Molly and I hurried after him. We had to struggle to keep up. He could move pretty damned quickly for an oversized mouse. Moving between the rows of Doors proved to be a creepy and even disturbing experience. I couldn't shake off the feeling that they were looking at me, and considering—and not in a good way. Some of them felt . . . attractive, as though tempting me to open them and see what they had to offer. Others felt alien, invidious, as though there was something lying in wait behind them, just waiting for someone foolish enough to open the Door. And some . . . I didn't even want to get close to. As though they were

Doors to places that shouldn't exist, or at the very least shouldn't have access to our world. I passed one Door that made all my hair stand on end. It felt like something was beating and hammering on the other side of the Door, trying to break it down so it could get into our world . . . to do terrible, unspeakable things. I gave that Door plenty of room, and hurried on.

Molly didn't seem too bothered by any of it, keeping her gaze fixed firmly on the Doormouse's back as he scurried ahead of us. So I just stared straight ahead too, and made myself concentrate on keeping up. Until finally the Doormouse came to a sudden halt, standing before one particular Door.

"There!" he said, gesturing grandly with one furry paw. "You see what I mean?"

I had to admit that I did. The Door before us was covered from top to bottom with a thick layer of ice, shining blue-white under the Storeroom's bright lights. The encased Door was only just visible, deep inside the ice. It radiated a bitter cold, so fierce I had to brace myself to take a step closer. I didn't try to touch the ice; I just knew I'd draw back a handful of frostbite. I walked around the Door, taking my time, looking it over, and there wasn't a crack or a flaw to be seen anywhere in the thick ice. Just a solid block, formed around a Door that had tried to go somewhere it was never meant to.

"I created this Door just like any other," said the Doormouse, his voice respectfully low. "It should have worked. The mathematics were sound, the science unchallenged. I had no reason to believe there would be . . . problems. But within moments after I finished this Door, and set the coordinates for Ultima Thule, the whole thing just froze over. Solid ice, from the coldest place in the world. Some places just don't want to be visited."

Molly sniffed loudly, conjured up a handful of hellfire, and threw it at the frozen Door. The blazing flames splashed harmlessly against the ice, fell away, and disappeared. Not a single drop of melted water ran down the ice covering the Door. Instead, the Storeroom's sprinklers opened up, directly over the Door. I jumped back to avoid being soaked, dragging Molly with me. The Doormouse had backed away the moment Molly conjured up her fires. He barked a command at the sprinklers, and they turned themselves off. The Doormouse looked pityingly at Molly.

"Like I hadn't already tried that . . ."

"Bet you didn't try this," I said.

I subvocalised my activating Words, and armoured up. The Doormouse made a high chittering noise and backed away several steps. Drood armour always makes a strong first impression. I stepped up to the Door, and was surprised to find I could still feel primordial cold radiating from the block of ice, even through my armour. It was protecting me, but I could still feel it. I hit the block of ice with my armoured fist, and it just glanced away, without doing the slightest damage. I could punch a hole through a mountain with my armour on, but I hadn't even cracked this ice. I hit the block again and again, all my armour's strength behind every blow, and my golden fist just jarred harmlessly against the thick ice.

I threw my arms around the frozen block and wrestled with it, and for the first time, the ice cracked. Thick shards fell away, to shatter on the floor. The Doormouse made a loud, shocked sound. Molly cheered me on. I threw everything I had against the ice, and it cracked again, a long, jagged line from top to bottom. But still it wouldn't break.

A thick layer of hoarfrost formed on the front of my armour, and I could feel the terrible cold creeping in. Forcing its way past my armour's defences. I struggled with the ice block, throwing all my armour's power against it, and the ice defied me. The awful cold sank deep into my flesh, into my bones. I was shaking and shuddering inside my armour, gritting my teeth to keep them from chattering, and to keep myself from crying out in pain and shock. Until finally I had no choice but to let go, and stagger backwards, before the cold penetrated my heart, and perhaps my soul.

I stood there, glaring at the great block of ice, breathing hard. The ice covering the Door had already repaired and restored itself, looking thicker and even more impenetrable than before. I had been defeated by the cold, by the winter of the world, Ultima Thule. I looked at the Doormouse, and he nodded slowly.

"So," he said. "Drood armour does have its limitations. Interesting to know . . ."

I armoured down, shaking and shuddering convulsively. Molly threw her arms around me and held me tightly to her, using the warmth of her body to drive the cold out of mine. I held her close, and the cold quickly fell away. The Doormouse stood off to one side, tactfully staring into the distance. I finally patted Molly on the back, to let her know I was all right again, and we let go and stepped back from each other. We shared a smile. The Doormouse cleared his throat loudly.

"Only a Drood would try to wrestle winter itself. Still, you actually cracked the ice of Ultima Thule! I am impressed, young Drood! Really!"

"That . . . was serious cold," I said, looking at the ice-covered Door with respect.

"Well, yes," said the Doormouse. "I mean, the clue is in the name. *Ultima Thule*, the ultimate cold. The unending winter of the world. And you're telling me you want to go there?"

"I don't want to brag," said Molly, "though I'm going to . . . I have been to the Antarctic, without any special clothes or equipment. I can handle cold."

"That's natural cold," the Doormouse said severely. "There is nothing natural about Ultima Thule. It's a pocket dimension, a created reality, a world within a world, with its own rules. I've always believed it was made to store something . . . I don't know what, and I don't want to. But I'd hate to think what might happen if it ever thaws . . . and gets out."

Molly looked at me. "We are going to need more than long thermal underwear . . ."

"I've got my armour," I said, "and you've got your magics. We can survive long enough to reach the Winter Palace." I looked at the Doormouse. "All right, we can't go direct. Is there an . . . indirect way of getting there?"

"Of course!" said the Doormouse. "If logic and reason aren't enough to scare you off, then I feel I have done all that can reasonably be required of me. I may ask you to sign something to that effect before you go. I can provide you with a Door that will drop you off on the Trans-Siberian Express! One of the last surviving steam trains still running in the world today, from Eastern Europe to Siberia, all the way across Russia, and beyond. Somewhere along the way, you will pass by a naturally occurring dimensional Door that opens onto Ultima Thule. I think it's a crack in the world, or perhaps even a mistake in the original calculations. Or maybe a back door into Ultima Thule left by the dimension's original designer. Very few people know it even exists. It isn't always there and it won't stay open for long, but it should be there for the next thirty-six hours."

"Should?" I said.

"Best I can do," said the Doormouse.

"We'll take it," said Molly.

The Doormouse bustled back through the long lines of Doors, and Molly and I went with him. I took the opportunity to ask him what he knew about the Merlin Glass, on the grounds that anyone as interested as in Doors as he is should have at least heard of it. The Doormouse was immediately so excited that nothing would do but that I get the hand mirror out and show it to him. He preferred not to hold the Glass himself, so I had to hold the mirror as he leaned forward, bent so far over that the tip of his muzzle almost touched the Glass. He kept his arms behind his back, so he could be sure he wouldn't accidentally touch the mirror. His eyes gleamed brightly, and his long whiskers went into full twitch mode. After a while, he backed carefully away and looked at me thoughtfully.

"Now that is interesting . . . Come with me, dear boy, and we'll take a closer look, in my laboratory."

"What about our Door?" said Molly.

"Patience, dear girl, patience! Now come along, come along!"

He scurried off, ducking and diving between the standing Doors, and we had no choice but to go after him. He took a sudden sharp turn to the left, and opened a fairly ordinary-looking door that I would have sworn wasn't there a moment before. I glanced at Molly, we both shrugged more or less simultaneously, and we went through the door after him.

We found ourselves in a large open workplace, a scientific laboratory with dozens of work-benches, all kinds of equipment, and enough different projects on the go to keep even my uncle Jack happy. The workstations were covered with all kinds of partially assembled high tech, some of it so advanced, alien, or just plain *other*, that I couldn't even recognise what it was, never mind guess what it might be for. Some were clearly functioning, flashing lights or making odd sounds, while others seemed to be moving on their own, to some unknown purpose. One had almost reached the edge of its bench, and the Doormouse absently pushed it back to the middle again. He smiled at me encouragingly, and gestured for me to set the hand mirror down on a work-bench already crowded with half-finished things. I looked for some open space, and the Doormouse swept it all away with one quick brush of his arm. Many things crashed to the floor, but the Doormouse only had eyes for the Merlin Glass. I set it down on the bench, and stepped back. He immediately leaned right over the mirror again, making soft humming sounds to himself.

"What do you know about the Merlin Glass?" I said bluntly.

"I have been aware of it for some time," said the Doormouse, not looking away. "Your uncle Jack and I do consult, from time to time, on occasion. On matters of . . . mutual interest. And I know something of the Glass' history, of course. It is one of the great Mysteries of the world, after all. You didn't know? I am surprised . . . The

London Knights had the Merlin Glass under lock and key for centuries, until one of them returned it to your uncle Jack a few years back."

"Wait a minute!" I said. "The London Knights had it? But Merlin gave the Glass to my family! Why did the Knights have it for so long? And why would they give it back?"

"Ask your uncle Jack," said the Doormouse.

"No, wait, hold on just a minute," I said. "I looked this up, in the family archives. Merlin Satanspawn made a gift of the Glass to my family, not the London bloody Knights!"

"Oh, he gave the Glass to the Droods, right enough," said the Doormouse. "But your family knew, better than most, that you should always beware sorcerers bearing gifts. At some point, they chose to give the Glass to the London Knights. For safekeeping, perhaps? Or in return for . . . something else? I really don't know. Perhaps you should go back and check your family archives more carefully . . ."

"Do you know why Merlin gave the Glass to my family in the first place?" I said.

The Doormouse looked at me, and if there was any expression on his furry face, I couldn't read it. "If you don't know, young Drood, I certainly don't."

He turned back to his work-bench, and reached out a fuzzy paw to the hand mirror. It slid smoothly away from him, across the bench. The Doormouse blinked a few times and then tried again, with his other paw. The hand mirror jerked back several inches, refusing to be touched. The Doormouse muttered something quite astonishingly obscene, and grabbed at the Glass with both paws. It shot back and forth across the bench, like a drop of water on a hot surface, avoiding his grasp no matter how quickly he moved. The Doormouse finally gave up and stood back, breathing hard.

"It has been acting up, just lately," I said. "Almost as though it has a mind of its own. I was told . . . there might be something alive or aware, hiding or imprisoned, inside the mirror's reflection. I can't say I've ever seen anything, but . . ."

"That's Merlin Satanspawn for you," said the Doormouse. "Always thinking three steps ahead of everyone else. I think . . . we need to take a closer look at this. Yes . . ."

He turned abruptly away from the work-bench, and hurried off to trot back and forth among the larger pieces of scientific equipment cluttering up his laboratory. He peered closely at some, patted others familiarly like old friends, rejecting one after another as he searched for something specific. There was something about the Doormouse's laboratory that reminded me irresistibly of the Armourer's workplace. Though thankfully there weren't any little mouse lab assistants scuttling around. I took the opportunity to look closely at several half-finished Doors standing off to one side. Bits and pieces protruded, strange tech that made no sense at all to me. Some of the Doors' insides were so complicated I couldn't even seem to focus on them properly. As though they possessed too many spatial dimensions for the human mind to cope with.

Molly wandered around, prodding things, until I asked her very politely not to.

The Doormouse came back, huffing and puffing as he pushed a huge piece of equipment ahead of him. It looked a bit like one of those really big telescopes you see in observatories, except for all the ways in which it didn't. The Doormouse pushed one end right up to the Merlin Glass, which was resting on the work-bench, apparently at peace for the moment, and then he retreated some distance, to peer through an eyepiece on the far end of the apparatus.

"What is that thing?" I muttered to Molly.

"Beats the hell out of me," she murmured back. "Just looking at half the stuff in this place gives me a headache. Why did you have to get him started on the Glass? We could have been out of here by now!"

I shrugged. I didn't really have an answer, except that I didn't like not being able to trust something I'd come to depend on so much. I glared at the Merlin Glass, hoping it would stay put if I just kept my attention fixed on it. I half expected it to jump up off the work-bench, and try to force itself back into my pocket. The Doormouse had his furry face screwed right up, his eye jammed against the eyepiece of the thing that wasn't a telescope. All the while muttering to himself and pulling distractedly at his whiskers. He finally came out from behind the thing and hurried over to stand with Molly and me. He glowered at the Merlin Glass, but didn't try to touch it again.

"Interesting," he said.

"What is?" said Molly. "What?"

The Doormouse looked at me carefully. "You've been using the Glass as a Door, mostly?"

"Yes," I said. That much I was sure of.

"The Merlin Glass has a great many other functions and capabilities built into it," said the Doormouse. "Some of which have apparently never been accessed, never mind activated. This is a very intricate piece of work . . . I looked inside it, and it just seemed to fall away forever . . . There are layers upon layers, levels within levels. Merlin always was ahead of his Time. I can't even say for sure what the original purpose of the Glass was. What he intended it to do for the Droods. Or to them . . ."

"Is it . . . I don't know—alive, or aware?" I said.

"I didn't see anything to suggest that," the Doormouse said carefully. "Though it does seem to have a strong survival instinct built in. I suppose Merlin thought it would need that if it was going to hang around with Droods."

"Is there anyone, or anything, present in the reflection?" I said.

"Oh yes," said the Doormouse quite casually. He seemed to be concentrating on something else. "I saw it, briefly, looking back at me. Don't know what it was, though. Or why it's there. It seemed to be hiding from my equipment, though before today I would have said that was impossible. So! The Merlin Glass has been operating quite efficiently as a Door?"

"Yes," I said.

"Then I should just use it for that," said the Doormouse.

"So there's nothing to worry about, with the Glass?" said Molly.

"I didn't say that," said the Doormouse. "I'm just fed up looking at it. Damn thing's given me a headache."

I picked up the hand mirror from the work-bench. It didn't try to avoid my touch. I looked into the mirror, and my reflection stared innocently back at me. I looked carefully at what lay behind me in the reflection, but I couldn't see anyone, or anything, that shouldn't be there. I put the Glass away.

And then we all looked round sharply, as a heavy iron

bell began to toll loudly somewhere in the background. The Doormouse's ears stood straight up, and he clasped his paws together in front of him, almost as though he was praying. His eyes were very wide.

"What is that?" said Molly.

"The cloister bell," said the Doormouse. "General alarm. Panic stations. Something bad is coming, so run like hell while you've still got a chance."

He sprinted out of his laboratory and into the Showroom, not even glancing back to see if Molly and I were following. I had to run at full pelt just to catch up with him, while Molly pounded determinedly along behind me. The Doormouse shot through the Storeroom and back into his reception area, and then slammed to a halt so suddenly I almost crashed into him. He stood very still, head up and whiskers at a slant. Molly caught up with me, clapped a hand on my shoulder, and leaned heavily on me.

"What?" she said breathlessly. "What the hell . . . is going on?"

"Someone is trying to force their way into my establishment," said the Doormouse. He was staring down the length of the reception area, his gaze fixed on his front door. "Even though I put up the *Closed* sign! People have no manners these days . . ."

He moved slowly forward, trembling and twitching. I gestured to Molly, and we moved forward on either side of him. The closed front door had a large section of frosted glass, through which I could just make out a single dark shape standing outside. It looked human, and it didn't seem to be moving. But there was something about the shape . . . like one of those indistinct threatening figures you see in nightmares, full of awful significance. And the iron bell was still tolling mournfully in the background.

"Is this the Door that gives you access to the Nightside?" Molly said quietly to the Doormouse.

"Yes," he said, staring transfixed at the shape outside his door. "I don't care who that is. They can't get in. They can't! No one could get through all the layers of protection I've put in place! It's just not possible . . ."

There was a loud, harsh sound, like a great pane of glass shattering. Followed by another, and another.

"He's breaking through my shields!" said the Doormouse, almost hysterically. "Even Walker couldn't do that!"

"Do you want to run?" said Molly, practical as ever. "Choose a Door and just disappear?"

"I can't," whispered the Doormouse. "This is my place. My shop, my home. I won't be driven out of my own home."

"You work for the Droods," I said. "That means you're protected by the Droods. No one messes with anything that belongs to us. You stand your ground, Mouse. If they want to get to you, they have to get past me first."

"I find that a perfectly acceptable arrangement," said the Doormouse.

He reached inside his lab coat, and produced a monocle, a single gleaming lens set in old ivory. He screwed the thing into his left eye, and studied the door before him. And the dark figure standing motionless on the other side. The Doormouse scowled, concentrating, and then he straightened up suddenly, his eyes wide and staring. The monocle fell out, and he caught it absently and tucked it away again.

"Oh hell," he said miserably. "It's him."

"Run?" said Molly.

"No point," said the Doormouse. "There's nowhere we could go where he couldn't find us."

The front door swung open, quite casually, and in walked a man I'd never met before, and never wanted to. There are people in my line of work, people who operate exclusively in the hidden world, that everyone knows about but no one ever wants to meet in person. Hadleigh Oblivion, the Detective Inspectre, was very definitely one of those people. He stopped just inside the reception area, and smiled politely at the Doormouse and Molly and me. As though he'd just dropped in to see how we were. The front door slowly closed itself behind him. I suddenly realised the iron bell had stopped tolling, as though it had realised there just wasn't any point any more. The enemy was inside the gates, the wolf in the fold. I looked at Molly.

"I know who that is," I said.

"So do I," said Molly.

"This is bad, isn't it?" I said.

"You have no idea," said the Doormouse.

"He used to be Walker," said Molly, staring steadily at Hadleigh. "He used to represent the Authorities, here in the Nightside. All through the Sixties and into the Seventies, Hadleigh Oblivion was The Man. And then something happened . . . that he has never been able to talk about. Something too extreme even for the Nightside. He was never the same afterwards. He went a bit strange, they say, and gave up being Walker to walk his own path. Strange and awful paths, forbidden even in the Nightside.

"And then, they say, Hadleigh went underground. All the way underground. He studied at the Deep School, the Dark Acadamie, the one place you can go to study the true nature of reality. He came back disturbingly powerful, and strangely transfigured. He walks in shadows now, between Life and Death, Light and Dark, Law and Chaos. The Detective Inspectre, who only ever investigates the very worst crimes, where reality itself is under threat."

"You know a lot about him," I said.

"Know thy enemy," said Molly.

"But . . . do you really believe all that?"

"No one knows what to believe when it comes to Hadleigh Oblivion," said Molly. "Except that he is seriously scary. And if I'm saying that . . ."

"We can stop him," I said. "I mean, come on, you're Molly Metcalf and I'm Eddie Drood!"

"Eddie, I don't think you or I could even slow him down, on the best day we ever had."

"Okay," I said. "That's what comes of spending too much time in the Nightside. You start to believe all the weird shit they talk here. Besides, if he only turns up when reality itself is threatened, what the hell is he doing here?"

"I have a horrible suspicion we are about to find out," said the Doormouse.

"I am still very much in favour of beating a hasty retreat," said Molly.

"Molly . . ."

"This is Hadleigh Oblivion!" said Molly.

"No point in running," the Doormouse said glumly. "Wherever we ran to, he'd already be there, waiting for us. No one escapes the Detective Inspectre. I'd wet myself if this wasn't a new carpet."

"Why?" I said, honestly baffled by their reaction. "All right, he's got a bad rep. I've heard some of the things he's supposed to have been involved in. But what's so special about him? What can he do?"

"Anything he wants," said the Doormouse.

I glared at the man still standing patiently before us. "Well?" I said loudly. "Is any of that stuff true?"

"Believe it," said Hadleigh Oblivion. "I am the man who can't be stopped, or turned aside. The man who will do whatever is necessary, whatever the cost. It says so on my business cards. I am the Detective Inspectre, Eddie Drood, and you should not have come here."

He smiled calmly at me, not moving at all, wearing a long black leather coat so dark it seemed to have been made from a piece of the night itself. He had a bone white face, a long mane of jet-black hair, deep-set unblinking eyes, and a coldly cheerful, colourless mouth. He looked as though he was contemplating doing awful things in the name of the Good, and enjoying them. He looked starkly black and white, because there was no room left in him for shades of grey. He gave the impression that wherever he was, that was where he was supposed to be. He appeared surprisingly young, barely into his twenties, though if he'd been Walker in the Sixties, he would have to be in his eighties now.

Power burned in him. I didn't need my mask to see it.

"What did they do to you, Hadleigh?" said Molly. "Down in the Deep School, in the Dark Acadamie?"

"They opened my eyes," said Hadleigh Oblivion.

"What are you doing here?" I said bluntly. "What do you want?"

He ignored me, turning the full force of his dark eyes on the Doormouse, who shuddered suddenly.

"Hello, Mouse. Been a while, hasn't it? Made any more Doors you shouldn't have?"

The Doormouse looked startled. "How did you know about that?"

"I know everything," said Hadleigh. "It's in my job description."

"Everything?" I said, not even trying to hide my scepticism.

"Well," Hadleigh said easily, "everything I need to know."

"Whatever Doors the Doormouse may or may not have made," I said, "that's Drood business. And we will deal with it."

"We?" murmured Hadleigh. "But you have been declared rogue, Eddie Drood. Rejected and repudiated by your family. And you have entered the Nightside illegally, in defiance of long-standing pacts and obligations."

"No, he hasn't!" Molly said immediately, ready as always to defend me. "The House of Doors isn't in the Nightside, not as such. In fact, by walking through that Door into the Doormouse's establishment, technically speaking you have left the Nightside! So you don't have any jurisdiction here, do you?"

"That is a technicality," said Hadleigh. "But let us agree that we are all of us outside the Nightside. It doesn't matter. Unfortunately for all of you, I have jurisdiction wherever I go."

"Who gave it to you?" Molly challenged him.

"It was decided where all the things that matter are decided," said Hadleigh. "In the Courts of the Holy, on the Shimmering Planes. And in the Houses of Pain, in the depths of the Pit."

None of us had any answer to that. I was beginning to get a very bad feeling about the situation.

"I won't let you take me back to my family," I said.

"Dear Eddie," murmured Hadleigh. "Always so single-minded. That's not why I'm here. It has been brought to my attention that you and the witch are looking to gain possession of that most unpleasant of Mysteries, the Lazarus Stone. And that is a threat to reality itself. Because it can rewrite and undo History. No man or woman was ever supposed to have such power. It always ends badly. You can't be allowed to have it, Eddie Drood."

"I don't want it for myself," I said.

"Doesn't matter," said Hadleigh. "No one can be allowed to possess the Lazarus Stone."

"What about the Lady Faire?" said Molly.

"She never wanted to use it," said Hadleigh. "So it was safe enough with her."

"You don't understand why I need it!" I said.

"I don't care," said Hadleigh. "No man or woman can be trusted with the Lazarus Stone."

"Not even you?" said Molly.

"I would only want it to destroy it," said Hadleigh. "Now, you must come with me, Eddie Drood."

"So you can hand me over to the Authorities?" I said. "You think my family will stand for that? Rogue or no rogue?"

"I haven't served the Authorities in a long time," said Hadleigh. "You must come with me, to the Deep School."

And something in the way he said that, and something in the way Molly reacted, sent a cold chill racing down my spine.

"Why?" I said. "Because your people have always wanted to get their hands on a Drood torc? On Drood armour?"

"No, Eddie," said Hadleigh, still smiling that cold, calm smile. "Because we have always wanted to get our hands on a Drood. We have so much to learn—from your flesh, your armour, and your mind. Your history and your secrets. Your education is about to begin, Eddie. I can't promise you'll enjoy it, but it will ... open your eyes. The Dark Acadamie will make a new man out of you."

"Well, there's a kind offer," I said, fighting to keep my voice calm and conversational. "But I think I'm going to have to decline. I don't have the time right now."

"You don't have a choice," said Hadleigh.

I gave him my best cold smile. "I think you'll find I do, Hadleigh. I always have a choice. That's what being a Drood is all about. Now, you're worrying my girlfriend and terrorising the Doormouse, and I won't stand for that. I think you should leave here, now. While you still can."

"Oh, Eddie," said Hadleigh. "What fun we're going to have, breaking you."

I armoured up, my golden strange matter encasing me in a moment. The Doormouse yelped and fell back several steps, looking quickly around for something to hide behind. Molly laughed out loud, shot Hadleigh the finger, and moved quickly to one side to give me room to work. I walked slowly towards Hadleigh, and the carpeted floor shook and shuddered under the weight of my armoured tread. Hadleigh looked into my featureless golden mask and didn't budge an inch. He raised one milk white hand, and snapped his fingers imperiously. I stopped, and braced myself, but nothing happened. Hadleigh looked startled. He snapped his fingers again, the sound of it loud and forceful in the quiet, but still nothing happened. Molly laughed mockingly, behind me.

"How very odd," said Hadleigh. "That should have forced your armour back into your torc and put it to sleep. It worked on Droods before ..."

I grinned broadly behind my mask. A sudden new shot of confidence rushed through me, as I realised Hadleigh wasn't up to date. He didn't know about the new Drood armour. Didn't know about Ethel, and her other-dimensional strange matter. Which meant he wasn't infallible after all. Which was good to know. I started towards him again.

Hadleigh thrust out an open hand, and it felt like I'd crashed into an invisible wall, stopping me dead in my tracks. I strained against it, with all the strength my armour could provide, but I couldn't move an inch closer to the Detective Inspectre. I stopped trying, and looked at him. He was frowning with effort. I extruded a long, gleaming sword from my golden hand, concentrating on the edge until it was the sharpest thing I could imagine, and then swung it with both hands. The golden blade sheared clean through the invisible barrier, and there was the sound of a great glass pane shattering. I grinned again behind my faceless mask, and pulled the sword back into my hand. I raised one golden fist and showed it to Hadleigh. And then I raised thick golden spikes out of the knuckles and walked towards him.

He thrust out his hand again, scowling with concentration, and it was like being struck in the chest by a mountain. It stopped me dead again, and it was all I could do to stay upright. Hadleigh thrust his hand at me, and this time my whole armour boomed, like a struck gong. I looked down at myself, and to my utter astonishment I saw long, slow ripples move across the surface of my armour. The kind you get when you throw a pebble into a pond. The ripples rose and fell in the surface of my armour, radiating out and then back again, until finally . . . they settled down, and disappeared. The surface of my armour was still again.

I'd never felt anything like it before. My armour

felt . . . shocked. But it was still there. It had survived. Bless you, Ethel.

Hadleigh was looking at me oddly. As though he wasn't used to having his will, or his power, defied. That made me feel good. I laughed at him.

"That the best you've got, Detective Inspectre?"

"Hell no," said Hadleigh Oblivion.

He started to raise his hand again, and Molly moved quickly forward to stand between him and me. I was expecting her to hit him with a handful of hellfire, or blast him with one of her storm winds . . . and I really didn't think either of those old reliables would work this time. But instead, she raised her voice and said one commanding word.

"Tree!"

And just like that, out of nowhere, one of the great old trees from her primordial forest slammed into being, right in the middle of the Doormouse's reception area. Its upper branches flattened against the high ceiling, while the rest spread out to fill the area. It brought the scent of wood and leaves and growing things with it, rich and overpowering, and its sheer presence dominated everything. Hadleigh just stood there and looked at it, openly bemused. For the first time he looked genuinely caught off balance. A squirrel came running down one of the long branches, to glare at Hadleigh with sharp, beady eyes. It had grey fur with a wide red-brown streak down its back and tail. It peered disapprovingly at Hadleigh, and then turned its head to wink at Molly.

"Don't you worry, girl!" it said loudly. "You get the hell out of here. We'll slow him down for you, see if we don't. *Hey, rube!*"

Dozens of squirrels burst out of the leafy depths of

the tree, scampering along its many branches. And every single one of them pelted Hadleigh with handfuls of nuts. Hundreds of them shot through the air, thrown with incredible force. Hadleigh started to say something, and then stopped as a nut hit him in the forehead with such force that even I winced. Hadleigh fell back a step in spite of himself, holding one arm up to protect his face, and a whole barrage of nuts hit him in the ribs, hard enough to knock all the wind out of him.

The nut barrage intensified, filling the air. I didn't know where the squirrels were getting them from, but not one missed its mark. I don't think I've ever seen so many angry squirrels in one place before. And I certainly don't think I've ever seen a man look so surprised before. Molly grabbed my armoured arm.

"You heard the squirrel! Let's get the hell out of here!"

"I have come around to your way of thinking," I said. "Running is good."

"Sounds like a plan to me," said the Doormouse.

The three of us sprinted back through the door at the back of the reception area, and on into the Storeroom.

The Doormouse slammed the door shut and locked it with a barked command. He looked quickly around, at the long rows of standing Doors. I armoured down and looked at him, and then at the locked door.

"Will that stop him?" I said.

"Almost certainly not," said the Doormouse. He looked at Molly. "You will get that Tree out of my reception area at some point, won't you?"

"It'll go home when its job is done," said Molly. "It was just the quickest way of summoning the squirrels.

They've always had a soft spot for me. Don't worry. They'll disappear along with the Tree. Though it might take you a while to gather up all the nuts and get the squirrel shit out of your carpet."

The Doormouse looked at her, started to say something, and then thought better of it.

"Why are we hiding in here?" I said. "Do you have a Door that can take us somewhere he can't follow?"

"No," said the Doormouse. "But we should be safer, hidden among so many Doors. They impact on so many realities, just the sheer number of possibilities should help confuse Hadleigh. For a while."

"You really think we can hide from him?" said Molly.

"I don't know!" the Doormouse wailed plaintively. "This is the Detective Inspectre we're talking about! Oh shit . . . Listen. He's coming."

"Take us farther in," said Molly. "Deeper among the Doors."

"There must be something here we can use," I said.

"Against him? Against Hadleigh Oblivion?" said the Doormouse.

"Stop hyperventilating right now, or I will make you breathe into a paper bag," I said sternly. "He thought he could take me, and he couldn't. So he's not unbeatable."

"Have you had an idea?" said the Doormouse, looking at me hopefully.

"Not yet," I admitted. "But I am working on it."

"Come on," Molly said to the Doormouse. "Eddie's a Drood, I'm the wild witch, and you're a Master of Doors. Between us, we should be able to come up with something."

The Doormouse nodded quickly and scurried off between the rows of Doors. He stopped before one, chosen apparently at random, and pulled it open. He gestured frantically to Molly, and she hurried through. I went after her. The Doormouse followed close behind, all but shoving me, and once we were all through he slammed the Door shut behind us.

Rows and rows of Doors stretched off into the distance, for as far as I could make out and quite a bit farther, but in front of us was just a blank wall, of so pure a white it was essentially colourless. The Doormouse worked frantically on a combination lock set into the Door, and then sighed heavily and stepped back.

"There! I've just scrambled the spatial coordinates. No way he can follow us through that Door! We're right at the extreme end of the Storeroom. Should take him a while to catch up with us. We're as far away from Hadleigh as we can get and still be inside the House of Doors."

I looked at Molly. "Hadleigh Oblivion is pretty damned powerful, and maybe just a bit scary, but I still don't like running from an enemy."

"I do!" said Molly. "When it's the Detective Inspectre his own bad self in person, I am fully in favour of sprinting for the nearest horizon, and going to ground in a whole different reality! If you'd heard some of the stories I've heard, your heart would be jumping right out of your chest too."

"Really?" I said.

"Yes! Really!"

"Oh, come on," I said. "We've faced down the Most Evil Man in the World! What makes Hadleigh so different?"

"You haven't been paying attention, have you, Eddie?" Molly stopped herself short, closing her eyes briefly as she fought for control. "Damn, I'm hyperventilating now. And that is not like me."

"No, it isn't," I said. "So if you're that worried, I'm that worried."

"You should be," said Hadleigh Oblivion.

We all spun round, to find the man standing politely just a few feet away. He hadn't come through the Door the Doormouse had blocked, and though I looked all around me, I couldn't see any other Door standing open. Hadleigh didn't seem to have been running. He wasn't even breathing hard.

"You're getting on my tits," I said to Hadleigh.

He smiled. "I get that a lot."

"Shut up and run!" howled the Doormouse. He shot off between the hovering Doors, with Molly and me right on his furry heels. The Doormouse yanked open every Door he passed, revealing shifting views of a dozen different destinations, some of them quite definitely out of this world. I could hear Hadleigh behind us. I risked a glance back over my shoulder. He was just trotting along, not hurrying, not pushing himself, but still keeping up with us effortlessly. He was smiling, like he was just out for a pleasant afternoon run.

The Doormouse looked back too, and saw that Hadleigh was ignoring all the opened Doors. The Doormouse barked a command at one Door, in a language I didn't even recognise, and the Door swung open just as Hadleigh drew abreast of it. A blast of superheated flame shot out of the opening, as though the Door had opened onto the surface of the Sun. Hadleigh ran right through the terrible flames without even slowing. And came out the other side entirely unaffected. The Door slammed shut.

The Doormouse yelled another command at another

Door, and a great jet of water shot out, under intense pressure. As though this Door had opened somewhere deep under the Sea. And again, Hadleigh just ran on through the solid jet of water like it was a pleasant summer shower, and when he came out the other side he wasn't even damp.

The Doormouse yelled at another Door. It burst open, and a giant mutant killer bee flew out. Just the one, but so damned big it had to force its way through the opening. Twelve feet long from proboscis to stinger, and almost half as wide, with great flapping wings, a vast black and yellow body, and arched, spiky legs. And a buzz so deep it sounded like a roll of thunder. With its huge faceted eyes, it saw Hadleigh approaching, and its stinger pulsed in anticipation. Drops of poison fell from the stinger, to hiss and steam on the floor like acid. Hadleigh strolled right up to the bee without even pausing and punched it so hard in its oversized face that his fist slammed right through the skull and ended up arm-deep in the bee's head. Its buzz shot up into a pained squeal, and its wings flapped hard as it tried to pull itself away. Hadleigh yanked out his hand, in a flurry of steaming ichor, placed his other hand flat on the bee's distorted face, and pushed the creature firmly back through the Door. He then slammed the Door shut, and came after us again.

The Doormouse made a high whining noise, of almost spiritual distress, and tried again. Another command opened another Door, and a freakishly long, thick, and warty tentacle shot out and wrapped itself around Hadleigh. The tightening coils stopped him in his tracks, but then shuddered suddenly. The tentacle withered and shrivelled away from the Detective Inspectre, falling to the floor in twitching coils. Hadleigh stepped easily out of them and carried on. The tentacle whipped back through the Door, and it slammed shut.

I hadn't realised how long I'd been running while looking back over my shoulder, until Molly stopped right in front of me and I crashed into her. The impact threw her headlong on the floor, hard enough to drive all the breath out of her. I had to pick her up and stand her on her feet again. Up ahead was another blank wall. Long rows of Doors still stretched away in every direction, but there was nowhere left to run.

I looked behind me again. Hadleigh had slowed to a walk. He could see he had us cornered. I looked at the Doormouse, who was peering frantically this way and that, unable to make up his mind. He saw Hadleigh coming, pointed a stubby furred finger at the Door nearest Hadleigh, and shouted a single command.

"Eat!"

The Door flew open, and something behind it bellowed hungrily. Hadleigh paused, and looked into the opening. The bellow shut off abruptly, and the Door closed itself, almost apologetically. The Doormouse whimpered, and yelled a series of high-pitched commands. All the Doors between Hadleigh and the three of us opened at once. He walked steadily forward, and every single Door closed itself as he approached, ignoring the Doormouse's increasingly hysterical commands.

A Door appeared suddenly in the floor right in front of Hadleigh, dropping open like a trap-door. Hadleigh walked across the open space as though it wasn't there, not even glancing down. Two Doors came flying forward out of nowhere at fantastic speed, on either side of Hadleigh, sweeping in like two great wooden flyswatters. Only to slam to a halt at the very last moment, as though they'd run into an invisible wall. I knew the feeling. Hadleigh looked at each Door in turn, and they vanished.

"You'll pay for that, Hadleigh Oblivion!" screamed the Doormouse. "Full price!"

Molly stepped forward, rolled up her sleeves, and raised both arms in the stance of summoning. The Doormouse put a gentle paw on her shoulder.

"Don't," he said, making a great effort to take command of himself again. "You haven't got anything that could affect him. And the backlash . . . would be unpleasant. Nothing can stop him."

"Why?" I said, honestly baffled. "He's just one man! What makes him so special?"

The Doormouse leaned in close to me, fixing me with a terrible frightened gaze.

"They say he's *realer* than us."

While I was still trying to get my head around that, the Doormouse turned away and fiddled with the combination on the front of a nearby Door.

"There," he said quickly. "This will deliver you onto the Trans-Siberian Express. Somewhere along the Siberian route. Stick with the train until you feel the presence of the natural gateway. Then get off the train. You'll have to jump; it doesn't stop anywhere there. Don't worry — you'll know the gateway when you get close enough. Whether you want to or not. Now go! Best of luck, send me a postcard, don't look back."

"No," I said.

"No?" said Molly, stopping just short of the Door. "Really?"

"Really," I said. "I'm not leaving you to face Hadleigh on your own, Mouse. I don't leave friends in the lurch.

Not even if the enemy is the Detective bloody Inspectre. Just can't do it."

"You're crazy," said Molly. "But you're right. Running is one thing; running out on a friend is quite another. Don't know what I was thinking."

"It's Hadleigh Oblivion," said the Doormouse, as though that was all the explanation anyone needed. And maybe he was right.

I turned to face Hadleigh, armoured up, and crossed my golden arms over my armoured chest, blocking his way. Molly moved quickly in beside me, glaring at the Detective Inspectre unswervingly, stray magics spitting and sparking around her fists. The Doormouse hid behind us. Hadleigh strolled forward, crossing the remaining space like we were just good friends meeting in the park. He was still smiling easily, not in the least affected by anything he'd been through. He finally came to a halt, an acceptably respectful distance short of me. He looked my armour over like he was thinking of renting it, and then ignored me to smile coldly at Molly.

"Step away from the Drood, witch," he said. "You can't protect him. If you even try . . . I'll have you banned from the Nightside. I might even have you banned from your own private forest. Don't think I couldn't."

"Nuts," said Molly, and his smile flickered for a moment.

I took a step forward, and his dark eyes turned immediately to me. I unfolded my arms and let him see my spiked golden fists.

"You really shouldn't have done that," I said. "No one threatens my Molly and gets away with it."

Hadleigh started to say something, and I lunged forward and took hold of his throat with one golden hand.

He grabbed at my wrist with both hands, and then his eyes widened as he found he couldn't break my grip and he couldn't get his breath. His lips moved soundlessly, and strange energies flared all around my armour, but none of them could touch me. He summoned forces and powers to batter and assault me, until reality itself seemed to ripple around me, but none of them could reach me. He fought me with everything he had, and it wasn't enough.

I shook him hard, to get his attention.

"I don't care who or what you think you are, Hadleigh," I said. "You never met a Drood like me."

I threw him backwards, and he fell on his arse. He sat there on the floor, looking at me with something very like shock.

"What . . . ?" he said. "I don't . . ."

"Shut up and listen," I said. "I am a Drood in my armour, and we exist to stop people like you from throwing their weight around. Let me remind you, Hadleigh: to threaten one Drood is to threaten the whole family. And you really don't want to go there."

"You're rogue," said Hadleigh. He scrambled back onto his feet again, and I let him. He stared into my faceless mask. "Your family has disowned you."

"I was declared rogue before," I said calmly. "And I came back to rule my whole damned family. It doesn't matter what they think I've done; they'll learn better. It doesn't matter how angry they are; they'll get over it when they learn the truth. My family and I may disagree from time to time, but in the face of a mutual enemy it's always going to be one Drood for all, and all for one. Are you really ready to go to war with all the Droods, Detective Inspectre?"

He glared at me, and considered the question for a

long moment. He actually thought about it, before slowly shaking his head.

"You're right, Eddie Drood. You're not worth fighting a war over. I'll wait till you've done all the hard work and claimed the Lazarus Stone, and then I'll take it away from you."

He bowed stiffly, to me and Molly and the Doormouse, and then he turned and walked away, disappearing between the long lines of Doors.

"Damn," said Molly. "Damn! Eddie, you just faced down the Detective Inspectre! I am seriously impressed!"

I armoured down so I could smile at her. "When in doubt, go for brute strength and ignorance, and baffle them with bullshit. And a little applied psychology."

"Did you know your armour could protect you from the Detective Inspectre?" said the Doormouse.

"Of course," I lied.

He shook his furry head slowly.

"Will your family really go up against him for you?"

I shrugged. "Probably. Once I've got them back on my side. But for that I need the Winter Palace, the Lady Faire, and the Lazarus Stone. In that order."

"Then the sooner you're out of my establishment, the better," said the Doormouse. "You are bad for business, Eddie Drood. My nerves may never recover. Now, off you go. The Trans-Siberian Express is waiting for you. No charge for the service, best of luck, why aren't you two moving?"

CHAPTER EIGHT

Murders on the Trans-Siberian Express

The Doormouse's Door dropped us off in a long wooden carriage, full of crates and boxes, suitcases and other luggage, and lots of shadows and shifting light. Molly and I had to cling to each other as the speeding carriage lurched back and forth, throwing us this way and that. The air was thick with dust and the smell of unvarnished wood, and freezing cold. I looked back at the Door, but it was already gone, as though to make sure we couldn't change our minds.

"Well," I said, as lightly as I could manage, "welcome to what appears to be the baggage compartment of the renowned Trans-Siberian Express."

Molly laughed and clung to my jacket lapels with both hands so she could grin right into my face. "You just faced down the Detective Inspectre, Eddie! I am so proud of you! But if you ever scare me like that again, I will slap your head right off. What do you mean, *baggage compartment*?"

"I have never known anyone who could change direction so often, and so fast, in the same conversation," I said. "So, in order, thank you, understood, and take a look around."

We finally got our balance and let go of each other, so we could properly investigate our new surroundings. We'd arrived in a narrow railway carriage, constructed almost entirely from wooden slats, an unpolished wooden floor thickly covered in sawdust, and a rough, curving wooden ceiling. Two bare bulbs swung in the gloom overhead, unlit, but bright light punched through slits and holes in the carriage walls, filling the long open space with great blasts of flaring light, more than enough to push back the constantly shifting shadows. Crates and boxes and expensive leather luggage were piled up everywhere, and crammed tightly into shelves that ran the whole length of the carriage. Much of it had the look of expensive designer brands, while the carriage itself was deliberately old-fashioned. A blast from the past, in the service of tradition and nostalgia.

Molly staggered up and down the rattling carriage, looking closely at anything that seemed expensive or interesting and getting into everything. She didn't seem particularly impressed by our new surroundings. I said as much.

"You don't seem too impressed by our new surroundings, Molly."

"Oh, come on!" she said, not even glancing back at me. "It's a dump! Whoever put this place together had never even heard of style or comfort, except as something other people did. Look at all this unfinished wood, I'll get splinters, I know I will."

"It's traditional," I said. "It's supposed to be . . . basic. The whole journey is a throwback to the grand old days of steam travel. This kind of in-depth historical re-creation is very popular these days. And extremely expensive. It costs a lot of money to look as authentically crap as this. I'm sure the passenger carriages are much more stylish, and comfortable. In a determinedly old-fashioned way, of course. Steam trains are considered very romantic, mostly by people who've never actually travelled on one. You have at least heard of the Trans-Siberian Express, Molly, haven't you?"

"No," Molly said shortly, idly testing the locks on a suitcase. "Sounds very much a boy thing, steam trains."

"The journey starts off in Eastern Europe," I said patiently. "Runs from one side of Russia to the other, including Siberia, and then down through China, to its farthest coast. The height of old-time luxury, I'm told, for those who can afford it."

"Then what are we doing in the baggage car?" said Molly.

"Hiding out," I said. "We don't want to be noticed, remember?"

Molly sniffed loudly, giving all her attention to a pile of designer luggage with entirely insufficient defences. Given that this was the luggage of very rich and important people, I have to say most of it was painfully badly protected. The bigger crates and boxes were just held together with elastic cables, leather straps, and the odd length of baling wire. And the locks weren't anything I couldn't have opened in a moment, if I'd been so inclined. I looked thoughtfully at one long rectangular box, pushed up against the far wall ... which gave every appearance of being a coffin. Wrapped in heavy iron chains. I drew Molly's attention to the coffin, and we stood together, to consider it.

"Are those chains there to keep thieves out, or whatever's inside in?" wondered Molly.

"Let sleeping mysteries lie," I said. "And since there aren't any seats or chairs in here ..."

We sat down on the coffin lid, side by side. The baggage car continued to throw itself violently back and forth, as the train hammered along the tracks. The air was close, and the cold was starting to bite, but for the first time it felt like I could relax and feel safe. Or at least not immediately threatened by anything. It felt good, to be somewhere no one was looking for us. Molly stared unblinkingly at the expensive suitcases piled up opposite us, and I sighed inwardly as I recognised a familiar mercenary gleam in her eye. Molly was considering going shopping, and not in a good way.

"I will bet you there are all kinds of serious valuables in those cases," said Molly.

"Could we think about that later?" I said, even though I knew a lost cause when I saw one right in front of me.

"No time like the present," Molly said cheerfully. "You're the one who didn't inherit any money from his grandmother. One of us has to be the provider."

"I'm really not going to like this month's bills, am I?"

"Oh, hush, you big baby. It's only money." Molly looked around her speculatively. "There's got to be a safe in here somewhere, where they lock up the really tasty stuff."

"We don't want to set off any alarms," I said sternly.

"Or alert people on the train that we're here. We need to be quiet."

"What's all this *we* shit, kemo sabe?" said Molly. "A girl has to look out for her best interests . . ."

"We are on our way to a place that doesn't officially exist, to steal something that almost certainly doesn't do what it says on the tin, from a person who isn't even a person, to buy my parents back from someone we don't even have a name for!" I said. "While every secret organisation in the world, very definitely including my own family, wants us dead! We don't need any more complications, Molly!"

"Oh, all right!" said Molly. She sat back on the coffin lid, stuck out her lower lip, and glowered at me. "I can remember when you were fun . . ." She looked around the baggage car some more, and a deep frown slowly etched itself between her eyebrows. "You know, Eddie, there is some seriously strange stuff in here. I'm picking up all kinds of magical emanations, leaking past a whole bunch of quite unusual wards and protections."

"All the more reason not to go messing around with them," I said.

"I'm just curious . . ."

"Oh, that is always a bad sign."

Molly was already up off the coffin lid and on her feet again, staggering across the lurching floor to peer closely at this piece of luggage and that. She knelt down opposite a large hatbox and considered it thoughtfully. The hatbox had been sealed with all kinds of pretty ribbons, tied in really intricate bows, along with several lengths of delicate silver chain and one really heavy steel padlock.

"Molly . . . ," I said warningly.

"I want it."

"You don't even wear hats!"

"It's the principle of the thing," said Molly, still staring intently at the hatbox. "How dare the world hide things from me . . ."

She snapped her fingers smartly, and the padlock flew open. I braced myself, ready to dive for cover, but nothing happened. Molly smiled sweetly, and pulled the silver chains away, dropping them casually on the floor beside her. She undid the pretty ribbons with nimble fingers, and then opened the lid. Only to immediately fall backwards onto her haunches, as a very large hat covered with all kinds of brightly coloured feathers flew up out of the box and fluttered vigorously around the baggage car. It bobbed this way and that and then flapped upwards, where it bounced back and forth along the curving wooden ceiling. The hat rose and fell and turned itself around, as the fluttering feathers tried to drive it in a dozen different directions at once. It seemed cheerful enough, for a flying hat.

Molly glared at it. "Get back in the box!"

The hat ignored her, flitting up and down the length of the baggage car at considerable speed, clearly having the time of its hatty life. And probably setting off all kinds of security alarms. I got up off the coffin, grabbed several small useful items, and lobbed them at the hat, trying to bring it down. The hat avoided my efforts with almost insulting ease. Molly scrambled up off the floor and we pursued the thing up and down the carriage, while it fluttered back and forth, always just out of reach. The jolting floor didn't help, throwing Molly and me all over the place. I crashed into some piled-up bags and sent them flying. A few broke open, spilling their contents across the sawdust floor. Clothes and books and assorted valuables, and one brass cage containing one very large black bat. The cage broke open on impact, and the bat saw its chance for freedom and took it. It flew swiftly back and forth, its leathery wings making a sound very like gloved hands clapping. And then the bat saw the hat, and went for it. The bat and the hat threw themselves at each other with clear mutual loathing, and not a little viciousness. They crashed together, spun round and round the carriage several times, and then separated, to regard each other ominously from a distance.

Molly lost her balance, and grabbed at the nearest shelf to steady herself. Her hand missed the shelf and fastened onto a bottle bearing a handwritten sign that said simply *Gin*. The bottle slipped out of her hand and smashed on the floor. A great cloud of purple smoke billowed up, taking on a vaguely human form, with a grinning bearded face at the top. Not *Gin*. *Djinn*. Nothing causes more damage than a bottle of cheap djinn. The gaseous figure quickly spread out to fill the whole carriage. It had enough physical presence to knock me off my feet and send me staggering backwards, until I crashed up against the far wall. I could just about see through the purple fumes to where Molly was pinned up against the opposite wall. Her arms flailed through the gassy body without doing any damage. The bat and the hat fluttered helplessly together, pressed against the ceiling. The giant bearded face grinned nastily, and piled on the pressure as it continued to expand.

"Get this thing off me!" yelled Molly. "I can't move! It's crushing me!"

I forced myself down the carriage wall, until I could crouch with my arse on the floor. I could hear the djinn laughing. I pushed myself forward until I was lying on the floor, and then I crawled forward on my belly, setting all my strength against the pressure of the djinn's gaseous body, until I reached the sliding door set into the carriage wall opposite me. I tried to force it open, but it was locked shut. I armoured up my hand, smashed the lock with my golden glove, and gave the sliding door a good shove. The door flew open, and the djinn's gassy body was sucked right out through the opening. I just caught a glimpse of a shocked and surprised bearded face, and then the djinn disappeared, sucked away and dispersed in the rushing wind.

The bat and the hat flew out after it. I waited till I was sure they were safely gone, and then sat down in the opening with my legs dangling over the side and watched the scenery rushing past. Molly came lurching forward, and sat down heavily beside me. She leaned against me companionably, as we both got our breath back, and then we just sat there together and enjoyed the world speeding past. It was very . . . scenic. An endless sea of snow, stretching away in all directions as far as the eye could see. Rising and falling but frozen in place, just a great expanse of gleaming white, without even a single tree or shrub to break the monotony.

"Where are we, exactly?" said Molly, after a while.

"Siberia," I said. "Somewhere. It's a big place. Covers a lot of ground."

Molly shuddered. "Damn, it's cold! I mean . . . really cold!"

"And this is just Siberia," I said. "It's going to be a whole lot colder once we pass through the Gateway into Ultima Thule."

Molly looked down at her long white dress. "I'm really not dressed for the occasion, am I? Hold on while I break open the suitcases and have a good rummage round for something more suitable. Preferably with furry bits of dead animal attached."

"I think we've let loose enough annoyances for one day, don't you?" I said. "God alone knows what else they've got packed away in here."

"Good point," said Molly. "I'll just find a passenger on the train who's wearing something seriously furry, lure her to a quiet place, and then mug her. My need is greater."

"How very practical," I said.

Molly shuddered again from the cold, so I helped her to her feet and slammed the heavy sliding door back into place. I squeezed the lock shut with my golden glove, and then sent the armour back into my torc. I was shivering now too from the cold that had got into the baggage car, and my breath steamed on the air, along with Molly's. We went back to the coffin and sat down, hugging ourselves tightly. Molly banged on the coffin lid.

"Are you awake, Count Magnus?"

"Can't take you anywhere," I said.

She glared at me. "Explain to me again why we're having to do this the hard way?"

"Once more, then," I said, "For the hard of learning at the back of the class. This train will carry us to a naturally occurring Gateway, somewhere in the snowy depths of sunny Siberia, and this Gate will in turn deliver us to Ultima Thule, the Winter Palace, and eventually, the Lady Faire."

Molly sniffed loudly. "And how long is it going to take to reach this Gateway?"

"I don't know," I said. "Hours, I should think."

"What?" said Molly, sitting up straight. "Hours?" She

stood up abruptly and planted herself before me with her fists planted on her hips, the better to glare down at me. "I am not sitting here, in this dump, freezing my tits off, for hours on end! And . . . I am hungry! Very seriously hungry. Eddie Drood, we are going to the restaurant car. Right now!"

I stood up, and smiled at her. "Your relentless logic has defeated me. I will admit, I am feeling just a bit peckish myself."

"Then let's go!" said Molly.

"Can we at least try to keep a low profile?"

"Who's going to know us here? Let them look."

"You've never been one for hiding your light under a bushel, have you?"

"Listen," said Molly, "I am so hungry right now, I could eat a bushel."

The door between the baggage car and the next compartment was of course very firmly locked, but a little firm pressure from a golden glove was all it took to persuade the door to open. Having Drood armour is like possessing a free pass to everywhere. Molly slipped her arm through mine, and we strode proudly on into the passenger carriage, which turned out to be a much warmer place, and far more civilised. A perfect re-creation of an early-twentieth-century railway carriage, with every conceivable comfort and luxury, and every relevant detail carefully preserved. Or at the very least, cunningly duplicated. The old original gas lamps in fact contained carefully concealed electric light bulbs, while hidden central heating soon took the chill out of our bones. The richly gleaming beechwood panels were stamped at regular intervals with the golden crest of the Trans-Siberian Express Company. The carriage was made up of spacious separate compartments, with padded leather seats and specially reinforced wide windows through which the rich and important passengers could enjoy glorious views of snow-covered scenery. Very nice views. If you liked snow. And not much else.

Molly and I sauntered down the narrow aisle, arm in arm and heads held high, as though we had every right to be there. The few people we encountered just smiled and nodded pleasantly to us. Molly and I nodded and smiled in return. No one raised a fuss, or asked any questions, because since we gave every appearance of belonging there, then obviously we must.

And there you have it. How to be a secret agent, in one easy lesson.

A steward in a blindingly white uniform with lots of gold piping and serious braid on his shoulders and rows of gleaming buttons came bustling forward to meet us. He smiled and bowed, and inquired how he might best be of service, in formal Russian he'd clearly learned from a book. I answered him in English, and he immediately responded in English he'd clearly learned from a book. Molly dazzled him with her smile, and asked for directions to the restaurant car. The steward bobbed his head quickly.

"Just follow the corridors through carriages second and third, honoured sir and lady, and you will emerge immediately into the restauranting car. Second serving of the day is just beginning."

I gave the steward my best dazzling smile, to make up for the fact that I didn't have any suitable money about me with which to tip him, and Molly and I moved on. The steward was gracious and understanding about it, and made a rude gesture at our backs that he didn't realise I could see in the mirror on the wall. I wasn't worried he might say something. The rich are often notoriously poor tippers. It's part of how they got to be rich.

We reached the restaurant car without further mishap, and it turned out to be barely half full. Perhaps the constant lurching of the train had made the other passengers travel-sick. At least it meant we had no problems getting a table. Molly and I just marched down the aisle with our noses stuck in the air, and none of the exquisitely dressed people already at their tables paid us any attention at all. I chose the very best table, picked up the *Reserved* sign and threw it away, and pulled out a chair for Molly to sit down. She sank elegantly into it with a gracious smile, and I sat down opposite her and studied the setting details as the spoils of conquest.

Gleaming white samite tablecloth, luxurious plate settings, and first-class cutlery, all of it stamped with the Trans-Siberian Express company crest. I shook out the heavy napkin, dropped it in my lap, and pocketed the silver napkin holder. I glanced out the window, just in case anything had changed. Snow. Lots of snow. And even more snow. For a moment I thought I saw something moving, but when I looked more closely I realised it was just the train's shadow, racing along beside us. Molly caressed the inside of my thigh with her toes, underneath the table, and smiled at me demurely.

I picked up one of the oversized menus. The heavy paper stock was bound in red leather, and everything on offer was in French. I can read French, but it was a sign the food was almost certainly going to be overcooked and underwhelming. That kind of food nearly always is, outside of France.

"There aren't any prices," said Molly, running her eyes rapidly over what the menu had to offer.

"If you have to ask the price, you can't afford it," I said. "That goes as standard, in places like this. Ah, there's an English translation at the back, if you need it."

Molly glowered at me over the top of her menu, and withdrew her foot. "I'll back my French against yours any day."

"Splendid idea. Bring her on," I said. "Baguettes at dawn?"

Molly giggled, and we turned to the menu's back pages, honour satisfied. The English-language translation was in very small type, as though it was being presented only very grudgingly. I couldn't say I was particularly impressed by any of it. Just because something is rare and expensive and fashionable, it doesn't necessarily follow that it's going to be in any way tasty. I can remember when baby mice stuffed with hummingbirds' tongues was all the rage, in the most-talked-about London restaurants. I once outraged a celebrity chef by asking if I could have mine in a sesame seed bun.

"Oh look!" said Molly. "There's going to be a caviar and vodka tasting later this afternoon."

"Don't get too impressed," I said. "Unless it's the real Beluga stuff, all caviar tastes the same. Salty. The trick is to get them to provide you with enough dry toast to eat it on."

"Snob," said Molly, not unkindly.

"I'm a Drood!" I said cheerfully. "We're entitled to the best of everything the world has to offer. It says so in our contract."

"You have a contract with the world?"

"Oh yes," I said. "Of course, we don't let the world see it."

"Of course," said Molly.

"You can't talk," I said. "All the time you were staying with me at Drood Hall, you insisted the kitchens provide you with six boiled eggs for every breakfast, just so you could choose the best one."

"I got the idea from Prince Charles," said Molly.

"You've never met Prince Charles!"

"I read about it, in *Hello!* magazine. And if it's good enough for him . . . Have you anything witty and informative to say about the vodka?"

"Only that vodka usually only tastes of whatever you mix it with. I've had peppermint vodka, paprika vodka, chocolate vodka . . . What an afternoon that was. I do remember a story my uncle James told me, from his time in Russia during the Cold War. He said he always used to drop a little black pepper onto the surface of a glass of vodka, let the pepper sink to the bottom, and then knock the vodka back in one, so that the peppered dregs stayed in the bottom of the glass. Because in those days you got a lot of homemade bathtub vodka showing up in Moscow, even at the best parties, a lot of it spiked with fuel oil. The fuel oil floated on the surface of the vodka, and the black pepper attached itself to it, and took it to the bottom of the glass. Made the stuff safe, or at least safer, to drink. *Blind drunk* wasn't just an expression in those days."

"You know such charming anecdotes," said Molly. "Better not try that trick here; I don't think it would make a good impression."

"Of course not," I said cheerfully. "Only the very best for us, because we're worth it."

"I love to hear you talk," said Molly. "You've lived, haven't you, Eddie?"

"Not as much as you," I said generously.

Her earthy laughter filled the air, and well-manicured heads came up all around us. I don't think they were used to hearing the real thing. Perhaps fortunately, a train conductor came bustling into the carriage just then. Wearing a sharp and severe black uniform, with lots and lots of gold buttons down the front, and a stiff-peaked cap. He looked quickly round the restaurant car, fixed his gaze on Molly and me, and headed straight for us. He had that look, of a small man with a little power, determined to abuse it for all it was worth. And make everyone else's life as difficult as possible, just on general principles. It was clear from his expression that he didn't like the look of Molly and me. We weren't dressed well enough, didn't look rich or powerful enough, to be eating in his restaurant car, on his train. The likes of us had no place in such a salubrious setting.

He walked right up to us, ignoring all the other diners seated at their tables, and everyone else sensed trouble coming and determinedly minded their own business. Molly studied the conductor lazily as he approached, and smiled a quietly disturbing smile.

"Want me to turn him into something squelchy?"

"Not in front of the passengers," I said quickly. "We're trying not to draw attention to ourselves, remember?"

"All right," said Molly. "I'll try something subtle."

"Oh good," I said, wincing. "You always do so much more damage when you're trying to be subtle."

The conductor slammed to a halt at our table and drew himself up to his full height, the better to puff out his chest and sneer down his nose at us.

"Yes?" I said, drawing the word out in my best aristocratic English, so that it sounded like an insult. "Is there something you need, fellow?"

He'd clearly heard that kind of English before, and it threw him a little off balance, but one look at our clothes reassured him that we were definitely not the right sort. He glared at me unblinkingly, ignoring Molly. Out of the corner of my eye, I could see that going down really badly with Molly.

"Pardon me, sir and madam," he said, in only lightly accented English. "I am afraid I must insist you show me all your tickets and passes. Including your reservations for dinner at this serving. If you cannot, you must explain yourselves immediately! I hope it will not be necessary for me to summon the security guards. They can be . . . most unpleasant."

"Well, we wouldn't want that, would we?" I said. "Molly dearest . . . ?"

"Of course, darling," said Molly. She snapped her fingers imperiously, to draw the conductor's attention, and then fixed his gaze with hers. His face went blank, and his jaw dropped, just a little. Molly held out an empty hand to him. "There. See? We have first-class tickets. And reservations. And everything else we need. So you don't need to bother us ever again. Do you?"

The conductor started to say something, and then his mouth snapped shut as Molly frowned. The conductor looked at her empty hand, and then smiled meaninglessly at Molly and at me.

"Of course . . . madam and sir. Everything is in order. You will not be troubled again."

"We're not the diners you're looking for," I said.

"Quite so, sir . . ."

He turned abruptly away and marched off, looking completely convinced and terribly confused. He rubbed at his forehead with one hand, as though bothered by something he couldn't quite place, or something in his head that shouldn't be there. He glared at everyone he passed as he hurried back down the aisle, looking for someone to take out his unease on, but everyone had the good sense to keep their heads down and say nothing. Molly looked around for the nearest waiter and caught his eye, and the young man immediately snapped to attention and hurried forward to take our order.

In the end, Molly ordered one whole page of the menu, and not to be outdone, I ordered everything on the opposite page. Just to increase the odds of ending up with something worth having. The waiter actually lowered himself to look seriously impressed. The bill for that much food was probably more than he and his fellow waiters on the train earned in a week. I then raised myself even further in his estimation by blithely ordering him to bring us a bottle of the best Champagne the Trans-Siberian Express could offer. The waiter smiled and bowed quickly, several times, and then hurried off to place our order and tell his fellows all about it. Obviously anticipating a really good tip, because clearly money meant nothing to such wealthy patrons as us.

Molly and I threw aside the menus, sat back in our comfortable seats, and looked about us. It was all very calm, very civilised. Very peaceful. Not a hint of piped music. Though if they sent a gypsy violinist in to serenade us, I was fully prepared to punch him in the head repeatedly until he gave up and went away again.

"We should do this more often," said Molly. "We never seem to find the time to just kick back and enjoy ourselves. Pamper the inner person . . . Though I have to ask, are you actually planning to pay for all this, or are we just going to have to break a window and jump for it?

I mean, I never pay for anything on principle, on the unanswerable grounds that the world owes me. But I have to say, confusing a conductor is one thing, but confusing a credit card reader could prove problematic . . ."

"Not to worry," I said. "I have a whole bunch of credit cards, courtesy of the Armourer. All part of an agent's legend, once he's out in the field. I was supposed to hand them back in, but after the way my family treated me, somehow it just slipped my mind . . ."

"Won't they have shut those cards down, now you're disowned?" Molly said carefully.

"They can't," I said cheerfully. "They're not real cards. They're good enough to fool any machine, anywhere in the world, but the best of luck to anyone actually trying to get money out of them . . ."

Molly looked at me accusingly. "Why haven't I heard about these cards before?"

"Because you'd only have abused them," I said.

"Of course!" said Molly. "That's what credit cards are for!"

"It's people like you that undermine economies," I said. "Now then, I can only use each card once, and then they self-destruct so they can't be traced. And since I can't go back to the Armourer to ask for more, we're going to have to make them last." I stopped for a moment to consider the matter. "I still believe I can go home again, eventually. That I can put things right with them. When I explain about my parents, and the Voice, and the Lazarus Stone."

"After everything your family has put you through, you still want to go back?" said Molly. "After all the terrible ways they've treated and mistreated you, you still think you have to explain yourself to them? You let your family walk all over you, Eddie."

"Of course," I said. "That's what families are for."

I looked out the window again. Snow. I looked up and down the restaurant car, studying the other passengers. They all seemed very prosperous, very comfortable, and happy enough with the food in front of them, if not necessarily with each other's company. There was barely a murmur of conversation going on in the whole carriage. Most of the diners had the look of couples who'd been together for some time and had said everything to each other that was worth saying. So they sat, and ate, and didn't look at each other. I hoped Molly and I would never get to that stage.

It also occurred to me that there was an awful lot of expensive and impressive jewellery on open display, because after all there couldn't be any dangers in a place like this ... I turned back to Molly and found she was also studying the jewellery, with the look of someone doing mental arithmetic. She caught me looking at her.

"Relax, Eddie. I'll be discreet. They'll never know what hit them. Yes, I know, we're not supposed to draw attention to ourselves, but who would be looking for us here?"

"Who wouldn't?" I said. "It feels like everyone in the world is after us. Very definitely including whoever is really responsible for the murder of all those people at Uncanny. We still don't have a clue as to who that was. We're the only ones who can find out, because we're the only ones looking. Everyone else is convinced it was us. There are a lot of people out there who'd do anything to punish us for what they think we've done. The Regent of Shadows did a lot of good for people in his time. He still has a lot of friends out there. Then there are all the people who'd love to get their hands on a rogue Drood and his armour. And finally, people like the Detective Inspectre, who think they can use us to get to the Lazarus Stone."

"I'm not sure there is anyone like Hadleigh Oblivion," said Molly.

"You could be right there," I said. "But you get the point."

"How could I not, after you've explained it all so laboriously? I am keeping up with things, Eddie! Honestly, you'd think I'd never been on the run before . . . So, basically, we're hiding from absolutely everybody?"

"Basically, yes," I said. "Just like old times."

We shared a smile, remembering how we first met. When my family denounced me for the first time, and tried to have me killed, and the only people I could turn to for help were those I'd previously considered my enemies. Molly and I had already tried to kill each other several times, earlier in our careers, so she was one of the first people I turned to. The only person who knows you as well as an old friend is an old enemy. Who knew the two of us would get on so well . . . ?

The waiter came hurrying forward, proudly bearing a bottle of Champagne in an ice bucket. He placed the bucket reverently on the table and then opened the bottle with practised ease. He poured me a glass, and presented it to me with a grand gesture. I think I impressed him, and perhaps even faintly scandalised him, by not even glancing at the label on the bottle. I took a good sip, and nodded nonchalantly. I gestured to the waiter to pour a glass for Molly. He did so quickly, and Molly took the glass and downed it in one. She smiled sweetly at the shocked waiter.

"That's the stuff. Pour me another, sweetie. I've got

my drinking cap on, and my liver is going to take some real punishment this evening."

The waiter looked at me imploringly, but I just gave him a *What can you do?* shrug. He sighed, quietly, in a *Barbarians Are at the Gate* sort of way, and refilled Molly's glass. She knocked that one back too.

"I can't help feeling you're not getting the most out of that," I said.

"I'm thirsty!" Molly said loudly. "It's been a busy old day." She glared at the waiter, and he hurried to pour her a third glass. He then put the bottle in the ice bucket and ran away before he could be forced to participate in any more appalling behaviour. Molly sipped at her Champagne, little finger delicately extended, grinned at me, and looked out the window. At all the endless, unmarked snow rushing past. I looked too, just to keep her company. There still wasn't a single tree or landmark to be seen anywhere, even along the distant horizon. No sign of life, let alone civilisation.

"It's like looking at a dead world," Molly said quietly. "Like looking at the surface of the Moon . . . Siberia. You were here once before, weren't you, Eddie? On that case you still don't like to talk about."

"Yes," I said. "The great spy game. Somewhere out there, beyond the horizon, buried deep beneath the Siberian tundra, lies one of my family's greatest secrets and most terrible horrors."

"What?" said Molly.

"Hush," I said. "Keep your voice down. We don't want to wake him."

"Your family history never ceases to appal me," said Molly.

But there must have been something in my face . . .

because she stopped asking questions. We both have our pasts, and our secrets, places we cannot go. Molly looked out at the empty landscape again, resting her chin on her hand.

"How are we supposed to find this Gateway?" she said morosely. "How are we supposed to find anything, in all this . . . wilderness?"

"The Doormouse said we'd just know," I said. "That we'd sense where it was, the moment we were close enough, whether we wanted to or not. Which is, of course, not in the least worrying."

"What can you do?" said Molly. "He's a Mouse."

We stopped talking, as the food finally arrived. So much food, in fact, that it had to be wheeled to our table on several large trolleys, by several large waiters hoping to share in a really big tip. Or perhaps because they wanted to see what kind of idiots would order so much more food than they could possibly eat. The waiters took it in turn to lay out plates and bowls, dishes and tureens, and all kinds of steaming-hot food, until they ran out of room on the table and had to start overlapping things. I just sat back and let them get on with it. I have to say, everything smelled pretty damned good. Molly started making cute little hungry sounds, and clapping her hands together. When the waiters finally finished, they stood back and stared respectfully at the magnificent repast they'd delivered, and then they all looked expectantly at me and Molly. Molly looked right back at them, and they all suddenly remembered they were needed urgently somewhere else, and ran away as slowly as their dignity would allow.

Molly and I tried bits and pieces of everything, stabbing things with forks or just picking them up with fingers. To the accompaniment of appalled noises from people around us, who couldn't believe what they were seeing, I chewed enthusiastically at this and that, only occasionally spitting things out. Because there are limits. A lot of what we'd ordered turned out to be regional specialities, and strange delicacies from local cultures. Mostly hotly spiced meats, and unfamiliar vegetables beaten and boiled to within an inch of their lives. Some was just unidentifiable bits of animal, whole organs swimming in sauces thickened with fresh blood. More like a road accident than a meal.

"I think this . . . is yak," I said, chewing determinedly on something purple, served on a bed of bright pink rice and grey peas. "On the grounds that just eating this fills me with an overwhelming impulse to shout *Yak!* in a loud and carrying voice."

"I think what I've got here is Mammoth," said Molly. "It's certainly big enough. Could this be its trunk, do you think?"

"No," I said judiciously. "That looks like a much more intimate part of its anatomy. You're going to eat it, aren't you?"

"Damn right I am!" said Molly. "I'm hungry! You sure I can't tempt you to try just a little bit?"

"No," I said. "I would wince with every bite."

"I wonder if they had to tenderise it first, with a mallet?" said Molly, smiling wickedly, and I had to cross my legs and look the other way.

We ended up eating a hell of a lot of the food, and drinking all of the Champagne, before finally throwing in the napkin and leaning back in our seats, happily replete and more than a little stuffed. Molly fixed me with a sly grin.

"You know, I could probably use my magics to convince the conductor we have reservations for a first-class sleeping compartment. How would you like to join the Hundred-Mile-an-Hour Club?"

"Nice thought," I said. "But I am so full right now, all I'd want to do with a bed is sleep in it. My body is completely preoccupied with digestion."

"Getting old, Eddie," said Molly. "But we could just sleep, if you like. It has been a long, hard day . . . We could take it in turns, one sleeping while the other stays on guard. If we really are in any danger, this far from everyone and everything . . ."

"We're in danger wherever we are," I said. "And perhaps especially here. If word has got out that we're going after the Lazarus Stone, they'll expect us to go through Ultima Thule. So there are bound to be people lying in wait along the way . . . Hoping to intercept us, or follow us, or just pick us off from a distance. People who would just love to catch us napping . . . No, Molly, we can't sleep, we can't take it easy, and we can't take our eye off the ball. Even for a moment."

Molly looked out the window again. "There's no one out there, Eddie."

"No one we can see."

Molly sniffed, and gestured rudely at the other diners. "I can't see much of a threat coming from any of these overprivileged nostalgia freaks. Unless they plan to smug us to death."

And then we both sat up straight, as shouts and screams and sounds of open violence suddenly exploded from beyond the closed door at the end of the restaurant carriage. The door we'd come in through. The other diners looked up, startled, and began to babble nervously among themselves. One large gentleman stood up, rather officiously, and started toward the door to investigate. He'd almost reached it when the door was smashed inwards with such force that the whole thing was blasted off its hinges and out of its frame. It flew down the aisle to slam into the large gentleman, knocking him off his feet and onto his back. He lay groaning on the floor, with the door on top of him.

One of the white-uniformed stewards came flying through the gap where the door had been, tumbling bonelessly down the narrow aisle between the tables, until finally he crashed to a halt. There was blood all over the torn white uniform, and it was suddenly horribly clear that the body had no head. The ragged wound at the neck suggested the head had been torn off by brute force.

Blood from the severed neck had been thrown everywhere as the body tumbled down the aisle, splashing the furnishings and fittings, and soaking into the expensive clothing of those diners sitting in the aisle seats. Their cries went flying up like startled birds, and they shrank back in their seats, away from the awful thing that had so violently invaded their comfortable lives. I looked at Molly, and we both got up from our seats and moved out into the aisle, to face whatever might be coming. We stood side by side, confronting the dark opening. Molly shot me a quick grin, ready for anything, and I had to smile back at her.

It would feel really good to hit something. To take out the day's frustrations on whatever poor fool was stupid enough to interrupt our downtime.

The first man to step through the doorway was dressed all in red. Blood-red leather jacket and trousers, with a dark red mask covering his entire face, with just the eyes showing. There was something about the eyes . . . Too fixed, too fierce, too intent. He stood in front of the doorway with fresh blood dripping from his bare hands, his long lean body almost quivering with nervous energy. You had only to look at him to know that he was here to fight, and kill . . . and that he would enjoy every bloody moment of it. He wasn't a soldier, or even a mercenary; he was a killer.

He stepped quickly forward, and half a dozen more men came quickly through the doorway after him. Six more lean and hungry men, dressed in blood-red.

"Why are they all wearing masks?" Molly said quietly. "Are they afraid we might recognise them?"

"There's something odd about the way they all look," I said. "The way they move. They all have exactly the same body language. Weird."

And then we glanced behind us, as the rear door to the carriage slammed open. Two armed security guards, in much the same black uniform as the conductor, came running in. They shouted at Molly and me in Russian, telling us to get the hell out of their way. They were both big muscular types, carrying heavy machine pistols. They looked like they knew how to use them.

Molly and I moved hastily back out of the way, and they ran straight past us, training their guns on the men in red and yelling for them to surrender. One of the blood-red men stepped forward, raising his bloody hands, and both security men opened up on him at once. The bullets raked him from chest to groin and back again, but he just stood there and took it. I saw the bullets go in, but he didn't bleed at all. Didn't even stagger back, from the repeated impacts.

He came forward, incredibly fast, and hit the nearest

security man in the head so hard it broke the man's neck and sent his head swinging all the way round to stare over his shoulder with empty eyes. The body was still crumpling to the floor when the blood-red man turned on the other guard, who was still emptying his gun into the quickly moving target. The blood-red man snatched the machine pistol out of the security guard's hand, reversed it, and smashed the stock of the gun into the man's chest so hard, it sank half its length into his body. Blood flew out in a jet, soaking the blood-red man's jacket. The security man let out a single agonised grunt. The blood-red man pulled the gun back out, in a fresh flurry of blood, and the security man fell to the floor. The blood-red man tossed the gun carelessly aside, and looked at me again. With those mad, fierce eyes.

And I just knew I'd seen them somewhere before.

The other passengers scrambled up out of their seats, screaming and shouting, and ran for the rear door. Molly and I stayed back to let them pass, not taking our eyes off the blood-red men. The passengers slammed into one another in the narrow aisle, fighting hysterically as they tried to make their escape. Molly and I stood together in the aisle, blocking the blood-red men's way. I could hear diners struggling to force their way through the far door. Finally the last shouts and cries died away as they disappeared into the next carriage. Molly and I were left alone with the blood-red men.

I looked them over carefully, and the more I studied them, the more identical they seemed. Same height, same weight, same body language. The way they held themselves. And they all had the same intent, fanatic's eyes . . .

"Who are these guys?" Molly said quietly.

"Beats the hell out of me," I said. "But they're not just uniformed thugs, like MI 13's shock troops. They're stronger than anything human should be, and faster, and from the way that one just soaked up bullets . . . Augmented men? Specially created soldiers? Clones?"

"Ask them," said Molly.

"Worth a try, I suppose," I said. I took one careful step forward, and all their eyes moved to follow me. "Who are you?" I said loudly. "What do you want with us?"

"I would have thought that was obvious," said Molly.

"I have to ask," I said, not looking back. "You know how the bad guys always love to boast. And it is always possible there's been some terrible misunderstanding."

"You think?" said Molly.

"Not really, no. But you have to cover every possibility . . . Look, do you want to come forward and take over the questioning? I don't mind. Really."

"No, no, you carry on," said Molly. "Though I would just point out that not one of these arseholes has answered you yet. Which is just rude. I say we forgo further questioning and move straight on to the arse-kicking. Just on general principles. We can always ask questions afterwards, to whoever's still conscious."

The blood-red men surged forward, moving incredibly quickly. More of them came bursting through the open doorway, until a small crowd of blood-red men filled the end of the carriage. An army of fanatical killers, all dressed the same, all looking and moving exactly alike. They stood unnaturally still, their gaze fixed on me, ignoring Molly. Poised and ready, as though just waiting for the order to attack.

"Okay, Molly," I said steadily. "I count twenty-three of them now. And I have this horrible feeling there are probably even more of them on the other side of that doorway. They're all looking at me, but I'm pretty sure they'd be just as happy to take you down too, so I have to ask, Molly, are you back to full strength?"

"Are you?" said Molly. "You were the one complaining you were too full to do anything physical."

"I have my armour," I said patiently. "Do you have all your magics back?"

"Not all of them, no, but . . . enough. Come on, Eddie, there are twenty-three of them against two of us, so for all practical purposes we outnumber them. Let's do it."

"Sounds like a plan to me," I said.

I armoured up, and golden strange matter flowed all over me in a moment. I felt stronger, faster, my mind suddenly running at full speed. Putting on Drood armour is like suddenly emerging from a doze to full wakefulness, or like coming out of a dream to sharp reality. Like a blast of adrenaline to the soul. I always feel more alive, more aware, more me, when I'm in my armour. Ready to take on the whole damned world.

Interestingly, not one of the blood-red men reacted at all. They didn't even flinch. Which was unusual. Most people jump half out of their skin the first time they see a Drood armour up. It's basically just self-preservation instincts kicking in, because if a Drood's turned up, everyone else is in real trouble. The blood-red men just stood their ground and stared at me with their over-bright eyes, as though this was what they'd been waiting for.

Molly got fed up with being ignored, stepped forward, and thrust out a hand at the blood-red crowd. She spoke a couple of really nasty Words, and I winced inwardly as I recognised her favourite transformation spell. I have seen

Molly turn whole armies of very rude unfortunates into so many confused-looking toads with that spell. Which made it all the more interesting, and upsetting, when nothing happened. The blood-red men just stood where they were, entirely unaffected. Molly slowly lowered her hand.

"They must be protected," I said.

"No!" said Molly. "You think?"

"Don't get ratty with me," I said. "It's not my fault your spell didn't work."

"Might be," said Molly. "You don't know."

"Look, let's go straight to the ultra-violence," I said. "That'll cheer you up. I'm going in. You watch my back."

"You got it," said Molly.

I surged forward with all the strength and speed my armour could provide, and the blood-red men came to meet me. There was a terrible vicious energy in their movements. I punched the first one in the head so hard I heard his neck break, but his masked face just seemed to soak up the punch, and he didn't fall. In fact, I heard his neck bones crack and creak as they repaired themselves. So I kicked his feet out from under him, let him fall to the floor, and just walked right over him to get to the next target.

I lashed about with spiked golden fists, and bones broke and shattered under my armoured strength. I punched in heads, punched out hearts, grabbed arms and shoulders and crushed them with my terrible hands, and not one of the blood-red men cried out, or made a single sound of pain or shock. I hit them hard, sending them flying this way and that, but they just kept coming, pressing silently forward, trying to overwhelm me and drag me down through sheer force and weight of numbers. I couldn't seem to hurt or damage any of them, no matter how hard I tried. I knocked them down and they just got up again. I broke them, and they put themselves back together. They swarmed all over me, hitting me from every direction at once, clinging heavily to my arms and legs.

It was like fighting in some awful nightmare, where nothing you do seems to have any effect and there's no end to the silent, faceless enemy.

I grabbed hold of the ones clinging to me, pulled them loose one at a time, and threw them away. They slammed into tables and chairs and partitions, but they always got up again. I grabbed one, picked him up bodily by the ankles and used him as a flail, swinging him round and round, smashing into the others. I had some vague idea his body might be able to affect those like him. But although I heard his bones break, and theirs, as I used him as a living club ... when I finally dropped him to the floor neither he nor his targets had any problem putting themselves back together again.

I took hold of a red-masked face with both golden hands, and ripped the head right off. No blood erupted from the ragged neck, and the fierce eyes behind the mask still glared at me mockingly. I threw the head away, and its body went lurching after it, arms outstretched. I felt like laughing hysterically. You can't see things like that, such brutal disregard and contempt for all natural laws, without losing some self-control. But when in doubt ... If your tactics aren't working, change your tactics.

The Sarjeant-at-Arms taught me that.

So I grabbed hold of the nearest blood-red man, and hurled him at the nearest window. The thick glass shattered and the body went flailing through, into the cold outdoors, to be left behind as the train roared on. One less enemy to fight . . . is one less enemy to fight. Freezing-cold air blasted in through the shattered wooden frame, so cold I could feel some of it even through my armour. Interestingly, I could see breath steaming on the carriage air, seeping out from behind the blood-red masks. Which suggested my attackers were still sort of human after all. I grabbed another one and threw him out the window too.

The blood-red men pressed forward, and I struck them down, hauled them off me, and threw them out the broken window. I whittled the crowd down to less than a dozen, and suddenly a whole new crowd of blood-red men came charging through the open doorway, as though summoned by some unheard call. More and more of them, forcing their way into the restaurant car, squeezing through the narrow doorway, determined to get at me. All of them dressed in the same crimson leathers and full face masks, all of them looking exactly the same and packed full of the same endless energy. They never said a word and they never made a sound. I counted thirty of them before I lost track, with still more crowding in through the doorway.

All the time I was fighting I could hear Molly behind me, chanting Words of Power. Her magics spat and crackled on the air as they fought to get some hold on the blood-red men's impervious bodies. Half a dozen of them suddenly burst into flames. They didn't seem to care, and it didn't slow their attack. Their burning leathers gave off an awful stench, but the jumping flames didn't seem to affect the flesh beneath. The blood-red men fought on, even as they burned, their flames setting light to tables and chairs and hanging curtains as the train's motion sent them lurching this way and that. Soon both sides of the carriage were on fire at that end, flames leaping up eagerly. A dark smoke drifted down the carriage, whipped up by the cold air still blasting in through the smashed window.

The blood-red men kept pressing forward, through the smoke and flames, while more and more of them plunged through the open doorway.

I kept hitting them, and they kept getting up again. I hit them with punches that would have demolished a house, but the damage just wouldn't take. They were all superhumanly strong, and inhumanly resistant to punishment. If I hadn't had my armour, they would have taken me down easily; as it was, all it could do was keep me in the game. They weren't strong enough to hurt me through my armour, but the sheer overpowering weight of their numbers drove me back, step by step. All the way down the restaurant car, with Molly forced to back up behind me, still lobbing the odd nasty spell over my shoulder, like occult grenades. They didn't do any lasting damage, but they did slow the enemy down. The blood-red men never said a word as they pressed forward, their unblinking gaze fixed always on me.

I kept grabbing individual attackers when I could, and throwing them out the window, but they were arriving faster than I could get rid of them. I hauled a table out of its setting and forced it into place across the aisle before me, then followed it with several more. Trying to set up a barricade. The blood-red men set their hands on the tables and tore the heavy wood apart like it was paper. They threw the pieces aside and came after me again. And I was getting tired. The armour makes me strong and fast, but it still relies on me to operate it. I grabbed hold of the nearest blood-red man and tried to tear his scarlet mask away, so I could see the face beneath. But there was no gap between mask and skin, as though they were sealed or fused together.

"Rip the mask off!" Molly yelled behind me.

"I don't think it is a mask," I said. "I think . . . it's his face."

"Rip it off anyway!"

And then we were interrupted by the sound of approaching feet behind us. I threw the blood-red man away and glanced quickly back over my shoulder, just in time to see a dozen or so train security guards come running in through the rear door. They wore the same black uniforms, but this time they were armed with all kinds of heavy-duty weaponry. Molly and I jumped back out of the way, to opposite sides of the aisle, and the security men opened up with everything they had, shooting at everyone in front of them.

They advanced steadily, blasting away at the blood-red men . . . who just stood their ground, soaking up the bullets as though they were nothing. They didn't flinch and they didn't blink, and they didn't fall back one single step. The noise of so many guns firing at once was deafening in the enclosed space. An occasional stray bullet hit my armour, which obligingly swallowed it up. I glanced across at Molly, but she was already hiding under a table. The security guards kept on firing, yelling half-incoherent obscenities at each other in military Russian, their eyes wide and shocked at what they were seeing.

Chests and heads exploded under the impact of heavy ammunition, only to repair themselves in moments, like film running backwards. And step by step, the blood-red men forced themselves forward, into the heat of the attack, against the terrible pressure of massed gunfire, until they were close enough to lay hands on the security guards. They tore the men apart, limb from limb, ripping off heads with horrid ease and throwing them away. The guards died quickly, smoking guns falling uselessly from their dead hands. The blood-red men didn't even bother to pick them up. Blood sprayed up to stain the carriage ceiling, then fell back in heavy crimson drops. More blood splashed across the fixtures and fittings, and ran in thick rivulets along the polished wooden floor. Until nothing was left of the security guards but a bloody mess in the aisle that the blood-red men kicked their way through as they came on.

Molly and I had taken the opportunity to fall back to the rear door. I looked down the length of the carriage, at the army of blood-red men striding through the debris of dead guards, with flames and smoke at their backs as fire consumed the whole back half of the restaurant car. They were still coming for me, relentless and implacable, like demons out of Hell.

"Well," said Molly, just a bit breathlessly, "I think we know now just who it was killed all those people at the Department of Uncanny. Men who can't be stopped, with inhuman brute strength, who don't use weapons ... Fits the bill, don't you think?"

"Undoubtedly," I said. "They killed all those people, looking for the Lazarus Stone. And they killed my grandfather. No mercy for these bastards, Molly."

"I have no problem with the sentiment," said Molly, "But I have to say ... I really don't see how we can stop people who won't stay dead when you kill them!"

"The ones I threw out the window didn't come back," I said. "So let's concentrate on the one tactic we know works. I mean, they've got to run out of numbers eventually. Haven't they?"

"Do you want the truth, or a comforting lie?" said Molly.

"Convince me," I said.

"This is a great idea!" said Molly. "I love it!"

We strode forward, laid hands on the first blood-red men we came to, and went to work. They had strength, but we had the element of surprise. I had my armour, and Molly had her magical protections. We picked the blood-red men up and tossed them out the carriage windows, one after the other. Half a dozen of them went flailing through the air, and out into the Siberian winter, before they even knew what was happening. But after that the blood-red men stuck close together, making it harder for us. And even as we thinned out the ranks, more and more of them came charging through that open doorway, appearing out of the smoke and flames as fresh reinforcements.

There had to be a dimensional Door back there somewhere. It was the only answer that made sense.

It was getting harder to see what I was doing. Half the carriage was on fire, with flames sweeping forward in sudden rushes, while thick black smoke hung heavily on the air. Molly's face was flushed, and wet with sweat, I hoped just from the growing heat. The blood-red men kept throwing themselves forward, clinging stubbornly to my arms and shoulders, trying to drag me down by sheer force. I straightened my legs and stiffened my back, and would not fall. Molly was forced back behind me again, using me as a shield. I crushed skulls with my golden fists, and threw men away, but they just swarmed all over me with nightmare tenacity. More of them had caught on fire from the surroundings, but it didn't slow them down.

We had to retreat; we had no choice. There were just too many of them, filling their end of the carriage, and forcing their way forward as more appeared. I backed away, step by step, with Molly behind me, until we slammed up against the rear door. I yelled for her to open the door, and then we both backed quickly through it. I slammed the door in the face of the blood-red men, and crushed the lock with my golden hand. Molly worked a quick spell to fuse the wood of the door with its surrounding frame. And then we both backed away some more. The door bucked and shuddered, and then tore apart as the blood-red men smashed right through it.

The other passengers, who'd thought they were safe from the madness, were shouting and screaming, running down the aisle to the far door and the next carriage on. Others retreated into the separate compartments, pulled the shades down, and locked the doors. Like that would help. One man stood his ground in the aisle, defiantly pointing a gun at the blood-red men coming through the broken door. His hand was shaking as he opened fire, and he barely missed Molly and me as we squeezed quickly past him. He soon ran out of bullets, but instead of doing the sensible thing and running with the rest, he just stood there and fumbled in his pockets for more ammunition. I grabbed at his arm to haul him along with me, but he just jerked his arm free and went back to his reloading. Molly was some way down the aisle, yelling to me, so I left him to it.

I caught up with Molly at the far end of the carriage. I hauled the door open and Molly darted through. I looked back just in time to see the blood-red men fall on the man who wouldn't run. They surged forward, into the face of his bullets, uncaring and unaffected, even as he fired into them at point-blank range. They pulled him down and trampled him underfoot, and moved on. He didn't scream for long. The blood-red men smashed in all the doors of the compartments they passed, and killed everyone they found. Again, the screams didn't last long.

I retreated through the door, and locked it. There was nothing else I could do. I hurried down the new aisle with Molly at my side, and we soon caught up with the retreating passengers, packed so tight now that they filled the aisle and blocked the way to the next door. They shoved and fought each other blindly, in their need to get away. The blood-red men burst in the door and fell into the new carriage, bringing with them the last dying screams of slaughtered men and women, and the thick coppery smell of freshly spilled blood.

"I don't think they intend to leave any witnesses," I said to Molly. "I can't let this go on. These people are dying because of us. Innocent bystanders. Just by being here, we're endangering these people."

"Well, what do you suggest?" Molly said roughly, her flushed face dripping with sweat. She was so exhausted she could barely hold herself up.

"I suggest we save as many as we can," I said. "We can't win this fight. There are too many attackers, and they won't stay dead. Which is cheating, in my book. So, if we're going to protect the other passengers, we need to lead the enemy away from them."

I turned to the door in the carriage wall at my left, and kicked it open. My armoured boot sent the door flying out of its frame, and it went bouncing down the track behind us. Through the open gap, the featureless snow-covered landscape rushed by. I stuck my head out the gap, took a good look around, and then looked back at Molly.

"I saw we take the fight upstairs. Care to follow me up?"

"Oh hell," said Molly. "Why not?"

I stepped out into the blasting wind, swung around, and clambered up the side of the heavily rocking carriage. The train's jolting motions did their best to throw me off, but I grew sharp golden spurs on the palms of my gloves, and sank them deep into the wood of the carriage wall. It took me only a few moments to climb up onto the roof, stand up, and look around me. My armour kept me balanced as I took in the view. Snow and more snow, under an empty blue-grey sky. One of the back carriages was now completely consumed by fire, burning fiercely. Thick black smoke billowed up, snapped back in long dark threads by the racing wind. The flames were already spreading to the carriages on either side. Apparently sprinkler systems hadn't been thought traditional.

Molly flew up to join me on the roof, soaring elegantly through the air. She landed hard beside me, as the last of her levitation magic ran out. She grabbed one of my arms to steady herself, and then quickly let go. She was shuddering hard in the bitter cold and the blasting wind. She was trying to maintain a layer of warmth around her, but it was already breaking down. Her magics were running out. But she wouldn't say anything, so I couldn't. It wasn't as though there was anything I could do. Except stand between her and the worst of the blasting air, as a windbreak. She nodded briefly, appreciatively, but she was still shivering.

The blood-red men came climbing up both sides of the carriage, hauling themselves up by brute strength,

quickly and without grace, punching holes in the outer
walls to make climbing aids. Apparently untroubled by
the rocking motion of the train, or the freezing wind.
More of them burst out through the carriage windows,
and out the doors at both ends. I moved quickly back
and forth, kicking their hands away as they reached the
roof, but there were just too many of them, and I couldn't
be everywhere at once. Molly tried to blast them away
with sudden bursts of storm wind, but with her magics
failing, her winds were quickly blown away and dispersed by the existing wind. All too soon there were
thirty, forty blood-red men assembled on top of the carriage roof, with still more climbing up the sides.

I could have gone to meet them, knocked them down
and kicked them off the speeding train, but I couldn't see
the point. Head-to-head confrontation didn't work. So I
turned to Molly.

"Run," I said.

"What?" said Molly. "Where?"

"Away from them!" I said.

I took her by the hand, and we sprinted down the long
metal roof. The blood-red men came running after us. We
reached the end of the carriage worryingly quickly, and
jumped the gap to the next carriage. I landed hard, still
holding on to Molly, and we ran on. My armoured feet
left heavy dents in the metal. Molly was breathing loud
and strenuously at my side, but she kept up. She shot me
a wide grin, and a laugh that was immediately torn away
by the rushing wind. We ran on and on, until we ran out
of carriages, and all that remained was the great steam
engine itself and its massive bunker half full of coal.

The noise from the engine was deafening, and great
blasts of blistering-hot steam shot past us, thick with fly-

ing cinders. Molly had to move quickly to stand behind me, one hand raised to keep the cinders out of her eyes. There was nowhere left for us to go, and the blood-red men were already charging down the last carriage roof towards us.

And, just like that, suddenly I could feel the presence of the Gateway. Off in the distance, not far ahead. A certain knowledge, like the pointing of a compass needle. Not a very pleasant feeling, knowledge of something that shouldn't exist, that had no right to exist, in the natural world. Like a vicious itch I couldn't scratch.

"Can you feel that?" shouted Molly, over the roar of the engine.

"Hell yes!" I said. "The train's finally brought us within the Gate's field of influence!"

"So what are we going to do?" said Molly. "We can't stay on the train much longer, in case it carries us past the Gateway. Come on, Eddie, you must have a plan. You always have a plan, even if it's usually a really bad one."

"I thought you liked my plans," I said.

"I promise I will love the arse off this plan, whatever it is, as long as it means we don't have to fight the blood-red men any more! They are seriously wearing me out."

"Okay," I said. "Jump."

Molly looked over the side of the jolting railway carriage, at the endless snowy plain rushing past us at speed. And then she looked back at me.

"Are you crazy?"

"We're a long way from where I'd hoped to be," I said. "But it feels like we're in walking distance of the Gateway. You can feel that, can't you?"

Molly nodded reluctantly. "Like dead cockroaches

crawling all over my skin. Unnatural bloody thing. You really want to do this, Eddie?"

"Not as such, no. Do you have a better idea?"

"No, but . . ."

"The snow will break our fall."

"All I'm hearing is the word *break*. It's all right for you—you've got your armour."

"You can fly down."

"I haven't got enough magic left to fly!"

"Some days, things wouldn't go right if you paid them," I said. "Please accept my apologies in advance."

I picked her up in my arms, cradled her against my armoured chest, ignored her outraged cries, and jumped off the edge of the speeding carriage. We seemed to hang on the air for a long moment as the train shot past, carrying the blood-red men with it. And then the snow leaped up to meet us. We hit hard, the sheer weight of my armour driving me into the snowy bank like a nail into wood. My legs absorbed most of the impact, though Molly shook and shuddered in my arms. She'd sworn harshly all the way down, but the jolt of our sudden stop shut her up. I ended up sunk in snow almost to my waist, still holding Molly tightly. The moment she got her breath back she demanded I put her down, in a strained and rather dangerous tone. So I lowered her carefully onto the snowy bank.

She sank only a foot or so into the snow, but it was enough to make her cry out in shock at the bitter cold. I hauled myself up out of the hole I'd made, and stood beside her. We watched the Trans-Siberian Express race off into the distance, trailing flame and smoke. None of the blood-red men had jumped off the train to come after us. They were all standing unnaturally still, on top of the carriage, looking back at us.

The train quickly disappeared into the distance. I somehow doubted the blood-red men would still be aboard when what was left of the burning train pulled into its next station stop. It was all very quiet now, with the train gone. The freezing air was still, without even a breath of wind. Not a sound to be heard anywhere, and not a movement to be seen.

"Why didn't they come after us?" said Molly, hugging herself tightly to try to stop shaking from the cold. "Not that I'm complaining, you understand . . ."

"Maybe they're not equipped to survive in the wild," I said. "Or maybe their orders didn't cover leaving the train."

"Maybe they know something about this place that we don't," said Molly darkly.

"Wouldn't surprise me in the least," I said, looking around. "Desolate bloody location."

"I'll bet there are wolves," said Molly.

The more I looked, the more appallingly empty and deserted the snowy landscape seemed. Like a desert, covered with the perfect disguise. No trees or shrubs anywhere, no landmarks, nothing that stood out against the gently rising and falling snow, stretching off in all directions as far as I could see. And I could see pretty damned far through my mask. The sky was perfectly clear, just a pale blue, pale grey, cloudless cover. The sunlight was fierce and unrelenting, but gave no warmth at all. I could see Molly trying to summon her protections, to keep out the cold, but they were little more than a faint shimmer in the air around her. I considered armouring down, to join her, and then quickly pushed the thought aside. One of us had to be properly insulated from this appalling environment if we were to keep moving.

"How long do the days last up here?" Molly said suddenly.

"I don't know," I said. "It's not like my armour comes with built-in Google. Or even a compass. Since we're in Siberia . . . that means we're inside the Arctic Circle. Daylight could last for ages. Or, the sun could just go down and not come up again for weeks. I suggest we think positive, and get a move on."

Molly started to say something, and then stopped. Her head snapped around, to stare out across the snowy wastes. We both stood very still, and listened. And from off in the distance came the howling of wolves. A whole lot of wolves.

"Told you," said Molly.

"What the hell are wolves doing all the way out here, in this wilderness?" I said.

"Looking for food, probably," said Molly. "Let them come. I am so cold I'm fully prepared to rip the fur right off a wolf and wrap myself up in it."

I stared off in the direction of the Gateway, concentrating my Sight through my mask. I could feel the presence of the Gate stronger than ever, peering back at me. And suddenly I could See it — a great light, fierce and brilliant, blasting up into the sky like a spotlight, right on the edge of the far horizon. Like a beacon, calling us on.

"We're a lot closer to the Gate than I thought," I said. "Easy walking distance. Can you See it?"

Molly looked where I was pointing, and then scowled

and shook her head. "My magics are all but flatlined. I used them all up, fighting on the train. I can't even feel the Gate's presence any more. Though that's no great loss. Made my skin crawl. Let's get moving, Eddie. I am freezing my tits off just standing here."

"How much longer will what's left of your protections last?" I said carefully.

"Long enough. Let's go!"

I thought about Ultima Thule, the winter of the world, on the other side of the Gateway, where the conditions were bound to be so much worse . . . but I didn't say anything. I wouldn't be saying anything Molly didn't already know.

We started off through the thick snow. I went first, slamming through the snow with my armour, sending it flying to either side. I ended up blasting out a trench for Molly to trudge along in, behind me. It saved time, and made life easier for her. The sheer weight of the packed snow fought against me, but it was no match for my armour. Molly slogged along, not complaining at all, which worried me. That wasn't like her. When I finally glanced back over my shoulder, there wasn't a trace of her protections showing. She was shivering and shuddering, arms folded tightly to preserve what warmth she had, her mouth clamped shut to keep her teeth from chattering. Her breath leaked out in short bursts, steaming on the cold air, and there wasn't a trace of colour left in her face.

"I've been thinking about the blood-red men," I said, to try to keep her mind off things. "The way they all looked the same, moved the same . . . I think they were clones."

"Could be homunculi," said Molly, forcing the words

out past her pale lips. Even half frozen, she still had to be contrary.

"No one makes those any more," I said. "Too time-consuming, too expensive, and you just can't get the proper ingredients these days. But it seems like every-one's into cloning now. I blame Dolly the sheep. She made it look easy, even though it wasn't. Why clone a sheep, anyway? It's not like there's a shortage . . . Why not clone a giant panda, or something else we're in dan-ger of losing?"

"If you're trying to keep up a cheerful chatter to take my mind off the desperate situation you landed us in, please stop," said Molly. "As for the blood-red men, I'm sure I sensed some kind of outside control, back on the train. A single will, working through all the blood-red men at once. Which could mean we have a single enemy after us."

"I suppose that helps," I said, smashing through a tall snowbank with one sweep of my golden arm. Small pieces of snow pattered down all around. "A single en-emy, who can command a murderous army of things that don't know how to die. I don't suppose you have any idea who that might be?"

"Someone who wants the Lazarus Stone," said Molly. "Damn, my hands are screaming at me . . . Whoever it was, they're responsible for killing the Regent and his people. No wonder the place was such a mess. A whole army of unstoppable, inhumanly strong killers . . . The poor bastards at Uncanny never stood a chance."

"Not after a traitor opened the door for them," I said. "Somebody planned all this . . . Almost certainly the Voice who took my parents. But who? Why?"

"There you go again," Molly said grimly. "Asking

questions you know I don't have any answers for. Once upon a time, when it came to enemies with good reason to want us dead, I could have provided you with a really long list . . . But it seems to me that we wiped most of them out, these last few years."

"We have been busy," I said, checking the distance still to go, to the Gateway. The bright pulsing pillar of light on the horizon didn't seem any closer. "Seems to me the only way to identify our enemy is to discover as much as we can about the Lazarus Stone. That's the driving force behind everything that's happening. We need to know what it really is, what it really does . . . And maybe that will tell us why the Voice wants it so badly."

"A Stone that can snatch people out of Time, before History says they're dead," said Molly. Her voice was growing quieter, the words less distinct as her lips grew numb. "If you could do that, Eddie, if you could save someone, who would you choose?"

"My uncle James," I said immediately. "He was like a father to me for so many years, after my parents disappeared. He did so much for me, and did his best to protect me from the worst sides of my family."

"He would have killed you, at the end," said Molly. "We had to kill him."

"I know," I said. "He had to die. For the family to survive. But I do miss him. How about you, Molly? Who would you bring back?"

Before she could answer, we were interrupted. A great pack of wolves came running across the snow towards us. They moved at incredible speed, seeming to barely touch the surface of the snow. As though their sheer speed kept them from sinking in. Huge animals, twice the size of the average dog, long and lean with pale grey fur and mouths dropped open to reveal large, jagged teeth. They ran in silence, dozens of them, in perfect formation. Their eyes glowed red, fixed on Molly and me.

The pack split suddenly in two as it drew nearer, the wolves swinging out and around us, closing in from all sides, until they were running in a great circle around us. Molly and I moved to stand back to back. The wolves kept moving, speeding across the snow, endlessly circling. Watching us with unblinking crimson eyes, searching for some sign of weakness.

"They look . . . hungry," I said.

"Much as I hate to admit it," said Molly, "I am seriously low on magic, and running on fumes. I have a few useful items about my person, but that's pretty much it. And there are an awful lot of them . . ."

"Maybe if I kill a few, the others will get the message and leave us alone," I said.

"Worth a try," said Molly.

"Okay," I said. "Leave this to me . . ."

"Hell with that!" Molly said immediately. "I can handle a few wolves!"

"Wouldn't doubt it for a minute," I said. "But it's not just a few wolves. And you need to hang on to your remaining magics. Never know when you might need them."

I was thinking of Ultima Thule, and I knew she was too. When she spoke again, her voice was worryingly quiet.

"It's nice you're still assuming we'll both get that far, Eddie. But those are really big, really vicious-looking wolves, and you're the only one with armour. I'm not feeling as . . . dangerous as I usually do. I'm just . . . tired."

I'd never heard her say that before. Never heard her sound like that before. A chill ran down my spine.

"It's just the cold getting to you," I said. "Stay put, while I go teach these wolves a few manners."

I charged forward through the packed snow, sending it flying in all directions. Every single wolf stopped dead in its tracks to look at me, but I was bearing down on the nearest wolf before it had time to do more than bare its nasty teeth at me. I grabbed it by the tail, jerked it up off the ground, and swung it round and round my head. It howled miserably as I put some muscle into it, until it was just a grey blur on the air. And then I let go of the tail, and the wolf flew off into the distance. It travelled quite a way before it finally crashed back to earth, burying itself in the snow. All the other wolves turned their heads to watch it fly and land and not move again, and then they all turned their shaggy grey heads back to look at me. They held themselves perfectly still, as though communing on some deep level, and then they all moved purposefully forward, heading straight for me.

"Now, you see?" I said, my voice hard and flat on the quiet. "Any rational creature would have taken the hint. It's no wonder you guys are nearly extinct."

Half a dozen wolves surged forward, crossing the intervening snow with incredible speed. I stood my ground, waiting. They all hit me at once, each going for a different target. Their jaws snapped closed on arms and wrists, legs and groin, and one went straight for my throat. Their teeth clattered harmlessly against my armour, and they all fell back, yelping in a hurt and confused sort of way. I smashed their skulls, one at a time in swift succession, with brutal efficiency. I wasn't in the mood to mess around. Molly needed me.

More wolves hit me, from behind this time, scrambling all over me as they tried to force a way through my armour with their teeth and claws. I grabbed them, one at a time, snapped their necks, and threw the limp bodies away from me. Dead wolves lay broken in the snow all around. And still the rest of the pack held their ground, watching me with cold, implacable crimson eyes.

Two wolves shot in from the side, ignoring me and going straight for Molly. She threw something at them. There was a sudden explosion, and both wolves were blown apart. Bits of bloody meat and smouldering fur rained down across the snow, staining it in ugly scarlet Rorschach blots. Molly grinned at me.

"Incendiaries are our friends. Never leave home without them."

The wolf pack fell back on two sides, presenting us with an opening in the circle, a way out. I went back to Molly and offered her my hand, pulling her up out of the trench I'd made. I led the way slowly forward, heading for the opening, looking quickly back and forth, ready for any movement by the wolves. Molly trudged along through the snow, sticking close to me. The wolves let us pass, but we'd hardly made a dozen paces beyond the circle before they came stalking after us. Moving slowly, silently, maintaining a respectful distance but still following.

"They're not giving up," I said quietly to Molly. "Why aren't they giving up?"

"Why do you keep asking me questions you know I don't know the answers to?" said Molly.

"Just to annoy you," I said.

"Then it's working. They must be really hungry . . . Wait a minute—can you feel something?"

"Like what?"

"Hold up a moment."

We both stopped and looked around us. I couldn't see a damned thing anywhere in the whole snowy landscape, apart from the wolves behind us and the Gateway up ahead. But the wolves all had their heads up, looking nervously about them, ignoring Molly and me. They looked disturbed, and frightened, making darting little runs this way and that, as though not sure where to go for the best.

"Come on, you have to feel that!" said Molly. "Vibrations, deep in the ground, under the snow."

"Yes . . . ," I said. "Like an underground train . . . But there's no subway system all the way out here. Is there?"

"There you go with the questions again," said Molly. "The vibrations are getting stronger! Whatever's down below, it must be pretty damned big. And heading straight for us."

"You know," I said, "for a deserted Siberian tundra, there's a hell of a lot going on here."

The ground exploded before us, snow and earth and rocks blasting up into the air and falling back again. The wolves scattered and ran, as something huge and nasty burst up out of the broken earth to tower over us. Twenty feet tall and still rising, covered in dark brown scales, a living column four to five feet in diameter, a terrible creature from the depths of the earth, still rising up and up into the air before us. The great blunt head unfolded suddenly, blossoming like some fleshy flower, revealing flapping pink petals of dark-veined flesh, surrounding great circular jaws packed with teeth, swirling round and round like a meat grinder.

The creature made an insanely loud sound, like some awful factory siren in Hell. The thing had no eyes, or any other sensory organs, but it was obvious it could sense its prey. The great flowering head slammed down, the body bending in an arch, and the grinding teeth fell upon a running wolf, picking it off with flawless accuracy. The creature snapped up the wolf and swallowed it whole as it straightened up again, leaving just a few spatters of blood on the snow where the wolf had been, its paw-prints just suddenly stopping.

"What the hell is that thing?" said Molly.

"Siberian Death Wurm!" I said. "I thought they were extinct!"

"Has anyone told it that?" said Molly.

The ground shook heavily, and Molly and I had to grab each other to keep our feet. The earth exploded again and again, snow and dirt flying into the air, as more and more of the awful creatures erupted from below. Until we were surrounded by ten of the huge, openmouthed Wurms, their heads swaying high in the air above us. The wolves were running in all directions now, running hard for their lives, but the Wurms just slammed their heads down and picked the wolves off neatly, one by one. Swallowing them whole, to be ripped apart by the swirling, grinding teeth, until there were no wolves left at all. The Wurms swayed around us like a living forest of tall scaly columns, sending their deafening screams out to each other. They sounded horribly triumphant.

"Run," I said to Molly.

"Which way?" said Molly. "The bloody things are everywhere!"

"Head for the Gateway," I said. "Make for the light."

"What bloody light?" said Molly. "I don't see it anywhere!"

"Oh, I just know I am going to regret this later," I said.

I grabbed Molly and threw her over my shoulder, and

then sprinted for the horizon, forcing my way through the thick snow by brute force. I ran hard, accelerating to more than human speed, snow flying in all directions as I ploughed right through the packed banks, refusing to let them slow me down. Molly cursed me shakily, in between breaths forced out of her by my lurching progress.

"Put me down! Now!"

"Oh, shut up," I said. "I am saving your life!"

"This . . . is so undignified . . ."

"I'm faster than you are."

"Not fast enough. We're not out of them yet."

"Back-seat driver."

I ran between the last two towering Wurms, dodging back and forth as the great flowering heads came crashing down. They didn't even come close, but just the terrible impacts were enough to throw me off my feet for a moment. I kept going, not looking back. I could hear Molly breathing hard, as the continual impacts slammed the breath out of her, but she didn't say a word. When I was some distance away, and felt safe enough to stop, I let her down. I had to hold on to her for a moment, steadying her till she got her breath back. Then she pushed me away, and glared at me.

"We will have words about this, later."

"Understood," I said.

She looked about her. "I still don't see this damned light of yours. I can feel the Gate's presence, though. We're not far from it, are we?"

"Almost there," I said. "Ten, twenty feet, and we are out of here."

The ground ripped open between us and the Gate, sending me staggering backwards as a Siberian Death Wurm blasted up out of the earth. A shower of snow hit

Molly hard, throwing her to the ground. More snow splattered against my armour, and fell away. Molly scrambled back to her feet, plucked a charm off her ankle bracelet, and threw it at the Wurm's towering body. It slammed against the scales, exploding in fierce violet flames, and the Wurm didn't even notice it. The flames died quickly away, unable to get a hold. Molly looked at her charm bracelet as though it had betrayed her, and then looked at me.

"That's it!" she said. "I'm out! I haven't anything left that could even touch that thing!"

She was shaking and shuddering harder than ever, no longer protected from the awful cold by any of her magics. I looked back the way we'd come. The other Wurms were plunging down into the snow, throwing themselves back into the ground and burrowing towards us. I could feel the vibrations through my golden boots. I looked at the bright spotlight of the Gateway, stabbing up into the sky. Easy running distance, once we were past the Wurm before us. I didn't think it could sense us as long as we stood still, but the moment we started running . . . it would know. But we couldn't stay where we were for long. The other Wurms were coming.

"Molly," I said steadily, "I need a distraction. Something to hold the Wurm's attention, just for a few moments."

"Got you," said Molly, forcing the words out through chattering teeth. "I run for the Gate, it goes after me, and you take it out when it isn't looking."

"That's the idea," I said. "Trust me?"

"Forever," said Molly.

"Forever and a day," I said.

She ran for the Gate, plunging through the deep snow

as fast as she could. The Wurm's head whipped around, attracted by the movement, and the huge head came slamming down, its wide-petaled mouth stretching out to take her. I ran forward and threw myself at the creature as it came within reach. I hit the neck just below the head, hard, and the sheer impact of my armour, moving at speed, forced the head aside so that it missed Molly by several feet. The head surged back up into the air, and I rode along with it, my golden fingers plunged deep into its flesh. My legs dangled, until I grew spurs in my golden boots and plunged them into the scaly body.

The Wurm reared up to its full height while I clambered up the last of its neck until I was right below the mouth. The circles of grinding teeth whirled round and round, unable to reach me. I pulled one hand back and then thrust it deep into the flesh right in the gaping mouth, as hard as I could. My fist sank in deep, probing for the brain, until my arm was in all the way to the elbow. The Wurm convulsed, shaking its great head back and forth, trying to throw me off. I yanked my hand out, and dark purple blood spurted, steaming on the chilly air. The head whipped back and forth, and I hit it again, with all my armour's strength behind it. This time my arm sank in almost up to my shoulder.

The long, scaly body shuddered down all of its length, and then suddenly went limp. I'd found the brain at last. The head crashed down as the body collapsed, and I rode it all the way to the snow-covered ground, waving my free arm and whooping wildly. The snow came flying up to meet us, and I jumped free at the last moment. The ground shook as the Wurm measured its length on the earth, and snow jumped up into the air all around it. The Wurm just lay there, shuddering and twitching its whole length, the great grinding teeth slowing to a halt. I dug myself out of the hole I'd made in the snow, and strode back to join Molly.

"Show-off," she said. But she couldn't keep from grinning.

"Worms should know their place," I said.

"You want to tell that to the ones still heading our way?"

"What are they burrowing through, exactly?" I said. "The snow, the earth, the rock beneath?"

"If we hang around here long enough, you can ask them," said Molly.

"Good point," I said. "Follow me."

I led her the last few feet to the Gateway. Up close, it was just a light shining up into the sky, from no obvious source. Molly still couldn't see it, but she could feel it. She put her hands out to the light, as though to warm them.

"I can feel the power it's generating," she said. "Nasty, crawling sensation. Like sticking your hands into a dead body that isn't dead enough. How do we open the Gate?"

"I don't think it's closed," I said. "No one made this, it's a . . . phenomenon. A crack in the world. Like a geyser . . . I think we just walk through it. Ultima Thule should be on the other side."

"Should?" said Molly. "Really not liking the *should*. Something like this, we need to be sure."

"We can't stay here," I said. "Stuck in the middle of the Siberian wilderness, with a whole bunch of Death Wurms coming straight for us. There isn't anywhere else for us to go, Molly."

"You're right," said Molly. "After you."

I had to smile. "Whatever happened to *ladies first*?"

"Do I look crazy?" said Molly.

I looked at her as she shivered violently in the cold, and a hand tightened round my heart. "Molly . . . this is just the cold of the natural world. I don't know if you can survive the unnatural cold of Ultima Thule without your protections."

"You'll find a way to protect me," said Molly, meeting my gaze steadily. "I trust you, remember? I trust you to find a way to keep me alive in Ultima Thule. Don't let me down, Eddie."

"Never," I said.

The Siberian Death Wurms were almost upon us. I took my Molly by the hand, and led her into the light and out of this world.

Into Ultima Thule.

CHAPTER NINE

So Many Lovers, So Little Love

The cold hit Molly like a hammer, driving her to her knees. She cried out once, despite herself, an awful sound of shock and pain, and then she couldn't get her breath back. All the colour was forced out of her face in a moment, and her mouth and eyes stretched painfully wide. I knelt down beside her and took her in my arms, but she was shaking and shuddering so much I could barely hang on to her. A terrible cold wind buffeted us this way and that. I wrapped myself around Molly as best I could, trying to protect her from the cold and the wind with my body and my armour. She clung to me desperately, making horrible straining sounds as she fought for breath.

I couldn't help her at all.

There was no snow or ice, just black and grey rock, in a world more bleak and bare than anything I had ever seen before. I could feel the cold even through my armour. Molly had no magics left, no shields or protections. She was only human, in a place not meant for anything human to live. She collapsed against me. I called out to her, but she couldn't hear me. She was dying of the savage cold, in the place I'd brought her to.

I looked desperately around for help or inspiration, or just something that might serve as shelter, but there was nothing. We'd appeared some way down a narrow valley set between two great mountains thrusting up into a purple sky. No sign of people or civilisation anywhere. The valley channelled the raging wind, so that it howled and shrieked as it hit us like a battering ram, again and again. There wasn't a cave or a crevice, an overhang or windbreak. Nowhere I could take Molly to hide and protect her.

I had to do something; either I came up with some way to save her, in the next few moments, or I could watch her die. And all I had was . . . my armour. I seized on the idea. The armour protected me; there had to be a way it could protect Molly too. The armour came from my torc. I called on it, and it came out to cover me. But what if it could cover more than just me? I had learned to reshape my armour, through willpower, so what if I could make it cover both of us at once? I concentrated, and the golden armour surged and rippled all over me . . . but it wasn't enough. Ethel had created the armour to cover just me. One torc, one Drood. I raised my head and called out.

"Ethel! Please! You made this armour; help me use it to save the woman I love! Please, Ethel, I need to do this! For her!"

And from a world away, her voice came to me, quiet but distinct.

Oh, all right. Just this once.

I concentrated again, and the golden armour leaped out from me, surging forward to cover Molly in a glistening golden wave ... before contracting suddenly to armour her from head to toe. Sealing her off from the killing cold. She stopped shaking immediately, and I heard her draw a great, ragged breath. We were two golden statues, clinging to each other. She raised her head to look at me, and two featureless golden masks reflected each other. But I could still feel her gaze. And I could hear her laughing. She let go of me, and I helped her to her feet. And we stood together, side by side in Ultima Thule. Two suits of strange matter armour, linked by two fused golden hands. We couldn't let go; that golden umbilical cord was all that sustained Molly's armour. But as long as we remained linked, nothing Ultima Thule could throw at us could hurt us.

"You see?" said Molly from behind her mask. "I knew you'd find a way to save me. You should learn to have more faith in yourself. I do. Damn! This feels good! I feel better than good—I feel great! I could get used to this ..."

"Don't," I said. "This is a strictly temporary solution, to get us to the Winter Palace. There's a reason why my family introduces strict training from a very early age. Wearing Drood armour can easily become ... addictive. We're trained to control our armour, so it doesn't control us."

"I can cope!" said Molly. "Oh, it feels so good to be warm again! Been so long I'd almost forgotten what it feels like ..." She looked around her, taking in the desolate landscape. "Miserable bloody location. Worse than Siberia. At least that had snow. This is Ultima Thule, is it? Looks like the end of the world."

"The final winter of the world," I said. "The end of everything. Look at the sun."

We both looked up. In a bruised and empty sky, the sun was just a dull red circle, hanging low above the mountaintops. It looked tired and worn out, a dying star for a dead world.

"The heat is going out of this place," I said. "I don't think this pocket dimension was made to last. Unless it was made by someone who liked feeling miserable. I think we're in the far future of the world, in the dying days, when Entropy is King."

"But why?" said Molly. "I mean, really, why? If you could create a whole pocket dimension, why settle for this? What purpose does it serve?"

"Presumably," I said, "it provides a proper setting for the Winter Palace."

Molly sniffed loudly. "I don't see it. Are you sure the Gateway brought us to the proper location?"

I pointed down the long, narrow valley, and there, right at the end, set between two great towering precipices, stood a single massive structure, half as large as the mountains around it. Made entirely out of gleaming ice, wide and vast and impossibly intricate, its long projections branched endlessly in all directions. Like a single massive snowflake, half buried in the cold cold ground. Shining and shimmering, blazing with its own fierce light. Unlike anything a human mind might conceive, it was overwhelming in its perfection. And yet there was something about it that made me think of an ancient fairy-tale castle. The Winter Palace of the Ice Queen, who made everyone love her, whether they wanted to or not. Who summoned men and women to her with her siren song, and made them love her until they died of it.

"The Lady Faire built that?" said Molly.

"Hardly," I said. "The Winter Palace has been around a lot longer than she has. No, she just rents it, on occasion. Like everyone else."

"Rents it from who?"

"Good question. If you ever find out, do let me know. Come on, let's get moving. The sooner we get safely inside, the better. I'm not sure how long even Drood armour can protect us from such an extreme environment."

"Why have a palace in a place like this?" said Molly, not unreasonably.

"I don't know," I said. "Probably to discourage unwanted visitors. All the properly invited guests are teleported in, arriving safely inside the Winter Palace without having to brave the cold." I looked carefully around me. "I'm not Seeing any security fields, or force shields, or any kinds of protection set in place around the palace . . . No hidden mines, no floating curses, not even the most basic sensor arrays, to let people know there's anyone out here . . . Perhaps they believe Ultima Thule is all the protection they need. And with anyone else, they'd probably be right. Come on, we have to find a way in, infiltrate the Lady Faire's Ball without being spotted, and get our hands on the Lazarus Stone. Lots to do, lots to do . . ."

"And how, precisely, are we going to do all that?" said Molly.

"Once we get inside the Winter Palace, separately," I said. "We'll be far too conspicuous together. I'm hoping the Lady Faire will have invited enough guests that we can just blend in, and disappear in the crowd. But we can't risk drawing undue attention to ourselves. Which means I can't use my armour in there, and you can't use your magics."

"Oh poo!" said Molly. "I was just getting used to this armour. And I can feel my magics rushing back! I think being inside your armour is speeding up the process wonderfully."

"Drood armour is designed to keep its wearer invisible from pretty much anything, under normal circumstances," I said. "But the Winter Palace is bound to be bristling with all kinds of specialized security measures, to protect the guests from outside threats. And probably, from each other . . . My torc should be able to hide itself, as long as I don't call on it, but if you even try to summon your magics, you can be sure they'll hit you with everything they've got. Suddenly and violently and all at once."

"All right!" said Molly. "We have to be sneaky. I get it! We go our own ways once we get inside, first one to grab the Stone signals the other, and then we both leg it back to the real world, at speed. Anyone would think I'd never done this before." She stopped, and looked around her. "You know, I still can't see the Gateway we came through."

"That's because it isn't there, here," I said. "It's a one-way Gate; it only exists on the other side. So we can't use it to get back. We'll have to break into the Winter Palace's teleport stream to get home again."

"Wonderful," said Molly. "More complications. And the more I look at the Winter Palace, the less I see anything that looks like an entrance. What if the only way in is by teleport?"

"Look, if breaking into the Winter Palace was easy, everybody would be doing it."

"Someone got out of the grumpy side of bed this morning. So what does the Lazarus Stone look like?

What are we actually looking for? An earring, or a stone big enough to club someone over the head with?"

"No idea," I said. "I never even heard about the bloody thing till today. Does make things a bit tricky, doesn't it? I suppose it's too much to hope that it'll be out on display somewhere, with a really big sign saying *This Is the Lazarus Stone; Please Don't Touch* . . . Hmmm. I think our best bet is to locate someone inside the Winter Palace who does know what the Stone looks like, and get them to take us straight to it. Though of course when I say *us* . . ."

"I get it! Really! Separate ways, no looking back. Like I need you cramping my style . . ."

We started down the long, narrow valley, still holding hands. I did consider creating some kind of umbilical cord, but our link seemed precarious enough already, without adding any further strains to it. I didn't want to push Ethel's gift too far. We strode on, leaning into the teeth of the roaring wind, fighting its vicious gusting flurries with our armoured strength. The ground was hard and unyielding under our feet, cracked open in jagged splits and wide crevices. Some we could step over; others we had to jump. And sometimes I looked down and thought I saw sullen red lava, bubbling away at the bottom of the deepest cracks.

Apart from the howling wind, there wasn't another sound to be heard. Nothing moved but us. Not a living thing anywhere, not even vegetation. Not even any rocks or pebbles, as though everything had been worn down, reduced to its barest essentials. My hands and feet were numb, despite my armour. Ultima Thule's cold was seeping in. Which was . . . disconcerting. I'd never known any conditions that could get through Drood armour before, no matter how harsh or severe the environment. Which led me to believe this wasn't any ordinary dimension. If it was the end of the world, Earth's final days, then perhaps this was a spiritual cold. The touch of Entropy itself.

No one really knows the limits of my family's armour, because we've never encountered them. But Time brings all things to an end.

"How sure are we that the Lady Faire's security people don't know about the Gateway we came through?" said Molly.

"Not sure at all," I said, glad of some conversation to take my mind off things. "But I think if they did know, or even suspect, they'd have put some kind of defence in place out here, to deal with whoever came through, the moment they arrived. Take them out while they were distracted by the cold. I prefer to believe that since the Gateway doesn't exist on this side, it can't be detected from here. Believe what makes you happy, that's what I always say."

And then we both stopped, as the ground fell sharply away before us, revealing two long rows of ice blocks, stretching away, facing each other. Each block was around seven feet tall and three wide, solid ice containing a human form. Men and women, frozen in place forever. Molly and I helped each other down the steep incline; and then we walked slowly down the central aisle between the ice blocks, looking closely at the figures frozen inside. Dead faces peered sightlessly out through the ice, their features preserved in emotions that would last an age, in this awful place. Shock and horror, mostly. Clawed hands scrabbled desperately at the inside of the ice, caught in one last attempt at escape before the ice closed in on them. Clothes and outfits, equipment and weapons, from a hundred different times and countries. And much good any of it had done them.

"Warnings," I said finally. "Made from those who came before us. *Turn back, intruder, while you still can.*"

"Except we can't," said Molly. "Not that we would, of course, but . . ."

"Yes," I said. "It would be nice to have the option."

"So we're not the first people to try to break into the Winter Palace from Outside," said Molly. "You think these people came here through the Gateway?"

"No way to ask them now," I said. "They didn't have the advantage of Drood armour, so here they are. Preserved, permanent scarecrows."

"Except we don't scare," said Molly. "Still, I have to say, leaving them here, like this . . . That's cold."

"Yes," I said. "It is. I don't know who these people were, or why they came here, but they deserved better than this. I will make someone pay for this."

"Of course you will, Eddie."

Molly squeezed my linking hand, and we strode on between the two long rows of ice blocks. After a while I stared straight ahead, so I wouldn't have to make eye contact. You can't keep feeling sorry for people; it wears you out. And I was having a hard enough time feeling confident as it was. I hate missions where there are too many unknowns, too many variables, and this whole case was nothing but.

We left the ice blocks behind and moved on down the valley, slipping and sliding on ground polished like glass by the endless wind. The Winter Palace loomed up before us, growing larger and more intricate the closer we got. Dazzlingly huge, breathtakingly detailed. The biggest snowflake in the world, in the last winter of the world. I finally stopped, to look it over carefully. Molly was all for pressing on, impatient to get started, but we were still linked by our joined hands and I wasn't going anywhere till I'd thought about it some more. Molly stood reluctantly beside me, bouncing up and down on the soles of her golden feet.

"I am not seeing any door, or opening, or entrance anywhere," I said. "And since all the properly invited guests appear *inside*, it may be that there is no way in from out here."

"I told you that!" said Molly. "I suppose . . . we could break in."

"We're trying to be sneaky, remember?"

"Why should there be any openings?" said Molly, in her most irritatingly reasonable tone of voice. "I mean, it's a snowflake! Which are famous for not having holes. However, now most of my magics have returned, thanks to this marvellous armour of yours, I can sense the teleport stream the guests arrive through. I think I can tap into it, even from this distance . . . and get us inside. With a bit of luck."

I looked at her. "How much luck?"

"Well . . . We would be jumping blind. I'm pretty sure I can arrange for us to materialise in an open space . . ."

"Hold it!" I said. "I've got a better idea! The Merlin Glass! That's our way in!"

"Why didn't you think of that before?" said Molly. "We could have used it back at the Gateway, and avoided this bloody walk!"

"I got distracted," I said.

"Ah," said Molly. "Of course you did."

I eased my free hand through my armoured side, and

reached for the hand mirror, but the damned thing avoided my grasp again, refusing to cooperate. Presumably because it didn't want to be exposed to the cold of Ultima Thule. I could understand that. I chased the Merlin Glass around my pocket for a while, just on general principles, and then gave up. I removed my empty hand, and Molly shook her head sadly.

"Not again . . ."

"Once this increasingly infuriating mission is over," I said, "I am going to have a very firm talk with the Merlin Glass. In fact, once everything's been sorted out, and I have reestablished communications with my family . . . I think I'll take the Glass down to the Armoury and let the lab assistants play with it. That should frighten it."

"Shall I try my teleport spell now?" Molly said sweetly.

"How accurate can you be, working blind?" I said. "We don't want to materialise inside the furniture. Something like that can be very hard to explain."

"Trust me," said Molly. "That hardly ever happens. I have an instinct for these things. If I tap into the existing teleport stream and follow that, we should be perfectly safe."

"Should?"

"Look, do you want the truth, or a comforting lie?"

"Guess."

"Everything's going to be fine!" said Molly.

We appeared inside a very small room. So small we were standing face-to-face, surrounded by all kinds of objects pressing in on us.

"We're inside a broom closet, aren't we?" I said.

"It was the best I could do!" said Molly. "It was the only enclosed space next to the teleport station."

"It's a broom closet!"

"I know! It was either this or the toilets!"

I scrabbled along the wall with my free hand, found the light switch, and turned it on. Flat yellow light from a bare hanging bulb illuminated a space just big enough to contain the two of us and assorted cleaning products. I suppose even a Winter Palace needs janitorial staff. I armoured down, and Molly appeared before me. She smiled at me brightly, gave my hand one last squeeze, and reached for the door. I stopped her quickly.

"Hold it," I said. "Better check out who's outside first. Might look a bit odd for the two of us to just walk out of a broom closet."

"Not at the Lady Faire's Ball," said Molly. "I'll bet there are all kinds of furtive assignations going on here, in all sorts of places."

"I'll go first," I said. "Remember, no magics."

"Bet I get to the Lazarus Stone before you do," said Molly.

"Yell if you do," I said. "And then I'll race you to the teleport station."

"What if the station's locked down?" said Molly. "I got us in here, but there's no guarantee I can get us back to the real world."

"One problem at a time," I said.

I squeezed past her, eased open the broom closet door, and peered cautiously through the gap. All kinds of people were hurrying past, but they all seemed intent on their own business, and didn't even glance at the broom closet. And after all, why should they? I looked back at Molly.

"Okay, I am out of here. Give me a minute, and then it's your turn. Try not to kill anyone you don't absolutely have to, there's a dear."

"Teach your grandmother to suck . . ."

I slipped out into the corridor and closed the door firmly behind me.

The interior of the Winter Palace could have been any first-class, extremely expensive and very elite hotel, anywhere in the world. Lots of wide-open space, richly polished wood, gleaming marble, and deep-pile carpeting. Every conceivable luxury out on display. And well-dressed, very important people hurrying back and forth on their own very important business. No windows anywhere, though. It was comfortably warm, for which I was very grateful. I'd had more than enough of the cold of Ultima Thule. I could feel the last of the bitter chill seeping out of my bones, and out of my soul, as I strode quickly through the wide corridors of the Winter Palace.

I acted as though I belonged there, as though I had every right to be there, so everyone just assumed I did. It helped that as a field agent, I had been trained to have one of those faces that everyone thinks they half recognise. Just a familiar kind of chap, the kind you see every day, everywhere. I smiled and nodded easily to everyone I passed, and they nodded and smiled easily back. Because that was what you did in places like this. Where everyone was bound to be someone, and you were bound to have met them somewhere before . . . It never occurred to any of them that I might be an outsider, or an intruder, because they knew the only way to get in was through the teleport station. And for that, you needed an invitation.

There seemed to be a great many corridors, heading off in every direction. There were any number of signs and helpful directions on the walls, in all kinds of languages, but not one pointing to the Ballroom. Maybe the directions were on the invitation ... I couldn't just walk up to the reception desk and ask, without giving myself away. And I couldn't ask any of the guests. So I walked up and down, and back and forth, peering in through all sorts of doors, until it started to feel like I was walking in circles. I stopped, and looked thoughtfully about me.

In and among the many fine guests, in their formal attire and peacock displays, their designer dresses and fashion abominations, were a lot of people who were quite obviously not guests. They wore formal uniforms, neat and efficient with gleaming buttons, all of them topped with stylised white full-face masks, revealing only the eyes. Security people, hotel staff, all the rank and file you need to keep a place the size of the Winter Palace running smoothly. And all of them coming and going completely unchallenged, because if you were wearing a uniform you must be staff. And no guest would lower himself to notice mere functionaries. I looked the staff over carefully.

It was easy enough to spot the security people, in their sharp white leather uniforms. Something in the way they moved, in the way they held themselves, suggested they were used to taking care of problems. And the blank white masks had distinct possibilities ... I was reminded for a moment of the masked blood-red men on the Trans-Siberian Express, but these were all quite definitely different people.

I picked one at random, followed him at a cautious distance, and watched closely as he reported to the Head of Security. Who fortunately wore much the same uniform and mask as everyone else. Presumably a style thing. I followed the Head of Security through the bustling corridors, and he didn't even notice, he was so caught up in his own duties and responsibilities and in looking important. He had a bulky comm unit stuck in one ear, and was constantly talking loudly to somebody about something. I waited, choosing my moment carefully, and when he finally made the mistake of pausing in a deserted side corridor, I eased quietly in behind him and seized the back of his neck in a nerve pinch. His head lolled back, his eyes rolled up, and I caught hold of his collapsing body before it hit the floor. I slung one of his arms across my shoulders, and looked quickly around for somewhere handy to dump him. A well-dressed couple paused at the entrance to the side corridor, looking dubiously at me and the Head of Security. I gave them a cheerful smile.

"I'd give the shellfish a miss, if I were you."

The couple moved on. I found a convenient cupboard, hauled the door open, and bundled the unconscious Head of Security inside. There was just room enough in the cupboard for me to join him. I closed the door carefully. I was getting really tired of huddling inside small rooms. I changed clothes with the Head of Security, banging my elbows repeatedly in the confined space. Fortunately the Head was a rather larger person than me, so I could get into the uniform without straining. Though I did have to pull his belt right in to keep my trousers up. The stylised face mask peeled off easily, and slapped itself onto my face the moment I brought it close enough. Some kind of static cling deal. I wished briefly for a mirror. The uniform felt like it was flapping about me, and only fitted where it touched. Hopefully people would pay more attention to the uniform than to the man inside it.

I stuck the comm unit in my ear, and immediately a rush of overlapping conversations filled my head as everyone tried to talk to me at once, asking why I'd gone quiet for so long. Apparently they were used to being micro-managed. I growled something about maintaining security, and told them all to shut the hell up until I told them they could talk again. Everyone went quiet. Clearly the Head of Security ran a tight ship. I rummaged through my new pockets and came up with a small laminated ID pass, labeled *Burke Tallman*. I had to smirk. With a name like that, he pretty much had to go into the security business, if only in self-defence. I lowered my voice again, and growled into the comm unit.

"I want this channel kept clear until further notice, for emergency purposes. No one says anything until I say otherwise. Got it?"

There was a quick rush of hurried agreements, and then the earpiece went quiet. I shook my head. What kind of security force didn't even recognise their own Head's voice? They just assumed it had to be Tallman, because I was speaking on his channel. You'd never get away with that at Drood Hall. Still, it was good to know Tallman's staff was used to obeying orders they didn't necessarily understand. I should be able to take advantage of that.

I stepped out of the cupboard and closed the door carefully behind me. A few people walking down the side corridor looked at me curiously. I glared right back at them, and they hurried past. I went strolling through the corridors of the Winter Palace, and people fell back on all sides to give me plenty of room. No one messes with a Head of Security, be they guests or staff. The odds were that few of them knew Tallman by sight; they were just reacting to the uniform and the attitude. So long as I played the part and barked out orders with confidence, no one short of the Lady Faire was going to challenge me. I stopped the next security man I met, stuck my mask into his, and demanded directions to the Ball. He looked at me hesitantly.

"But don't you know? Sir?"

"Of course I know," I growled. "I'm just checking that you do! Now give me the directions, and be succinct! And do up those buttons!"

He quickly did so, then gave me detailed instructions on how to get to the Ballroom. I dismissed him with a look, and he hurried off, not looking back, eager to escape before I decided to quiz him on something he might not know. I smiled behind my mask. And went to the Ball.

The Ballroom of the Winter Palace turned out to be absolutely huge, overwhelmingly impressive, and almost obscenely opulent. It had been fitted out to look like a massive ice cavern, gleaming and shimmering, complete with stalactites hanging down from the arching ceiling and stalagmites rising up from the mirrored floor. Even the various fixtures and fittings gave every appearance of being made from snow and ice. All of it entirely artificial, of course. It might look convincing, but the whole place was more than comfortably warm, from some hidden heating system. And nothing was melting.

There were long tables with every kind of sophisticated buffet food, and tall towers of champagne glasses, the booze running down them like bubbling waterfalls. What looked like entirely authentic furs had been scattered across the floor, mostly polar bears and pandas. King-sized penguins waddled back and forth like miniature waiters, only revealing themselves to be automatons when they spoke to the guests. And there were guests everywhere, hundreds and hundreds of them, crowding the Ballroom and filling it from wall to wall. Who knew the Lady Faire had ... got about so much? I moved easily among the packed guests, and no one challenged my right to be there. Just having the Head of Security present made everyone feel that much safer, and protected.

It was hard to believe one person could have had this many lovers in one lifetime. Even if she wasn't, strictly speaking, a person at all, being a ladything. There were men and women, gods and monsters, and at least three aliens. Plus a whole bunch of famous names and faces, from all across the world. Politicians and celebrities, movers and shakers, and not a few Names that wouldn't have meant anything to anyone outside the hidden world. If they really were all past lovers of the Lady Faire, she must have been very busy down her extended lifetime.

Everyone seemed to be getting on well enough, chatting politely and even pleasantly with one another. Drinking fine wines and comparing party nibbles, acquired absently from waiters and waitresses carrying them around on silver platters. The waiters looked like butlers, and the waitresses looked like French maids.

The Ball boasted a wide and varied selection of Very Important Personages, who would have been at each other's throats anywhere else. But they all came together companionably enough to discuss the one thing they had in common. Their memories of the Lady Faire.

Music came from a small orchestra on a raised stage at the far end of the Ballroom. Fronted by a French singing sensation so famous even I'd heard of her—the inimitable Rossignol. She was singing some obscure French torch song, leaning heavily on the vowels and hitting the *r* sounds for all they were worth when I entered. But she broke off abruptly as a member of the hotel staff hurried onto the raised stage and murmured in her ear. She had a quick conference with the musicians, and then they launched into the old Petula Clark hit "Downtown." Followed by "Always Something There to Remind Me." Either it was Sixties Night at the Winter Palace or these were some of the Lady Faire's favourites. Nothing comforts an old soul like the popular music of one's youth. I knew the songs because Uncle Jack was always playing Sixties compilations in the Armoury.

I moved off to one side and put my back to a wall, the better to observe the guests. Some of them I knew immediately, because they knew me. As Shaman Bond, or Eddie Drood, or both.

Dead Boy was there, of course, imposing his appalling personality on anyone foolish enough to come within reach and not run away fast enough. He lurked beside a much-depleted buffet table, standing tall and Byronically dissolute in his deep purple greatcoat, with the usual black rose at the lapel. He always left the greatcoat hanging open at the front, so he could show off his autopsy scar. Apparently he saw it as a conversation piece.

For a returned soul possessing his own dead body, Dead Boy was a cheerful enough sort. And for a quite definitely deceased person, he was putting away a hell of a lot of party food, stuffing his mouth with one hand, and stuffing his coat pockets with the other, for later. A waitress passed by, bearing a tray of champagne glasses. Dead Boy took the tray away from her and drank the lot, one glass at a time.

Not far enough away, the Vodyanoi Brothers were putting on their usual obnoxious show. Two very large Russian gentlemen, in matching expensive black leather jackets and trousers, with shaven heads and nasty grins. Kicked out of the Moscow Mafiosi, for crimes far too unpleasant to discuss in civilised company, they travelled the world, hiring themselves out as shock troops and enforcers. They were werewolves, and complete arseholes. People stared at them in open disgust and repulsion, as the Vodyanoi Brothers did their best to command everyone's attention.

"Greetings, everybody!" said Gregor, the older brother. "We are being Vodyanoi Brothers! Pirates and adventurers, and very dangerous people! Oh yes! Show them how dangerous, Sergei!"

The younger Vodyanoi Brother turned abruptly into a huge humanoid wolf, with silver grey fur and massive muscles bulging under his thick pelt. Guests fell back, coughing at the sudden rank, musky scent on the air. The wolf grinned widely, the better to show off his vicious yellow fangs.

"Highly dangerous, I think you will agree!" said Gregor, smiling a smile with no humour in it at all.

None of the other guests seemed particularly impressed. It took more than a simple shape-change to impress someone who'd slept with a ladything. Most of the guests' expressions suggested that the Lady Faire must really have been slumming it when she lowered herself to sleep with those two. Or at the very least, in the mood for some seriously rough trade. Sergei noticed that being a really big wolf just wasn't cutting it, and so he shrank back to human shape again. He glared sullenly about him, and then spotted Dead Boy.

He strode right up to Dead Boy, and started to say something aggressive, only to break off as Dead Boy grabbed him by the throat with one pale hand, pulled

him close till they were face-to-face, and then bit off
Sergei's nose. The werewolf howled, struggled free of
Dead Boy's grip, and fell back several steps, both hands
clasped over the part of his face where his nose used to
be. Blood pumped thickly between his fingers. Dead Boy
chewed carefully, considering the taste, and then smiled
slowly. Sergei regarded him with wide eyes, and then
lowered his hands to reveal a regrown nose. Dead Boy
looked at him thoughtfully, and Sergei ran back to his
big brother. Gregor growled at Dead Boy, who smiled
happily back.

"I love Russian food!" he said loudly.

The Vodyanoi Brothers huddled together, and then
fell back, disappearing into the crowd. Dead Boy picked
something out of his teeth. I didn't stay to see what. I
moved on before he could spot me.

Jimmy Thunder, God for Hire, was trying to impress
an elven princess with the size of his hammer, Mjolnir,
and getting nowhere. Jimmy was a genuine descendent
of the old Norse Gods, at a great many removes and on
the wrong side of many blankets. A huge figure, with a
great mane and beard of fiery red hair, he had a voice so
low it seemed to rumble up from somewhere deep in his
chest. He wore much-used biker leathers, with gleaming
steel studs and hanging chains, and heavy boots with
steel toe-caps. He had a chest like a barrel, and shoulders
so broad he often had to turn sideways to get through a
door. The elven princess turned up her nose at him and
stalked away, and Jimmy fastened Mjolnir back on his
belt. Just as well. The hammer had been a famous
weapon in its day, but it was well past its prime now, and
getting senile. Word was, Jimmy never threw the hammer

any more, because he couldn't be sure it would remember who it was supposed to come back to.

Jimmy Thunder was a private investigator, bounty hunter, and supernatural bail bondsman. When he felt like it.

And then there was the original Bride of Frankenstein, along with her current paramour, the latest incarnation of the Springheel Jack meme. The Bride was seven feet tall if she was an inch, and very well-fleshed. The Baron had to make his earliest creations somewhat oversized, to be sure of getting all the bits in. Her face was pale and taut, as if stretched by too much surgery, though I knew for a fact she'd never let anyone touch her with a scalpel since her creation. She had huge black eyes that didn't blink nearly often enough, a prominent nose, and lips the colour of dried blood. She was striking rather than pretty, but quite definitely attractive, in a spooky and downright disturbing way. She wore her long black hair piled up in a beehive tall enough to put Amy Winehouse to shame, and she wasn't bothering to dye out the long white streaks any more. Or using makeup to cover the heavy stitch marks at her throat and wrists. She wore a flouncy powder blue blouse, cut deep at the front to show off her magnificent cleavage, over navy blue slacks tucked into thigh-length riding boots with heavy silver spurs.

Up close, I knew she would smell of attar of roses and formaldehyde.

Springheel Jack stuck close at her side, bestowing cold, considering looks on anyone he thought was getting too near. He was tall and slim, cool and calm, and handsome enough in a sinister sort of way. Dark and dignified, he wore the traditional black opera cape, flowing about him like folded bat wings, and an old-fashioned top hat. The look came with his inheritance of the old Springheel Jack meme, the deadly assassin of Old London Town, who predated Jack the Ripper by some fifty years. Springheel Jack was a terrible idea given shape and form, jumping from one generation to another in the same cursed family. Cold blue eyes met mine, briefly, and they were old, old eyes. It was the burden of his inheritance that he carried in his head all the experiences of his many predecessors. I couldn't see any sign of the long cut-throat razors that were the other part of his inheritance, but I had no doubt they were about his person somewhere, security checks be damned.

There were other guests I knew well, if only by reputation. The Replicated Meme of Saint Sebastian were swanning around in all their usual arrogant display. Six versions of the same personality, dwelling in six different bodies. Supposedly some kind of soul-share deal, one person inhabiting an endless series of bodies, co-opting new ones as the old ones wore out. They were all dressed in the same smart grey business suit, complete with the same Old School Tie. Their faces were hidden behind identical thinly beaten steel masks. Again, I was reminded unpleasantly of the masked blood-red men, but it was clear these were all very different body shapes. I watched them for a while, unobtrusively. There was something familiar about them . . . Even though I knew for a fact I'd never encountered the Replicated Meme of Saint Sebastian before.

According to the family files, they'd worked for us on occasion. Co-opting people we didn't want around any longer.

The Living Shroud was just a long, grubby winding sheet, of the kind used to wrap the dead before they went into the grave. The usual cerements of the dead, thick with dust and cobwebs, except there didn't seem to be anyone inside them. Certainly nothing I could see, and there aren't many things that can hide from me. But something was giving the Shroud its human shape as it drifted slowly through the crowd. Apparently entirely unmoved by, or uninterested in, the other guests.

The Living Shroud made a living, if that's the correct term, by haunting people for hire. Apparently you paid the Living Shroud to stalk people, at increasingly close quarters, until they gave up and paid what they owed. The current record for surviving the Living Shroud's presence was seventeen hours. I had to wonder, if the Living Shroud really didn't have a body, how could it be one of the Lady Faire's ex-lovers? Maybe she knew it before it became . . . whatever it was now.

Next up on my radar was the Lady Alice Underground. Everyone had heard of her. An elderly but not in any way frail dowager dressed in dull black Victorian mourning clothes, the Lady Alice was an explorer of the Underverse. Those spatial dimensions that exist beneath our own, populated exclusively by symbols and icons and archetypes. Her face was a mass of wrinkles, her thin grey hair pulled back in a tight bun, but her eyes were sharp and fey and wild, almost feral. She had the look of someone who'd spent too much time among things and people that weren't really people or things. The Lady Alice Underground was the last of the old school adventurers, the ones who went forth in a spirit of conquest.

And then there was the Last of Leng. Everyone had heard of that cruel and awful people, living in their ancient city on the Plateau of Leng. A vicious people, feared by all. Black Heir destroyed the entire city with a backpack nuke, some time back, and pretty much everyone in the world threw a party. Horrible place, horrible people. But one member of that appalling city survived, somehow. The Last of Leng. Walking alone in the world, because no one else wanted anything to do with it.

It walked alone at the Ball too. It went where it wanted, because no one dared turn it away, but it was always unwelcome. Certainly no one at the Ball wanted anything to do with it. The Last of Leng was a broad, hunched figure, its hooded head thrusting out before it, dressed in poison green robes, with long rags and tatters trailing out behind it. The hood was pulled well forward, to hide the face in impenetrable shadows. Just looking at the lurking figure made my skin crawl. I couldn't believe even the Lady Faire would have had . . . intimate knowledge of something as physically and spiritually foul as the Last of Leng.

I kept moving, hugging the walls of the massive Ballroom. I was careful to avoid the Vodyanoi Brothers, because they knew me as Shaman Bond. They'd currently retreated to a far corner, snarling at everyone. Sergei kept fingering the nose that had grown back, as though afraid it might fall off. Every now and again, they would call out to some passing waiter or waitress, for food or drink, but the staff was all careful to ignore the two werewolves. Until finally the Vodyanoi Brothers jumped on a waiter who'd strayed too close, pulled him down, and loudly announced their intention of eating him. They glared happily about them, defying anyone to stop them. Which was all the excuse I needed.

I used the Head of Security comm channel to send

out a general call ordering my security people to remove the Vodyanoi Brothers. At once, by force, by any means necessary. And then throw them out of the Winter Palace. Invitations revoked. Security people descended on the Vodyanoi Brothers from all directions at once, the guests falling back to give them room to operate. But not so far that they couldn't see what was happening. The security men and women quickly surrounded the Vodyanoi Brothers, who both turned wolf and glared defiantly about them. They sank their claws into the whimpering waiter, refusing to give him up. The white-uniformed security people closed in, and hit the Vodyanois with a dozen Tasers at once.

Electricity spat and sparked loudly on the air, and all the silver grey fur stood on end. It might take silver to kill a werewolf, but Tasers will still shock the shit out of it quite successfully. If you use enough of them, and keep your finger on the trigger.

Gregor and Sergei Vodyanoi convulsed violently, shaking and shuddering as they were forced back into their human shapes. They let go of the waiter, who was quickly dragged away. The security people shocked them some more, just on general principles, and then shut down their Tasers and moved in to give the Vodyanois a good kicking. The two twitching bodies were then dragged away.

Most of the guests applauded.

One of the security men came diffidently forward to report to me. "The problem has been dealt with, sir. Any further orders, sir?"

"Put them outside," I growled. Just to make sure. "Let them walk home."

"Of course, sir."

He hurried away. I was pretty sure the Vodyanoi

Brothers would turn up again, somewhere. They were harder to kill than cockroaches.

I continued moving around the perimeter of the Ballroom, keeping an eye on everyone and everything, still waiting for the Lady Faire to show her face. The only person in the Winter Palace I knew for sure knew what the Lazarus Stone looked like. As Head of Security, it shouldn't be too difficult for me to lure her away and make her take me to it. And I was curious to see what she looked like . . .

The guests had quickly recovered from seeing the security forces in action. Most were chatting quite cheerfully about it. The Bride and Springheel Jack were dancing with Dead Boy and a costumed adventurer from the Nightside, one Ms. Fate. No doubt exchanging gossip, swapping barbed bons mots, and discussing the possibility of getting together later. The Lady Alice Underground was swapping brittle smiles with Tommy Oblivion, the existential private eye, who specialised in cases that may or may not have actually occurred. He might or might not have slept with the Lady Faire; he probably couldn't be sure himself. The Replicated Meme of Saint Sebastian were keeping to themselves, and everyone else let them. The Last of Leng had got into a staring contest with a Yeti that looked like it could go on for some time. And everyone danced and chattered, ate and drank, and threw occasional tantrums . . . as they waited for the guest of honour to appear.

I kept moving, doing my best to appear inconspicuous, or at least not worth paying attention to.

And then I spotted Molly. She was wearing the French maid outfit, all stiff starched black and white with unnecessary bows, moving easily among the guests as just another waitress, offering a selection of smoked nibbles from her silver platter. Presumably to give her an excuse to get close to people, and listen in on their conversations. In the hope of finding someone who knew what and where the Lazarus Stone was. She looked . . . pretty damned good in the outfit. She had once offered to send off for a French maid outfit by mail order, but in the end I chickened out and said I wouldn't wear it.

Molly turned her head suddenly and looked right at me. She didn't smile, or even drop me a wink, before turning deliberately away and moving on. I made a point of moving off in the opposite direction.

Clearly neither of us was any closer to discovering the Lazarus Stone. And I wasn't sure how much time we had left before one or the other of us said or did the wrong thing and was discovered.

I finished a complete circle of the Ballroom, and stopped to look around me. If the Lady Faire didn't deign to turn up soon, I'd have to leave the Ballroom and go looking for her. Which presented its own difficulties. I still had no idea what she looked like, and it wasn't like I could ask anybody. The one thing everyone in this place had in common was that they all knew their hostess.

I moved back the way I'd come, passing a group of several leaders of small countries, and some who were now ex-leaders, all in deep conversation. Many were actually deadly enemies out in the real world, but here at least they seemed quite comfortable in one another's company. Several very well-known film stars had attracted their own circles of admirers. Every now and again the admirers would lose interest in their star and look away, hoping for the arrival of the Lady Faire, and then the film stars' smiles would vanish in a moment, reappearing only when their admirers' attention returned to them.

A butch dyke dressed only in assorted leather straps, a noted supporter of conservative family values in the real world, was dancing with Something from a Black Lagoon. An ex-pope who was supposed to have been safely dead for some time was dancing the Argentinean tango with an alien Grey. I passed by the Replicated Meme of Saint Sebastian, and they all made a point of turning their backs on me.

And then the Bride and Springheel Jack walked past me, and the Bride did her best to hide a double take as she recognised me. She might not be able to see my face through my security mask, but her more than normal eyes could See my torc. The Bride hurried Springheel Jack along. His face didn't change at all as he glanced at me. He did look like he wanted to ask the Bride a whole bunch of questions, but she just kept him moving. When a woman that big has you by the arm, you move.

I would have worried about them, but I was distracted almost immediately, because I had to move quickly to interrupt a fight between Jimmy Thunder and the Living Shroud. It seemed the Living Shroud had tried to cut in with Ms. Fate, and Ms. Fate had declined. The dead thing had insisted, and the Norse godling was now towering over it with Mjolnir in his hand. Jimmy never could resist being chivalrous when there was a young lady to impress. Everyone fell back as Jimmy told the Living Shroud to get lost, in a loud and carrying voice. The empty grave trappings stood its ground, trembling with anger, dropping cobwebs and dead spiders all over the floor. A cold malevolence emanated from the Living Shroud, like bad spiritual radiation. Jimmy shuddered abruptly, and looked briefly uncertain, and then he grabbed a handful of the Shroud's grave wrappings, to pull it closer. The rags just rotted and fell apart in the godling's hand, and he pulled a disgusted face. The Living Shroud slapped Jimmy Thunder across the face with an empty sleeve, and the sheer power in the blow sent Jimmy's head whipping round. There was definitely something solid inside the grave wrappings. Jimmy Thunder roared with anger and raised Mjolnir on high. All the watching guests leaned forward, eager to see some serious smiting.

The hammer came crashing down, and I stopped it in mid-air with a very briefly golden hand. I didn't care what happened to the Living Shroud, but I couldn't let it happen on my watch, or people might start to wonder why. And I didn't want anything to happen that might dissuade the Lady Faire from appearing. So I armoured up my hand, just for a moment, and thrust it in the way of the descending hammer. The golden glove absorbed all the impact, stopping Mjolnir dead in its tracks. And then I pulled the golden strange matter back into my torc before anyone noticed it was there. It was a risk using my torc, even so briefly, but I had no choice. It didn't seem to have set off any alarms.

Jimmy Thunder swore loudly, his whole arm twitching painfully from being stopped so suddenly. He stepped back, looking at me with shocked, startled eyes. I glared back at him, secure behind my security mask.

I moved in between him and the Living Shroud, and gave my full attention to the inhabited grave clothes as they flapped and fluttered agitatedly before me. They rose up, growing and expanding. Strange energies flared around them. And then Molly appeared behind the Shroud, and threw a tray of champagne glasses over it. The alcohol soaked quickly into the rags, and Molly set fire to them. The grave wrappings immediately went up in blue flames, burning fiercely.

The Living Shroud howled miserably and spun round and round, beating at its burning self with empty sleeves, which only seemed to encourage the flames. The Shroud went running up and down the Ballroom, burning brightly, while people fell back delightedly and cheered and applauded. Until finally the Lady Alice Underground put the Shroud out with a handy soda siphon. The Living Shroud stood very still, half its rags just scorched tatters, falling away in blackened lengths. There was still no sign of whatever might be inhabiting what remained.

I called the security people back to the Ballroom, and they quickly surrounded the Living Shroud. There was a tense moment, and then the Shroud allowed itself to be escorted out. Leaving a trail of dark smudges on the floor behind it. Some of the guests actually got down on their hands and knees to pick up charred bits of rag, for souvenirs. I glared at Jimmy Thunder, who just shrugged. He'd been glared at by far worse than me. He went back to join Ms. Fate, who gave him a stiff talking-to, on the grounds that she operated as a costumed adventurer in the Nightside, and thus could be considered quite capable of looking after herself.

I nodded to Molly. "Thank you. That was very helpful. You can return to your duties now."

She bobbed an almost convincing curtsey. "Yes, sir. Thank you, sir."

She moved quickly away. I was still getting my breath back, when I found myself suddenly confronted by the Last of Leng. It crouched before me, giving the distinct impression it was glaring up at me from under its lowered hood. Up close, the poison green robes and tatters smelled strongly of rotting flesh and ordure. My torc burned at my throat, trying to protect me against something.

"Where is the Lady Faire?" said the Last of Leng in a harsh, grating voice.

"I'm sure she'll be here, when she's ready," I said smoothly.

"Not good enough. Go. Tell the Lady Faire I am here. Tell her to come. Now."

"I am Head of Security," I said, careful to keep my voice calm and polite. "I have duties and responsibilities here. I'm sure the Lady Faire will appear, in good time."

"I gave you an order!"

"So you did. And this is me, ignoring it, because I don't work for you. Now be a good little last survivor of an appalling civilisation, and piss off. Before I throw an entire security force at you."

I shouldn't have lost my temper, but after all, this was the Last of Leng. There are limits.

"You dare!" shrieked the Last of Leng.

"Frequently," I said. "Famous for it. One more word out of you, and I'll have you thrown out into Ultima Thule, and you can spend the long journey home knocking icicles off your wrappings. Except you can't go home, because some sensible and public-spirited person blew it up. So beat it, you bum."

The Last of Leng started to say something, and then turned abruptly and strode away. Several guests nodded approvingly. They would have liked to applaud, but it was the Last of Leng, after all, and they weren't as brave as me.

I turned away, and there was Dead Boy, waiting for me, grinning all over his deathly pale face. I sighed inwardly. As if I didn't have enough problems ... Dead Boy had a tall glass of something dark and steaming in one hand, and a half-eaten dodo leg in the other. He dropped me a heavy wink.

"I knew it was you! I never mistake an aura. Don't worry," he said, in what he probably thought was a conspiratorial tone, "I've got your back."

"Oh good," I said. "I'm sure whoever you think I am is very grateful. Now will you please *go away* and ruin somebody else's day?"

"That's what I'm here for," said Dead Boy.

He dropped me another heavy wink, with his heavily mascaraed eye, and swaggered away. Dead Boy didn't care what I was doing here. He just thought it was funny. Being dead for so long has given him an odd sense of humour. I wasn't sure whether having his support felt comforting or not. I watched him latch on to a waiter with a new tray of party snacks, and launch himself in hot pursuit. Dead Boy had the attention span of a goldfish swimming in a bowl of liquid LSD. I sighed quietly again, and wondered what else could go wrong. I was attracting far more attention than was good for me. In fact, I was starting to wonder whether I should just leave the Ballroom and start bullying hotel staff until one of them told me where the Lazarus Stone was.

And then I spotted a face I knew, deep in the milling crowd. A face I recognised immediately, that I had thought never to see again. My heart hammered painfully in my chest, and I had trouble getting my breath. A tall, distinguished figure in a formal tuxedo moved easily through the crowd. He looked exactly like my uncle James. My *late* uncle James, the legendary Grey Fox. I hadn't seen him since he died right in front of me, in Drood Hall, all those years ago. He couldn't be here. He died. I went to his funeral. Unless . . . somebody had already used the Lazarus Stone.

Unless someone had rewritten History, bringing James back from the dead. But if History had been changed, I wouldn't still remember the way things used to be . . . would I? I had survived the destruction of the Sceneshifters . . . so I was the only person in the world who still remembered them . . . I plunged forward into the crowd, pushing people out of my way and ignoring their objections, but by the time I got to where I'd seen my uncle James, he wasn't there any more. I looked quickly about me, while everyone else stuck their noses in the air and made pointed comments about my rudeness, but I couldn't see Uncle James anywhere.

If he'd ever really been there.

I was seized with an awful sense of urgency, a need to do . . . something. If the Lady Faire, or anyone else, had started using the Lazarus Stone after all these years . . . we were all in real trouble. But deep down, I didn't believe it. If James' death had been undone, I wouldn't still remember him dying. Hell, I probably wouldn't still be standing here. So whoever it was I saw, it couldn't have been the Grey Fox. Just someone trying to pass as him. Unless . . . Could Uncle James have pulled off the greatest trick and comeback of his career? Faked his own death, back then? I saw him die, but so had a great many people, down the years, and he'd always bounced back, smiling broadly, refusing to explain how he'd done it. All part of the legend of the Droods' greatest field agent: the infamous Grey Fox.

But he wouldn't have done that to me . . . would he?

Or could it be some shape-shifter or face-dancer, pretending to be him? Wearing James' face to get into the Lady Faire's Ball, to get to the Lazarus Stone? I smiled coldly behind my security mask. If someone here was hiding behind Uncle James' reputation, I would have their balls.

I wished Molly was with me, so I could discuss this with her. She would have known what to say, what to do. She always was the professional one.

Then, quite suddenly, everything stopped. The noise broke off as everyone stopped talking. The music stopped and the singer fell silent. Everyone in the Ballroom stood very still. We were all looking at the Lady Faire, standing in the open doors at the far end of the Ballroom, come at last.

She held an effortlessly aristocratic pose, smiling on her gathered guests. Someone started applauding, and everyone joined in. I did too. Just couldn't help myself. People started cheering, and shouting happily. Some wept, quite openly. The great ice cavern filled with a joyous sound, overwhelming and overpowering. A spontaneous outbreak of good cheer and affectionate tribute. The Lady Faire was here at last, and everyone wanted to show how much they still cared for her. Perhaps the one great affair, or even love, of their troubled lives. The only person who had ever really mattered to them. The Lady Faire smiled graciously about her, accepting it all as her right. Her right of conquest, perhaps.

Everyone was looking at her in the same way, or at the very least, in varieties of the same way. Looks of love and hunger and lust, but more than that . . . They were the looks of a subjugated people, of those who had been touched by the Lady Faire and loved it. Or had been made to love it, by the perfect honey trap. The Baron Frankenstein had done his work well. The Lady Faire was so much more than an ex-lover to these people. She was a living goddess. Male and female and everything in between; they had loved her once and they loved her now, despite themselves. And having finally seen her, I could understand why.

The Lady Faire, that most infamous omnisexual and ladything, the most successful seductress in the history of espionage, the Ice Queen herself . . . was tall and stately and wore a perfectly fitted white tuxedo. Her hair had been shaped and dyed into a perfect re-creation of Jean Harlow's platinum bombshell. Her face was handsome and striking and beautiful, all at once, with a strong bone structure. She had golden-pupiled eyes, a pointed nose, and pink rosebud lips. Her smile was a practised thing, but charming as all hell. More a man's smile than a woman's . . . Shapes and movements inside the white tuxedo suggested a woman's body, and then a man's, both and neither and more.

There was no point in even trying to guess her age. She looked perfectly youthful, no more than her twenties. But there was a suggestion of age, of long experience, in her eyes and her smile, in every small movement, and in the grace and elegance that hung about her like a well-worn cloak. Much used, and invisibly mended. You could tell that here was someone who had been around. Who had seen things and done things, some of them awful. Not that she cared, and nothing she would ever apologise for. You just knew, from looking at her. She had a feminine glamour, and a masculine presence. There was nothing androgynous about her. She was quite definitely female. And male. And so much more.

The Lady Faire took your breath away, sweet as cyanide.

She certainly made one hell of a first impression. My torc was burning fiercely at my throat, or I might have fallen under her spell too. She—it was easier to think of her that way, less complicated—was overpoweringly sexual, seductively alluring, without even trying. I could feel the attraction burning off her, like the light that calls moths to throw themselves into the flame and perish. Looking at her was like staring into a spotlight aimed personally at you. And yet . . . there was something else there too. Like a maggot squirming deep in an apple. An almost arachnid revulsion, a bone-deep, soul-deep aversion to something that just shouldn't exist in the natural world.

Or maybe that was just me. After all, I've been around a bit myself.

I wanted to turn away, but I couldn't. I felt the same need, the same hunger, that drew everyone else to the Lady Faire. I fought it, drawing on the strength of my torc, and my armour, and my Drood training. To always be in control, and never the one controlled. I was half tempted to armour up, just so I could hide behind it. I thought of Molly, and all she had come to mean to me, and that helped. What was a living goddess in the face of the wild witch of the woods? There was no room left in my heart for the Lady Faire. But still, I couldn't look away. I knew the Lady Faire was a honey trap, and a danger to everything I cared about . . . but I was finding it hard to care.

She was just like the legendary Ice Queen. You looked at her, a sliver of her ice entered your eye, and you were hers forever.

Except I was a Drood. A field agent trained to never give in to outside influences. Trained from an early age to be loyal only to Droods. *Anything, for the family.* I concentrated on my torc, and immediately a tendril of golden armour shot up my neck to form a mask under my security mask. And just like that, I could See the Lady Faire so much more clearly.

No one else could tell, but I could See her pumping out pheromones on an industrial scale. Musk, mating signals, bypassing the conscious mind to appeal directly to the unconscious, affecting people on the most basic, fundamental level. No wonder I'd been having so much trouble thinking clearly. I breathed deeply through my hidden golden mask, and felt my head clear as though a cold wind was rushing through it.

The Lady Faire still looked just as impressive, but also . . . beautiful and horrible. Human and inhuman. As though two sets of impressions were at war with each other. She was still strikingly attractive, but no longer seductive. The brute force of her chemical appeal made her seem more like an Insect Queen than an Ice Queen. I could See cracks in her perfect face, in her practised composure. Age had taken its toll, after all, and she was no longer the great creation she had been.

And just like that, I could remember everything Molly meant to me. I could see her face and hear her voice, and there was no one else in the world I wanted as much as I wanted her.

It was a shock to the soul, to step back from the precipice I'd been ready to leap over. To realise how close I'd come to jumping off that cliff edge along with all the other lemmings. Molly was back, like she'd never been away. I didn't think I would ever mention this to her. How I'd felt, for those few delirious moments. I felt a certain sense of relief, now that I understood what had been happening to me. It wasn't all down to the pheromones, to the chemical impulses, but they had definitely got to me. The Baron had put a lot of thought into his creation. The bastard.

The Lady Faire finally got bored just standing there, and strode regally forward into the Ballroom. Her ex-lovers were all still cheering and applauding, trying to outdo one another and catch the Lady Faire's eye. She moved easily among her conquests, stopping here and there to favour this one and that, by remembering their name. And then she would remember a place or a time or a moment, and everyone hung on her every word and smile and gesture. Great men and women fawned over her openly, competed shamelessly for every glance, and debased themselves just for the chance of a smile. Sometimes she would lay a hand briefly on a shoulder, or caress a face with her fingertips, and the guests so favoured all but swooned.

But the Lady Faire never paused for long, always moving on, leaving a trail of broken hearts behind her. All over again.

No one made any move to touch the Lady Faire. Not, it seemed to me, because it was forbidden; they just didn't dare. Even with the maddening pheromones hitting these people full blast, she still had complete control over them. I looked carefully around the milling crowd, and even at the farthest edges of the Ballroom, where logic suggested the pheromones wouldn't even have reached yet, everyone still seemed perfectly dazzled and bewitched. Even so, a phalanx of uniformed security people followed close behind the Lady Faire, keeping an eye on things, clearly ready to slap down anyone who even looked like they were getting out of hand.

I was still thinking on how best to separate her out from her audience so I could grill her on the Lazarus

Stone, when the Bride took advantage of the general chaos to come over and join me for a quiet word. While everyone else had all their attention fixed on our hostess. The Bride nodded easily to me, while Springheel Jack hung back a little, ready to see off anyone who looked like they were trying to listen in.

"So," the Bride said quietly, "do I have the honour of addressing Shaman Bond, or Eddie Drood?"

"Neither," I said just as quietly. "I'm currently passing as the Winter Palace's Head of Security. Hence the uniform and mask. Try to look impressed."

"I thought it must be something like that," said the Bride. "You do have a tendency to show up at all the most interesting events, whoever you're being. I didn't think the Lady Faire was one of your past indiscretions . . ."

"I didn't think she'd be one of yours," I said. "Or is it Jack who's taken a stroll up that very well-worn path?"

"I'll never tell," said the Bride. "Not that I have any time for the Lady Faire, you understand. I don't think anyone outside her enchanted circle has, really. You don't love the Lady Faire; that's not what she's for. Everyone here likes to refer to themselves as ex-lovers, but it's really just another term for something far more basic. She and I are both creations of the Baron, but she thinks she's so much more. So much better than the rest of the Spawn of Frankenstein. She never turns up at any of the reunions."

"Then why are you here?" I said bluntly.

The Bride grinned. "She does throw the very best parties, darling. Wait till we play Twister later." She leaned in close, to kiss me chastely on the forehead. "Thank you, for all you've done for the Frankenstein family. We do not forget our debts."

She drifted away, accompanied by her faithful Spring-heel Jack, and they disappeared back into the crowd. I had to grin. Twister . . . a game that should only be played by adults, while drunk. Naked. Greased. And then my smile disappeared as I spotted someone in the crowd who shouldn't have been there. There was just no way on this earth that the Lady Faire would have lowered herself to sleep with Jumping Jack Flashman. That renowned short-range teleporter, infamous thief, and well-known scumbag. Jumping Jack would have boasted to everyone in the world about it if he'd ever got that lucky.

No, he hadn't been invited to the Ball. Odds were he was here for the same reason I was: to get his hands on the Lazarus Stone.

He wasn't exactly in disguise, but he certainly wasn't looking himself. He'd spent some serious money on some serious clothes, and had dyed his hair bright red. Presumably as a distraction. He was behaving himself for the moment, not picking anyone's pocket or lifting their jewellery. But I still couldn't have him here, running loose. Let the Lady Faire realise she had one uninvited guest, and she'd be bound to start looking for others. And once she knew there was a thief in the fold, who knew what kind of security measures she might place around the Lazarus Stone? No, I had to shut Jumping Jack Flashman down fast.

I went back on Tallman's comm channel, and told his people to very quietly bring all the anti-teleport systems online and isolate the Ballroom. No one in or out until I said otherwise. A brief rush of voices through my ear-piece assured me that this was being done. I sent out more instructions, to the security people inside the Ball-room, telling them who to look for. I only needed to mention Jumping Jack Flashman, and immediately men and women in white uniforms locked onto him and started closing in. No one wanted to take any chances with this particular slippery little devil.

The guests realised something was up, and fell back to give the security people room to work. Interestingly, none of the guests looked guilty, or evasive, as though they had something to hide. They all just immediately assumed the security staff must be after someone else. Jumping Jack's head came up sharply as he spotted the first few security people closing in on him. He sneered at them and tried to teleport out.

The look of shock on his face when he discovered he couldn't get out of the Ballroom was priceless. His eyes widened, his jaw dropped, and his whole body radiated panic. He flickered in place several times as he tried to force his way past the Ballroom's shields, but he didn't go anywhere.

He tried again and again, flickering on and off like an angry light bulb, and then he lost it big time as the security staff closed in. He went jumping back and forth around the Ballroom in a series of short-range teleports, appearing here and there among the guests, who all thought it was great fun. They laughed happily as he appeared and disappeared among them, and yelled his location to the security staff. Of course, by the time any of them got there, he was gone again. Shouts and cries went up everywhere, as Jumping Jack tried to find an exit that hadn't been blocked off, and the security staff ran themselves ragged trying to keep up.

Once the guests realised they were in no danger from Jumping Jack, they decided it was all just a game and started rooting for the underdog. They cheered Jumping

Jack on, and took open delight in not quite getting in the way of the pursuing security people. I looked to the Lady Faire and saw immediately that she wasn't in the least pleased about what was happening. Her own security people had her pinned up against a wall, so they could surround her. Just in case. Her face and eyes had gone quite cold. If only because Jumping Jack's appearance had stolen her thunder, and no one was admiring her any more.

I decided I'd better do something before she started looking around for the Head of Security and demand that he Do Something. I still had my armour in place under my white security mask, and I used the strange matter covering my eyes to slow down the passing of Time, so I could follow the teleporting more easily. Slowed right down, a pattern in the jumps quickly became obvious, and it was easy enough for me to figure out where Jumping Jack was going to appear next. He was following a familiar, well-rehearsed pattern, not nearly as random as it seemed. So I just needed to position myself carefully for his next appearance.

I eased my way through the crowd, and no one paid me any attention. They were all having far too much fun watching the security staff race back and forth. And laying down bets on where the teleporter would appear next. Jumping Jack materialised right where I'd calculated, and in the moment after his arrival, while he was still getting his bearings, I grabbed the back of his neck in a nerve pinch and he went out like a light. I caught him before he hit the floor, and looked reproachfully at the dozen or so security staff as they came panting and lurching through the crowd to join me. I handed the unconscious body over to them, and they hauled him away.

I did feel a bit sorry for Jumping Jack. If ever a man was out of his depth . . .

The crowd were all chattering quite happily with each other, enjoying the unexpected excitement. The general feeling was that this was the best Ball the Lady Faire had thrown in a long time. I got on my comm channel again.

"Put the teleporter somewhere safe and very secure," I growled. "I'll want to talk to him when he wakes up. Starting with how he got in. So don't damage him; I need him able to answer questions. You can drop the teleport shields now, but keep your eyes open! This shouldn't have happened! You people are seriously underperforming! Go check the perimeter; make sure the Winter Palace is secure. And yes, I mean all of you! Go! Go!"

A series of affirmations came quickly through my earpiece, as everyone headed for the farthest parts of the Winter Palace. Hopefully, to keep themselves busy and occupied, so they wouldn't notice me and Molly going after the Lazarus Stone. Wherever the hell the bloody thing was. It amused me that no one had challenged me yet. Apparently a uniform and a mask will get you anywhere if you just act arrogant enough. I was still congratulating myself on that when I looked up to find the Lady Faire heading straight for me. I felt like running, but I was in the middle of a crowd and a long way from the nearest exit. So I stood my ground, drew myself up, and nodded respectfully, as though there was nothing at all out of the ordinary here, nothing to be worried about.

With anyone else, that would probably have worked.

The Lady Faire planted herself right in front of me, looked at me thoughtfully for a worryingly long moment, and then gestured imperiously for her security people to withdraw. They did so, reluctantly. They'd been well trained to trust absolutely no one. The Lady Faire looked me up and down, and then smiled pleasantly.

"Hello. Who are you?"

I took a deep breath, in spite of myself. She really was very impressive up close, even with my armoured mask filtering out her pheromones. Having the Lady Faire smile directly at you was like taking a shot of adrenaline straight to the heart. From a rusty needle. My pulse was racing, and my hands were sweating. My torc burned fiercely at my throat, fighting her influence. The Lady Faire's proximity was smothering, dizzying. I made myself concentrate on my torc and my training, and just nodded casually to the Lady Faire.

She actually looked surprised, for a moment. She wasn't used to people not falling immediately under her spell.

"Who am I, my Lady?" I said. "I am Head of Security for the Winter Palace."

"No, you aren't," she said pleasantly. "I chose Burke personally to take charge of my Ball. He's one of my old conquests. I only have people around me that I know, and know I can trust. Don't worry, whoever you are. If you're good enough to get in here without an invitation, and without causing a fuss like the poor fool you just captured, you're certainly worth talking to. You're a Drood. I can See your torc. Which is presumably why you're not as . . . impressed, as most of the people I meet. I find that rather refreshing. One does so crave for something new, as one gets older. So why are you here, Drood? I don't think I've done anything to upset your family recently."

"This is personal," I said carefully. "I am Eddie Drood. I'm here because you knew my uncle James."

"Of course!" said the Lady Faire. "The Grey Fox. A

very interesting man. Almost as infamous as me. I was quite sorry to hear of his death."

"That's the point," I said. "I'm almost sure I saw him here, in the crowd, just a few moments ago."

The Lady Faire shook her magnificent head. "Unlikely. I don't allow ghosts to hang around. There are just too many of them, and they're all so clingy . . . I have regular exorcisms performed wherever I go, to clean house. It's the only way to get any peace. I make an exception for Dead Boy because . . . Well, because you have to. But you didn't come all this way to pursue a ghost, Eddie Drood. What do you want with me?"

I looked at her thoughtfully. Things were finally working out. "Is there . . . somewhere we could speak privately?"

She looked me over. "Yes. I think so. Come with me, Eddie Drood."

She led me out of the Ballroom, gesturing for her security people to keep their distance. They glared at me, but didn't even think of disobeying their Lady's orders. A great many of the guests looked impressed, or possibly jealous, as the two of us left the Ballroom. Some looked as though they would have liked to warn me . . . And it did worry me that I couldn't see Molly anywhere at all.

CHAPTER TEN

Everything Revealed at Last

he Lady Faire took me by the hand. She had long, feminine fingers, with a man's strength. She led me through the wide corridors of the Winter Palace like an older woman seducing a teenager, with the promise of knowledge of what it means to be a man. And I let her do it. It all seemed very quiet, away from the Ballroom, calm and peaceful after the roar of the crowd. Such close proximity to the Lady Faire was dizzying. I felt . . . many things, but mostly vulnerable. As though I was no longer in command of the situation. Perhaps the Lady Faire sensed what I was feeling, because she took her own sweet time taking me to where we could talk in private.

She turned suddenly down an unmarked side corridor, and just like that we seemed to have left the Winter Palace and were moving along an elevated walkway on the exterior of the building, with the ground far and far below. I knew we couldn't be, because the Winter Palace was after all a giant snowflake, with no smooth exterior anywhere . . . and because I already knew the extreme cold of Ultima Thule would have killed us both in moments. But the illusion was complete and convincing as we walked high in the sky, looking out over the great mountain ranges, set against the purple sky with its dying red sun. Like looking out on the last evening of the world, with the sun getting ready to go down for the last time. A feeling of loss and melancholy settled over me, as if I were saying good-bye to an old friend.

I made myself concentrate on the mechanics of the situation. Either it was just an illusion or we were being protected from the outside by some hidden force shield. It seemed to me that I was feeling some of the cold. Perhaps that was the intention, to titillate the guests with just a touch of what they were being protected from. The Lady Faire glanced back at me, to see how I was taking it all. I flashed her a meaningless smile. I couldn't help noticing that her breath was steaming thickly on the chilly air, far more heavily than mine. As though she was warmer than me, inside. I wasn't sure where that thought was going.

We left the outer walkway, and went back inside the Winter Palace. Into a bare and featureless corridor that seemed almost uncomfortably warm. I didn't have a clue where we were now, in relation to the Ballroom. The Lady Faire led me on, keeping just a little ahead of me, never once letting go of her grip on my hand. Every now and again she would squeeze my fingers lightly, and my heart would beat just that little bit faster. She stepped it out, elegantly, every movement more than usually sensual, sexual, and enticing. She walked like a man but moved like a woman. I could feel my hand sweating inside hers. Her hand wasn't sweating at all. She seemed perfectly relaxed and at ease, as though she'd done this many times before. As though it came to her as naturally as breathing. My heart was pounding hard in my chest, and my breath was coming more and more quickly. I tried to think of Molly, and my mission, my missing parents and why I was there, but it was hard to think of anything but the Lady Faire when she was this close.

I could tell she knew what I was feeling. She found it amusing.

Finally, we came to her room. The door swung open before us as we approached, apparently entirely of its own accord. And once we'd passed through, into the room beyond, the door closed itself quietly but firmly behind us. I listened for the sound of a lock engaging, but didn't hear it. That didn't mean it hadn't happened, though. Just as I'd expected, the Lady Faire's room was a bedroom. The great circular bed in the middle was so big it seemed to take up half the available space. The Lady Faire finally let go of my hand, and I stumbled to a halt just inside the door. As though only her encouragement had kept me moving. She moved over to the bed, still not looking back at me.

"Nice place." I said, fighting to keep my voice calm and steady.

"It suits me," said the Lady Faire. "Though I've known better."

"Why choose the Winter Palace for your Ball?" I said, just to be saying something.

"I rented it, from the Wulfshead Club management," said the Lady Faire. "We go way back. They always do me a good deal. And they do have access to such unusual properties."

"You know who they are?" I said. "The actual people?"

She finally turned around, and looked at me. Her glance, and her smile, was like a caress on my face. "Is that what you came here to talk about, Eddie Drood?"

"No," I said.

She wandered around her room, quite casually, trailing her fingertips across the various surfaces. Like a cat rubbing its body against the fixtures and fittings, to remind them who was in charge. She smiled at me, quite easily, as though I was just an old friend who'd happened to drop by. Her body seemed to press out against the restrictions of her white tuxedo, as though all the buttons might burst open at any moment, unable to handle the strain of containing everything that lay within.

"Relax, Eddie," she said. "Sit down. Make yourself comfortable. Would you like something to drink?"

"No, thank you," I said.

Disturbed that my voice didn't sound as assured as I thought it should, I deliberately looked away from the Lady Faire, and took an interest in her room. It was large and open and almost unbearably sybaritic, with every conceivable luxury and comfort to hand. Lots of soft surfaces, in soft pastel colours. Modern furniture, in smooth organic shapes. Bare walls, without a single print or painting, and not even the smallest decorative object on any of the furniture tops. The bed dominated everything. The bed was what the room was for.

And yet there was no personality to the room. Nothing to show that the Lady Faire had any interest in impressing her character on it. You couldn't say it was a woman's room, or a man's. No personal touches anywhere, to suggest the kind of person the Lady Faire was, in private. Perhaps there was no private person. Perhaps what you saw was what you got. God knew, that was impressive enough. Perhaps for the Lady Faire, being the ultimate honey trap that she was, a bedroom was just somewhere she did business.

When I looked at her again, she was bent over the mini-bar in the far corner. The gleaming white fabric of her trousers stretched tight across her bottom. And I caught my breath despite myself. She straightened up, taking her time, poured herself a tall glass of Perrier water, and slammed the door to the mini-bar shut with a careless bump of her hip. She took a long drink, her Adam's apple moving up and down sensuously slowly. She put down the glass, and looked at me again, and I knew immediately from her smile that she knew I'd been watching. Her golden-pupiled eyes were sparkling, teasing. She stood there, not saying anything, to put the pressure on me to talk, to break the silence. An old agents' trick. I didn't say anything.

She moved over to the huge circular bed. The fitted sheets had already been folded back invitingly. Waiting. The sheets were a dark pink, almost blood colour. Almost . . . organic. Presumably the Lady Faire just liked to have everything ready, for whatever the night might bring. Or whoever. She sat down on the edge of the bed, and looked at me. I looked around the room, at anything but the bed. She started to say something, and then stopped herself. I could still see her, out of the corner of my eye. She sat with her back straight, and her legs elegantly crossed. I couldn't help but feel I was in the presence of a practised performance. For an audience of one. Something she had done so often, she'd refined it down to just the barest necessary essentials. Much reduced, but still a display intended only for me. Aimed at me, like a weapon.

Her interest in me seemed real enough, but I was still sufficiently in control of myself to know I couldn't trust it. She let her hand move slowly across the taut bedsheet, as though stroking a favoured pet. She caught my glance, and leaned forward a little, to show off her smile and her eyes. I still couldn't get a sense of what her body might be like, under that expertly fitted white tuxedo. It curved out well enough, to suggest breasts and hips, but there was a masculine strength in the long arms and legs. Broad shoulders, but a swan's neck. A woman's grace, but a man's power. Ladything, omnisexual, male and female and everything in between. Up close, that was just words. She was simply magnificent. Desirable. Turned up to eleven.

"Come and sit beside me, Eddie," said the Lady Faire. "There's nothing to be afraid of."

"I'll bet you say that to all the boys," I said. And I made myself pull up a smoothly curved chair and sit down on it, facing the bed. I sat carefully upright, with my legs firmly crossed. Trying not to look too defensive. I had an erection so hard it was almost painful, and I was pretty sure she knew that, though she'd never looked. I suspected the Lady Faire wasn't fooled by anything I said or did. She really had seen it all before. I couldn't help feeling that the only reason I wasn't completely captivated by the Lady Faire, the legendary Ice Queen, was that she wasn't really trying.

"You're wondering what they all wonder," she said. "What lies beneath, when the outer trappings are discarded. Who and what the Lady Faire really is, when she's at home. The answer is, everything you could ever want. Everything you've ever dreamed of, especially the ones you never tell anyone about. I was designed to appeal to every taste, to be open to everything. I could take your breath away, Eddie. My body was made to quicken the heart and madden the senses, in every way there is. I could make you love me, Eddie Drood. Make you serve me and worship me, and make you enjoy every moment of it. You've never had a lover like me. I could make you mine, forever."

"Bet you couldn't," I said. My mouth was dry, but my voice was perfectly steady. "I already have a lover. My own true love. And she is more to me than you'll ever be. Because she gives a damn."

"The witch? Dear little Molly Metcalf? I don't think so."

"She would rip your heart out with her bare hands," I said. "And I hate to think what she'd rip off me . . ."

"It's all right, Eddie. She doesn't need to know. I won't tell her if you won't. Come here, and sit with me on the bed. How can we really understand each other, if we don't know each other intimately? How can we discuss anything, if we're not open with each other? You do want something from me, don't you?"

"Yes," I said. "But for what I have in mind, we don't need to understand each other that well. I'm just here to do some business."

"So am I!" said the Lady Faire. "I've been trying to tell you that all along, darling. For me, it's always about the give-and-take."

"I'm not here for you," I said.

"Don't you want me, Eddie?"

"You know I do," I said. "But what I want doesn't matter. You'd be surprised how often in my life what I wanted has never mattered."

"Now that's just sad," said the Lady Faire. "Come to me, and I'll make it feel all better. That's what I'm for."

I think I surprised her then, by laughing briefly. "You need new material, Lady. The old lines are getting worn out."

She sighed, and leaned back on the bed. "Very well, Eddie. We'll play it your way. What do you want from me? Why did you come all this way, to Ultima Thule and the Winter Palace, and my annual Ball, if not for me?"

"Tell me what you know," I said. "About my uncle, James Drood."

She shrugged quickly, just a little irritated, as though she didn't like to think about the past. Or her past lovers. Because the past, and everything in it, didn't matter to her.

"Of course I remember James. He wasn't everything his legend suggested, but he was a perfectly adequate lover. Of course he was getting on a bit, when I knew him. I don't age as normal people do. But then I don't do anything as normal people do. The Baron Frankenstein saw to that. You do know he was responsible for my creation . . . Of course you do. You're a Drood. Droods know everything. Many people have told me that I should have known the Grey Fox when he was younger, in his prime. And I did try! But he was always so very busy, and so very elusive . . . I had to wait for him to come to me. And of course he did, in the end, like everyone does. It is possible he had almost as many lovers as I did . . ."

"He certainly had more children," I said.

"I don't have children," the Lady Faire said coldly. "The Baron saw to that too. I was made from dead things, in his laboratory, made from pieces of old life, stitched together. And while every part of me functions perfectly,

I remain dead inside. It's not important. Children would only have got in the way for what I was made to be."

"I'm sorry," I said.

"Don't be," said the Lady Faire. "I'm not. James . . . Yes. He was fun to have around, for a while. We had a very pleasant time together while it lasted. What do you want from me, Eddie? You must have known him better and longer than I ever did. Or do you want me to tell you what your precious Uncle and I did in bed? What he liked me to do to him?"

"No," I said. "This isn't about that. He gave you something. Something he really shouldn't have. I'm here because I want it back."

She sat up straight on the bed, giving me her full attention for the first time. Her face was expressionless, her golden eyes utterly cold.

"So that's why you're here! The Lazarus Stone! I should have known . . . Well, you can't have it. It's mine. Mine! James gave it to me!"

"You must have known he wasn't supposed to do that. You must have known you wouldn't be allowed to keep it."

"You think you can just walk in here and take it?" said the Lady Faire, and her voice was deadly cold.

"Well, yes," I said. "I'm a Drood. That's pretty much what Droods do."

"My security people . . ."

"Are currently scattered to the farthest reaches of the Winter Palace," I said. "On my direct orders, as your Head of Security. And whilst you undoubtedly have many . . . abilities, I don't think you've got anything that would stand against Drood armour. So, where is the Lazarus Stone?"

The Lady Faire put her arms behind her and leaned back on the bed, giving me her best languorous, heavy-lidded look. "Are you planning to beat the information out of me? I might enjoy that."

"The word is out, in all the important places, that you have the Lazarus Stone," I said patiently. "I'm just the first to come after it. The first to find you. There will be others. A never-ending stream of others. And you can bet they won't be nearly as polite as me. You could go into hiding, I suppose. Dig yourself a really deep hole, drop in, and pull it in after you. But you're not ready to turn your back on the world and all its pleasures, to live the solitary life of the hermit. Come, my Lady. Be reasonable. You don't need the Stone that badly. So give it up. I mean, what would you use it for, anyway? Is there really anyone you would want to bring back, out of Time?"

"The Baron, of course," said the Lady Faire. "Because he was . . . my first. And no one does it like Daddy." She laughed softly then, at the look on my face, and something in the sound of that laughter raised all the hackles on the back of my neck. "Yes . . . I'd bring the Baron back, out of the dead Past. Just so I could thank him properly, for making me what I am. I'd keep him alive in constant agony for years, before I finally let him die."

"Then why haven't you?"

"Because I'm afraid . . . Afraid that if I did bring him back . . . even after all these years, he would control me again. And no one controls the Lady Faire."

"You're never going to use the Stone," I said. "Because if you were, you would have done it by now. So give it back. And put temptation behind you."

"No," said the Lady Faire. "You can't have it. It's mine. My property. And I never give up anything that's mine.

Why do you think the Ballroom is full of my ex-lovers? Because I just can't bear to let anything go."

She stood up abruptly, and advanced on me. I stood up to face her, and didn't retreat. She strode right up to me, and I put up a hand to stop her. She took my hand in both of hers and clutched it tightly. Her hands felt very soft, and very warm, and very strong. She was standing close to me now, only our linked hands separating our two bodies. I could feel the breath from her mouth on mine. Feel the forceful pressure of her breath on my lips. Her eyes stared into mine. She hit me with the full force of her influence, and whether it was the pheromones or her personality, it didn't matter. I could feel my will-power withering, like a moth in a flame. And there, in that moment, I wanted her like I'd never wanted anything else in my life. But I'd had a lot of experience in wanting things I knew I could never have.

So I did what I always do when I feel threatened. I called up my armour, and it flowed out of the torc at my throat and covered me from head to toe in a moment. Sealing me off from the world, and all the things in it that were a danger to me. The golden strange matter closed over my hand, gently forcing her hands away. And just like that, her power over me was gone. Swept away like a bad dream. She could tell. She stayed where she was, looking at her own face reflected in the featureless golden mask.

"So lovely," she said. "So lovely."

And then we both looked round sharply, as a whole bunch of alarms and sirens went off at once.

"Something's happened, back at the Ballroom!" snapped the Lady Faire, immediately all business again.

"That's the general alarm. Is this more of your doing, Drood?"

"I don't know," I said. "I'm here with you."

"Is it the witch?"

"Which part of *I am here with you so I don't know anything more than you do*, are you having trouble grasping?" I said. "I don't think Molly would start anything on her own, though."

"Then it's more thieves!" The Lady Faire actually stamped a foot in frustration. "While I'm wasting my time here with you! And I don't even have a Head of Security to protect my guests, do I?"

I armoured down again. It was clear we'd have to go back to the Ballroom to see what was happening, and I didn't think it would calm all the notable guests to know there was a Drood in the house. The Lady Faire headed for the door, and it swung quickly open before her. I went after her.

"This is all your fault!" she said loudly, not looking back. "Whatever it is, whatever's happened, I want you to know that as far as I'm concerned it's all your fault!"

"Of course," I said, hurrying out into the corridor after her. "It always is. I'm a Drood."

I have to tell you, when the Lady Faire feels like it, she can really run. She pounded down the corridors, arms pumping at her sides, taking turns apparently at random without ever slowing down, and it was all I could do to keep up with her. She never once looked back to see if I was still there. We ran at full pelt through a warren of interconnecting anonymous corridors, with all the bells and sirens still screaming their heads off. Whatever bad thing had happened, it was clearly still happening. I'd lost track of exactly where we were in the Winter Palace long ago, so I stuck close behind the Lady Faire, determined not to be left behind. The comm unit in my ear was full of raised voices, all shouting at once. I got the impression all the security people were heading back to the Ballroom at speed, but that no one knew why yet.

I got my answer soon enough, when a dozen blood-red men in their full face masks burst out of a side corridor and spread quickly out to block our way. The Lady Faire crashed to a halt so suddenly I nearly slammed into the back of her. The blood-red men stood very still, all of them looking squarely at me. The Lady Faire looked them over, and then turned to glare at me.

"Are they with you?"

"Very definitely not," I said. "We don't get on. Be careful; they're dangerous."

The Lady Faire threw back her head, shook her Jean Harlow hair defiantly, and glared at the blood-red men arrayed before her. "They all look exactly the same. What are they? Clones?"

"Probably," I said. "You try asking; I haven't been able to get a word out of them so far. But I have seen them kill a whole bunch of people, so maintain a cautious distance."

The Lady Faire sniffed loudly. "Dangerous . . . They're only men."

She stepped forward and smiled at the blood-red men, hitting them with the full force of her presence. Even standing behind her, I could feel some of it. Incredibly, the blood-red men didn't. They just stood their ground and stared right back at her. Entirely unmoved, and unaffected. The Lady Faire fell back a step, and looked at me, actually shocked. I don't think she'd ever

encountered such a situation before. She looked . . . lost.
As though the world had suddenly stopped making
sense to her. I moved carefully forward, to put myself
between her and the blood-red men. And she was so
shocked, she let me do it. Immediately, all the blood-red
men snapped their attention back to me.

"What are you doing here?" I said to them. "How did
you even get here? Did you use the Siberian Gateway?"

"Gateway?" the Lady Faire said immediately. "What
Gateway?"

"Later, dear," I said. "Hush now. Drood working.
Please don't distract me while I'm trying to negotiate
with the bloodthirsty and quite possibly criminally insane clone people."

The blood-red men surged forward, their hands reaching out with clawed fingers. I armoured up again and
punched in the face of the nearest man with such force I
heard his neck snap, as his head spun round to face in the
opposite direction. But he didn't fall. His head just turned
back again, with a loud ratcheting of repairing neck bones.
So I grabbed him and threw him at the blood-red men
behind him. They all went down in a great tangle, and
immediately started getting up again. I grabbed another
blood-red man and threw him at the nearest wall so hard
the sound of the wood panels breaking was actually
louder than the sound of broken bones. The rest of the
blood-red men came straight for me. I could hear the
Lady Faire breathing heavily behind me, but she didn't
run. She had confidence in me. Which made one of us.

I threw myself at the advancing blood-red men, lash-
ing out with spiked golden fists, putting all my armoured
strength into every blow. I hit them hard, smashing in
skulls and punching out hearts, snapping arm and leg

bones. I knew I couldn't kill them, so I concentrated on major damage. I broke them with my armoured hands, threw them to the floor, and trampled them underfoot. They never cried out, never made a sound of pain or protest. I threw them the length of the corridor, and they just picked themselves up and came back at me. So I picked them up and smashed them into the corridor walls, one at a time, wedging them into the holes they made. And while they were still struggling to pull themselves free, I grabbed the Lady Faire by the hand and we ran down the corridor, leaving them behind. The Lady Faire didn't say anything, but she held on to my gloved hand really tightly.

It didn't take me long to remember that I didn't know where we were going, so I armoured down and let her take the lead again. We were both breathing hard now, and not just from the exertions of the fight. There was something seriously disturbing about enemies who wouldn't stay down, and wouldn't stay dead. It turned out we were only a few corridors short of the Ballroom. As we approached the open door, all the alarms suddenly shut down, and I could hear cries and shouts and sounds of violence. I slowed to a halt, and the Lady Faire slowed with me. She realised she was still holding on to my hand, and let go. She looked more angry than upset at having her Ball ruined.

"How many of these red men are there?" she demanded.

"Usually as many as it takes to get the job done," I said.

"Are they an army?"

"Wouldn't surprise me."

"Don't you know anything about them?"

"They kill people," I said steadily. "And they just keep coming, until they get what they're after."

"Why are they here?" said the Lady Faire, almost plaintively. "Are they after you?"

"Wouldn't surprise me," I said. "But I think it's more likely they're here because they want what I want. The Lazarus Stone. I told you people would be coming for it."

"I should have cancelled the Ball," said the Lady Faire. "My horoscope said it was going to be a bad day."

"I do not believe in the stars," I said.

"They believe in you."

I took a deep breath and headed for the open entrance. Some conversations you just know aren't going to go anywhere useful.

When we finally crashed through the door and into the Ballroom, we found there was a riot going on. Security people, in their white uniforms and masks, were pouring into the great ice cavern through all the entrances at once, and going head to head with any number of blood-red men. The security people had all kinds of really nasty weapons, but the blood-red men had numbers, unnatural strength, and their awful unstoppability. Guns could damage them, but not kill them. Even the most terrible wounds healed almost immediately. And one by one they were wearing the security people down; when one of them fell, with blood staining their white uniforms, they didn't get up again.

The voices in my earpiece were going out, one by one. I wanted to shout at them, to warn them, but what could I tell them that they couldn't already see for themselves? They weren't my people, weren't even really on my side, but I was still proud of them. They could have run and saved themselves. But they stood their ground and fought on, to protect the guests. Because that was their job.

The guests were mostly hanging back, sticking to the far walls and the farthest reaches of the ice cavern. Keeping well out of the way, and basically treating the whole bloody struggle as just more free entertainment. Some were cheering one side, some the other. Many were placing bets. They hadn't realised yet the danger they were in. They thought they were exempt. The Lady Faire glared at the bloody debacle her Ball had degenerated into, and then turned abruptly to glare at me.

"Do something!"

"I'm open to suggestions!"

I looked around, and spotted a surprisingly familiar face standing alone. Unnoticed by the other guests, the security people, and the blood-red men . . . because he wasn't really there. And since I couldn't do anything about the blood-red men, I thought I might as well check out the one thing that stood out. I gestured for the Lady Faire to stay put by the doorway, and moved cautiously forward. For the moment both sides in the fight seemed too busy to notice I'd arrived, and I wanted to keep it that way until I'd figured out something useful to do. I quietly approached the shimmering figure by the wall, and its head came slowly round to look at me. The Phantom Berserker nodded slowly, and waited for me to join him.

For a ghost, he looked surprisingly solid, but then, my armour gives me amplified Sight on many levels. To everyone else he was probably just a shadowy figure, unclear and insubstantial, unless you looked at him directly. To me, he was a tall, bulky Viking figure with the traditional horned helmet and a bear-skin cloak. His deathly pale face was drawn and gaunt. He had haunted eyes. Word was, agents from the Department of Uncanny had dug him up out of some ancient burial mound in Norway, back in the Sixties, and he'd followed them home. They didn't have the heart to kick him out, so they made him an honorary agent, and he'd been with them ever since.

"Hello!" I said, raising my voice to be heard over the general bedlam. "Eddie Drood, remember me? The Regent's grandson. I thought you were dead? I saw your body lying among all the others, at the massacre at the Department of Uncanny."

"I was dead," said the Phantom Berserker. His voice was hollow, and strangely distant, as though it had to travel a long way to reach me. "For a while I was alive again. But it didn't last. Now I'm a ghost again. I'm surprised you can see me; no one else here can. But then, you're a Drood, and the rules don't apply to you, do they? It was all my fault, you know. What happened at Uncanny. All those deaths. All my fault."

"Talk to me," I said. "Tell me what happened."

"I was the traitor inside the Department," said the Phantom Berserker. "I opened the door, to let them in. This Voice came to me, out of nowhere, and it promised me things. Said it could provide me with flesh and blood, in a new body, so that I could breathe and move and feel again. A real live body, after so long as only a drifting spirit from another age. And I wanted that so very badly. I could materialise, from time to time, just long enough to be useful to the Department. But not for long. Never for long. And those brief flashes of feeling, of simple sensation, just made it so much worse when I had to go back to being immaterial again. My people knew what they

370 ° Simon R. Green

were doing, all those centuries ago, when they cursed me to be the Phantom Berserker. I was so desperate to feel again, to live again, that I said I'd do whatever the Voice wanted. In return for a body."

"Whose Voice was it?" I said. "Who did you make a deal with?"

"I don't know," said the Phantom Berserker. "The Voice put me to sleep, and when I woke up again, I was alive. I had a heart that beat and lungs that moved, and blood that coursed through my veins. I had hands that could touch, and a mouth that could taste. I think I went a little crazy then, for a while, indulging all my senses. After all the years of just watching people enjoy life and take it for granted. But it didn't last. I'd been alive less than a day when the Voice came to me, inside the Department of Uncanny. And told me it was time to pay the price for what I'd been given. All I had to do was shut down the Department's security systems and unlock the doors, and my debt would be paid. It didn't seem like much to ask. Just an information grab, I thought. Such a small thing, to pay for this new body, and all its pleasures. I wish I could say I hesitated. I opened the door and let them in. I didn't know what they were going to do. How could I?

"The bloody men swarmed in, an army of them. And the first thing they did was kill me, standing at the door. They struck me down with their bare hands, and just like that I was a ghost again. So weakened there was nothing I could do but watch . . . as they killed everyone in the Department. Everyone who'd been so kind to me . . . I watched them kill your grandfather. Watched them rip Kayleigh's Eye right out of his chest. There was nothing I could do. Nothing."

"Why are you here?" I said.

"Because the Voice still has power over me. Because I said yes to it, I have to serve it. Even though I swore to serve and protect your grandfather all my days. Do you know what it means, for a Norseman to betray his oath? I am in Hel, Eddie Drood. Still under the control of the man who ruined me."

"You don't have to serve him," I said. "Death breaks all oaths, all bonds."

"If only that were true," said the Phantom Berserker.

"I think I know a way out of Hel," I said. "Wait, and watch for your chance. And when you see an opportunity, take it. Whoever's behind the Voice, I don't think he'll be able to resist turning up here, in person. And then . . ."

"And then?" said the Phantom Berserker.

"That's up to you," I said.

The Phantom Berserker turned away from me, not saying anything. And I couldn't give him any more time, because I'd just seen Molly Metcalf, fighting fiercely in the middle of the crowd. I went to join her.

She'd conjured up a long sword of vivid blazing energies, and was using it to cut off heads as fast as she could get to them. Headless bodies of blood-red men went staggering this way and that, in pursuit of their lopped-off heads. No blood spurted from their necks. The heads went rolling here and there along the floor, kicked around like footballs. Now and then a body would find a head and clap it back into place, whereupon the wound would seal and fuse immediately. I wasn't sure the right bodies were finding the right heads, but since the blood-red men were all identical, I didn't suppose it mattered. All this was keeping a lot of blood-red men occupied, and taking them out of the fight, but not for long. And more of the blood-red figures were pouring into the Ballroom through all the entrances and exits. Dozens and dozens of them. They already far outnumbered the remaining security people, because all of the white-uniformed security staff who were coming had already arrived, and there seemed no end to the numbers of blood-red men.

Molly looked around and grinned briefly as I moved in to cover her back, and then we both went to work, cutting off heads and smashing in skulls with grim joy and great efficiency. The blood-red men should have learned to keep their distance from us, but something drove them on to attack us anyway.

"Where the hell have you been?" Molly said loudly. "As if I couldn't guess. So what does the Lady Faire look like, in the flesh? Does she have both sets of bits?"

"I have no idea," I said, wrapping myself in my armour and striking down blood-red men with vim and vigour. "She never undid a button while I was with her. All we did was talk."

"Did she tell you where the Lazarus Stone is?"

"No."

"Then maybe you should have undone some of her buttons," said Molly.

It's amazing how much damage you can do to people, with spiked armoured fists and a blazing energy sword. It was also amazing, and not a little disturbing, how fast the blood-red men could come back from so much damage. I scowled, under my featureless golden mask, thinking hard. There had to be a way to stop them . . .

The last of the security people were still fighting, well and bravely, but they were vastly outnumbered by blood-red men. The security staff had been forced into small defensive clumps, scattered across the Ballroom, firing bullets and poisoned needles and the occasional energy blast. But the blood-red men were still pouring in through all the doors, leaping across the bodies of their own fallen to get at the security people. Blood spread thickly across the ice cavern floor.

The mood of the watching guests quickly turned against the blood-red men. They shouted and jeered and threw things, and when it became clear that wasn't going to stop the slaughter of the security people, many of the guests decided it was time to do something.

Some guests tried to teleport out, only to look shocked and startled when they discovered they couldn't, because someone had reinstalled the anti-teleport shields. Some tried to run, only to find there was nowhere to run to. All the doors were full of blood-red men. Some tried to impress the masked invaders with their names and status, only to find the blood-red men didn't give a damn. And some of the guests fought fiercely, just because it was in their nature.

Dead Boy got stuck right in, wading into the fighting where it was fiercest, beating up blood-red men with his unfeeling fists, and happily ripping arms out of their sockets with his unnatural strength. His deep purple greatcoat flapped around him as he received and handed out appalling punishment. Dead Boy was almost as hard to stop as the ones he fought. But in the end they came at him from every side at once, piled on top of him, and just dragged him down by sheer weight of numbers. He went down still fighting, and continued to struggle even under a weight of bodies that would have held down an enraged rhino.

The Bride fought with more than human strength,

breaking bones and smashing in skulls with effortless
ease, while Springheel Jack guarded her back with two
nasty-looking straight razors. The Bride tore blood-red
men limb from limb, and Springheel Jack cut them up
like joints of meat. Until finally they too fell under the
weight of so many attackers, and disappeared from view.

Jimmy Thunder struck his enemies down with Mjolnir, and whoever the hammer hit did not rise again. Even
the blood-red men were no match for that mighty and
ancient weapon. The Norse godling strode through the
chaos with contemptuous ease, sending broken bodies
crashing to the floor, singing some old Norse song on the
joys of blood and slaughter. But in the end, the blood-red
men found his weakness. They ganged up on the costumed adventurer Ms. Fate, despite all her fighting skills,
and beat her savagely. Jimmy lost his temper and threw
his hammer at them. Mjolnir flashed through the air, and
just the impact of its arrival killed half the blood-red
men, but then the hammer dropped to the floor and lay
there. Jimmy called desperately for it to return to his
hand, but either the hammer didn't hear him or it had
forgotten how. The blood-red men hit Jimmy Thunder
from every side at once, and eventually they pulled him
down. For all his strength and fury.

Most of the other guests didn't last long. And when
they saw the blood-red men tear the Living Shroud
apart, unravelling and scattering its rags and tatters until
there was nothing left . . . they surrendered. The Lady
Alice Underground sat down and put her hands on her
head. The Last of Leng retreated to a corner and
crouched there, snarling. Everyone else put their hands
in the air, or ostentatiously dropped their weapons to the
floor. Surprisingly, the Replicated Meme of Saint Sebas-

tian hadn't got involved at all. They just stood together by a far wall, watching silently from behind their impenetrable metal masks.

Molly and I stood back to back in the middle of the room, not actually surrendering but no longer fighting. There just didn't seem any point. We were surrounded by rank upon rank of blood-red men. A dozen or more came forward, encircling the Lady Faire and urging her on. She didn't appear to be hurt, but there was no doubt she was no longer in charge. She went where the blood-red men indicated for her to go. She strode along with her head in the air, projecting icy dignity. She shot me a cold and angry look, as though I'd betrayed her by not fighting to the death. Molly made her blazing sword disappear, and I armoured down, to keep her company. Fighting against the odds had taken us as far as it was going to. All that remained now was to stand down and see what happened next.

The Ballroom was still and quiet, with blood-red men in control everywhere. I couldn't see a single white-uniformed security person still standing. I hoped they weren't all dead. They'd fought well. I realised I was still wearing the white face mask of the Head of Security. I peeled it off and threw it away, along with the comm earpiece. Voices rose on every side from among the guests, as some of them recognised me. Or at least the torc at my throat. The voices died quickly away again as the blood-red men stirred dangerously. The guests were split up into small groups, surrounded by silently watching blood-red men. The Ball was over; it remained to be seen what would replace it.

To discover what this had all been about.

"Really don't like the odds here, Eddie," Molly murmured. "Please tell me you've got something up your sleeve."

"Just my arm," I said quietly. "On the bright side, I think we're finally about to find out who's been running the blood-red men all this time. The villain behind the Voice. Hopefully, we're about to get some answers to a whole lot of questions. You know how bad guys love to boast."

"He's going to make a speech, isn't he?" Molly said gloomily. "I hate speeches."

"Even when I make them?"

"Especially when you make them!"

"Oh, that hurts," I said.

And then a man came walking through the crowd towards us, wearing James Drood's face. The blood-red men fell back, to open up a wide aisle for him to walk through. The closer he got, the less like Uncle James he looked, though the face stayed the same. He didn't move like James, or act like him. The face . . . was just another mask, in a Ballroom full of masks. And yet . . . there was something familiar about this man. I did know him from somewhere. He walked right up to me, ignoring Molly standing at my side, and stopped right in front of me.

"You're not James Drood," I said roughly. "Nothing like him. Who are you, really?"

The face flickered and disappeared, like the illusion it was, and standing before me was Laurence Drood. The Drood from Cell 13, free at last. He laughed softly at the look of surprise on my face.

"Oh, come on," he said. "I can't believe you didn't guess it was me all along. I mean, who else was there? Who had better reason than me to want the Lazarus Stone?"

"How did you get out?" I said numbly.

"I could have left any time," said Laurence. "I know everything the family knows, remember? How could they build any jail that could hold me? I just never had a reason to leave before."

"Why did you choose to look like my uncle James?" I said, and he grinned again at the anger in my voice.

"Because he was the Drood I always wanted to be. Oh yes. The man who got to go out into the world and have adventures, and beautiful women, and make a legend of himself. I always wanted to be the Grey Fox. Didn't you, Eddie? He got to live the life, while I remained stuck in my Cell, living my half life ... But I don't want to talk about that now. I want to talk about us, Eddie! Because this has all been about you and me."

"I told you," Molly said resignedly. "He's going to make a speech. Boast about his triumphs, and explain his motives. Like we care. We know why you did all this, you miserable little scrote! It's because you're a sick scumbag who gets off on hurting people!"

"If she speaks again," Laurence said to me, "I will have my people sew her lips together. It's up to you."

"She'll be quiet," I said quickly. "Talk to me, Laurence. Because there's a lot going on here that I don't understand."

"Hoping to buy some time, Eddie?" Laurence said cheerfully. "Thinking perhaps that while I'm talking, people aren't dying? Or just hoping you can use the time to put together some brilliant plan to defeat me, at the very last moment? I don't think so. I know everything the family knows. Including you. That's why I've been one step ahead of you all along. Now shut up and listen. I've had a lot of time to think about what I would say when I finally got out."

Molly growled under her breath, but said nothing. The blood-red men stood very still, all around, every single one of them fixing me with the same intent glare I saw in Laurence's eyes. That meant something. Though I wasn't sure what, yet. So I just stood there and looked interested, while Laurence talked. His voice rose and fell and he waved his arms around a lot, because he wasn't used to talking to people face-to-face.

"I wanted to be put away, to be locked up securely, all those years ago," he said earnestly. "When the accident first happened. When I suddenly knew everything, all at once. It was such a powerful experience, horrifying and overwhelming. It took me a long time to get my head back together again, to think only my own thoughts. And by then I'd been the Drood in Cell 13 for such a long time that most of the family had forgotten I'd ever been a person in my own right. I'd become just a cautionary tale for those who ran the family. *Don't let anyone try to know too much* ... I could have left Cell 13 at any time once I was back in control of my own mind, but where would I go? What could I do? The world had moved on and left me behind. And it wasn't like I could put my burden down and walk away from it. The whole of the family's knowledge filled my head, and it kept flooding in, more and more, never ending. Even if I did leave, the family would be bound to send agents after me, to track me down and drag me back. For fear of the damage my knowledge might do in enemy hands. So I stayed in Cell 13, studying all the information in my head, and planning my revenge. And finally I learned about the Lazarus Stone. And saw a way out of my horrible half life."

He suddenly pulled open the front of his shirt, to show me Kayleigh's Eye, fused to the flesh of his chest.

A great glowing amulet, with a golden alien eye se...
centre. Staring at me unblinkingly. Just as it had on...
stared at me from my grandfather's chest. Tears stung my
eyes, but I wouldn't let them fall. Not in front of the enemy. I glared at Laurence, and when I finally trusted my
voice again, I let him hear the rage and contempt that
burned within me.

"You killed the Regent of Shadows," I said. "You
murdered my grandfather, you crazy piece of shit. I will
make you pay . . ."

He smiled easily, entirely unmoved, and rebuttoned
his shirt with quick, fussy movements.

"Well," he said, "I didn't kill him personally . . . Though
it was my will that moved the hands that killed him, and
tore the Eye from his chest through brute force. The only
way it could be taken. So, yes, I suppose you could say I
am responsible. It doesn't matter. Really, it doesn't! I've
killed lots of people, just recently. Indirectly. To get here,
to this place and this moment. I just wanted you to understand, Eddie, that there's no point in attacking me. You
can't hurt me and you can't stop me. You must understand, I will do anything, absolutely anything, to get what
I want."

"Well, what do you want?" said Molly.

I tensed, half expecting the blood-red men to attack
her for interrupting their master. But Laurence just
laughed, and waggled his fingers in her face mockingly.

"All in good time . . . I have so much to tell you, Eddie.
My story has been going on a lot longer than you realise.
So hush now. Listen, and consider. After the attack on
Drood Hall by the Accelerated Men . . . you do remem-
ber that, don't you? Of course you do . . . One of the Ar-
mourer's precious lab assistants found his way down to

Cell 13 to talk with me. What was his name ... Oh, I can't remember. It doesn't matter. He was very bright, but not very sensible. He thought he was using me, the poor fool.

"He had been struck by the idea of creating Accelerated Droods, you see. The perfect, unstoppable field agents. He couldn't find the information he wanted in any of the official family files, or in the Library. The Council had suppressed the information for reasons of its own, that I probably don't need to explain to you, Eddie. Anyway, the lab assistant wondered if the Drood in Cell 13 might know ... So he came down into the depths to talk to me, to make his deal with the Droods' very own Devil. Typical lab assistant, ready to risk everything in the pursuit of knowledge. And never really thinking about the price he'd have to pay in return.

"I didn't know anything about the Accelerated Men, as it happened. But I did know many other fascinating things that I could use to bewitch a simple lab assistant. You don't need to know what those things are, Eddie. Secret things! Hidden things! Oh, if you only knew! The family has always had more sides to it, more levels within levels, than you ever suspected. But they were just the thing to enchant and seduce a young lab assistant's mind. More than enough to sucker him in, and keep him coming back for more.

"I persuaded him to contact the Doormouse, using secret Drood code phrases, so it seemed my orders came from the old Matriarch, Martha. I never liked her. She came all the way down to Cell 13 the day she was made Matriarch, just to tell me to my face that she would see to it I was never released. Awful person. Anyway these orders, apparently from the highest authority within the Droods, instructed the Doormouse to create a number of very special Doors, giving access to the Hall grounds from outside. And then sell them on, to an approved list of customers. Not to any actual official enemies of the Droods, of course. That would have raised suspicions. Just to certain interested parties, who could be trusted to make use of the gift so suddenly dropped into their laps."

"Like the Wulfshead Club management," I said.

"Yes! Exactly! Though it seems I outsmarted myself there." He stopped for a moment, to scowl and sulk like a thwarted child. "I've spent so long rehearsing this speech! Don't interrupt me! I won't have you taking any of the fun away! Now. Where was I . . . Ah yes. The orders told the Doormouse that the Droods wanted these Doors made, and used, to test their defences and security measures. All quite reasonable. Actually, I just wanted the Doors used to keep the family distracted. The idea being that so many unexpected incursions from outside would seize the family's attention so they wouldn't notice what I was up to behind the scenes. But the Wulfshead Club management had to go and be clever, didn't they? How could I know they'd be smart enough and suspicious enough to look a gift horse in the mouth, and tip you off to the existence of the Doors?

"But it didn't make any difference, in the end. I'd also had the Doormouse create a private Door, so the lab assistant could visit me directly, without attracting unwanted attention. And so I could get out, whenever I chose, without anyone knowing. You know the first thing I did? I went for a walk in the Hall grounds. They'd changed so much since my day, but there were still many things and places I recognised. From when I was just another Drood. It felt so good, the wind and the sun on my face, and the green grass under my feet . . . I walked all the way across the lawns to the front gates and that was where I stopped. I stood there, looking through the heavy iron bars, looking out at the world. I could have just left, but I didn't. I realised ... It had been so long since I'd seen the outside world, that it frightened me. I knew everything about the family, but nothing about the world. I was so scared ... and I couldn't have that. I turned around, went quietly back across the lawns, and returned to Cell 13.

"Where I felt safe.

"I had the lab assistant take a sample of my DNA down to the Armoury, where he used it to make a whole bunch of adult clones. To serve me directly, to walk about in the world on my behalf, so I could experience the world through them. They were designed to be mindless, you see, just blank slates with nothing inside their heads but me. I controlled them all, my mind in their bodies. I was, after all, used to thinking about a lot of things at once. I sent my clones out into the world in my place, to make the world frightened of me.

"The lab assistant had his own assembly line running there, tucked away in the deepest recesses of the Armoury, and no one ever noticed. You'd be amazed at what goes on in the Armoury every day that never gets officially noticed. Or perhaps *amazed* isn't the right word. *Horrified*—that's closer.

"I sent my clone army to the Department of Uncanny, where my very own suborned traitor let them in. You can always find someone ... and I used one clone's hands to tear Kayleigh's Eye out of your grandfather's chest, Eddie. To make me invulnerable and untouchable. And my clones too, to a lesser degree, because of the spiritual distance ... or something. Injure and damage them all you like, but they'll always bounce back. As you've no doubt noticed. Aren't they splendid?" He leaned forward, conspiratorially. "That's why the masks, of course. Because they've all got my face. Bit of a giveaway there . . ."

"Why did you kill everyone at Uncanny?" I said.

He shrugged. "Exuberance? Once you start, you just can't stop . . ."

"But why were you still in your Cell, when we came to see you?" said Molly.

"She's talking again," Laurence said to me. "How do you put up with her?"

"I think she's posed a perfectly reasonable question," I said carefully.

"Is it? Oh, very well . . . What was the point in leaving, back then? If I left Cell 13 and didn't go back, the family would be bound to notice and start looking for me. And I couldn't afford to be noticed. Not with so many things left undone, or unfinished. Do try to keep up, Molly! It's all about the Lazarus Stone, you see. From the moment I knew of it, I knew it was what I needed to escape my fate. I waited years for the damned thing to show up. I didn't know James had given it to the Lady Faire. Because the Grey Fox had such excellent mental shields. Oh yes. He put a lot of hard work into them, because he had so much he needed to hide from his family. Including what really happened to his wife . . . He never told the family who he'd given the Stone to, because he knew they wouldn't approve. Well, I mean, would you? Unnatural creature . . . Even the Armourer didn't know, back then. Until he met up with someone in the Nightside, at the oldest bar in the world, and they told him, I think just to see the look on his face. And even then, I didn't know! Because the Armourer has his own very powerful mental shields. If you think the Grey Fox had secrets, they were nothing to what dear old Jack Drood has hidden away from the family all these years. It's hard to hide anything from me, you know. Secrets leave holes in the information stream, and it's amazing what I can deduce, just from the shape of the holes.

"But, finally, the Armourer mentioned the Lazarus Stone, within the hearing of my pet lab tech. Who misheard that the Regent had it. He couldn't wait to tell me all about it. I knew I had to have the Lazarus Stone, the one thing that could put an end to my endless half life. That's why I sent my clones to Uncanny, to get the Stone from the Regent. I was heartbroken when it turned out he didn't have it. And then you and Molly showed up there, and I saw a way to blackmail you into finding where the Stone really was, and getting it for me. And it worked!"

"Hold it," said Molly. "What happened to this lab assistant you've been talking about? Why isn't he here, with you?"

Laurence sighed loudly, and dropped me a wink. "Women, eh? Always focusing on the one little detail that doesn't really matter. Very well—once I had my Door, and my clones, and my information on the Lazarus Stone . . . I didn't need him any more, did I? So now he's sitting in Cell 13, thinking he's me, looking like me, so no one in the family will know I've left until it's far too late."

"At least you didn't kill him," I said.

"Why should I?" said Laurence. "I wasn't in a merciful mood." He giggled briefly. "And now! It's time to put an end to all this . . . I have enjoyed making my little speech. I knew I would. Thank you for leading me here, Eddie. I'll take over now."

"Wait!" I said. "You've got what you want. You don't need my parents any longer. Please, let them go."

"Oh, I don't have your parents, Eddie. I never did." Laurence grinned broadly. "That was just bluff, so I could motivate and control you."

A cold hand clenched around my heart, and I looked at him stupidly. "But you must know where they are! You know everything. Tell me!"

He waggled a finger at me. "Don't shout at me, Eddie," he said mildly. "I have no idea where your parents might be. Which is just a bit odd, I'll admit. I should know, shouldn't I? I can only assume your parents are so very thoroughly lost that no one in the family knows . . . Never mind, Eddie. Don't be a nuisance! I'm busy."

He beckoned to the Lady Faire, and when she didn't come forward quickly enough to suit him, two of the blood-red men grabbed her by the arms and hustled her roughly forward. They forced her into position before Laurence, and held her firmly in place while Laurence looked her over, thoughtfully. He didn't seem to be at all affected, or impressed, by her presence.

"Don't waste your dubious charms on me, Lady," he said finally, almost absently. "I am fully in control of myself. I have to be, when there are so many of me running around at once. And besides, I wouldn't know what to do with you. That part of me died long ago."

"Don't you miss it?" said the Lady Faire.

Laurence surprised me then, by taking the time to consider her question. But in the end, he shook his head firmly.

"No," he said. "There are many things I do miss, but that isn't very high on the list."

"I could make you remember how sweet it was," said the Lady Faire.

"No thank you," Laurence said politely. "You have only one thing I want."

"No wonder I had no effect on your clones," said the Lady Faire. "They're all just like you. No one home, inside."

Laurence laughed in her face, quite suddenly, and it was a nasty, mocking sound. Many of the watching guests stirred, affronted by his contempt for their beloved Lady. Some of them actually started forward, intent on doing something, and the nearest blood-red men clubbed them viciously to the ground. Dark pools of blood spread slowly across the floor. I wanted to do something, and I could feel Molly tensing at my side, but I stopped her with an unobtrusive hand on her arm. This wasn't the time to start anything.

Laurence glowered at the Lady Faire. "You have only one thing I want. Give me the Lazarus Stone. Now."

"You didn't really think I'd bring it with me to the Ball, did you?" said the Lady Faire.

"I know you did," said Lazarus. "You couldn't trust it, away from you. Not with so many powerful people here. And besides, I can feel its presence. So hand it over. Or would you rather I have my clones tear your clothes off, until they find it?"

"Anywhen else, I might have enjoyed that," said the Lady Faire. "But you have a way of taking all the fun out of things. There is such a thing as dignity, I suppose."

She reached carefully into an unobtrusive pocket on her tuxedo jacket, and brought out a small shiny object. Everyone in the Ballroom leaned forward for a better look. They just couldn't help themselves. I did too, and was disappointed to discover that the legendary and much-sought-after Lazarus Stone . . . was just a small sphere of unimpressive alien tech. Nothing glamorous or impressive about it. A pockmarked ball of some unfamiliar metal, two or maybe three inches in diameter. Except, the more I looked at it, the more it seemed to me that there was something . . . slippery about it. Something that made the Lazarus Stone strangely hard to look at, hard to pin down in any of its details. As though it had too many spatial dimensions for this world. Perhaps because it had been made by a species with far more than human senses, or less limitation in their thinking. All I knew was that just looking at the Stone made my head hurt.

Laurence reached out an eager hand to take the Lazarus Stone, and the Lady Faire drew back her hand.

"Why do you want the Stone?" she said. "What would you use it for?"

"I will use the Stone to reach back in Time, and grab myself," said Laurence. "Rescue myself from History, before the awful accident happens. Save myself, so I won't have to spend all those horrible years being the Drood in Cell 13. Being me."

"I thought the Stone could only be used to save people from the point before they died?" said the Lady Faire.

"You people," said Laurence quietly, contemptuously. "Always so limited in your thinking. And besides, I'm as good as dead anyway, aren't I? You couldn't say that I've had a life. But I will have."

"You would undo centuries of History," said the Lady Faire. "The world as we know it would just disappear!"

"I know," said Laurence. "And I don't care. Why should I? When did anyone in the whole world ever care about the Drood in Cell 13? That's why I keep saying it doesn't matter. Because nothing does, because I will make it all never happened. All the lives lost, all the lives ruined . . . won't matter at all. Let the whole world vanish, if that's what it takes for me to have a real life. Now give me the Lazarus Stone, Lady, or I'll have my clones take it. And you really won't like how I'll have them do it."

The Lady Faire put forward her hand, offering him the alien tech, and then she opened her hand and let the Stone fall on the floor between them. Laurence sneered at her, and bent forward to pick up the Lazarus Stone. And the Lady Faire kicked him square in the left eye, with the tip of her elegant white boot. A lot of people in the room winced, and some cried out despite themselves as they saw and heard the boot strike home. I was one of them. Laurence fell backwards, crying out abjectly as he clapped both hands to his face. The Lady Faire laughed at him.

"Didn't see that one coming, did you? I am not predictable!"

But what interested me was that all around the great ice cavern of the Ballroom, all the blood-red men had clapped their hands to their crimson masks. They had felt in their eyes what Laurence had felt in his. Slaved to his will, what he experienced, they experienced. And while Laurence might have Kayleigh's Eye fused to his chest, like my grandfather the Regent . . . it didn't protect Laurence as well as it had protected the Regent. My grandfather had been immune to all pain and damage; Laurence just repaired himself. As long as he felt pain, he was vulnerable. And through him the blood-red men . . .

I was just getting ready to jump Laurence, and try out

a whole bunch of violent theories, when a glowing form appeared out of nowhere, right in front of Laurence. He lowered his hands, and looked at the ghostly figure through watering eyes. The Phantom Berserker smiled at his erstwhile master, and it was not a good smile.

"Time for me to perform one last act of penance, Laurence Drood. To pay for my betrayal of all those who were so kind to me, at Uncanny. One last act of vengeance, on the one who betrayed me."

The Phantom Berserker thrust a glowing hand into Laurence's chest. It plunged in deep, and then materialised just enough for the glowing fingers to close around the glowing amulet. The Phantom Berserker tore Kayleigh's Eye out of Laurence's chest, by brute force. The only way it could be taken. Laurence screamed, but the sound was drowned out by the Phantom Berserker's triumphant laughter. He held the amulet up, so everyone in the Ballroom could see it, still dripping with its previous owner's blood. And then the ghost just vanished, taking Kayleigh's Eye with him. There was a long pause. Laurence slowly straightened up, panting harshly. The great wound in his chest was still bleeding heavily. He looked . . . like he couldn't believe what was happening.

All around the Ballroom, the blood-red men were clutching at their own fresh wounds.

"Well," I said loudly, "this is interesting, isn't it? You're not untouchable any more, Laurence. And neither are your clones. When you get hurt now, you stay hurt. And so do they." I looked around the Ballroom. "Ladies, gentlemen, others . . . I think it's time for a little violent revenge. Don't you?"

Laurence glared around him. "Stay where you are! I still outnumber you!"

"What are numbers?" said a new and very familiar voice, "in the face of retribution?"

The Replicated Meme of Saint Sebastian strode forward, together, all six of them. And something in their natural authority made everyone else fall back to let them pass. They strode forward to join us, Molly and me, Laurence, and the Lady Faire. And then, one by one, they removed their stylised metal masks, and immediately I understood why they'd all seemed so familiar. They weren't the Replicated Meme at all. They were my uncle Jack, the Armourer; the Sarjeant-at-Arms; William the Librarian; Callan, Head of the War Room; and Capability Maggie, the new Matriarch. And the most powerful telepath in the whole world, joined to us by marriage, Ammonia Vom Acht. Uncle Jack smiled at me cheerfully.

"Stand ready, my boy. The cavalry just arrived."

"How the hell did you get in here?" It wasn't much, but it was all I could think to say.

"I still had James' old invitation," said the Armourer. "I was able to use that, to track down the Ball's current location. And then it was easy enough for us to get in, hidden behind the masks of the Replicated Meme of Saint Sebastian. Who were only too willing to give up their current invitation and let us come in their place, after the Sarjeant had a few quiet words with them. Threatening, vicious, brutal words, I'm sure. Sorry we couldn't let you know, Eddie, but . . . we had to save the element of surprise for just the right moment. You didn't think we really believed all that nonsense about you being responsible for the killings at Uncanny, did you? You didn't really think we'd leave you out in the cold again? We know you better than that."

"We just let the world think we saw you as rogue,"

said Capability Maggie. "So we could operate quietly in
the background, working out what was really going on,
while everyone else was watching you."

"You did good work against the False Knights, boy,"
growled the Sarjeant. "You must have seen me look at
you, and let you go?"

"And we brought a little something with us!" William
said brightly. "Something to even up the odds!"

"Don't boast, darling," said Ammonia. "You're better
than that."

William nodded quickly. "It's true. I am."

"We brought a Door," said Callan, smiling unpleas-
antly about him at the blood-red men. "A dimensional
Door, to link the Winter Palace to Drood Hall. The
Doormouse was most eager to make amends."

The Armourer snapped his fingers imperiously, and a
Door appeared in the middle of the Ballroom. Just an
ordinary-looking wooden door, standing tall and wide
and upright, and apparently completely unsupported. It
swung open and a whole army of Droods in full armour
came storming through into the Ballroom. Dozens, hundreds of golden-armoured Droods. More than enough to
match the numbers of the blood-red men.

The Lady Faire's guests fell back, hugging the far
walls. They could see a massive clash between two armies
about to happen, between golden masks and crimson
masks, right in front of them . . . And they really didn't
want to be involved. They knew a grudge fight when they
saw one. Laurence glared around him. He straightened
up, his hands clenching into fists, and all the blood-red
men did the same. And just like that, it was on.

The Droods and the clones slammed together, no
quarter asked or given. Laurence tried to snatch the

Lazarus Stone away from the Lady Faire, who had it clasped firmly in both her hands. She backed quickly away from him, losing herself in the crowd, and he went after her. I went after him.

Golden fists clubbed down blood-red men, and extended golden swords cut and hacked. The blood-red men fought fiercely, but they had no weapons. They'd never needed them before. And even their unnatural strength was nothing when set against Drood armour. The clones fell in bloody heaps all across the Ballroom, and they did not rise again. Some of them turned on Ammonia Vom Acht, seeing her as an easier target. She just looked at them, and they all fell dead. You don't mess with the world's most powerful telepath.

The Droods beat the hell out of the blood-red men, all across the room. I pushed my way through the fighting, ignoring the various struggles. I wasn't even armoured up. I followed Laurence, until finally he caught up with the Lady Faire again by one of the exits, already blocked by Droods. He wrestled with her, crying angry tears of frustration as he tried to pry the Lazarus Stone out of her grasp. She fought him off, with a man's strength. I grabbed Laurence by the shoulder and pulled him away from her. He jerked free, and spun round to face me. He had the red puffy face of an angry, thwarted child.

"It's over, Laurence," I said. "Time to go home. I'm sure they've still got your old Cell waiting for you."

"I can't go back," he said. "I can't."

I sighed, despite myself. "We left you alone too long. So in a sense, we made this rod for our own backs. Time to let the Armourer and his lab assistants have a look at you. We've come a long way, since you were first locked up. There must be something we can do for you, by now."

Laurence shook his head slowly, fixing me with his bright, fierce eyes. "They want me dead. Because I know things. All the awful secrets, all the hidden deals, all the terrible compromises . . . Let me go, Eddie, and I'll tell you something you need to know. Something the whole family needs to know."

"Laurence . . ."

"Let me go and I'll tell you who's really looking out from inside the Merlin Glass!"

Molly moved in beside me. "You can't trust him, Eddie. He'd say anything. Kill him."

"I can't," I said. "Not in cold blood."

"Why not?" said Molly. "He killed your grandfather, and he lied about your parents. He would have messed up the whole world and not given a damn as long as he got what he wanted. And he'd do it again, first chance he got."

"Yes," said Laurence, nodding quickly. "Oh yes . . . They can't hold me in Cell 13 any more. I'll get out, and I'll kill you all, kill everyone. You'll see!"

"Put him out of everyone's misery," said Molly.

I could hear the fighting dying down behind me. I looked back, just in time to see the last few blood-red men go down. Laurence was all that was left now. If I was going to do something before my family did, I had to do it quickly. I reached into my pocket and the Merlin Glass leaped eagerly into my hand, snuggling against my fingers. I took out the hand mirror and Laurence looked at me oddly, his head cocked slightly on one side.

"For everything you've done, and for what you would do, given the chance," I said. "For all our friends at the Department of Uncanny, and all the innocent bystanders on the Trans-Siberian Express. For all the blood on your hands, directly and indirectly, it's time for judgement."

"You won't kill me, Eddie," said Laurence. "You haven't got it in you. Think of all the knowledge that would die with me." He waited, and when my face didn't change he spat at me. "I'm not sorry! I'm not! I only wish I could have killed more Droods. Because it was never an accident. There was no accident! They did this to me on purpose! I'm the victim here! You can't kill me!"

"Anywhen else, you might have been right," I said. "I like to think of myself as an agent, not an assassin. But after everything I've seen, I'm not in a merciful mood."

I activated the Merlin Glass, and held the hand mirror out before Laurence. He looked into the Glass and froze at what he saw looking back. A slow, terrible horror filled his face. And as he stood there, I shook the Merlin Glass out to full size and slammed it down over him, and sent him away.

I brought the Glass back down to hand-mirror size and put it away. There were shocked gasps all around the great Ballroom as all the blood-red men, the wounded and the dead, suddenly disappeared, leaving only dark scorch marks on the floor. The Droods looked around them, and started to armour down.

"Eddie?" said Molly. "What did you just do?"

"I sent Laurence into the sun," I said. "I needed to be sure he was dead and gone, and all his secrets with him."

"Ashes to ashes, and less than ashes," said Molly.

"We Droods have always known how to clean up our own messes," I said.

I turned to consider the Lady Faire, and then put out my hand. "Give me the Lazarus Stone, please, my Lady. It's over. The Stone belongs to the Droods. And just like you, my family never gives up anything that's rightfully ours."

The Lady Faire nodded slowly, and dropped the small pockmarked metal sphere onto my hand. It felt heavy, more than naturally solid, as I closed my fingers around it. The Lady Faire gave me an enigmatic smile.

"I'll always remember you, Eddie. The one who got away."

She smiled sweetly at Molly, and then turned and walked away, to talk with her guests. Molly looked after her, and then at me.

"I won't ask," she said.

"Best not to," I agreed.

And then Molly snatched the Lazarus Stone out of my hand, and teleported away.

CHAPTER ELEVEN

What Really Matters, at the End

I stepped through the Merlin Glass and into Molly's private forest. The wild witch's very own wild woods. Shafts of dazzling sunlight fell down through the packed trees, like spotlights pushing back the gloom from the overhead canopy, and, after the artificial cool of the ice cavern, the warm air of the endless summer was like a caress on my face. I shook the Glass down and put it away, never once taking my eyes off Molly, sitting quietly on the grassy bank overlooking her favourite pool. She didn't look round, though she must have known I was there. She just stared into the deep dark waters of the pool, her face empty, her eyes far away.

I'd instructed the Merlin Glass to take me straight to Molly, and it hadn't even hesitated. Molly hadn't tried to hide where she was going. I stayed where I was, looking slowly and cautiously around me. We were not alone. All kinds of wildlife surrounded us—beasts and birds and other things. Some showed themselves openly, studying me with wary eyes. Others were just bright-eyed shadows, moving restlessly in the dark between the trees. All of them ready to rush in and protect Molly from me, should it prove necessary. I moved slowly forward, and Molly didn't stir. I sat down beside her, on the grassy bank overlooking the pool.

She was holding the Lazarus Stone in one hand, almost carelessly, not even looking at it. She didn't look at me, even as I arranged myself carefully beside her. She just stared into the deep dark waters before her, as though they were the most important thing in the world. As though they held all the answers to all the questions . . . We sat quietly together, side by side, as we had so many times before. This quiet setting had always been her favourite place in all the woods, where she would come to think and reflect, when she felt troubled. We sat so close our shoulders almost touched, but didn't. I could have just reached out and taken the Lazarus Stone away from her, with or without my armour's help, but I didn't. Such a betrayal of trust would have ended everything between us.

"You knew I'd find you here," I said, finally.

"Yes," she said.

"Your favourite place. Your safe place. And even with the Merlin Glass to guide me, I don't think I could have entered your woods without your permission. You let me in here. So why did you run?"

"Because I needed time to think," said Molly.

"You always meant to snatch the Stone, first chance you got," I said. "For yourself."

"Yes," said Molly.

"Why? Why do you want the Lazarus Stone? Who do you want to bring back?"

"My parents, of course!" Molly said angrily, looking at me for the first time, tears glistening unshed in her eyes. "I want my mum! I want my dad! You got your parents back; why can't I have mine?"

"Because if you were to bring them back," I said carefully, "to rescue them from their sudden deaths on Trammell Island . . . History would change so much, the odds are you and I would never meet. Never fall in love. And then think of all the amazing things we accomplished together. We saved the world, saved Humanity itself, from the Hungry Gods and the Great Satanic Conspiracy and so many other things. We saved my family from itself . . . The world is a better place because of us."

"I know."

"And we wouldn't have each other, any more."

"I know! Damn you, Eddie Drood. For making me choose."

She gave me the Lazarus Stone, placing it carefully on my outstretched hand. It was very heavy for such a small thing. Heavy with the weight of potential responsibilities, perhaps. I held the Lazarus Stone for a long moment, and then I armoured up my hand and crushed the Stone to dust. It didn't try to resist. I opened my golden glove and let the dust fall away, into the deep dark waters of the pool. It vanished in a moment, leaving no trace of its passing. Molly let out her breath in a long sigh, and then looked at me.

"Wasn't there anyone you wanted to bring back, Eddie?"

She didn't mention my uncle James. She didn't have to.

"No," I said. "There's no one I want more than you."

She slipped her arm through mine, and leaned against me, and we sat together by the pool for a long time, thinking of many things.

"Come on," I said finally. "We can't just sit around here forever."

"I'm game if you are."

"We have to get back to Drood Hall."

"We do?" said Molly. "Why?"

"Since apparently I'm not a rogue after all, I need to bring my family up to date on a few things," I said.

"Cut the apron strings, Eddie. Be your own man! You don't need them."

"They need me," I said.

"Hold everything," said Molly, sitting suddenly upright. "Whatever happened to that little box, the one your grandmother left you in her will? Do you still have it?"

"In all the excitement I'd forgotten all about it," I said. I reached into the pocket dimension at my side, found the box, and brought it out. I studied it carefully, with Molly leaning in close for a good look. Just a small, oblong black-lacquered box, about a foot long and four by three inches. Gold-leaf filigree, in intriguing patterns, but no lock or hinges, and no obvious way to open it. I shook the box gently, but it didn't rattle.

"According to Grandmother Martha's will," I said, "something inside this box could make me undisputed Patriarch of all the Droods. No one in the family would be able to stand against me."

"Why would she leave you something like that?" said Molly. "I mean, she never liked you."

"More important, she never approved of me," I said. "Or any of the things I believed in. Still, family love can be . . . complicated."

"Maybe it's booby-trapped!" said Molly. "Set to blow you to pieces if you try to open it!"

"The Armourer thought not," I said. "And I've always trusted my uncle Jack."

"So what the hell is inside the box?" said Molly. "One of the Forbidden Weapons? Secret information on where all the bodies are buried? Blackmail material?"

"See?" I said. "You're learning to think like a Drood."

"Don't be nasty. What do you think is inside the box?"

"I don't know," I said. "Grandmother made it very clear in her will that I was to be given the box only if I formally agreed to give you up. To never see you again. That was her price for the power to make me Patriarch."

Molly looked at me. "You're telling me this, with the box in your hand?"

"Relax," I said. "I stole it when they weren't looking."

Molly laughed. "See? You're learning to think like me." She looked back at the black box. "You really believe that what's in there could set you in charge of your family?"

"I don't know," I said. "But it certainly put the wind up the Council . . ."

"Do you want to be Patriarch, Eddie?" Molly said carefully.

"You know I don't," I said.

I threw the little black box into the pond, and it disappeared into the dark waters. We sat and watched for a while, just in case, but it didn't reappear.

"Are you going to tell your family you did that?" said Molly eventually.

"No," I said. "Let them worry."

Read on for a preview of Simon R. Green's
next Shaman Bond Novel,

From a Drood to a Kill

Available now from Roc.

I t was a surprisingly pleasant day. Bright summer sun-
shine, a cloudless blue sky over sweeping grassy lawns,
the cries of peacocks and gryphons loud and clear on the
still air. Along with the quiet putt-putt of a steam-
powered autogyro chugging by overhead. Just another
day at Drood Hall, ancestral home of my long-established
family, and training ground for those who would protect the
world. I stood outside the main entrance door with my lady
love at my side. Molly Metcalf—wild witch of the woods,
supernatural terrorist, Hawkwind fan . . . and the only one I
trust to always have my back. We looked at each other and
grinned.

"Ready?" I said.

"Always," said Molly.

"Once we start," I said, "we don't stop. For anything.
Until we get to where we're going."

"Got it," said Molly. "We keep going, no matter what."
She looked at me carefully. "Are we really going to do

this? Take on the most powerful family in the world, on their own home ground?"

"Isn't that what you always wanted?" I said.

"Hell yes! But are you sure this is what you want?"

"Hell yes," I said.

Her grin widened. "Your family isn't going to know what's hit them."

"Let's do it," I said.

"Love to," said Molly.

I subvocalised my activating Words, and golden armour flowed out from the torc around my neck, covering me in a moment from head to toe in unbreakable, unstoppable strange matter. My family's greatest secret weapon. I felt strong and fast and fully alive, as though I'd just woken up from the long doze of ordinary living. Molly struck a sorcerous pose and was immediately surrounded by coruscating wild magics, spitting and sparking as they discharged on the air. The knight in armour and the wicked witch, determined not to be denied any longer. I raised a golden foot, kicked in the entrance doors, and the two of us slammed into Drood Hall.

Alarms and bells and sirens broke out everywhere all at once, and men and women froze in place along the whole length of the entrance hall, caught off guard. No one ever invades Drood Hall, home to the most feared and respected family in the world. It just doesn't happen. So they simply stood and stared, like rabbits caught in the headlights of an oncoming car, while Molly and I strode on. Two unstoppable forces for the price of one. A few of my family started forward to try to intercept us; some ran away; but most just stood and stared blankly, waiting for someone to tell them what to do.

A handful of security guards finally appeared, charging

down the hallway, yelling for everyone else to get out of their way, and armouring up as they came. I didn't slow down, just hit them head-on. Some I shouldered aside; others I knocked down and walked right over. They might have been armoured like me, but I was the one with the field training and experience. More armoured guards burst out of side doors. Molly called up vicious storm winds, and they blasted up and down the long entrance hall, picking Droods up and throwing them this way and that. Most of the family either grabbed for something secure to hold on to or ran for their lives. They didn't armour up or reach for weapons. I was seriously unimpressed. It was clear to me that the family needed to run more practise drills so everyone would know what to do when the impossible happened right in front of them. If this had been a real invasion, by outside forces, we would have been in serious trouble.

An armoured Drood blocked my way, reaching for me with golden hands. I hit him hard, slamming my shoulder into his chest. There was a loud clang of colliding metals as he was thrown backwards. I back-elbowed another in the side of the head, and swept the feet out from under a third. And kept going. I wasn't worried about hurting them while they were in their armour, but hopefully I'd knocked the breath out of them and bought us some time. Molly danced happily along at my side, throwing fireworks and concussion spells in all directions, just to keep everyone on their toes.

"Has anyone ever got this far inside before?" she asked.

"It has happened," I replied. "But we don't like to talk about it. Might give people ideas."

Molly was still sending Droods tumbling this way and that with her roaring storm winds. And perhaps enjoying herself just a little too much. Not everyone was armoured. I shot her a hard look from behind my featureless golden mask, realised that wasn't going to help much, and raised my voice to be heard clearly over the howling sirens and alarm bells.

"Take it easy, Molly! These people are family!"

"I know," said Molly.

"My family!"

"Not mine."

"They could be," I said. "One day."

"You say that like it's a good thing."

"Molly . . ."

"Sometimes you want too much, Eddie," said Molly. Not even looking at me. We pressed on, into the heart of Drood Hall.

The Serjeant-at-Arms appeared suddenly before us, wearing his traditional formal outfit of stark black and white. He would have looked very like a traditional old-fashioned butler if it hadn't been for the two extremely nasty-looking guns in his hands. The Serjeant is the first hard line of defence against any hostile intruders, and I was pleasantly surprised that we'd got this far before he turned up to stop us. He immediately recognised both Molly and me, but the guns he had trained on us didn't waver at all. I knew he'd have no hesitation in shooting if he thought it necessary. But I also knew he was so confident in his own abilities, it would never even occur to him that he needed to armour up to protect himself.

So I gave the nod to Molly, and she jabbed a specially prepared aboriginal pointing bone at the Serjeant. And just like that, he was gone. Teleported right out of the Hall and onto the grounds outside. Quite a long way off, to be exact—on the far side of the ornamental lake. By the time he could make his way back to the Hall, this should all be over. One way or another. Molly looked at the pointing bone in her hand. The sheer strain of what it had been asked to do had charred and cracked it from end to end. It's not easy, making a Drood go somewhere he doesn't want to go. Molly shrugged, tossed the bone aside, and we moved on.

We strode quickly through open halls and wide corridors, blasting our way through what little opposition there was. They say you can't go home again, but you can if you carry a big enough stick. The alarms and bells and sirens were deafeningly loud, but I could still hear armoured feet hammering on polished wooden floors as people headed toward us from all directions. But so far we were still keeping well ahead of them.

The Hall's interior security systems kicked in automatically once we passed a certain point, and all the doors ahead and around us slammed shut and locked themselves to try to contain the problem. With anyone else, that might actually have worked. Molly snapped her fingers at each door we came to, and it leapt open to let us pass. Until the anti-magic protocols activated and that stopped working. So instead I just lowered my armoured shoulder again and hit each closed door like a battering ram, smashing my way through. The heavy wood cracked and broke apart; sometimes the entire door was thrown right off its hinges. The world can be a very fragile place when you're wearing Drood armour.

Concealed trap-doors suddenly fell away in the floor before us, revealing dark bottomless depths. I knew where they were, so I just stepped around them. Molly walked straight forward across the open spaces, not even deigning to look down, defying gravity as she defied everything else that argued with her. The trap-doors closed behind us with quiet, defeated sounds.

"I have to say, I was expecting your family to put up more of a showing," said Molly. "Something more impressive, like energy weapons or force shields . . . high explosives. That sort of thing."

"My family will be very reluctant to use anything that destructive inside the Hall," I said. "For fear of damaging all the expensive paintings and sculptures we've accumulated down the centuries. Tribute from a grateful and rather scared world. That's what I was counting on. Luckily I don't have that problem. I've never liked the Hall."

"Even though it's where you were brought up?"

"Especially because it's where I was brought up."

I said that very loudly, for the benefit of anyone who might be listening and still planning on stopping us. I wanted them to believe I didn't care how much damage I did. And to be fair, Molly probably really didn't. But I was being careful to do no more damage than I had to— to the Hall, and to my family. Because while I might be mad at them right now, I still had to live with them afterwards. I'd put a lot of thought into this particular home invasion, and it was all about the shock and awe, and moving too quickly for any serious confrontations.

Half a dozen armoured Droods turned up with at least some idea of how to fight and a willingness to get stuck in. Good for them. But I was a trained field agent, with many years of hard experience and all kinds of nasty tricks tucked up my armoured sleeves. I knocked them down and kicked them around, and Molly hit them with eldritch lightnings if they tried to get up. They ended up scattered the length of the corridor, wondering what had hit them and whether it was ever going to stop. Poor bastards. They never stood a chance. Which was just as well. Because I would have damaged them if I'd had to. No one was going to stop me this time.

The farther into the Hall Molly and I penetrated, the faster we moved. By the time we approached the centre of the Hall and its hidden core, the Sanctity, we were both running at full pelt. I wanted to leave my family well behind, so there wouldn't be any . . . accidents. I was trying to make it clear to everyone that I was here for a purpose, and determined to get to where I was going. That I had no intention of being stopped . . . and that it really would be better for everyone if they just got the hell out of my way and let me get on with it.

Finally, we rounded a corner and there was the Sanctity, straight ahead of us. At the far end of a long stone corridor. The heart of the Hall, where all the decisions that matter are made. I slowed my pace to a determined stroll, and Molly drifted dangerously along beside me. No more smiles. This was serious business. I felt a sudden harsh tingling in my throat. I'd been expecting that. It was a standard defence, designed to deal with any Droods who went mad or rogue, by taking their armour away from them and pushing it back into their torc.

"Ethel?" I said, subvocalising so only she could hear me.

The warm and friendly voice of the Droods' very own other-dimensional patron and protector came clearly to me, inside my head.

"You know, I really should just shut you down, Eddie. That's what everyone else is shouting at me to do and I do wish they wouldn't. Tell me you have a really good reason for causing this much commotion."

"I have a really good reason."

"Really? Cross your heart?"

"Trust me."

"You know I do. But you don't make it easy."

"I know," I said. "But I do make it fun."

"Yes, you do. I'm looking forward to hearing what this is all about. Hint, hint."

"You'll enjoy it," I said.

"I'd better."

The tingling around my throat went away, and I relaxed, just a little. I'd been fairly confident I could convince Ethel—but it's hard to be sure of anything when you're dealing with an other-dimensional entity.

The way to the great double doors that were the only access to the Sanctity was blocked by two very large armoured guards who stood their ground. They showed no intention of moving or of being moved. I slowed to a casual stroll, with Molly close at my side. She gestured impressively at them, trying to teleport them away, as she had with the Serjeant-at-Arms. But without the pointing bone, she hadn't a hope of moving two Droods in their armour. She scowled, and stuck out her lower lip sulkily.

"Come on," I said. "That was never going to work."

"It might have!" she said. "I put hours into researching that spell."

"You didn't really think you could overcome Drood armour all on your own, did you?"

Molly smiled dazzlingly. "A girl can dream, can't she?"

The two guards stepped forward, long golden sword blades extending from their armoured hands. I was glad to see they'd been practising. Drood armour can be reshaped by the will of its occupant, but it takes a lot of concentration to hold the new shape. It was clear from the way the guards stood that they knew what they were doing. They looked practised and prepared, and properly dangerous. Everything a Drood should be. Good for them. I reached through the golden armour at my hip, into the pocket dimension I keep there, and brought out the Merlin Glass. One of the guards had just enough time to say, "Oh shit," before I shook the Glass out to Door size and clapped it quickly over each guard in turn, sending them through the Glass and out into the Drood grounds. Where they could probably have a very interesting conversation with the Serjeant-at-Arms. I shook the Merlin Glass back down to hand-mirror size and put it away again.

"So," said Molly. "That thing has decided to start working again, has it?"

"When it feels like it," I said.

"What would you have done if the Glass hadn't worked?"

"Improvised," I said. "Suddenly and violently and all over the place."

"Always works for me," said Molly. She stopped and looked at me thoughtfully. "Okay, why did the Glass work against the armoured Droods, when my magic wouldn't?"

"It's the Merlin Glass," I said. "Can't help feeling the clue is in the name."

We stood together before the closed Sanctity doors. One last barrier standing between me . . . and what I'd come for. The alarms and bells and sirens were still giving it their all, and I could also hear a great many feet heading in our direction, but for the moment we had the corridor to ourselves. I looked at Molly.

"You ready to do this?"

"Of course," said Molly. "Looking forward to it."

I tried the door handle, and as I suspected, the door was locked. I raised my voice.

"Ethel! Open the doors, please. If you wouldn't mind. I'd hate to have to seriously damage anything."

"Speak for yourself," said Molly.

I felt as much as heard a quiet, resigned sigh, and then the doors unlocked themselves, swinging slowly open before us.

I strode into the Sanctity with my head held high, Molly moving proudly at my side. The massive open space of the old wood-panelled chamber was almost completely deserted, and suffused with a rose red glow that emanated from no obvious source. The only physical manifestation of Ethel's presence. Under normal circumstances the rose red light was soothing and calming to the troubled soul, but I was so full of anger and a deep sense of injustice that I barely felt it. I don't think Molly has ever felt it. She's not a calm person. She stopped just inside the entrance, as the doors slowly closed themselves, so she could block the way against anyone who might come in after us. I walked slowly forward, and there, waiting for me, was the family's new Matriarch. Margaret.

She stood alone, staring defiantly back at me, unsupported by any member of her advisory Council, unprotected by any guards. Margaret was a short, stocky blonde, with hair so close-cropped it was almost military. She wore a battered bomber jacket over seriously distressed jeans, and much-worn work boots with trailing laces. She might have been taken away from her beloved grounds and gardens, and forced to run the family as the next in line; but no one was ever going to make her like it. Or look the part. Margaret had a firm mouth, fierce eyes, and a general air of barely suppressed fury.

"All right!" she said sharply. "You've got my attention. Now what is so important you had to force your way into the Hall and insist on seeing me, even though I already told you I was far too busy? Have you come back to take my position as head of the family by force, Eddie? Like you threatened to, the last time you were here? Because if you want it, you can have it. And I can go back to my gardens. I'm sure they miss me."

"I don't want to run the family," I said, very firmly. I armoured down, so she could see my face and see that I meant it. She relaxed, just a little.

"I hate being the Matriarch," said the woman who not that long ago used to be called Capability Maggie. When all she had to worry about was maintaining the Hall's extensive grounds and gardens. "Far too much responsibility, no time to myself, hardly ever a free minute to stroll round the flower beds and see how the new seedlings are coming along. I'd quit in a minute if they'd let me."

"Hell," Molly said calmly, "I'll take the position, if no one else wants it. Just think what I could do to an unsuspecting world with a whole army of Droods to back me up."

The Matriarch and I both looked at Molly, thought about it, and winced pretty much simultaneously.

"That . . . is a truly disturbing thought," I said.

"You could never take charge of the Droods," the Matriarch said coldly to Molly. "You're not family. Even if you should eventually marry Eddie, which a whole lot of us doubt, that still wouldn't make you one of us. Only a pure-blooded Drood can be Matriarch."

"Yeah," said Molly. "Because that's always worked out so well in the past."

"If we could just tiptoe back into the realms of reality," I said. "We have something important to discuss, Matriarch. I came here to talk to you about something specific, and I will not be stopped or diverted."

"You've made that clear enough," said the Matriarch. "I can't believe you've done this to us, Eddie. Untold damage, injured family members, and chaos everywhere. All because you couldn't be bothered to make a proper appointment, like reasonable people."

"There's no point in being reasonable with this family," I said. "I have tried it, and it never works. Because it takes two to be reasonable."

"What do you want, Eddie?" said the Matriarch, meeting my gaze unflinchingly.

"You know what I want! You promised me the family would use all its resources to track down my missing parents! It's been months since they vanished from the Casino Infernale in France; and you haven't come up with a single damned lead!"

"We've been busy!" said the Matriarch. "The world doesn't just stand still because you've got a problem! We have to hold Humanity's hand and blow its nose, and protect it from a thousand different threats it doesn't even know exist, all day and every night with never a break. And there are, after all, very real limits to this family's time and budget. We deal with the most important matters first. Everything else . . . has to take its place in the queue. Charles and Emily aren't even officially members of the family any more. Like you, Eddie. You walked out on us, remember? Turned your back on family duty and responsibilities so you could run off to work with your precious grandfather in the Department of Uncanny. Who, let us face it, have never been more than second-raters in the secret organisation stakes. And you think you have a right to demand full access to the family's limited time and resources?"

"After everything I've done for this family?" I said. "Damn right I do."

Even I could hear the dangerous chill in my voice. The Matriarch looked away, unable to meet my gaze.

"The general feeling is," she said finally, "that if Charles and Emily are still missing, it's because they want to be."

"Don't give me that," I said. "This family can find anyone, if they want to. Ethel!"

"Yes, Eddie!" said the warm, comforting voice, from everywhere at once. "Welcome home! Always good to have you around. You do liven things up so. Did you bring me a present? You know I love presents."

"Yes," I said. "But you're very difficult to buy for. What do you get the other-dimensional entity who is everything? Come on, Ethel. Why can't you just See where my parents are? I thought you said you could See anything, anywhere."

"I can! I can See everything that exists, and a good many things that shouldn't. I can See things you humans don't even have concepts for. But your parents remain . . . stubbornly elusive. They don't have torcs, so I can't track them that way; and when I try to look for them . . . wherever I look, they aren't there. So I can only assume they're no longer in this world."

A cold hand clutched at my heart. "Are you saying . . . they're dead?"

"I didn't say that. There are, after all, all kinds of realities. Some so distanced from this one, or so carefully concealed, that even I can't look into them. My abilities are very limited by my current circumstances. You have no idea what I've given up to take care of you Droods."

"If you want all of our resources turned loose on your private problem, Eddie," said the Matriarch, refusing to be left out of the conversation, "if you want to ask a personal favour from the family, you're going to have to do a favour for the family."

I looked at her slowly, consideringly, and to her credit she didn't flinch.

"I just knew that was coming," said Molly. "Didn't you just know that was coming?"

"A favour?" I said. "Like what?"

The Matriarch stirred uncomfortably, at something she heard in my voice. She chose her words carefully.

"We do have a case pending that the family needs to deal with but that we would prefer to keep at arm's length. Essentially straightforward, but ripe with pitfalls for the unwary. A case that could quite definitely benefit from your ... special touch."

"Hold it," said Molly. "I've just remembered something I wanted to ask! Do you know what's happening with the Department of Uncanny? Have you heard who's going to be put in charge?"

The Matriarch looked at her. She would have liked to be impatient, but everyone knew there was no point in trying to push past Molly when she had something on her mind. She had a tendency to throw things. Often large, jaggedy, pointy things. The Matriarch did allow herself a loud sigh, just on general principles.

"As far as I know," she said, "the Government hasn't decided whether they're going to keep Uncanny going, as a separate Department. It was almost completely destroyed, and most of its people killed. The Government might just fold what's left into MI 13, or replace it with something new. I understand Black Heir is very keen to take on Uncanny's responsibilities, and expand their area of influence in the hidden world."

Molly snorted loudly. "Black Heir? That bunch of vultures? Picking over the technological trash aliens leave behind when they have to get the hell out of Dodge in a hurry. They're just looking to increase their power base."

"Well, yes," said the Matriarch. "That's what Government Departments do. I understand there's a lot of interdepartmental jousting going on right now, as everyone fights it out for promotion. There are careers waiting to be made out of situations like this." She looked at me steadily. "Do you still consider yourself part of Uncanny, Eddie?"

"No," I said. "I only went along to be close to my grandfather. Now the Regent of Shadows is gone . . ."

"So who are you with now?" said the Matriarch.

"Remains to be seen," I said, not giving an inch. "Doesn't it?"

"You're family, Eddie," said the Matriarch. "You can always come home." She paused to glare coldly at Molly. "Even if you do bring some baggage with you."

Molly's head came up immediately. "Eddie! Tell me she did not just call me a baggage!"

"She did not just call you a baggage," I said.

"Yes, she did! I heard her!"

"Then why did you ask me?" I said.

"To give you a chance to say the right thing!"

"Now, you know very well I'm never any good at that," I said. "Can't we all just agree that everyone must have misheard and move on?"

Molly was still pouting dangerously, so it was probably just as well that the Sanctity doors burst open and the Serjeant-at-Arms launched himself into the Sanctity, armoured up and guns in hand, ready for action. And then he stopped, and looked around, as he realised there was no obvious trouble going on. He saw I wasn't wearing my armour any more, and immediately armoured down himself, rather than be outdone by me in the calm and controlled stakes. The guns in his hands remained pointed at me and Molly. We both made a point of appearing conspicuously unimpressed, while being careful to make no sudden moves. They were very big and very impressive guns.

"Stand down, Serjeant!" the Matriarch said loudly. "I am perfectly safe, and completely in control of the situation!"

The Serjeant didn't look like he believed a word of that, but he nodded reluctantly, and the guns disappeared from his hands. He drew himself up to his full height, looking more than ever like the world's most dangerous butler, and glowered coldly at me and Molly. We glared right back at him. Never show a moment of weakness to anyone in my family. They'll only take advantage.

"If it was up to me, I'd have you shot on sight," the Serjeant said flatly. "Every time you come home, Eddie, you bring trouble with you. When you aren't starting it yourself. I demand to know what has happened to the black box the previous Matriarch left you in her will! The contents of which could supposedly put you in complete control of this family, against all opposition!"

"Oh, that box," I said. "It's around somewhere. I'm sure I could put my hand on it if I felt I needed to."

"It belongs with the family!" said the Serjeant-at-Arms.

"But it was left to me," I said. "If my grandmother had wanted you to know about it I'm sure she would have told you."

"You must know you can't be allowed to keep it," he

said. "It's an open threat to the family! What if someone else got their hands on it?"

"Who's going to take it from me?" I said.

"You can go now, Serjeant," said the Matriarch in her most commanding voice. "I need to speak privately with Eddie. And Molly. You need to go calm the family down and check out the security situation. Make sure no one tries to take advantage and sneak in while we're all . . . distracted. And for God's sake shut those bloody alarms off! Can't hear myself think!"

The Serjeant made a quick gesture with one hand, and all the alarms and bells and sirens shut down. The sudden peace and quiet was an almost physical relief. The Serjeant scowled at me, and then at the Matriarch.

"He broke into the Hall! Threw the whole family into confusion, did all kinds of property damage, and made a joke of our defences! Are you really going to let him get away with that?"

The Matriarch stood her ground and stared him down. "Yes. I am. Because if you hadn't let internal security become so slack, this would never have happened. He should never have been able to get this far! I'd say we owe him our thanks for demonstrating so clearly all the shortcomings in our current defences. It's high time we ran more practise drills."

"I thought that!" I said.

"I know," said Ethel. "I heard you."

The Serjeant-at-Arms stared at the Matriarch with a look of betrayal, then abruptly turned around and stomped out of the Sanctity. Not quite slamming the door behind him.

"That man desperately needs more fibre in his diet," said Ethel. Just a bit unexpectedly.

"Can we please now return to the subject at hand?" said the Matriarch. "Because the case I was talking about is just the tiniest bit urgent."

"All right," I said. "What is this new mission that I'm so perfectly suited for?"

"And if it's so straightforward," said Molly, "why does it have to be Eddie?"

"Because there are . . . complications," said the Matriarch.

"Of course," I said. "Aren't there always? What kind of complications are we talking about? Things or people?"

"Let's just say I could use a Drood who isn't really a Drood," said the Matriarch.

"Ah," I said. "Are we talking plausible deniability?"

"Possibly," said the Matriarch. "If this should go wrong, suddenly and horribly and embarrassingly wrong, I don't want the repercussions coming anywhere near this family. It doesn't matter if you do something to upset the Government. They already hate and loathe you, with good reason. But I have to work with these people. The days when we could just tell Governments what to do are, unfortunately, behind us. Thanks to you."

"You're welcome," I said.

"You took away our authority! You neutered the family!"

"I saved our soul!" I said, not backing down an inch. "We were only ever meant to be Humanity's shepherds, not their owners! I did what was necessary to prevent us from becoming worse than the things we fight. Now, what kind of case are we talking about, exactly? Bearing in mind I still haven't committed myself to anything yet."

"Just a simple infiltration and information-gathering

assignment," said the Matriarch. A little too smoothly for my liking.

"Good," I said. "Because there's something important I need to tell you first."

The Matriarch looked quickly from me to Molly, and back again. "This isn't going to be anything good, is it?"

"I have decided," I said, "that from now on . . . I'm not going to kill anyone. I have had to do that too many times. I am a field agent, not an assassin."

The Matriarch looked at me searchingly, not sure where this had come from or where it was going. "Has something happened, Eddie? You've killed your fair share in the service of this family and never said anything before."

"More than my fair share," I said. "More than enough."

The Matriarch looked at Molly.

"Don't look at me," said Molly. "I haven't changed my mind. He's the moral one here."

"This case calls for an agent's skills," the Matriarch said carefully. "Nothing more."

"All right," I said. "Give me the details."

"Then you'll do it?"

"Give me the details."

"The Prime Minister made contact with the family, earlier this morning," said the Matriarch. "Begging for our help. World leaders might like to boast to each other that they're free from Drood influence these days, but they still know who to run to when it all goes pear-shaped. Ethel, be so good as to play back the recording of my conversation with the Prime Minister."

"Hold everything," I said. "Ethel, since when have you been recording conversations inside Drood Hall?"

"Welcome back, Eddie! I knew it had to be you, once

I heard all the alarms. This place is always so much more fun when you're around. Run the question by me again. I must have missed something. Why shouldn't I be recording conversations?"

"You've been recording *everything*?" I said pointedly.

"Well, not everything. Just the important things, that the Matriarch wanted an official record of, for the family files. I have eyes and ears everywhere, after all, and infinite capacity, so . . ."

"We are only talking about things that take place in a public setting," said the Matriarch.

"I haven't forgotten all those long, boring lectures of yours, about respecting people's privacy, Eddie. Even if no one has properly explained the concept to me yet. Or what it's for."

"Show me the recording," I said. "But we will be talking more about this later."

"Oh joy. Wildly looking forward to it. I'll bring popcorn."

A vision appeared, floating on the air before us like a disembodied monitor screen. I didn't ask Ethel how she was doing it. On the few occasions when I had been unwise enough to ask questions like that, I'd rarely understood the answer. And when I had, I'd usually ended up wishing I hadn't. She is an other-dimensional entity, after all, a Power from Beyond. That's all I needed to know. Though I would have quite liked to understand exactly why Ethel had chosen to stick around here, in our limited reality, just to be near my family.

One side of the vision showed the Matriarch sitting calmly behind her desk, in her office, while the other showed the Prime Minister sitting at his desk in his office. She seemed entirely relaxed; he didn't. The Prime

Minister was trying hard to look like a man of High Office and a World Leader, but he couldn't seem to meet the Matriarch's steady gaze for more than a few moments at a time. I got the feeling he was more distressed about the situation he was in than about having to beg the Droods for help. Something had seriously upset the man. And not just because he must have known that if we did agree to help him out, he was going to have to pay a high price for it in the future. The Prime Minister started speaking, and I listened carefully.

"You have to do something!" said the Prime Minister. "Important secret information is being leaked from our most secure listening centre."

"I take it we're talking about one of those places where the Government spies on people who'd be very upset if they ever found out they were being listened to," said the Matriarch.

"Well, quite," said the Prime Minister. "The majority of the information being leaked from this particular station is of a highly sensitive nature, and it seems clear that only a very important person could be doing it. Because only that sort of person would have access to this level of classified data. We need a Drood agent to go in undercover, find out what's going on, and put an immediate stop to it."

The Matriarch smiled, briefly. "I think we can arrange that. Which particular listening centre are we talking about?"

"The very latest, and most important," the Prime Minister said quickly. "The most up-to-date establishment in the country. We spent a great deal of money on Lark Hill. We can't afford for it to fail so soon. It's our most wide-ranging eavesdropping operation, unofficially called the

Big Ear. Their purpose is to monitor all forms of communication. They have a new extremely powerful and most secret device that allows them to listen in on absolutely everything without being detected. Phones, e-mails, computers, everything! Nothing is safe from this new device. The Big Ear is officially tasked and licensed to listen to everyone. Public and private, no exceptions. Including, of course, the most secret and secure information from every kind of source."

"No wonder you came to us," said the Matriarch. "If the people of this country find out that you've been spying on them . . ."

"It's for their own good," said the Prime Minister. "For their own protection."

"They might not see it that way."

"Which is why they must never know." The Prime Minister tried a knowing smile, but quickly let it drop when he realised it wasn't working. "We need a Drood field agent to go in and investigate the situation inside the Big Ear, because we can't trust anyone inside the centre and we can't call on anyone from the usual security organisations. Because they're not supposed to know the Big Ear even exists. We need to know if someone inside Lark Hill is selling secrets for money, or politics, or for what they think is a higher morality. The last thing we need is for this kind of information to show up on WikiLeaks! God save us from well-meaning people . . ."

"And," said the Matriarch, "you're worried about this new device of yours."

"Of course we're worried about the new device!" said the Prime Minister. "Sorry! Sorry . . . Didn't mean to raise my voice, but I'm really very concerned. If some disaffected person has gained access to it . . ."

"If we agree to do this," said the Matriarch, cutting firmly across his carefully rehearsed speech, "you will agree to owe us. I will tell you what and I will tell you when. And you don't get to whine about it."

The Prime Minister nodded immediately, trying his knowing smile again. "Of course! Understood. Yes. I'll leave it to you to sort out the details, shall I . . ."

The Matriarch cut off the connection; and the vision disappeared from the rose red air.

"He expects this to go wrong," I said. "He wants someone from outside in the frame, to lay the blame on."

"Of course," said the Matriarch. "He's a politician. But I need you to do this, Eddie. Partly because we need the present administration to owe us a favour, something we can hold over them in the future — and partly because I want to know more about this new eavesdropping device they have that can do so much. They shouldn't have access to anything that powerful."

"Why do you want me specifically?" I said.

"Because you are not officially part of this family at present. Everyone knows you're affiliated with the Department of Uncanny. Which should make it just that little bit harder for the mud to stick, if it starts flying. If . . ."

"If what?" said Molly.

"If I knew that, I could send one of my own people," said the Matriarch. "There's clearly something going on at the Big Ear that the Prime Minister isn't telling us, so . . . go in and sort it out, Eddie. Do whatever you have to, to get to the heart of things and put this right. While doing your very best to keep the family out of the line of fire. I've already made arrangements with the Armourer to sort you out a suitable cover identity with all the proper paperwork. You can go in as a security consultant from some real but minor organisation that won't even know its identity has been hijacked until it's too late. Do this favour for the family, Eddie . . . and you'll get what you want."

ABOUT THE AUTHOR

Simon R. Green is a *New York Times* bestselling author. He lives in England.

SIMON R. GREEN

FROM A DROOD TO A KILL
A SECRET HISTORIES NOVEL

Eddie Drood is on a mission to find his kidnapped parents,
who signed over their souls in exchange for the power to fight
the forces of darkness. Now his ladylove, Molly, his parents, and
other major players have been taken so they'll pay up—or
participate in the "Big Game." The rules are simple as are the
consequences: the winner's debt is paid in full, and the losers
will get themselves permanently lost, body and soul, forever.
To save his loved ones, Eddie will become a ringer in this deadly
contest that's undoubtedly rigged by the Powers That Be...

Praise for the Secret Histories novels:

"The action never stops...James Bond-style secret agent hijinks
with urban fantasy. Fun, escapist fare."
—*Library Journal*

R0202